GOLDMAN'S ANATOMY

Also by Glenn Savan

WHITE PALACE

GLENN SAVAN

Goldman's Anatomy

D O U B L E D A Y
New York London Toronto Sydney Auckland

PUBLISHED BY DOUBLEDAY
a division of Bantam Doubleday Dell Publishing Group, Inc.
1540 Broadway, New York, New York 10036

DOUBLEDAY and the portrayal of an anchor with a dolphin are
trademarks of Doubleday, a division of Bantam Doubleday Dell
Publishing Group, Inc.

Library of Congress Cataloging-in-Publication Data

Savan, Glenn, 1953–
Goldman's anatomy/Glenn Savan.—1st ed.
p.   cm.
I. Title.
PS3569.A837G65   1993
813'.54—dc20   92-25496
CIP

ISBN 0-385-42607-0

1   3   5   7   9   10   8   6   4   2

FOR MAYU

ACKNOWLEDGMENTS

I WANT TO THANK the following people, without whose expert advice, assistance, encouragement and nagging I never would have gotten this book done.

Rebecca S. Bierman, D.O. B.C., General Psychiatrist; Gary Hansen, Ph.D., and Barbara Hansen; Bernard Hulbert, M.D.; Ken Kroll and Erica Levy Klein; Carol North, M.D.; David Neumann; Dean L. Rosen, Psy.D.; Terry Savan, R.N., M.A.; Barbara Silverstein, Ph.D.; Mimi Smith; Malcolm Bliss Health Center; St. Mary's Hospital; and, as always, Barbara and Sidney Savan—whose faith still astounds me—as well as my two indispensable muses in New York, Deb Futter and Gail Hochman.

And as for sickness: are we not almost tempted to ask ourselves whether we could get along without it?

—Fredrich Nietzsche

PART ONE

One

ON THAT SEPTEMBER AFTERNOON more than ten years ago, when my life hung the curve from which it has yet to straighten out, I was feeling about as good as a man in my condition could feel. I was on my way home from a gem and mineral show in Kansas City (where I'd made out like a Barbary pirate) and speeding toward St. Louis in a car I'd recently paid for in cash: a brand-new boatlike, lipstick-red '81 Toronado, equipped with a special mechanism on the steering column that enabled me to drive using only my hands. It was quite a device, the sort of clever contraption, I liked to think, that a Benjamin Franklin or a Thomas Jefferson might have concocted for himself had he faced the same problems I did. From the right of the steering column a skeletal steel arm stuck out like an extra stick shift; you twisted the ridged plastic grip forward to accelerate, twisted back to slow down, and pushed ahead to brake; a fat twirling knob on the wheel let you swing it 180 degrees in either direction with your left hand while you worked the brake-accelerator with your right; the whole Rube Goldbergian affair was attached to the floorboard with a thicket of wires and rods. Thanks to that device, I could zip in and out of traffic with the ease of any normal driver, while my legs—stiff and swollen with arthritis—could remain as motionless as the pair of aluminum crutches I kept stuck at a slant, within easy reach, between the passenger seat

and the door. It had set me back almost twelve hundred dollars—but what the hell? At the age of twenty-five, I was already
basking in the comfy tax bracket I'd once hoped to reach, with
determination and luck, by the time I was in my early or middle thirties. And on that sunstruck Saturday afternoon, when
everything, without my knowing it, was about to change utterly, I was fetching home what was probably the single richest
haul of my career.

On the seat behind me sat two nylon backpacks stuffed carefully full (because of my crutches, backpacks were the only sort
of luggage I could handle) of such rare and costly items as
blood-red cinnabar from northern China, silvery needles of
stibnite from Japan, Mexican geodes bristling at their cores
with gorgeous white-capped amethyst, and a dozen Siberian
opals of such an intense celestial blue that my mouth had literally watered as I packed them—all of which, I figured, could
net me a solid twenty grand, provided that I found the right
buyers, worked the right deals.

And to top it off, the pain of my arthritis was at its lowest ebb
in months. My knees, which could swell to the size of canta-
loupes when my disease was raging full force, were only
slightly puffed and reddened, and my hips, where the pain
was often the most malicious, were giving me almost no grief
at all. On Friday at the trade show I'd managed to stay seated
behind my display table (where I'd artfully arranged my most
eye-catching specimens against a backing of dark blue velvet)
and haggle with potential customers for nearly four straight
hours before I finally had to struggle to my feet and work out
the kinks in my knees and hips; by this morning, miracle of
miracles, I was able to limp from booth to booth in that
packed, clamorous, earthy-smelling convention hall from the
opening bell at nine until well past two in the afternoon, picking up beautiful deals along the way as easily as picking up
shells along a beach. And while some stiffness had returned
today, the pain was so blessedly minimal that I was working
the gas pedal—but not the more resistant brake—with my very
own right foot.

Just why my arthritis had chosen to back off on this particular weekend was, as always, a total mystery. Aside from its
incurability, rheumatoid arthritis (which I came down with at

the age of nine, despite its rarity in young males) is as unpredictable as the St. Louis weather. Sometimes you're fairly functional, at other times you're immobilized with pain, and all those outside factors people love to speculate about—diet, stress, humidity—have about as much to do with your condition on any given day as the positions of the planets above your head. From my first childhood attack, until about the time I started to shave, I was confined to a wheelchair; since then I'd gotten around on the sort of waist-high aluminum crutches you see poster children leaning on; last week I was in a crucifixion of agony, this week I was damned near healthy, and there wasn't a rheumatologist, New Age healer, or witch doctor on earth who could begin to tell me why.

Every so often I'd twist down the rearview for another glance at my fat and lumpy backpacks—a sight that set me tingling with greedy joy. But don't get the wrong idea. I was greedy, all right, but not primarily for money. It was always beauty first, and beauty most powerfully, that fired my acquisitive lust. Whether I was eyeing a sea-green crystal of rocket-shaped tourmaline, a fine silk necktie, a gleaming new car on a dealer's lot, or much more problematically, a woman, if it wasn't a superlative example of its kind, I couldn't be bothered—and if it was, I was instantly reduced to the mentality of a barnacle. I had to attach myself to it; I had to have it. Maybe it's a trait I share with all connoisseurs. But I've often wondered if there isn't something else at work, some compensatory urge in shoddily made creatures like myself (just look at the lame god Vulcan, incongruously hitched to the goddess of love and beauty, or at poor Quasimodo, forever slobbering after his gypsy girl) that makes us yearn for the whole and the perfect. Of course I don't really know. I can only tell you that my pangs of anticipation were practically sexual as I barreled toward St. Louis, just squirming to get home and, like a sultan with a fresh shipment of harem girls to ogle, unpack and fondle my dazzling new beauties.

But first I had to stop off at my parents' house in suburban Creve Coeur, and attend to some more mundane business. I turned off Highway 270 and ran the gauntlet of depressingly cheerful postmodern shopping centers that lined both sides of Olive Street Road, and then descended, with my usual twinge of nostalgia, into my parents' low-lying subdivision. Until I graduated from Washington University here in St. Louis and finally moved out on my own (with both a B.S. and a master's in mineralogy, earned in five straight unrelenting years) this was the only neighborhood I'd ever lived in. The subdivision, named Tempo, had gone up in the waning days of the Eisenhower administration—that halcyon era when a tailor like my father and a high school English teacher like my mother could still afford a modest home on a six percent loan. The Goldman residence, on Flair Court, was a structural clone of its neighbors, a one-story shoebox with a false brick front and a carport to the side, distinguished only by the fancy Gs cut into the awnings, our name on the mailbox, and the concrete slope that eased down from the front step, which my father had laid in with his own hands when I was ten, so I could roll in and out of the house unassisted in my wheelchair. I parked in the carport (my father wouldn't be back from the tailor shop until this evening) and made my way down the walk with that peculiar, spidery, four-legged gait (a crutch, a foot, a crutch, a foot) recommended by my physical therapists to prevent the leg muscles from atrophying.

I was, as you might expect, an oddly built young man. Owing partly to my constant use of crutches, and partly to my long dependence on steroids (fifteen milligrams a day of prednisone, an anti-inflammatory, for the past fifteen years), my upper torso was massively bulked, with buffalo shoulders and a Schwarzeneggian chest, while below, in a sharp mismatch, my hips were barely there, my legs were twisted sticks, and my pelvis hung at a weak crooked tilt, like that of a limp marionette. I also had the cherubically puffy red face that cortisone can sometimes produce. And that, along with my thick girlish eyelashes, my rather pouty mouth, and the disarming effect of my crutches, often led people to assume that I was younger and more guileless than I was—not a bad secret weapon to have on hand, by the way, when negotiating with dealers who had yet to get to know me.

My mother, who's mad about posting notes around the house, had taped a message to the door, printed in her firm, masculine hand.

Arnie:

Welcome home. Hope you've had an enjoyable trip. I assume it was a lucrative one, as usual. You'll find me in the basement, slaving away on your laundry like the dedicated mother that I am. See you there.

Typically, my no-nonsense mother hadn't bothered to sign her note—just as she never belabored the obvious by identifying herself over the phone when she called.

I poked into the house, through the book-and-magazine-cluttered living room, past the dining room table littered with my mother's school materials and lesson plans, and paused at the lip of the broad, gracefully swooping concrete ramp that stood in place of the old basement stairs. Like the concrete slope in front of the house, this was a relic of my wheelchair-bound childhood, and one I couldn't help viewing, sentimentally or not, as a monument to my parents' long self-sacrifice. They'd had it built so I could reach my enormous rock collections downstairs, but at what crushing expense I never did find out, for both my parents had always stonewalled me on that question. For all I knew, they were still paying it off.

I spider-walked as softly as I could down the ramp. My mother was standing at the Kenmore washer and dryer that had been my gift to her on her fiftieth birthday, folding the last of the laundry I'd dropped off on my way to Kansas City. She wore a pair of jeans that, despite her age, didn't look half bad on her compact rear end, and a red-checked headscarf that incompletely covered her lank silver hair. On the floor stood piles of folded clothing, stacked around my flat red backpack, which lay waiting to be filled.

At that time I was living independently—but only to a point. I worked my crutches with the plastic-coated handles that jutted from the shafts, making it impossible, while standing up, to use both my hands at once. And although I'd had my little house in Maplewood outfitted with stainless steel handrails—above the kitchen counters, beside my bed, along the top of the bathtub, the inside of the shower, and the sides of the toilet—there were still certain tasks I was helpless to perform on my own. I could manage such basics as taking my own baths, leaks and craps—thank God—and while steadying myself at the handrails in the kitchen, could pour drinks, fix sandwiches, make coffee, and so on. But when it came to any real cooking, the major cleaning, and my laundry, I was as dependent on my mother as an infant.

I meant to sneak up behind her and surprise her with a kiss. But the rattling of my crutches must have given me away. She flashed a smile over her shoulder, dropped the shirt she was folding, and embraced me, the top of her kerchiefed head just reaching the base of my throat; I could only partially return the hug. It still astounds me to remember how that tiny woman, who's never weighed above a hundred pounds, used to push me, drag me, hoist me around in that wheelchair for so many years—even when I was in my early teens, and must have weighed half again as much as she did. But luckily for the both of us, Doris Goldman was built as tough as an ant.

She started fussing with the collar of my shirt. "How are you feeling, Arnie?"

"Just fine," I said.

She inspected me rather suspiciously with her slightly bulging, shrewd gray eyes. "What do you mean, just fine?"

"Almost fine, how's that? I'm having a banner day, Mom. Believe it or not, I was actually using my feet while I was driving just now."

"Really? Well, that's wonderful, Arnie. Let's hope it keeps right up."

"It won't," I said.

"You don't know that. Who can say what might happen? You were never supposed to get out of your wheelchair, don't forget." She smiled. "You just might confound the experts yet."

"I'm not holding out for any miracles, Mom."

"Well, I am. If that's all right with you." She turned back to her laundry. "So how did you make out in Kansas City? Did you make a killing?"

"It was a massacre," I said.

She laughed. "Well, thank God somebody in this family is out there making a killing. Instead of the other way around."

I frowned at my mother's deceptively frail-looking back. That remark was a not-so-veiled jab at my father, whom my mother has never really forgiven for his lifelong mediocrity.

Henry Goldman still worked in the same stifling little tailor shop in University City where he'd been altering and pressing suits since before I was born (as an only child who came along very late in their lives, I'm sure I was a mistake, although my mother has always denied this), and after more than twenty-five years at the job, he had yet to become partners with old Mr. Handler, or even to acquire a piece of the business. And the worst of it was—from my mother's point of view, anyway—my poor *shlub* of a father didn't really seem to *mind*. Soft-spoken, hunch-shouldered, sweet-natured and sad-eyed as a beagle, my father was the very image of incurable resignation. How his ineffectual genes had managed to bypass me entirely, without leaving a discernible trace behind, was anybody's guess. But I was so clearly the son of my hard-driven, obstinate mother, I might have sprung fully armored from her head.

She stuffed the piles of finished laundry into my backpack, zipped it up, and as she stood, expertly hoisted it on.

"For chrissakes, Mom—I can handle that myself."

She ignored me and started for the ramp. "So tell me about Kansas City."

I clanked behind her. "There's not much to tell. Basically all I saw was the inside of the convention hall, my hotel room, and a shitload of rocks."

My mother, starting up the curved white ramp, was almost completely hidden by that big red backpack—except for her elbows sticking out to the sides, her skinny legs scissoring below.

"Did you come up with any museum pieces?" she asked.

"Yeah, I think so, as a matter of fact. This one terrific lot of blue Russian opals in particular. I'm thinking of trying Bill Conway at the Chicago Natural History Museum. I know he doesn't have anything like them."

"Blue opals. That sounds lovely."

"Would you like one?"

She paused at the top of the ramp. "What?"

"Hell, I've got a dozen of them, Mom. I could have one set into a pendant for you practically at cost—"

"Are you insane? Something you could sell to a museum—

around *my* neck? Where would I wear it, Arnie? To my PTA meetings?"

She was leading the way toward the living room now.

"You'd better learn to curb that crazy extravagance of yours," she went on. "Especially if and when you ever decide to get married. You'll turn your wife into a monster."

"Mom, I enjoy being extravagant. It gives me this exhilarating sense of power."

My mother snorted as she slung off the backpack, and set it down on the floor near the door. She rubbed at her shoulder as she looked at me. "So did you meet anybody at this trade show?" she asked.

I smiled and squeezed my crutch grips. "Uh, meaning what?"

"Meaning did you meet anybody. Like a female."

"Mom, the only kind of women you meet at rock shows all have blue hair, wear orthopedic shoes, and live in camper vans."

She gave me a disgruntled look, then started back toward the kitchen. "You want some coffee? I started a pot."

In the kitchen I took a seat, slipped my wrists from the clamps of my crutches, and leaned them against the side of the table. My mother brought me my coffee—black as tar, the way I like it—then went over to the rolltop desk where, as always, there lay a thick confusion of bills, junk mail, coupons to be clipped. She fished around.

"I saved something here I want you to look at."

"Oh Jesus, Mom . . ."

"Oh Jesus what? You don't even know what it is."

I grunted, and sipped my coffee.

"Now, I'm asking you to take a look at this, Arnie. And please. Will you not make up your mind until you've given it some fair consideration?"

She handed me a letter.

I didn't have to read it to know what kind of letter it was. My mother periodically made small contributions to various organizations—self-help groups, singles clubs, athletic associations, and so forth—that catered to various categories and subcategories of the handicapped—paraplegics, quadriplegics, arthritics, you name it—and all for the underhanded purpose of keeping herself on their mailing lists. Like most of what my mother did, this ruse made perfect sense. She knew that if such mail came to my house, I'd chuck it in the trash without a second glance. But by having this stuff mailed to her instead, she could at least make sure to corner me on the subject every so often. She poured herself some coffee, sat at the table, and eyed me like a cobra.

I finished scanning the letter and set it down beside my coffee mug.

"Well?"

"Sounds like fun," I said. "For people who find that sort of thing fun."

"Arnie, you know I haven't bothered you about anything like this for a very long time."

I smiled at her. "And then you just couldn't stand it any longer, could you?"

Her eyelids came down a notch. "I may as well tell you, Arnie. They asked for an RSVP, and I took the liberty of sending it in for you. Along with twenty-five dollars."

"You did *what?*"

"You heard me." She rubbed at the finely wrinkled skin at the base of her throat. "I've never understood your intransigence in this area, Arnie. It's a party—a mixer for young people, that's all."

I picked up the letter again. "Mom, did you *read* this? Did you see what they're *calling* this thing? Just listen to this. *You're invited to a Fall Funfest for the Physically Challenged.* For the physically challenged! I mean, shit!"

"What? What are you objecting to?"

"You *know* what I'm objecting to! I mean, why can't these mealy-mouthed jerks in their PR departments ever just call a cripple a cripple? Hell, I don't mind the term. I *like* it, in fact. Cripple. There you go. There's no disputing what *that* means. It's clean, direct, honest—"

"What has that got to do with anything?"

I threw up my hands. It wasn't as if my mother hadn't heard me rave on about this issue before—which never failed to light a fire under me. "I'm sorry, Mom. But I just don't *like* the idea of being euphemized out of existence. I mean, first I was handicapped. Remember back when I was handicapped? And

then I was *disabled*. And then, all of a sudden, I was *special*—
whatever the hell that means—and then for godsakes, I was a
special needs person. And now it turns out that I'm *physically
challenged!* Well, shit! Who wouldn't *want* to be physically challenged? It puts you right there on the cover of *Parade* magazine! It makes you sound wonderful, heroic—as if all the normal slobs out there getting around on their own two feet just
aren't *trying* hard enough! As if you're supposed to be *admired*
for your—"

"Arnie, you're flying way off the handle!"

That shut me up, momentarily. Probably I *was* overdoing it.
I was stroking the tops of my thighs now—from the knees to
the crotch to the knees again—which was an old nervous habit
of mine, and a dead giveaway that I was on edge. I left off
massaging myself and sank forward over my crossed arms.
"Look, Mom, I just want to make it in the real world, all right?
I'm not interested in making it in a phony one."

"What's phony about people with similar needs and con-
cerns getting to know each other?"

"Why should I want to surround myself with other cripples?
To *remind* myself I'm crippled? Jesus, that's the last thing I
need to dwell on!"

"Nobody's saying you have to dwell on it, Arnie."

"Why, of course they are! Why else would anyone be there?
They'll probably all be wearing name tags saying, *Hello, my
name is blah-blah and my disease is blah-blah-blah.*"

"My God, Arnie—just what do you think you are?"

"I'll tell you what I'm not," I said. "And that's a guy who
goes to Fall Funfests for the Physically Challenged."

My mother looked at me flatly for a beat. Then she came
over and took up my cup. "You want this warmed up?"

"Please."

I assumed the argument was over. But my mother, not so
easily outdone, tried another tack.

"Arnie, what could it hurt to just go have a look? And then,
if you don't like it, leave. What's the big deal?"

"If it's not such a big deal, why are you making such a big
stink about it?"

My mother set down the coffee pot; her bony shoulders

sagged. "Because I'm worried about you, Arnie. You're not
. . . balanced."

"You think I'm crazy?"

"No, Arnie. No, all right? I'm astounded sometimes at how
very sane you are, given everything you have to contend with.
I mean balanced in your life." She brought my coffee over,
then clunked down in her chair. "You live all alone in that
slummy little house—"

"It's only slummy on the outside, Mom."

"Just let me finish. And you work yourself like a slave, and
you read your books, and except when you come over here for
dinner, I don't know what else you *do*. You never get out."

"I'm out with my clients all the time."

"Well, all right—but can you call any one of them a real
friend?"

"Sure. Desmond Garlick."

"Desmond Garlick lives in *Wales*. He visits here maybe once
a year, at most."

"You're forgetting about Redso," I said.

Redso Wolff—his given name was Arthur—had been my
closest friend, maybe the only true friend I'd ever had, since
high school.

"Wonderful!" my mother said. "There's another one who
lives halfway across the world!"

"Pittsburgh isn't halfway—"

"The point is, he's been away at drama school for the past
two years. When was the last time you saw him? At Christmas?"

I shrugged.

"Anyway, you know that's not what I'm talking about. What
I'm talking about is the lack of any women in your life. I mean,
besides me."

"Hey, don't sell yourself short, Mom."

"When was the last time you had a girlfriend, Arnie?"

I sighed.

"There was that one back when you were in graduate school
I remember—what was her name?"

"Brenda."

"Brenda. That's right. I never understood why you
dropped her. But anyway, who has there been since then?"

"No one," I said. I was stroking the tops of my thighs again.

"Arnie, will you please listen to me? Maybe you think you're plenty strong and self-sufficient—and maybe you are. But you're also human. And if you don't let go of this stubborn pride of yours, if you keep holding out for what you can't have, I guarantee you, you'll wind up with nothing."

"Mom, all I want is a nice, attractive, intelligent woman with two arms and legs that function. Is that really so much to ask?"

"Yes," my mother said emphatically. "Arnie, I know you're wonderful, and you know you're wonderful, but you can't expect women—especially young women—to be saints. Now, I'm sorry if that sounds harsh—"

"You don't need to apologize."

"Will you *please* just go to this party and take a look around? There are bound to be plenty of young women there with problems similar to yours—"

"Mom, don't you get it? I don't *want* a young woman with problems similar to mine. Isn't that clear?"

My mother shrugged. "It's clear," she said.

"So there's just . . . nothing left to discuss."

Almost in tandem, like two exhausted wrestlers giving up the fight, my mother and I both heavily sighed. Then I shifted in my seat, winced as I raised my hip, plucked my wallet from my pocket, and withdrew a five and a twenty. I pushed the money toward her.

"What's that?"

"Reimbursement. I'd hate to think you threw twenty-five bucks out the window."

My mother crumpled her mouth. "You're hopeless, you know that?"

"You're absolutely right, Mom." I dredged up a small smile. "So why don't you just give it up?"

I DROVE HOME with my buoyant mood of an hour ago in ruins. Even my legs seemed to know it. My right knee had gone so stiff that I could no longer use it to work the gas pedal. Pain grumbled and whined in my hips.

My mother had zeroed right in on the sorest point in my psychology. I wasn't nearly as complacent in my solitude as I wanted her to believe. The dull pain of my loneliness, in fact, was almost as chronic and nagging as the pain of my arthritis. And there were plenty of times, mostly when I wasn't keeping busy, when it sank me.

Until I'd gone to college my love life (to stretch a term) had been little more than a long and exhausting parade of hopeless crushes, always aimed at the loveliest and least accessible girls at my schools—and relieved only by my twice-daily or thrice-daily stroke sessions, aided by the cold smiling nudes in the pages of my men's magazines. It wasn't until my final year in graduate school, when I was twenty-three, that I finally lost my virginity, and then with an extremely drunken girl named Mary, about whom (as drunk as I was when I bedded her) I remember almost nothing else, except that in the sallow light of morning I judged from her looks that she was probably just as desperate as me. Then there was Brenda—poor Brenda, as I can't help thinking of her. She was a geology student, we met in crystallography lab, and soon after that we were sharing, on most nights, her narrow dorm-room bed. But while Brenda was bright and kindly, with a very keen wit, she was also, I'm sorry to report, shaped like one of those Stone Age carvings of a *zaftig* fertility goddess, all bulges, folds and sags. I tried, for a couple of months, and as best as I knew how, to maintain the lie that I was in love. But Brenda's looks, such a world away from my ideal, were simply more than I could take, and my hypersensitive esthetic finally reared its tyrannical head. I backed off with some lame excuse about not being ready for a real commitment, whereupon poor Brenda, who must have been inured to such disappointments, plucked up what dignity she had left, and waddled with barely a protest out of my life. Since then, aside from a date or two that my mother had drummed up for me through her network of busybody friends —and the less said about those nervous, socially inept, hopelessly unattractive women, the better—I'd been alone.

And maybe I deserved what I was getting.

But what could I do? I was a physical wreck, enslaved by my notions of physical beauty. The irony wasn't lost on me, of course. But unless I put out my eyes, or rewired my brain, I saw no possible way out of my predicament.

And yet I had hope. I knew how the world tended to work. And about one thing my mother had been flat wrong; I wasn't holding out for what I could never have. One of these days, and it wouldn't be so long now, I would have rolled up so much money from my gem and mineral trade that some female somewhere—some lovely two-legged paragon of normal, healthy womanhood—was going to overlook my spectacular deficiencies (or be blinded by the dollar signs flashing in her big blue eyes), be lured into my gem-encrusted lair, and settle for me just as I was.

I was prepared to wait, and to suffer while I waited. For if my arthritis had taught me anything, it was how to wait and suffer. Sooner or later I would claim my consolation prize.

That was the secret solace of my early adulthood—however seldom it actually consoled me.

WHILE I COULD have afforded a much nicer place in a more affluent area of St. Louis, I'd chosen, for reasons of security, to take a house in one of the more run-down sections of the run-down old suburb of Maplewood—a gritty blue-collar neighborhood of dark corner taverns, warehouses, liquor stores and auto body shops, where the squat red brick houses and the more rambling ramshackle wooden ones were all jumbled together, like drunks leaning shoulder to shoulder, on narrow potholed streets. Frequent American flags, jacked-up cars, banged-up pickups, and plenty of preposterous lawn ornaments all added to the philistine ambience. My house on Oxford Street was one of the squat red brick ones (although much bigger on the inside than it looked), sitting back from the street behind a rampantly overgrown lawn, which I purposely never watered and only occasionally hired a neighborhood kid to mow. I meant for the place to look as seedy and destitute as possible, for like one of Potemkin's hollow villages, my house was an exercise in deception. No passerby in the street, and no burglar worth his jimmy (or so I hoped) would have any reason to suspect that behind that shabby facade lay an eye-popping repository of gemstones, fine crystals, and irreplaceable fossils whose total cash value I could really only guess at. Naturally the ugliness of my surroundings got me down on occasion. But I had no plans to move. When it came to my rocks, it was safety above all. At the end of this week, in fact, I had a long overdue appointment to see about getting an alarm system installed.

I bumped down the pocky driveway, and as always, discreetly parked my shiny new Toronado in the back. I took up my crutches, got out of the car, opened the back door, sat on the seat, and shrugged on the first of my rock-laden backpacks. I clumped up the rotting back porch, and when I reached the door, damned near almost blacked out.

It was standing slightly open—a slice of the green and white tiled floor showing obscenely between the door and the step.

I stared down in slack-jawed amazement.

It was impossible, inconceivable, that I could have been so brain dead as to leave the back door standing open for the whole time I was in Kansas City!

But either that, or I'd been robbed.

I almost smiled at the bitter joke—if the bastard had only waited another week, he would have tripped my expensive new alarm system—then carefully lowered my backpack to the porch. I filled my chest with air, clenched my jaws, and clumped inside, through the kitchen and into the dining room, where the lion's share of my finest rocks was set out on display.

It was like dying an excruciating death, only to find yourself abruptly in paradise. For whatever I'd been robbed of, it hadn't been these rocks. There they all were, my faithful beauties, my glittering rockettes, all lined up right where they belonged on the steel shelves that filled the room. Almost lost, and yet not lost at all, they seemed haloed by a shimmering hyperreality. I crutched past them slowly, then past the matching, chest-high, amethyst geodes that flanked the entrance to the living room like a pair of jeweled gates, and over to the hand-built redwood specimen cabinet in the living room, where my priciest specimens were secreted, and which made the whole house smell a little like a hamster cage. I unlocked it and slid out each of the shallow drawers. My rubies, my garnets, my jade and my jets, my lapis lazuli and sapphires and aquamarines, my beryls and onyx and tiny turds of native copper and silver and gold, all lay as snug in their labeled and cotton-lined boxes as babies asleep in their cradles. I exhaled in a fury of relief.

But then, as I was relocking the cabinet, I heard a groaning of pipes behind the walls, and the sound of rushing water in the bathroom down the hall, gushing full throttle into the sink.

So he was here after all! The son of a bitch had been caught short, had had to take a leak before ransacking my house—and now he was washing his hands! But could a criminal be so dainty? Why, sure. Why not? Where burgling was concerned, stealth and daintiness were all. I was evidently in the company of a nerveless professional.

But was he armed?

I glanced down at my fists where they gripped the crutch handles. The knuckles bulged white, but the crutches held steady. I was possessed by an irrational calm. I moved quietly to the nearest rock shelf and coldbloodedly made my selection: a rod of petrified wood, about ten inches long—heavy and solid enough, I figured, to crack a skull without cracking itself. But did I actually have it in me to brain a human being? I had no idea. I only knew that my rocks, my rocks, were everything—not only my whole life's work, but my whole life's hope—and that I wasn't about to give them up without a struggle.

I jammed the rod of petrified wood down the back of my pants, through the belt, and advanced down the carpet to the bathroom. The fizzy cascade of water from the sink should have drowned out any clanking from my crutches; still, I took it as gingerly as I could. The bathroom door stood ajar a few inches. I softly set my right crutch against the wall, plucked my weapon from my pants, and leaned in for a look.

It wasn't quite what I'd expected.

A naked woman, damp and rosy, was bent forward almost double, bracing herself on the steel handrail that stood alongside the tub. Her face was lost behind the shower curtain. But oh, I could drink in the sight of the rest of her; the rounded white goose-pimpled thighs, the patch of black pubic hair bristling between them, the puckered folds of her belly and the udderlike swinging of her full heavy breasts as, behind her, my old friend Redso Wolff slapped himself into her backside with the sort of rocking, languorous rhythm you might use to push a child on a swing. Redso's eyes were shut. His white teeth were bared in a grimace of pleasure. Water droplets clung like tiny diamonds to his bush of red-orange hair. The cords of his neck stood out, and the quiltlike muscles of his chest rippled, relaxed, and rippled again as he kept rocking away in his ecstasy.

I backed off, stuck my rod back down my pants, and beat a retreat down the hallway. My hands were so sweaty I could barely keep hold of the slick plastic handles of my crutches.

Heated through with shame—yet what had *I* done to be ashamed of?—I crutched out into the dazzling sunlight to fetch my backpacks. Once I had them safely inside the living room, I decided I could use a drink; my heart was pounding like a buried kettledrum. Two bottles stood out on the kitchen counter, one of Glenlivet, one of Cuervo Gold (Redso must have taken them from the cabinet where I kept my booze), and steadying myself at the handrail, I poured myself a shot of scotch. Drink in hand, I hop-skipped over to the table and set my crutches against the edge. I tasted my whiskey, and shuddered.

So Redso Wolff was back.

Redso had always gone in for dramatic entrances—just as he had on that day back in high school, ten years before, when he'd first shown the daring, or the imagination, or the generosity of spirit, to befriend me.

I don't know when I've been more badly in need of a friend. I had recently undergone two jarring transitions that would have shaken anyone's sense of himself, let alone a crippled fifteen-year-old. During the preceding summer, my illness had taken a shocking and unexplainable turn for the better. Within a space of weeks, confounding my doctors, I had moved out of my wheelchair and onto a pair of shiny new aluminum crutches. And now it looked like I would be starting my sophomore year at the regular public high school in the fall. As was so often the case in my life, my fate had been determined by a matter of mere bodily mechanics.

Few public institutions in those days (the late sixties) were equipped with ramps for wheelchairs. And for that reason alone, I'd been stuck for five nightmarish years at the Litzinger Special School, the sole facility for handicapped children in the area, where the student population was about two-thirds retarded, and the rest, like me, were classified as "orthopedic"—and which I loathed with such a passion that I referred to it in conversations with my mother (knowing full well how much it hurt her) as "the concentration camp." It's not true, by the way, that people can get used to anything. Pain, for example—even to chronic pain sufferers like myself —never loses the fresh sting of its surprise. And certainly I never got used to the Litzinger Special School—to the humiliation of boarding that runty yellow bus so publicly every morning when it stopped in front of my house, the windows filled with the blithely smiling faces of retarded kids, or to that hellish cafeteria, with its mingled stinks of institutional cooking and imperfectly controlled bladders and bowels, or to the insulting easiness of the classes, designed for kids who could barely concentrate, or to the painful tedium of physical and occupational therapy, or to the eeriness of the playground during recess, when I would sit out in my chair on that quiet and listless blacktop among my classmates—some of them perpetually squirming in the grip of cerebral palsy, some with the partially formed, or flipperlike, or wholly missing limbs resulting from thalidomide, others with more unusual birth defects (I remember in particular one little boy whose knees bent in backward, like a stork's), and some, with their emaciated bodies and their shining, otherworldly, unforgettable eyes, slowly and imperceptibly dying of MS. I was among them, all right, but in my own defensively proud and stubborn mind, I wasn't *of* them. While *their* conditions might have been hopeless, while *they* might have been stuck here for the long haul, I had no doubt at all that sooner or later *I* would be flying the coop —by virtue of the fact that I was me, Arnie Goldman, and clearly slated for better things. Naturally there were some children I became friends with. But none of those attachments ran very deep—and by the time my crutches freed me from that wasteland of broken young bodies, I left them all behind me without a flicker of regret.

Yet my return to the regular public school system—contrary to my joyful expectations—left me just as miserable as before. I found myself stunned, intimidated, virtually paralyzed with culture shock. Central High had been baby-boomed into a lively overcrowdedness, and within those thundering hallways between classes, engulfed by an excess of animal vitality and high spirits that I could scarcely comprehend, I felt, as I plugged along on my crutches, hugging the walls for safety, as vulnerable as a tortoise amid a herd of stampeding horses. For months, until well past the Christmas break, I wasn't myself. I kept my mouth shut in my classes—something completely unprecedented. I took my lunches alone in the cafeteria when I could find an empty patch of table, and when I couldn't, settled in uncomfortably with other taciturn rejects like myself—the grossly obese, the profoundly sullen, the pathologically shy. I sometimes considered taking my mother's sound advice, and getting involved in some after-school activity where I could more easily make friends: the literature club, the chess club, the debate team. But a new and mortifying timidity restrained me. I had moments of pure panic: where, if anywhere, would I ever fit in? In the company of cripples I felt defiantly normal, while in the company of normal teenagers I only saw myself as crippled and disdained. There were times in my self-pity when I even succumbed to a certain nostalgia for the old Special School—where at least I hadn't stuck out like a freak.

Naturally I couldn't take part in athletics. But due to a hare-brained notion of "mainstreaming" that was then all the rage among educators, it was a policy of Central High that every student, able-bodied or not, had to show up and dress out for gym class. So each day at two I would do my four-legged crutch-walk behind the other trotting boys—senselessly decked out in my sneakers, shorts and Central High T-shirt—and out to the playing fields, where nobody expected me to play. Sometimes I'd pass the hour by watching the other boys run track, play softball, and so forth (but without real envy; it had been that long since I'd participated in any sport), and once in a while I'd trade a few words with Coach Kessler, who, judging by the way he always squinted off at anything but *me* when he spoke, I seemed to make distinctly uncomfortable. Mostly, however, I sat alone, up in the stands overlooking the football field, and buried my discomfort in a book.

One spring afternoon I looked up from my copy of *Slaughterhouse Five* to see, far below my perch at the top of the stands, a student by the name of Redso Wolff loping in my direction, his puffball of bright orange hair bobbing energetically against the green of the field. He wore the requisite gym clothes, but his outfit made no more practical sense than my own, for his left arm was in a cast, and flapping uselessly in a sling. With his good arm he gave me a wave, then came bounding up the rows of concrete seats, taking them two at a time.

While I'd never said boo to Redso Wolff, I could hardly help knowing who he was; he was as famous, or notorious, as any student at the school. At the start of the spring semester, the Central High *Round-Up* had done a front-page feature article on him, replete with a grainy photograph, trumpeting the news that Arthur Wolff, better known to his friends as "Redso," had been the recipient of the much vaunted National Council of Teachers of English Award—the only student at Central High to have done so, and one of only eleven winners in the entire state of Missouri. Adding further to his laurels, Redso had just landed the part of Billy Bigelow in the upcoming student production of *Carousel*, which was something of a school record, as he'd already played the lead "to unanimous critical acclaim" in the last two plays the Drama Club had staged. "How far will Redso Wolff ultimately go?" the article asked. "Only time—and talent!—will tell!"

And yet he wasn't exactly your model student. Earlier that same week during gym class, while an electrical storm kept us confined to the auditorium, Coach Kessler had filled the hour with a booming, heartfelt, meandering speech on Good Student Citizenship (punctuated every so often by an accommodating drumroll of thunder) in which he singled out Arthur Wolff as his cautionary example. The reason Arthur was absent on this Monday, Coach Kessler informed us, was that he'd been involved in an accident on Saturday night; he'd driven his car straight into a tree, on Ladue Road, less than half a mile from the school. The coach had spoken to the police, and thus had it on good authority that the alcohol levels in Redso's blood had been high enough to "knock a horse unconscious." There was also good reason to believe that he'd been smoking pot. The car had been totaled, and Redso's arm had been fractured in two places; he was lucky to be alive at all. Furthermore, Coach Kessler went on, it was common knowledge around Central that pot wasn't the only drug that Redso Wolff indulged in, that some of the opinions he expressed in class were "just plain anti-American," and that you couldn't trust him as far as you could throw him in the company of respectable girls. The real tragedy, of course, was that Arthur had it in him to become one of the inspirational leaders of the high school. He was undeniably intelligent and talented, and was even, Coach Kessler had to admit, a natural on the basketball court. But his stubborn refusal to lend his talents to the team was just one more indication that Arthur lacked the character of the true athlete. "I don't think I need to remind you boys that drinking and driving don't mix," Coach Kessler reminded us during his peroration. "But neither—are you listening to me, gentlemen?—neither do rotten apples and good ones."

And now this genius-criminal, the Jean Genêt of Central High, was standing right in front of me with a broad invasive grin. Along with his other natural advantages, Redso was a compellingly handsome young man. He was one of those redheads whose skin was pale, but unfreckled. Below that mass of fiery hair, his features were almost too large, almost too sharp, and yet somehow harmonious—a big hawkish beak of a nose, strong high cheekbones, a squared assertive chin, and a pair of pale blue eyes set at a slightly Asiatic tilt, rather like those of a Tartar, or a Finn. Below his left eye the flesh was puffed and purplish; a rough red skid mark ran from the bottom of his ear to the side of his mouth—obviously results of his accident.

He went on grinning at me. "So is this idiocy, or what?" Redso said.

I shifted my aching hips on the cool concrete. "Uh, is what idiocy?"

"Having to show up for gym in the condition we're in."

Already I was warmed by Redso's suggestion, dubious or not, that we were both somehow in the same boat. "It's idiocy, all right," I said. "Hell, even if you croaked, they'd probably still make you show up and dress out."

Redso laughed. "No kidding, man. Stuffed like a bird in your Central High T-shirt." He scratched at his cast, then put out his good hand. "Redso Wolff," he said. "Although all my enemies call me Arthur."

I told him my name, and we shook.

"Goldman. Is that Jewish?"

"Yes."

"Ah, that's great! That's *perfect!* See, I'm Catholic. German Catholic. And my theory is, Jews and Catholics understand each other. I mean, we both grew up *meshugah,* right?"

I laughed. "I sure did, anyway."

"Yeah, I'll bet you did." Redso's tone was kindly. "So? What're you doing way the fuck up here in the clouds, anyway? Feeling sorry for yourself again?"

He might as well have kicked me in the solar plexus. I hunched my shoulders and scowled at the playing field. The boys at the far end were doing jumping jacks.

"Hey, sorry, man. I only brought it up because that's all I've seen you *do* around this place. You know, poking along on those crutches with that tragic look on your face. And . . . I dunno. I just thought you might be getting a little sick of it by now."

Something fell clean away from me then.

"You're damned straight I'm getting sick of it," I said.

Redso threw back his head and hooted. "That's the spirit! *Non carborundum illegitimi est.* Don't let the bastards grind you down! That's one of my father's favorite sayings, and he should know. He's the biggest bastard who ever lived. So? You mind if I take a seat?"

"No. Hell, no. Sit down."

Redso plopped down onto the concrete—so carelessly that I winced for his broken arm. "So anyway," he said, "I just figured we ought to get acquainted, seeing as how we're going to be sidelined together for a while. They tell me it's going to be eight weeks before the cast comes off. Not that I mind. Shit, it's going to be a pleasure, not having to take orders from Commandant Kessler for a change. Is that guy a Nazi, or what?"

"He's not too wild about you, you know."

"Yeah, so I heard. And it breaks my heart, believe me." Redso glanced at my crutches. "So what's the story on those things? Or do you mind my asking?"

"No. I don't mind. I've got arthritis."

"What? At your age?"

"Well, it's not the same kind that old people get. That's osteoarthritis. What I've got is called rheumatoid arthritis."

"Huh. Never heard of it. Are you in pain?"

I hesitated. "Yes."

"All the time?"

"Most of the time."

"Bad pain?"

"Well, it's not good pain," I said, with a smile. "Anyway, what about you? You can't be feeling too great."

Redso partially lifted his cast from his sling. "You mean this? Shit, I can't feel a thing. I'm flying high on codeine right now, if you want to know the truth. I've got a whole bottle of it back in the locker room, if you think you could use any. Great stuff. Good for whatever ails you."

"Um, no thanks."

"Well, you just say the word." He frowned at my book. "Vonnegut, eh? You a Vonnegut fan?"

"I wouldn't call myself a fan, exactly. He's pretty entertaining, I guess. But he's not really all that deep."

"No? Well, who is?"

I mentioned, not without a little pride, some of the authors I'd recently been reading (I'd been on a Russian kick)—Dostoevsky, Chekhov, Gogol.

"Oh, man, you've got to be kidding! It's about *time* I met somebody in this fucking hole of a school who's got some taste in literature! I'd given up hope! So you must read a lot, am I right?"

"Probably too much."

Redso narrowed his slanted blue eyes at me. "Yeah, well, I guess you don't get out a whole lot, do you?"

"No. I guess I don't."

"Well, shit, Goldman. It looks to me like we're going to have ourselves a fine time, ducking gym class together. So? What other subversives have you been reading lately?"

Redso's arm took almost eight weeks to mend, which added up to eight weeks, every schoolday afternoon, of the kind of intense, wide-ranging and exhilarated discourse, peppered with universe-solving epiphanies, that maybe only two bookish adolescents can very long or very seriously sustain. By the time his cast came off, and he had to join the other boys down on the field, Redso was already in the habit of grandly proclaiming that we were destined to remain best friends for life.

I still wonder what he saw in me then. There Redso was, the observed of all observers, with more pals, girlfriends and fawning hangers-on than he could possibly know what to do with, and yet it was me, a friendless gimp, that he chose for a soulmate. Of course, at first I was almost slavishly grateful for his attentions, which couldn't have hurt. And I was probably his best audience—for who else among his peers could keep pace with him intellectually, catch his allusions, or so knowingly applaud the loopy acrobatics of his mind? The very fact that I was crippled might have been part of the lure, providing Redso with a very noticeable stage where he could flaunt his disdain for convention (no social arena on earth is more conservative than a high school) and to display, like a peacock, the wide-spreading glory of his generosity. For whatever his motivations, pure or mixed, Redso was wonderfully generous to me.

He swooped me into his world. I met his dizzyingly wide assortment of friends (pure democrat that he was, Redso consorted with whomever he pleased, with nerds and druggies and honor society students, as well as with jocks and prom queen types); he got me drunk, stoned, silly and sick, and all for the very first time; he swept me along on riotous outings to bowling alleys, ice-skating rinks, and teen dance halls, never mind that I couldn't for the life of me dance, ice skate or bowl. And never once did I detect in Redso the slightest hint of embarrassment or apology at having a cripple in tow. Such magnitude of spirit was amazing to me, not to mention deeply flattering. In Redso's eyes, apparently, I wasn't a freak at all, but just a regular guy who happened to be on crutches. For once I'd met someone whose view of me corresponded absolutely to my own—so how could I help but love him? He even went so far as to drag me along on some of his dates, keeping it an evenhanded threesome for as long as we were at the movies, the burger joint, or drinking beer on the banks of the Missouri River, and dropping me off at my house only when, as he put it, "the moment of truth" was impending. Of course I carried my secret lusts for each and every one of his perfumed, vivacious, coltishly long-legged girlfriends. But none of them could match one fraction of the devotion that flamed in my heart, and would always flame there, I was certain, for Redso.

AND SO EVEN NOW, as I finished off my drink and waited, barely breathing, for Redso to finish with his business in the bathroom, I was ready to forgive him his appalling *chutzpah*. Aside from my rocks, my books, and my few brief unhappy entanglements with women, it was Redso Wolff who had supplied nearly all the scant color in my life. And in the two years since he'd been away at the drama conservatory at Carnegie Mellon, there were times when I'd missed him with all the forlorn intensity of a lover.

The shower went silent, and soon Redso came loping into the kitchen (true to his name, he had the loose, hungry, head-bobbing gait of a wolf), saronged in one of my plush yellow towels. He stopped short, his eyes rounded. "Arnie! You sneaking gimp! What the hell are you doing in here?"

I cracked a grin. "Shouldn't I be asking you that question?"

"Ah, shit! Brother, is it good to see you!"

Redso charged me, stooped, and embraced me where I sat. I returned his hug the best I could (he was bent down in an awkward position) and then, either losing his balance or forgetting who he had in his arms, Redso oafishly leaned to one side, and nearly dragged me off my chair. I bellowed with pain.

He leapt back. "Whoa! Jesus, Arnie! You all right?"

I shot him a look of hot resentment as I rubbed at the sides of my hips—for I'd not only been hurt, but shocked by his clumsiness. While Redso had always been an exuberant, unembarrassed toucher—damned near Russian in his readiness to grab you, kiss you, clap you in a bearhug—over the years he'd learned how to handle me, fragile package that I was, with special care. Only my mother had a better sense of where and how to touch me.

I went on rubbing at my throbbing hips.

"Say something, Arnie. Jesus! Your face is as red as an apple. Did I really hurt you bad?"

I shook my head no—never mind that he *had* hurt me

pretty badly. "But Christ, Redso. When did you get so ham-handed?"

"I'm just a little overly excited, that's all. I mean, we haven't seen each other in so damned long—well, *Gott in Himmel!* Aren't you a tiny bit overly excited yourself?" Redso showed me one of his trademark ingratiating white grins, and yanked his towel tighter around his slim waist. He seemed to have lost a lot of weight back in Pittsburgh—so much that I wondered if he might have been sick. His ribs were apparent, his belly concave. His features were sharper, more hawklike than ever, the pale skin drawn tight across the bones. "So tell me the truth now, Arnie-boy. Didja miss me?"

"I missed you a lot."

Redso slapped his toweled hips. "Ah, that's what I wanted to hear! Sweet music to my ears!" Now he squatted down in front of my chair, and grinned up at me. "Goldman, do you realize you're the only man in my life?"

I laughed.

"Hey, laugh if you want. But it's true. I don't know what it is about you, buddy—maybe some extra touch of humanity that comes from being crippled, who the fuck knows? But lately I've been finding that I can't really *talk* to other members of my gender. Not like we talk. Not like we've always been able to talk. I mean with our hearts right out there in the open, pumping away on our sleeves. And I've missed the hell out of it, Arnie. Christ, if it weren't for you and the company of women, I'd be lost in this world. And that's the god's honest truth, pal."

How Redso got away with it—how he'd always gotten away with such unabashed expressions of emotion—I wasn't quite sure. But those words, which would have sounded maudlin in just about anyone else's mouth, had come through with a simple credibility. Maybe what lay behind it was Redso's utter lack of shame. He was never the slightest bit embarrassed by anything he said, and so neither, in most cases, were his listeners. And I had no trouble replying in kind. "Shit, Redso. You know I feel the same way."

His grin widened, and he shot upright. "I gotta tell you, man. All that time in Pittsburgh without you—nobody to lend me money interest free, nobody to swing a crutch at my head whenever I got out of line—it's a miracle I even survived. So? *Qué pasa? Come cómo va?* How're you doing there, pal? How's the dread disease been treating you? The legs doing all right?"

I gingerly shifted my hips; the throbbing had mostly died down. "Actually, they haven't been too bad, in general."

"Oh yeah?" Redso raised his hands high above his head and snapped his fingers. "Care to tango?"

"They're not that good, either."

Redso stood there, still grinning, and rocking slightly from heel to bare heel. "I've missed that chipmunk face of yours, buddy. It's been too long." Again he snapped his fingers. "So, hey? What the fuck are we doing, just standing here? This is a reunion! This calls for a drink!"

He spun away, and made for the tequila on the counter.

It came to me rather foggily—after all the distracting brightness that Redso had been flashing around—that I had a bone to pick with him. "Redso, what the hell is going on here, anyway?"

"What do you mean?"

"Are you kidding me? I just got home from Kansas City and found the back door standing open—wide open. I thought for a minute I'd been robbed."

"Ooh," Redso said, swinging around with the bottle in his hand. "That must've been traumatic."

"It *was* traumatic."

"Well, sure, sure. Hell, if anybody knows about your obsessive-compulsive attachment to your precious stones and baubles—*mein Gott!* You must've pissed your widdle pants."

I frowned at the odd hostility in that remark. "Just how did you get in here, anyway?"

Redso shrugged. He was working a fist around the neck of the tequila bottle like he was trying to twist it off. "I cannot tell a lie. I chucked a brick through one of your basement windows."

"You did *what?*"

"Hey, don't get all apoplectic about it, Goldman. I'll reimburse you for it, I swear to God."

I smirked at him, despite my irritation. Redso, in his own unthinking generosity, presumed that everyone around him was just as carefree with their property as he was. Or, put another way, he was a mooch. "Come on, Redso. When have you ever reimbursed me for anything?"

"What can I say? *Mea culpa. Mea maxima culpa,* all right? I mean, Christ—I had to get into the house *somehow,* didn't I?"

Now I saw again—in a vivid, upsetting flash—that naked woman bent forward over the bathtub, her melon-heavy breasts swinging to and fro as Redso so deliriously banged her from behind. She was somewhere in the house; but where, and doing what? I nearly brought the matter up—but caught myself. How could I know that Redso was here with a woman unless I'd seen what I shouldn't have seen?

Redso drank straight from the tequila bottle, his Adam's apple pulsing. He wiped his mouth with the back of an arm and let out a long rumbling belch.

"For godsakes, Redso. There's a lime in the fridge, some salt in the cabinet, and a shot glass over there by the sink. If you're going to do it, do it up right."

"Gotcha," he said, plunking down the bottle on the counter. He loped to the refrigerator, swung open the door, and ducked behind it. A slice of his frizzed orange hair hovered over the top. "I know, I know, I know," he said. "You don't have to tell me, Goldman. I know it was just plain criminal, breaking into your house like this. But you've got to understand, I didn't have any choice. I mean, I get off the bus last night without a nickel in my pocket, I find your house deserted, and so what's a poor fellow to do? Sleep in the street? Turn himself into the Harbor Light Mission?"

"Why didn't you try your mother?"

Redso seemed not to have heard the question. He shot upright, slammed the refrigerator door, and rubbed his lime against the taut skin of his belly as if he were polishing an apple. As he strode back to the counter, I was struck again by his emaciation. He had the look of a starving jittery dog as he prowled along the length of the gleaming handrail. "You got a knife around here anywhere?"

"Try the drawer to the left of the sink. Redso?" I waited a beat. "Hey, Redso."

He grunted.

"Why didn't you stay at your mother's house?"

He clanked around in the drawer. Then he drew out a

butcher knife, gave it a high triple-flip above his head, and caught it, thank God, by the handle.

"Redso, do you think you could answer a simple question?"

"Sure, sure. Fire away."

"Why didn't you stay at your mother's house last night?"

"*Ach,* for godsakes, Arnie! *You* try staying at Frieda's place for more than two minutes. Hummel dolls, sentimental samplers, pictures of my dead sadistic father stuck up on every wall— Christ! I'd rather be forced at gunpoint to sit through *The Sound of Music* again."

Now the obvious finally occurred to me. "But what are you even doing back here? Didn't your semester already start?"

"That's over and done with, pal. *Finito* and *kaput.*"

"What?"

He was prowling the counter again. "Shot glass, shot glass, shot glass . . ."

"In the dish drainer."

"Aha!" Redso plucked it out. He zipped back to the table, set the shot glass down with the lime and the knife, and stared critically at the arrangement for a moment. He slapped a thigh. "The salt!" he shouted. "The salt! The salt! My kingdom for the salt!"

He made for a cabinet, swung it open, and started rooting.

"Redso, could you slow down for half a second and *talk* to me? Are you saying you quit the conservatory?"

"That's exactly what I'm saying."

"But you—that doesn't make any sense. You said in your last letter—"

"That was months ago, pal. Things change. Things fall apart, the center cannot hold—well, you know the rest. Sorry about not writing for so long, by the way. But there was this insane Fellini-esque circus going on back at Carnival Mellon like you wouldn't—shit! Where's the salt? This place used to be as organized as a library."

"In the cabinet in front of you," I said, watching him very carefully now. "In the canister marked Salt."

Redso laughed, shook his head, whipped down the salt, and scooted right back to the dish drainer. "Now, where's that fucking shot glass?"

I picked it up and showed it to him. "Right here," I said. "Where you left it."

"I did?"

"Redso, are you all right?"

"What do you mean?"

"You seem—I don't know. Frantic. Distracted."

"Shit, Goldman—I feel fantastic! Terrific! Omnipotent! Like a big strong brilliant motherfucker ready to take a bite right out of the ass of the world!" He grinned and scratched vigorously at his protruding ribs. "You ever hear that crazy story about Yeats? Sounds apocryphal, but it's absolutely true. When he was sixty-five, maybe seventy, he had this experimental operation performed on him—had a pair of monkey's gonads implanted in his balls. And the next thing you know, he's writing the best damned poetry of his career. Stuff like *Why should not old men be mad?* And *I spit into the face of time!* Well, don't ask me why, but that's *exactly* how I've been feeling since—Christ, since I don't *know* when. Like I woke up one morning with an extra set of balls—the balls of a nine-hundred-pound gorilla! Man, I'm so full of piss and vinegar and nitroglycerin—"

"You look awfully skinny," I said.

"Hell, I'm just finally in fighting trim, that's all." Redso slapped his sunken belly as if to prove it. Then he zipped to the table, plunked down the salt, snatched up his shot glass, grabbed a chair, spun it around, and thunked into it backward, crossing his forearms over the top. "So, where were we? What were we talking about?"

"You and the drama conservatory."

"Right, right, right. So here's what happened. One day I'm walking to a rehearsal—the play's *Othello,* I'm Iago, and the director's a fucking incompetent—and bang, it hits me. Just like St. Paul getting zapped on the road to Damascus. Suddenly, I just *knew.*"

Redso's right knee was bouncing frantically, like a jackhammer.

"Knew what?"

"Knew I'd had it with jerking my meat, had it with the whole fucking program. It's high time I started *working,* Arnie

—and who needs a pack of washed-up, envious acting coaches to do it? So, *voilà*. I quit."

"You quit? Just like that?"

"Just like that." Redso hung over the back of the chair, grinning like an ape. His knee kept madly bouncing.

"But you only had one more semester to go."

"Yeah, so?"

"What about your scholarship money?"

He snapped his fingers. "Gone with the wind."

"Redso, that's crazy."

"Crazy like a fox, maybe."

I peered at my old friend. He was like someone I recognized, and yet didn't recognize at all, in a dream. "I'm not understanding this, Redso. You say you came back to St. Louis to work? What kind of work is there for an actor in St. Louis?"

"Shit work, commercial work, all right. But that's secondary, Goldman. Purely secondary." He leaned forward. "See, I've got this play I'm about to write. This play that's been *screaming* to get out of me—and I realized back in Pittsburgh that I had to be close to my sources to do it. Because get this. You're going to love this, Goldman. Guess what I'm writing about? I'm writing about my brutal fascist swine of a father, and my poor addled kitsch-crazed mother, and my whole twisted Prussian upbringing in my dear old Dutchtown neighborhood. In fact, that's the working title. *Dutchtown*. Not bad, eh? Now all I have to do is figure out the opening scene, and get the damned thing written, and I'm telling you, man—it's going to absolutely *blind* everybody who sees it!"

Now both his legs jackhammered—so rapidly the kneecaps were a blur. I had the urge to reach over and still them.

"So why the paternalistic scowl of disapproval?"

"Well, Jesus, Redso—what do you expect? You've been wanting to study acting at Carnegie Mellon for as long as I've known you. I mean, doesn't this strike you as just a little bit rash?"

Redso sprang to his feet and headed to the counter for the tequila. He swung the bottle to his mouth—apparently forgetting all the complicated meanderings he'd undertaken to collect his shot glass, lime and salt—and took a heroic chugging swallow.

" '*I wasted time / Now time has wasted me.*' Richard the Second, Act Two, Scene—well, who *gives* a shit what scene it was? The point is, Carnegie Mellon was wrong from the start—wrong, wrong, wrong, wrong, wrong—and I'd *had* it. Simple as that. *Verstehen?*"

"Redso, it can't be as simple as all that."

"Hey, partner. Spare me the fucking third degree. I told you what I told you, and that's all there is to tell."

"Who was giving you the third degree?"

Redso laughed—and damned if I knew why. His slanted eyes gleamed with an unfamiliar, almost hostile incandescence. I noticed that he was padding his bare feet around in a ceaseless, antic box-step, like he was standing on burning hot asphalt. I'd never seen him like this before. But what was I seeing? He'd already killed off a good portion of that tequila, easily enough to get drunk on. Yet I knew Redso, drunk or sober. This was something else.

But now a change came over him. His dance steps dwindled to a stop—and he smiled at something, or someone, past my shoulder.

I shifted around in my chair.

Leaning against the inside of the doorway, and watching him with a wary half smile, was Redso's lover, or pickup, or whoever she was, now endowed with a face, and a face so exquisite—oval-shaped, butter-soft, butter-white—that it pained me a little to look at her. She looked sleepy, as if she'd just stirred awake from a nap. There was a drowsy sheen in her black almond eyes; the lids above them sleepily drooped; the lids below pushed up against the whites like slim curved pillows. Her thick black hair, spilling in tangles all the way to the backs of her thighs, was streaked and peppered with gray —premature gray, surely, for she couldn't have been much older than Redso or me. The ripeness of her figure was nicely contradicted by the masculine outfit she wore: jeans, a scruffy gray corduroy jacket, and beneath that, a loose black T-shirt, against which the orbs of her full breasts swelled. She looked both young and mature, sleepy and alert, slightly mannish in that jacket and yet utterly, juicily female—and while I knew that I should have stopped staring, I couldn't. She showed me a smile, pressing her teeth into the plum-colored flesh of her fat bottom lip. My throat drew tight at the base. Whoever this woman was, I thought, she would never be a mere torso to me again.

"You must be Arnie."

"Yes. And you're . . . ?"

"Billy."

"Billy, meet Arnie Goldman, my best buddy in the world, the sole proprietor of the Maplewood Topkapi Palace, and a shining inspiration to money-grubbing crippled people everywhere! And Arnie, meet Billy Rubin. Christ, is she something, or what?"

Billy flashed a concerned look at Redso, then found her smile again, and approached me. She moved her shoulders in a funny, swaggering way. "Nice to meet you, Arnie."

She stuck out her hand. We shook. I had to swallow before I spoke.

"Nice to meet you," I said.

"Actually, I sort of feel like I already know you."

Her voice was a marvel; a rich, husky, soothing contralto that sounded, somehow, brown.

"You do? Uh . . . how's that?"

"You should just *hear* how Redso goes on and on about you, Arnie. I think you're the only other person in the world he admires as completely as himself."

"Ain't it the truth, ain't it the truth." Redso plopped into the chair behind me, seized my right shoulder, and leaned forward as he pulled me back; his tequila-scented breath pumped past my cheek. "We met at Carnegie Mellon," he said, "and right from the start, it was the real McCoy! I'm telling you, Goldman, the fucking genuine article! Billy was the only other student in the program from St. Louis—and now, glory be to God and saints be praised"—he was speaking in a thick Irish brogue—"she's thrown in her lot with me, boyo, and followed this happy bugger home!"

Billy had her hands pushed into her jacket pockets (I could see by the bulges they were fisted) and was observing Redso closely.

"And she's one hell of an actress, Arnie—and I mean one *hell* of an actress." Redso squeezed my shoulder so hard that I winced. "And get this. She's the daughter of a *rabbi*. An *Ortho-*

dox rabbi, no less. Of course, she's not exactly kosher anymore, or she wouldn't be hanging out with a *shaygetz* like me. But can't you see it in her, Goldman? Can't you just picture her as one of those exotic Old Testament babes—some Delilah or Bathsheba or Jezebel—putting starch under the robes of some filthy old Semites as she bends down over a well?"

Billy laughed—against her will, it seemed. "All right, Redso. How about slowing down a little?"

"Slow down? Slow down? Shit, I'm just getting started!"

She seemed to make a point of turning to me. "Anyway, Arnie, I hope you're not too angry about us breaking into your house. It was nervy of us, I know. But last night . . . well, we just didn't have anyplace else to go. We tried calling from Pittsburgh, and then from Illinois. But nobody answered."

I was so enthralled by the rich brown velvet of her voice that I'd barely comprehended the words. "I . . . well, it's nothing to worry about now. And anyway, you're more than welcome here. Both of you."

"You sure?" she said.

"Well, of course. And anyway, I've got the sneaking suspicion the breaking-and-entering stuff wasn't your idea."

"That's awfully generous of you."

"Yeah, that's Arnie for you. The sport of all sports. The most magnanimous of cripples! The great-hearted gimp—"

"*Redso,*" Billy said.

"What?"

"You're being really obnoxious, all right? Take a deep breath or something."

Redso shot to his feet, grabbed the butcher knife from the table, and began to saw ferociously into his lime. "Of course, we didn't *have* to stay here. We always could've stayed at Billy's Daddy's house." He snatched up his lime quarter and gave Billy a toothy challenging grin. "That is, if you can stand living in a thirteenth-century Jewish ghetto. You wouldn't *believe* the way this woman grew up, Arnie! Talk about fanaticism! I'm telling you, her father makes the Ayatollah Khomeini look like a bleeding-heart secular humanist! Of course I have yet to meet the fart . . . but anyway, anyway . . ." Redso popped the lime quarter in his mouth and noisily chewed. "Sho what I want to know ish, how did two people from shuch shcary fucking backgroundsh turn out to be sho damned adorable?" He tossed his sucked-out lime to the table, slapped his hands on his hips, and as he sassily wagged his shoulders, began to sing: "A, I'm adorable, B, you're so beautiful—"

"Redso," Billy said. "What are you doing?"

"Doing? Why, I'm singing! Gotta sing, gotta dance! What are *you* doing, Miss Rubin?"

"Watching you," she said.

"Yeah? How do you like my act so far?" Redso executed a series of nimble soft-shoe steps, then spun around and dropped to his knee, his arms outstretched, Al Jolson style. "Oh, Mammy! It's your blue-eycd Aryan boy from Alabammy! Hot-cha!" He shot upright with a shit-eating grin. "So? What do you think? You think I'll make it to Carnegie Hall at this rate?"

Billy gave him a steady look of warning, then plucked her hands from her pockets and made for the counter, her shoulders intently swinging. "All right if I fix a drink, Arnie?"

"Sure."

"How about one for you?"

"Um . . . yes. Thanks."

"How do you take it?"

"Just straight up."

"She makes a hell of a good nurse, doesn't she?" Redso tugged his towel tighter at his waist. "You can't imagine how efficient she is, Arnie—a true mistress of detail in every task she undertakes. Oh, Nurse Ru-bin! Oh, Nur-sie! Could you please come to my bedside and readjust my catheter?"

"Knock it *off,* Redso." Billy moved to the refrigerator and opened the door to the freezer.

"Oh, Nurse Ru-bin! I'm right over here in bed sixty-nine! *Why* do you ignore my plaintive calls? Can't you tell I'm suffering the tortures of the damned?"

Billy slid out a tray of ice.

And then Redso lunged for her. He swung her around by the shoulders, pinned her to the refrigerator, and forced his growling face to hers, his toweled hips grinding in lewd insistent circles. The tray hit the floor. Several ice cubes skittered out.

With a choked sound of protest, Billy shoved him away, her back thumping the refrigerator door. "No!" she shouted, giving an angry toss to her spill of salt-and-pepper hair. "My God, Redso—what's *wrong* with you?"

"Oh, come on, Rubin! Don't play the good little Rabbi's Daughter with me! I know what you like!"

"We're not alone, all right?"

"You—Wait! Stop the music! *Oy, gevalt!* Will you look what you've done to me? Jesus H. Christ! Will you *look?*"

Then Redso let loose with his *coup de grâce.* He opened his towel and thrust his pelvis forward. I was shocked to see that he was partially erect, his thick curved prick arching out with menace, cobralike, from its nest of red-brown hair. He wagged his hips. His prick flapped. "Ooh-la-la! Will you look? Just *look* at how John Thomas yearns for you!"

Billy stalked out of the kitchen.

Redso threw back his head and hooted. Then he wrapped his towel back around himself, and without a glance at me, followed after her.

I took up my crutches.

They were standing face to face in the living room, between my colossal amethyst geodes. Billy was hiked up on her tiptoes. She had one hand clamped over his mouth; the other gripped the back of Redso's neck. Redso was rocking himself from foot to foot, steady as a metronome—and of all the inexplicable antics he'd been up to so far, that steady robotic rocking was the most unnerving. He looked positively catatonic.

"Shh," Billy said, as if she was hushing an infant. "Shh . . ." She tipped Redso's face closer to hers, compelling him to look her in the eyes. "Try and relax," she told him in that dark soothing voice. "Can you relax?"

"I've just got this volcano inside me . . ."

"I know, baby. I know. Just breathe deeply, and try to let it go . . ."

Billy moved as Redso moved, swaying from side to side, so that she didn't lose contact with his eyes—which looked confused now, and a little frightened. "Shh," she kept saying. "Shh . . ."

Redso's rocking slowed.

She dropped down to the flats of her feet.

"All right now?"

He shrugged and nodded.

Billy turned to look at me. Somehow she'd known that I was watching them from behind. "Arnie?" Her eyes were shining. "Do you think you could leave us alone for a few minutes?"

It was the sort of request a nurse might have made as she briskly drew the curtains around a hospital bed.

And like a bewildered, embarrassed, helpless visitor, I did as she requested, and withdrew from my own living room.

Two

I WAS A MESS the next morning. Not only was I hung over, but my hips were killing me, the pain in the joints bubbling up at a slow constant boil; I must have passed out in an awkward position. It came clear to me, as I groaned myself upright against the headboard, that my misery was the result of all the reckless drinking I'd done the night before—in a vain attempt to keep up with Redso's bizarre and galloping excitement. Sluggishly, the general outline of things took shape. Following his shocking performance in the kitchen, Billy had seen to it, like a nanny, that Redso got dressed. Then she announced that they were going for a walk—around the block, she said, and then around it again, until they'd walked some of this crazy energy out of him—and managed to drag a still-jabbering, still-gesticulating Redso out the door, and into the warm September twilight. I was bleakly nursing another drink when the two of them finally returned, maybe an hour later. They probably should have taken a few more circuits around the block, it seemed to me, for Redso was every bit as charged up as before. We ordered a pizza (I paid) and Redso, with more pressing things to do, apparently, than eat, took a grand total of two bites. For the rest of the evening, as Billy mostly kept a watchful silence, and I sat on the sofa, appalled and bewildered, barely able to slip a comment in edgewise, it was all Redso's show: a nonstop, jazzed-up, freewheeling extrava-

ganza of talk, talk, talk—about his play, about the hostage crisis, about Tennessee Williams's loathing of his home town of
St. Louis, about Ronald Reagan's third-rate acting career and
what it boded for the next four years, about the flaws in the
Big Bang theory, about the hairsplitting theological disputes
that had torn apart the early Christian Church—about whatever happened to snag in the flooded rushing river of his
consciousness—and all the while, as Redso knocked back his
shots of tequila, and paced, and roared, and joked, and sang,
and wildly elaborated idea after overheated idea, I kept putting more scotch in my glass, and without really intending to,
drank myself into a stupor.

I wasn't used to drinking like that, or to suffering the conse-
quences. I seemed to remember that there was some old Alka-
Seltzer stashed somewhere in my medicine cabinet; but what I
really needed was my prednisone. I gripped the steel handrail
beside my bed, bore down on it, and as I wincingly dragged
my stiff legs across the mattress, the damned thing broke clean
out of its socket on the wall. It swung around on the leg still
bolted to the floor and cracked into the side of my night table;
there was a bad jolt, and I cried out.

Soon there was a soft insistent rapping at my door.

"Arnie? Are you all right in there?"

I recognized that husky female voice—and remembered,
with a stab of shame, how Billy Rubin in all of her vividly
recollected nudity had performed the starring role in my masturbatory fantasy of last night.

"Arnie?"

"I'm . . . fine."

"What was that banging noise?"

"It was . . . nothing."

There was a pause.

"Can I bring you anything?"

I licked my parched lips. Actually, that wasn't such a bad
idea. I dreaded having to get up to my feet.

"Could you maybe bring me a glass of water?"

"Of course."

"Also . . . there's a pill bottle on the sink. Marked
prednisone."

"Prednisone. You've got it."

I closed my eyes and sank back against the headboard.

Billy entered, wearing jeans and a baggy gray Carnegie Mellon sweatshirt, her gray-peppered hair yoked back into a ponytail. Her beauty hit me as a fresh revelation; my memory had underestimated her. She was carrying, of all things, a glass of beer. She approached the side of my bed with that intent, shoulder-swinging walk, and handed it to me. "I put a raw egg in it, plus some other stuff. It works like a charm, believe me. Don't think about it. Just drink it."

I gave the glass a suspicious swirl. The yolk, bobbing around in that gassy yellow liquid, looked vaguely fetal.

"Drink it," Billy said again.

Had it not been this exquisite bossy woman telling me what to do, I'm sure I would have flatly refused that evil-looking concoction. But I drank it like a good boy.

"Don't talk yet. Just let it sit."

I followed those instructions too, and tried, unsuccessfully, not to picture that obscene egg yolk lying and dissolving in the hollow of my stomach.

Billy scrutinized the label on the pill bottle. "What are these for?"

"Pain."

She frowned. "How many do you take?"

"Three should do it."

She was inspecting the label again. "Prednisone. That's cortisone—a steroid, isn't it?"

"Right."

"But aren't there side effects?"

"Oh, yes. Slews of them."

"Like what?"

"It's addictive, first of all. Your body produces cortisone naturally in the adrenal glands. But when you're taking cortisone, the glands just sort of give up and let the medicine do the work. So if you stop taking it abruptly—well, all hell can break loose."

"What happens?"

"Intense fatigue. Your blood pressure can plummet. You can go into seizures—it can get pretty nasty."

"Huh. Well, what about side effects?"

I explained that prednisone could screw up practically everything in the body—the heart, the kidneys, the liver, the bones—but that so far, I seemed to be lucking out. "Mostly it's just responsible for this lovely face I've got."

"What do you mean?"

"The red complexion. The chipmunk cheeks. See?"

"Oh, you're being too sensitive, Arnie. You're not a bad-looking man at all."

My heart leapt—although I knew her little compliment had been perfectly innocuous.

Now Billy was scowling at the broken handrail. "What happened here?"

"Hell if I know. The damned thing just broke off in my hand."

"Just now? It wasn't broken before?"

"No."

"Well, shit," Billy said, and then did something surprising. She dipped to her hams, like she was curtsying, and studied the end of the hollow steel rod. Then she squatted still lower, inserted her face between the night table and the mattress, and poked around in the socket on the wall. She jiggled something. Then, with a grunt, she got down on her knees and fished around the floor, under the bed. "Aha," she said, coming upright. She had two infinitesimal screws trapped between her thumb and forefinger. "Got 'em. And look here." She swung the end of the handrail toward me. "See? It just got bent. That can probably be fixed with a hammer. And these screws gave way. They look like pretty standard issue—easy enough to find at a hardware store."

I blinked at her.

Billy slipped the screws into her jacket pocket. "I'll take care of it later, all right?"

"You will?"

"Well, sure. I mean, it *was* our fault." She seemed to fight against an inward-curling smile. "I think."

I didn't want to try and imagine whatever wild sexual gymnastics might have gone on in my bed last night (yet what *could* they have been doing to wrench that handrail out of the wall?) and changed the subject.

"I uh, really could use those pills."

She shook out three, and held out her open palm. I downed

them, as was my custom, without water. Then I asked her where Redso was.

Apparently that was a touchy point. She sucked in her cheeks, turned away, and frowned off at my wall of bookshelves on the far side of the bed.

"You're not going to like it."

"I'm not?"

"God, I'm sorry, Arnie. I mean, we've *already* taken such unfair advantage of you—"

"What are you talking about?"

She sighed, and plucked from her pocket what looked like the receipt from last night's pizza. "Here. He left it on the kitchen table. You may as well read it yourself."

On the back of the receipt Redso had scrawled a dense note.

Arnie, dearest:

Mea culpa! Mea maxima culpa! But I was tackled by a gang of pushy Muses, and couldn't wait. I have to get alone for a while, drive to bum-fuck East Jesus or wherever to seek my vision, figure out the opening scene of *Dutchtown,* and get the fucker nailed down. But I won't be gone long, maybe a day, maybe less, so don't panic, and don't despair, and in the meantime, you make sure and treat my lady nice, all right? Sorry about the unsolicited loan, by the way. I'll make it up to you, I swear.

Love and kisses,
REDSO

I crushed the receipt into a ball, and asked Billy, in a low rumbling voice, if she could please hand me my crutches. As always, I'd left them propped by their clamps on the front edge of the night table; the impact of the handrail must have knocked them to the floor.

She handed me my crutches and discreetly turned away. I bared my teeth as I struggled out of bed. All I had on were my pajama bottoms, and despite my outrage and pain, I couldn't help hoping, in some self-serving corner of my mind, that Billy would be impressed with my well-muscled torso—should she ever turn around and take a look.

But she was staring off again, as if transfixed, at my bookshelves.

I went to my bureau, where, like an idiot, I'd left nearly a hundred dollars in cash sitting out. All that was left was a lone twenty-dollar bill. And the keys to my spanking new Toronado had also disappeared.

"Christ! I don't *believe* this! What the hell is the *matter* with him?"

Billy took the chair in front of my desk, and bit down with apprehension on that bitable fat bottom lip.

I was crutching back and forth in front of my bed, despite the boiling pain in my hips. "First he breaks into my house, then he steals my car—what is he, a juvenile delinquent? Did he tell you where he was going?"

"No. He was gone when I woke up."

"Well, where did you sleep?"

"On the floor. We got some sheets and blankets from your closet, and I remember him lying down with me last night—but I have the feeling he didn't sleep at all."

"Go*ddammit!*" I hollered. "I only bought that car two *weeks* ago! I swear to God, if he puts so much as a dent in that thing—"

I stopped crutching—the pain in my hips was now unendurable—and lowered myself to the edge of the bed. Only then did I realize what Redso had left behind, almost as a kind of pirate's ransom, to keep me company—and my outrage abated wonderfully.

I spoke more reasonably now. "Billy, have you ever seen him like this before?"

She hesitated. "Have you?"

"No. God, no. I mean, Redso's always been pretty wild, pretty flamboyant—but nothing like this."

"Huh," Billy said, and said nothing more.

I shifted my pounding hips on the bed, and tried another way in.

"You were living with Redso, right?"

She nodded.

"For how long?"

"Since a little after Christmas."

"So you've had your eye on him for quite a while."

She nodded again.

"And you don't have *any* idea what's happening to him?"

"Oh," she said. "I have some ideas."

"Well, would you mind sharing a few with me?"

"Arnie—" She sighed, shut her eyes, then looked at me. "I'm sorry. But I'm just not ready to talk about this yet."

That flummoxed me. "Why not?"

"Well, for one thing, you and I are practically strangers."

Why that hit me so hard, I wasn't sure; it was certainly true enough.

"And for another, I just don't *know* enough yet. And if I start analyzing it out loud, without really knowing what I'm talking about, I'm just afraid I'll get myself twice as screwed up. Sometimes talking is the *worst* thing you can do, you know? I just . . . need more time."

Billy hunkered over her crossed arms, looking as alone with her knotty problem, and as stonily impenetrable, as Rodin's *Thinker*.

"Well, could you do me one favor?" I asked her. "When you do hit the jackpot, will you make sure and let me know?"

Billy showed me a sad smile. "Of course I will," she said.

And so, for the rest of that day, even as his nagging, unignorable ghost kept hovering at our backs, we barely mentioned Redso again.

That was more than fine with me. Redso was gone with my Toronado until very late that night, and in the meantime a sort of holiday atmosphere prevailed, an enforced yet pleasant coziness, as if Billy and I had been marooned together, or snowed in by an impassable blizzard. And while I still had plenty of bothersome questions popping around in my skull, that first indelible day that Billy and I spent together, stranded all alone in my house, turned out to be one of the happiest days of my life.

Redso's theft of my car barely inconvenienced me at all. It was Labor Day weekend, for one thing, and there was no pressing business for me to transact. And anyway, much of the time I could make my phone calls, write my letters, do my books, clean and trim my crystals, and pack my shipping boxes full of expensive delicate specimens without ever having to step foot outside my house.

It was soon clear that, despite her drowsy looks, and in her own far more practical and controlled way, Billy was nearly as supercharged with crackling energy, and as tightly wound up, as her mysteriously overwrought boyfriend. When I got out of the shower, I saw that she'd changed the sheets on my bed, and made it up as snugly as a hotel maid. She'd moved their two duffel bags out into the living room, where she'd also cleaned up the detritus from last night's drunken soiree. And although I protested that I could handle it myself, Billy brewed a fresh pot of coffee, and while she was at it, threw together from the eggs, cream cheese, cauliflower, and green onions she found in my refrigerator one of the best omelets I'd ever tasted, golden and frothy and perfectly ovoid on the plate, which she served with buttered toast and fried potatoes. Between bites I pumped her for information, feeling free, for some reason, to poke around in areas that were probably none of my business. Maybe her beauty should have intimidated me; but there was something about this sleepy-eyed, velvet-voiced woman that put me at my ease.

I learned that Billy was a little older than I'd guessed (she'd be turning thirty in October) and that she'd grown up in University City—an older suburb of St. Louis that bordered Washington University, and at one time had harbored most of the city's Jews. She wasn't sure what her immediate plans were, except that she figured she could pick up some work doing local commercials; she'd made good money that way while attending the conservatory in Pittsburgh. She had an older brother, named Frank, who ran a secondhand bookstore up in Chicago, and was apparently something of a loser. "Think of Raskolnikov from *Crime and Punishment*," she said, when I pressed her for a description. "Sort of a *nebbish*—but with a dangerous glint in his eye." Her mother had died when Billy was a child, her father still lived in town—and it was here, when I began to ask about her father, that Billy turned coy. Was I always this curious, she wanted to know? No, I said. She showed me a dismissive smile, then got up to clear the dishes.

Later I took her on a tour of my rock shelves. She seemed impressed enough at first, but once she'd come through with the obligatory oohs and ahs, her eyes began to look a little glazed. Trying another tack, I asked her if she'd like to see the earrings, pendants, rings, and unset stones I kept in a special cabinet in my bedroom; it was the kind of princely stuff, I promised, that she wasn't likely to see in any jewelry store. Well, maybe some other time, Billy told me. The truth was, jewelry had never really turned her on.

After that, somewhat deflated, I gave up on trying to dazzle her with my treasures. Leaving Billy to her own devices, I carried my backpacks into the area of my bedroom that I used as combination office and lab, and unpacked, trimmed, catalogued, and labeled all the sparkling new lovelies I'd brought back from Kansas City. But I did so without my usual covetous lip-smacking.

Another kind of beauty, it seemed, had usurped my fascination.

LATER THAT AFTERNOON I found Billy in my bedroom, on her knees, her long ponytail shifting from shoulder to shoulder as she banged away with a hammer on the broken handrail.

"Uh, when you get through with that," I said, "you think you could take a look at the air conditioner? It's been making some funny noises lately."

Billy looked at me over her shoulder. "What kind of noises?"

"I was just kidding, Billy. Jesus—you mean to say you could fix an air conditioner, too?"

"Well, yes, depending on the problem. I mean, if it's something like a clogged filter, sure."

I took a seat at my desk, astonished. Of course I was an easy one to impress when it came to such handyman stuff. Hobbled as I was by illness, I'd never been asked to do so much as hammer a nail. "Where'd you get the screws?" I asked her.

"At the Venture Store, across Big Bend." She started whacking away with that hammer again.

"How in the world did you ever learn about this stuff?"

"From my father."

"But I thought he was a rabbi."

"He is. But he hasn't been a practicing rabbi—you know, had his own congregation—since I was a little girl."

"Well, what does he do now?"

She explained that her father managed some apartment buildings—slum properties, really, mostly up in North County

—that he'd inherited long ago from her grandfather. "He's always loved to work with his hands," she said. "And when I was a kid, he used to drag me along on his jobs—you know, and show me how to do things. Plumbing, painting, wiring, you name it. I was sort of his unpaid apprentice."

Billy had already fit the handrail back into its socket, and was craning forward to tighten a screw, her upraised valentine of an ass wagging at me unnervingly. I forced my gaze to the window.

"It sounds like you and your father were close."

"Probably too close." Billy sat back on her heels. "After my mother died, I sort of became all things to him. His cook, his maid, his assistant, his best buddy. It all got . . . pretty suffocating."

"Didn't your brother take up any of the slack?"

"Frank? God, no. They loathed each other. Still do. For one thing, Frank refused to study for the rabbinate—and my father's never forgiven him for that. They barely even talk nowadays."

"Huh," I said. "And you grew up Orthodox, right?"

"Oh, yes."

"That must've been a barrel of laughs."

"You wouldn't believe how regimented it was, Arnie. I mean, just to give you an example, every Friday afternoon before *Shabbos* started, I had to tear the toilet paper into squares, and stack it on the windowsill under this little bronze paperweight. God, I'll never forget that thing! It was shaped like the Star of David. Sitting there on a stack of toilet paper, right? Talk about inspiring feelings of piety."

"But why would you—? I don't get it."

Billy swiveled around. "I thought you were Jewish, Arnie."

"I am. But my parents were about as assimilated as Ozzie and Harriet."

She twisted a corner of her mouth. "Lucky you," she said. "Anyway, we had to use that toilet paper—and *only* that toilet paper—on the Sabbath. Apparently tearing things is considered work. Although I'd sure like to see the Talmudic passage that applies to toilet paper." She snorted, shrugged. "Anyway, I'm a fallen Jewess now. About as fallen as they get. I mean, just look at me—eating pepperoni pizza, going out with a German Catholic . . ."

"But how did you come to fall?"

Billy narrowed her eyes. "Really, Arnie. I feel like I should be handing you my résumé."

I clammed up then—feeling hurt all out of proportion to the injury.

As if sensing that, Billy set down her screwdriver, and said, "Basically with my father it was all the *letter* of the law. I never *saw* any spirit in it. The God I grew up with was basically just this petty tyrannical drill sergeant with hundreds of crazy rules. That's all."

"Well, what about now?"

"You mean my religious ideas?"

"Yes."

Billy gave out a long sigh. "I don't know," she said. "There's compassion, I suppose. Or love, if you want to call it that."

"And?"

"And that's about it. Everything else—well, did you ever hear that famous story about Rabbi Hillel? You know who he is, don't you?"

"I'm not totally ignorant, Billy. Just sacrilegious."

"Well, anyhow, the story goes that somebody challenged Hillel to explain the entire essence of the Torah while he was standing on just one foot. And what he came up with was the Golden Rule. You know, do unto others? And everything else, he said, was nothing but commentary." Billy paused. "And I agree. Beyond feeling for other people—well, it seems to me that everything else is just a lot of superstitious bullshit."

I watched Billy go on screwing in her screws, impressed with the clarity of her position—and just as impressed with the heart-shaped, jean-filling rump she so innocently presented to me. I didn't want to feel it, but I did, and in spades—an aching congestion in my chest that definitely wasn't compassion.

"So now it's your turn, Arnie. What are your religious ideas?"

"Hell, I'm a skeptic. I don't have any ideas."

She laughed.

I went on gazing at her hindquarters, and aching.

"Well, there you go," Billy said, and wobbled to her feet. "All fixed."

THAT EVENING Billy rather shamefacedly borrowed the twenty-dollar bill that Redso hadn't absconded with, and walked to the Kroger store a few blocks away to pick up the fixings for dinner. She prepared, as if to point up not only her talents as a cook, but her disdain for Mosaic law, a glorious pork tenderloin in a Marsala wine sauce, vermicelli with garlic and olive oil, and a bibb lettuce salad with a vinaigrette dressing that she whipped up right on the spot. I wasn't used to such cooking outside of restaurants (my mother never ventured into the terra incognita that lay beyond meat loaf and roast chicken) and piled on the compliments as thick as the food on my plate. For dessert we had ice cream. Then, drawing out the cork on a second bottle of wine, I challenged Billy to a game of Monopoly.

Maybe Billy wasn't quite so purely sweet and compliant as she'd seemed these past two days, I began to think, for once we'd passed Go a few times, I could see that she was out for blood. She was fiercely concentrated, calculating, and ruthless right up to the point of unfairness. She refused, for example, to even consider any real estate deals until I was desperate enough to give up the store—at one point she had me backed into such a corner that I traded Park Place for a measly two utilities—and her luck with the dice was nothing less than supernatural. I'd always prided myself on my Monopoly game (which was, after all, a game of deal-making, like my business) and yet within three hours Billy had efficiently blown me right off the board. And she wasn't exactly magnanimous in victory, either. Even after we'd put the game away, and settled down in front of the television with our glasses of wine, she went on analyzing with relish how she'd finessed me on several key trades, and pointing out what moves I should have made, but didn't, to save my ass. So here was something else I could add to my fledgling file on her character: Billy, kindly and soft as she might seem, played to win. And I had the feeling it wasn't solely at parlor games. Not that I really minded, of course. If it gave her that much pleasure to take me apart piece by piece at Monopoly—while I sat across from her all evening, drinking in the intoxicating sight of her—she could destroy me in that fashion just as often as she liked.

We sipped at the last of the chianti as Billy flipped around the channels with the zapper.

"Hold it right there," I said, leaning toward the set.

It was Jerry Lewis, undergoing his annual coast-to-coast martyrdom on his Muscular Dystrophy Telethon.

"You want to watch *this?*" Billy said.

"Oh, yeah. Don't touch that zapper. This is something I love to hate."

Lewis, his voice shot, his tuxedo shirt ruined, his rubber face shining with sweat and exalted suffering, was limping back and forth across the stage like some wild animal hunted to exhaustion.

"Oh, brother!" I said. "Will you look at this? If he wants to raise money for charity, fine. But why does he have to turn this into his own personal crucifixion?"

Billy smirked. "Come on, Arnie. It's called ratings. What could be more fascinating than watching someone in the process of falling apart? Especially when you know it's for real?"

I frowned at her, and thought about that.

"Anyway," she went on, "he *does* do good work. Even if it is in bad taste. You've got to hand him that."

I grunted, and went on squinting at the television.

Now Lewis was introducing his next guest, who, he promised, had something truly miraculous to share with all of America. The performer was a bearded young man in a cowboy hat and a gaudy western outfit, who, not incidentally, was armless. He sat on a low stool, barefoot, over his electric guitar that lay face up on the floor, and began to strum the thing with his left foot while he somehow formed the chords with the toes of his right. Pretty soon he was actually picking out notes. The song was "Amazing Grace," and naturally the audience was in paroxysms.

I was just about fainting myself. "Oh, man! Is this beautiful? Is this the fucking penultimate? Will you *listen* to this? The poor pathetic shmuck can't even *play.*"

Billy laughed. "Well, what do you expect, Arnie? He's playing with his toes."

"Then he shouldn't be playing at all," I said. "Not unless

he's every bit as good with his toes as any other musician is with his hands. Otherwise it's nothing but a *freak* show. Hell, I don't care if people want to gawk at freaks—as long as they're honest about it. But pretending to some lofty *compassion*, when all you're really after is some crummy voyeuristic thrill—"

"My God, Arnie! This really has you worked up, doesn't it?"

"This kind of bullshit always gets my goat. Take it from a real live cripple, Billy. There's nothing more insidious than sentimentality."

"No?"

"It's the flip side of cruelty. I mean, who was more drippily sentimental than the Nazis?"

"Now you sound just like Redso."

"Yeah, well, Redso and I have always seen eye to eye on this. You start reducing human beings to adorable little stuffed animals, and the next thing you know, you're sticking pins in them. Just look at what we're looking at right now. Christ, if this isn't cruelty, what is?"

"It sounds like you've given this some thought."

"I've had to, believe me. Otherwise they would've turned me into Tiny Tim a long time ago."

"What? Who would've turned you into Tiny Tim?"

"All the sentimental old ladies out there—which is practically everybody. They don't have anything *against* cripples, of course, but they don't want to be *disturbed* by them, either. They'd much rather cuddle up with the idea that we're nothing but harmless, sexless angels. Hell, Dickens knew what he was doing when he invented Tiny Tim. He knew what kind of pap would sell. I mean, can you imagine a realistic Tiny Tim? One who's capable of getting a hard-on, for instance?" Here my voice snagged, for I'd given myself a jolt. I hadn't meant to broach the subject of sexuality—certainly not my own, and certainly not with this stunning and absolutely unavailable woman right here on the sofa beside me. But there was something about Billy, some air of tolerance, of permission, that had me feeling as if I could say damned near anything in her presence. Still, I thought it might be wise to add a different twist to my argument. "And then, nowadays, it's not enough to be a saint. You've also got to be a *hero*. You ever notice how nobody in the media ever *suffers* from a disease anymore?

They're always *battling* it. *Bravely.* And if the cancer or whatever finally gets them, it's not some example of meaningless,
arbitrary unfairness. It's a *tragedy.* As if just being sick endows
you with some kind of Shakespearean status! I mean, the bullshit just never stops. Do you—Am I making any sense at all,
Billy?"

Billy, leaning back against the arm of the sofa, her knees
drawn up, was smiling at me now. "Uh-huh," she said. "And
you know what else I think?"

I waited.

"I think I'm going to like hanging out with you, Arnie."

I smiled at Billy—but didn't dare try to speak.

We went on watching Jerry Lewis operatically deteriorate.
Billy was sitting up now, and consciously or not, had her thigh
warmly pressed against mine. When she leaned forward for
her wine, I felt the broad mass of her thigh muscles flicker—
and then felt myself flush, luckily under cover of darkness.
Well, God bless us everyone, I thought. Tiny Tim was getting
a hard-on.

SOMETIME IN THE NIGHT, an explosion of yellow light
jarred me out of sleep.

"Sorry, pal. I won't be a second here. I'm just gonna grab
this typewriter and scoot, and you can go right back to your
beauty sleep."

I fought my way, like a swimmer, to consciousness.

Redso, in a filthy sleeveless T-shirt, his hair sticking out in
stiff orange clumps around his skull as if he'd been yanking at
it with his fists, was rummaging around on my desk.

I rubbed at my eyes with the heels of my hands. "What is
this, Redso? Where've you been?"

"Oh, driving up and down in the earth, and going to and
fro in it, blah de blah de blah."

"Could you be a little more specific?"

"The Ozarks. How's that? It's lovely this time of year. All the
chinless products of hillbilly incest are out in force, the dears,
with their pickups and gun racks and swastika tattoos—"

"Is my car in one piece?"

"What? Why sure, sure. Where the hell do you keep your
typing paper, anyway?"

"Bottom right-hand drawer."

Redso dropped to his haunches and yanked it open.

"Are you planning on writing *now?*"

"Why not now? Inspiration calls! Grab opportunity by the forelock—or the foreskin, however the fuck the saying goes."

"What the hell time is it?"

"Shit, I dunno. After midnight, before dawn—"

"Where are you planning on writing?"

"The kitchen, I guess."

"You—are you crazy? You're going to wake Billy up."

Redso bounced to his feet and spun around, a full ream of paper in his hands. There was something unwholesome about his grin. "Yeah? So? Why the proprietary interest in my girl-friend, Arnie-boy? You decided to become her guardian angel in my absence, or what? By the way, how *did* you two get along while I was away? Did you both make nice-nice?"

I pushed up a little higher against my headboard. A hard bubble of something like grief had formed in my throat. I swallowed, but it wouldn't go down.

"Redso," I said. "What's the matter with you?"

"Why the fuck do you keep *asking* me that? Jesus!" Redso slammed the ream of paper on top of my old black Royal, and hoisted his heavy load to his chest. "Here I am, on the biggest, most glorious roll of my *entire existence,* and all you can do is *grill* me about it like I'm some fucking criminal suspect! My supposed best friend! So what's the matter with *you,* Goldman? Does it *rankle* you to see me at the top of my form, or what?"

That crazy outburst knocked what little stuffing I had out of me. I sank down heavily onto my pillows.

"Just get out of here and let me sleep, all right?"

"Uh-oh. Now I've done it. Now I've gone and made Arnie mad."

"Redso, what possible reason could I have for being mad at you?"

He laughed. "Yeah, well, sweet dreams." As he headed for the door, he added, "Jerk off an extra time for me, okay?"

Redso disappeared—and, naturally, left the door standing wide open, the lights blazing overhead.

I lay there for a spell, immobilized by the ugliness of our exchange. What was happening to him? What *was* it? I forced myself into a sitting position. Whatever it was, I wasn't going to crack the mystery tonight. I took up my crutches from the night stand. Thanks to Redso, I had no choice now but to drag my aching body out of bed to close the door and turn out the lights.

Three

BILLY AND I lay side by side on lawn chairs beneath the big oak tree that dominated my tiny backyard, listening in the dark as Redso attacked his play. His typing erupted in short staccato bursts, like a machine gun.

"God, just listen to him!" Billy said. "He's been working like this for three straight days without a break—and he's *still* going like a nuclear reactor."

"This is all he's been doing since I went to Chicago?"

"Arnie, he hasn't even been sleeping. Or eating. Unless you count the sunflower seeds and the Snickers bars and all the gin and tonics he's been washing them down with I'm just . . . worried he's going to get very sick."

I took up my can of beer from the strip of overgrown grass between our chairs. "He didn't eat the chili you brought down to him before?"

"He wouldn't even *taste* it. And God, you should have heard him! *Oh, Christ, here comes Meals on Wheels again! Can't you see I'm trying to fucking concentrate, Rubin? I'll eat when I'm hungry, verstehen?* And on and on. You would've thought I was trying to poison him or something."

I had to marvel at Billy's dead-on imitation of Redso. She'd not only gotten his diction down, but had altered something in her throaty voice to vividly suggest his tonal quality. Several times before I'd heard her mimic him like this; it seemed to slip out of her as unconsciously as laughter.

There was another furious flurry of typing.

"Jesus," I said. "How can he possibly keep this up?"

Billy morosely shrugged, popped her can of Budweiser, and sank against her lawn chair. Dusk was giving way to darkness, and the row of lit basement windows, behind which Redso raged, splashed half the lawn in a lurid yellow glow. One of those windows was brand new—installed by Billy's own clever hands to replace the one that Redso had shattered with a brick on the night they broke into my house. It was almost inconceivable that only a week had passed since then. A year's worth of enormous changes, it seemed, had been crammed into those eight days.

I'd just returned that evening from a business trip to Chicago (where I'd sold my entire lot of blue Russian opals, for a very nice price indeed, to Bill Conway at the Natural History Museum) and was still in the process of catching up. But all through dinner, and now as she lay in the gloom beside me, Billy seemed deeply preoccupied, as though she were carrying on two dialogues at once: one with me, and a silent, far more urgent one with herself. I was sure she was withholding something from me.

I took a swallow of my beer and peered up into the dense black confusion of branches above us.

From the instant Redso flung his brick through my basement window, our new living arrangements were probably a foregone conclusion. Neither one of them had any money, they both needed my largess, and I was just as loath to say no to Billy as I was to my best friend. I offered them a rent that was virtually a handout: just a hundred a month, utilities included, along with the understanding that they would inherit those household chores that I couldn't handle myself, and had previously assigned to my overburdened mother. Immediately Billy snapped into action. By Wednesday night she'd already cleared out an island of space in my basement, amid the scores of boxes containing my mediocre or duplicate rock specimens, and furnished it with a battered brass bed, an old black safe to serve as a night stand, and a broad and scarred-up writing desk for Redso—all of which she'd picked up in a U-Haul she'd rented for the purpose before beginning her rounds of that morning's garage sales. By Friday afternoon, when I left for Chicago, she'd not only signed up with a talent agency, but had auditioned for and landed what she assured me was a very plum job; her magnificent dusky voice would now be the voice that delivered, in computerized fragments, the time and the temperature across the whole vast territory covered by Southwestern Bell.

Meanwhile, Redso was blasting ahead with his own agenda, content to let Billy and me pay his way as he devoted himself full time, and in a fury of monastic concentration, to the writing of his autobiographical play, *Dutchtown*. His strange euphoria had evaporated; now the agony of creation was all over him. He might have been an alchemist just one step away from discovering the philosopher's stone—wild-eyed, grizzle-cheeked, rank-smelling, short-tempered, and so utterly consumed by his project that he seemed to take the most innocuous conversational openings as philistine assaults on his fragile concentration. You ran into him upstairs as he was taking a break from his typewriter, pacing, muttering, mixing another gin and tonic, pulling on another cigarette (he'd started chain-smoking filterless Camels that week), and you told him good morning, or hello, and Redso would stop in his tracks and gape as if you'd cursed him in Swahili. Only Billy had any luck in communicating with him, and even then, most of their exchanges were cut short by one of his unprovoked and mean-spirited outbursts.

We tried to get away from him in the evenings. One night Billy went out with some old high school chums; on another night I joined one of my clients, Jack Grisbrook, and his wife for dinner; on another night Billy and I went to see *Raging Bull,* and afterward lingered at a bar, avidly dissecting that wonderful movie, right up until closing time. And on Friday, when it was time for me to leave for Chicago, I could hardly have been more relieved to put those 250 miles between Redso and me.

And yet . . . and yet . . . however weird, tense, or distorted our domestic situation was, it *was* a domestic situation nonetheless—and as close as I'd ever come, since moving from my parents' house, to the cozy bourgeois normalcy I longed for. For once, the house was alive, with a distinct human buzz in the air.

And so what (as I kept telling myself) if Billy was Redso's lover, and not mine? She seemed to genuinely like me, we had books and movies and theater and food and Redso to discuss, and if we didn't share in the ultimate physical intimacy, we were already friends, and were sharing in most of the others. In fact, as Redso, in his preoccupation, had steadily withdrawn from me, Billy, in a sort of emotional counterpoint, had steadily drawn closer. So how could I help being pierced by occasional moments of happiness—even as I was witnessing the inexplicable mental collapse of the man I loved most in the world?

Billy stirred in her lawn chair, and her breasts, like two fat little animals with minds of their own, rearranged themselves under her T-shirt. It struck me again how terribly easy it would be to simply reach over and give one of those critters a squeeze—or to touch her on just about any other part of her buxom and proximate anatomy I chose. I mentally groaned and turned away. As strained as things were between Billy and Redso while they were up on their feet, once in bed they were apparently getting along like gangbusters. Of course I wasn't exactly an expert on human sexuality, but it seemed to me that the frequency and ferocity of their fucking bordered on the pathological. I heard them in the mornings behind the buzz of my electric toothbrush. I heard them in the afternoons as I haggled with my clients on the phone. I heard them sometimes twice a night—as hard to ignore as a marching band down in the drumlike hollows of the basement—and while I easily could have left the house at such times, or simply pulled a pillow down over my ears, I chose instead, in an agony of envy and longing, to listen.

Nor was all my surveillance passive. One night I stood motionless in the kitchen beside the open basement door, and contemplated, like a piece of heartbreaking music, their yips, groans, exhalations, and bellows, all cruelly magnified by the surrounding concrete walls. And on another occasion, I'm sorry to admit, I abandoned all self-respect, worked myself down to the third or fourth basement step, and observed them from above. I even tossed out my old collection of skin magazines. Who needed them, when I could rely on my own private stock of pornographic loops featuring Billy?

I looked at her now in the waning light, her profile gray against the darker gray of the yard; her fat lips were pushed out so poutily I had to throttle an impulse to pinch them. I was fairly sure that Billy had no inkling of my monstrous lust —and absolutely sure that she thought of me only as a friend. Well, I wasn't about to blow that friendship with some idiotic— and hopeless—declaration of my love. And of course, there was Redso to consider. Even if I did have the wherewithal, somehow, to betray him, I was sure that my loyalty would win out, that I could draw on my deep reserves of integrity and self-discipline . . . But oh, what was the point of even speculating? Redso had no more to fear from me than an elephant did from a mosquito—and a flightless mosquito at that.

"Have you read any of his play?" Billy asked me.

"What? God, no. Not that I wouldn't love to see it. But he'd probably bite off my nose if I asked." I turned to her. "Have you?"

"Yes. While you were away in Chicago. He'd already finished the first act."

"You're kidding. How'd you get him to show it to you?"

"I didn't. Redso made the offer."

That stung. Granted, Billy was Redso's lover. Yet he'd known her for less than a year—while he and I had our entire adult lives in common. I squirmed in my chair. Wonderful, I thought. So now I was jealous of Billy as well as of Redso. I was batting a thousand, all right.

"Is it any good?" I asked her.

"It's so good," Billy said, "that it scares me."

I squinted at her through the gloom.

She sighed. "You don't know this about me, Arnie. But I'm a terrible sucker for talent. I'll excuse almost anything for it, I think. And Redso's play is so damned good . . . well, it's almost *okay* with me if he's like this. I mean, if that's what it takes." She picked up her beer, but only brushed the rim of the can across her lips.

"Let me make sure I'm understanding you, Billy. Do you mean to say that if you were Vincent van Gogh's nurse, for instance, you might decide to withhold his medication and let him suffer? For the sake of art history?"

Billy didn't answer right away. "Maybe I would."

Well, I thought, it was an interesting argument—not that I believed for a moment that she *would* have withheld poor Vincent's medicine. But I certainly wasn't ready to pump up Redso's situation, whatever it was, to that mythic level.

I asked her to tell me about the play.

"It's frightening. It's funny. It's tight. It's one of the best damned things I've ever read—and I'm not just saying that because Redso wrote it."

I shivered. "Well, hell," I said. "Maybe this *is* the way he has to do it."

Billy shifted her weight. "Oh, don't romanticize it, Arnie. Even geniuses have to eat once in a while, you know."

The sharpness—and the plain unfairness of that remark, given what she'd just been telling me—made me sit forward with a wince. For the first time it occurred to me that maybe Billy wasn't quite so seamlessly put together as she appeared.

Redso's typewriter erupted again.

"Is it true about his father?" Billy said. "That he was an interrogator for the army during World War Two?"

"Yes. As far as I know. He didn't come to America until he was fourteen or fifteen—so he still spoke fluent German. It only made sense that they'd use him in Intelligence."

"And was he really brutal to Redso physically?"

"According to Redso, he was. His father used to beat him all the time, he says—and in places where the bruises wouldn't show. Apparently he still remembered his old tricks. But Redso says that was nothing compared to the psychological terror."

Billy was silent for a spell. "And what about his mother? Was she really that ditzy and passive—always pretending that nothing out of the ordinary was going on?"

"Sounds like Frieda to me. She's never really played with a full deck of cards."

"Because the thing is—" Billy's voice caught. "I don't *want* him to have had a childhood like that. Maybe it sounds crazy, but I want to just grab hold of it somehow—and tear it *away* from him, you know?" She paused. "That does sound crazy, doesn't it?"

I carefully set my beer down on the thick matted grass between our chairs. I'd just been given a glimpse into the real depths of Billy's love—and it made me feel petty, ridiculous, small.

Billy pushed up heavily to her feet, and told me she was going for another beer. Did I want one? I did. I turned my head to watch her go. She drifted like a gray sleepy ghost through the dusklight.

I killed off my beer while I waited, and grieved for myself as maybe only a lover can—rather enjoying the flavorful bitterness of it.

Redso roared like a wounded lion in the basement.

I strained to hear what followed. But while it clearly involved two voices, the words were indistinct. I pushed up to my crutches and poked across the lawn.

The basement was lit up like a stage. Just below the window was Redso's writing desk; a chaos of dirty glasses, coffee cups, ashtrays, and crumpled balls of paper engulfed my typewriter. The rest of their living space was just as trashed—books and magazines and newspapers scattered all over on the floor, clothes flung everywhere, the bed a violent tangle of sheets. Redso was on his feet and pacing, wearing the same ratty brown terry-cloth bathrobe he'd been living in all week, his cigarette jammed up between his middle and index fingers. There was something oddly anachronistic in the way he smoked; each time he took a puff he cupped his hand over his mouth, like a movie tough from the thirties. Billy was leaning against a steel strut, another bowl of chili in her hands, glaring defiantly at Redso.

"You've got to eat," she said.

"Oh, Jesus! Don't start in with this Jewish mother routine! Just don't start!"

"You're going to get sick—"

"Hey! *Hey!* You want to really fuck up this relationship real good, Rubin, you just keep right on with this Sophie Portnoy crap! Christ! Do I look like I'm starving to you?"

"Yes!"

"Then I'll starve! *Verstehen?* Now get off my goddamned *back!*"

Billy marched over and placed the bowl of chili on a corner of his desk. Redso followed right behind her and struck it away with the back of his hand. The bowl hit the floor; the stuff bloomed across the concrete in a steaming brown island, stopping just inches short of Billy's tennis shoes.

"You—" She didn't finish her sentence.

"Me *what*, Rubin? Well? Come on! Me what?"

Billy strode off toward the stairs, and I lost sight of her. Redso spun back to his desk, his pale face sagging with rage. I moved away from the window before he could spot me and poked back to my lawn chair, where I got myself stiffly arranged, and let my crutches drop into the grass. After a while the screen door slammed and Billy appeared beneath the porchlight. She was holding a liquor bottle by the neck. For a few seconds she didn't move. Then she came down the steps, across the glowing lawn, and stopped in front of me, her hair haloed by the porchlight behind her, her face lost in shadow. "I've got your bottle of Glenlivet," she said, her voice oddly flattened. "Is that all right?"

"Of course. Is uh, Redso all right in there?"

"No."

"Are *you* all right, Billy?"

She didn't answer. She sent a shiver through her hair. "I have to get away from here," she said. "I don't care where. Anywhere. Can we go for a drive, Arnie?"

"Well, sure."

"Because . . . there are some things I have to tell you."

I DROVE AIMLESSLY around the narrow gloomy streets of our Maplewood neighborhood—mostly just taking rights, as we had no particular destination. Billy kept silent, her whiskey bottle jutting upright between her thighs. Jagged shapes thrown off by the passing streetlights slid slowly down her form, slipped across her lap and past her knees onto the floorboard, and started up once again at the crown of her head, like watery pieces of a jigsaw puzzle. Billy took a nip from her bottle and offered it to me. I shook my head no. She clamped it between her thighs again. She was wearing shorts, and I couldn't help imagining how cold the bottle must have felt against her skin.

"While you were gone," Billy said, "I went to the Wash. U. medical school library and did some reading."

I looked at her. She had her face to her window now.

"He's a manic-depressive," she said.

My heart seemed to pump in my throat.

"Although, of course, we haven't seen the depressive part of it yet."

I drove with great caution, for the old-model cars and pickups that lined these narrow streets made the passage very tight. That word, manic—like something festering below the surface of our careful circumlocutions—had been overdue to pop. Not that I was convinced that Billy was right. Not yet. I decided I should play the devil's advocate.

"What was it you read, exactly?"

"Psychiatric handbooks, that sort of thing. And it fits, Arnie. I mean, it *all* fits."

"You think Redso's actually, clinically insane?"

"He's been acting insane, hasn't he? Don't you think that's a pretty good indication?"

I didn't answer.

"Anyway, I know the same thing must have occurred to you."

"I've been . . . considering it."

"That's a pretty cautious choice of words."

"Well, shit, Billy. I'm trying to *be* cautious. You think I *want* to believe my best friend is a mental case? Especially before we have any proof?"

"You've been watching him crawl the walls for two weeks now, Arnie. How much more proof do you need?"

I widened my eyes at the street. The brake-accelerator felt wobbly, unreliable in my hand.

"When did this first occur to you, anyway?"

She was unscrewing the cap of the bottle. "Back at Carnegie Mellon."

"That long ago? For godsakes, Billy—why didn't you say anything until now?"

"Because I was waiting until I was sure. And now I am."

She tipped the bottle to her mouth, shuddered as she

brought it down, and offered it to me again. This time I took a small biting swallow, and handed it back to her.

"What the hell was going on back in Pittsburgh, anyway?"

Billy scooted down a little lower, rested her head against her seat, and as she talked on in that dark transfixing voice of hers, I kept taking rights through the gloomy maze of streets.

Redso's strange agitation, she said, had been apparent since they first became lovers, around Christmas. "And I'll tell you the truth, Arnie. I think it was one of the things that made me fall in love with him. He was so *alive*—so entertaining and funny and surprising—so incredibly exuberant and optimistic. Nothing could get him down. Every damned day was a holiday. It was just like—God, like being caught up in a whirlwind! And then, Redso's such a tremendously gifted actor . . . Well, I think I wrote it all off at first as part of his artistic temperament. His genius, if you want to call it that." She weakly shrugged. "Anyway, I liked it. And I mean, I liked it a *lot*."

Billy gave me a challenging look, as if to dare me to condemn her for that.

"But then it wasn't so much fun anymore. He started getting just like he is now. Not eating, not sleeping, temper tantrums, all of it. And it was affecting his work. We were doing *Othello*. He was playing Iago, and I was Desdemona, and the director . . . Well. We'd had a little thing before I fell in with Redso. It didn't last long, and it didn't amount to much. But Redso knew all about it. His name is Larry Klein. Maybe you've heard of him. He's an actor. Used to do old 'Twilight Zone' episodes, things like that?"

"I don't recall."

"Anyway, at first I thought Redso was doing it just to get at Larry. And maybe he was."

"Doing what?"

"He was getting very testy and argumentative during rehearsals. He wanted line readings from Larry. He *didn't* want line readings from Larry. He wanted help with his blocking. He wanted to figure out the blocking himself—it didn't matter. No matter what Larry suggested, Redso was right up in his face about it. And it wasn't just embarrassing. It was destroying everybody's morale. Everyone but Redso's, that is.

Nothing could destroy *his* morale, right? Anyway, when we finally went into performance, well, that was when Redso really pulled out the stops. He started ad-libbing."

"What? Ad-libbing *Shakespeare?*"

"You've got it. And the unbelievable thing was, he was *good* at it. He had the Elizabethan diction down, and the meter, and it even made *sense*. If you didn't already know the text, you wouldn't have *known* he was making half of it up as he went along. But of course, it was throwing all the other actors way off, just wrecking the play. So after that first performance, Larry gave him this huge chewing out, right in front of the whole crew—and I mean, he really let it rip. But that didn't stop Redso. The next night he'd stopped writing his own lines, all right. But *now* he was delivering half his lines in this thick German accent. And throwing in these German words. Can you imagine? He sounded like something out of 'Hogan's Heroes.' *O bevare, mein Herr, auff chelousy / It isst der green-eyed monster vich doth mock der meat it feeds on.* Well, you get the general idea."

I couldn't help laughing. "Come on, Billy. That's just too much to believe."

"Believe it," she said.

I gave a low whistle. "Man. What I wouldn't give to have seen that!"

"Oh, it was entertaining, all right—if you weren't on stage with him, trying to get through your part. Anyway, that did it. Larry called a meeting with the head of the department, and evidently Redso made another scene *there*. And so they kicked him out."

I looked at her. "They kicked him out?"

"Oh, yes. They don't put up with stunts like that at Carnegie Mellon."

"But Redso told me he quit."

Billy stared at me. Her eyes, in the gloom, appeared to be all shining black pupil. "Is that what he said?"

I nodded.

"Oh God."

We drove on for another block or so.

"I'm missing a piece of this, Billy," I said. "What are *you* doing here? Did you quit the program yourself?"

She stirred uneasily beside me.

"Of course I quit the program," she said.

"But what about your career?"

"People can leave something and then come back to it, can't they?" Her voice sounded squeezed.

"Well, sure. But it—" I shook my head. "I don't know, Billy. It just seems awfully—"

"What was I supposed to do, Arnie? Stay in Pittsburgh, finish my degree, and just hope that Redso didn't destroy himself in the meantime—a thousand miles away from me? What would you have done?"

"I have no idea," I said.

She dropped her head back against her seat.

"Anyway," she said, "that's the decision I made."

We had come full circle now, and were back on our own shabby street. Billy took another pull off her whiskey bottle (I wondered why she didn't seem at all drunk by this point) and said, as she recapped it, "So do you still need proof?"

I gave that some thought before I answered.

"I'll tell you what," I said. "I think I should go to the medical school library, and have a look myself at whatever it was you were reading."

"Fine. I'm not doing anything after my recording session tomorrow. You're giving me a lift home anyway, right? We can go then."

"That's a deal," I told her.

We bumped down my uneven driveway and parked behind the house.

Billy edged a little closer to me—I could smell her whiskey breath—and placed her hand, very lightly, on my right thigh. My head damned near exploded.

"Arnie, I want you to know . . . I'm just awfully glad you're around right now. I don't know if I could handle this all by myself."

I licked my lips.

"I think you're a good man," she went on. "A sweet man. And I just . . . Well. I just wanted you to know that."

She squeezed my thigh.

I winced. But I managed not to make a noise, and didn't move my leg a centimeter. Perverse as it might sound, I actually would have actually been glad for another stab of that very same pain.

"'BOUNDLESS ENERGY. Psychomotor agitation. Decrease in appetite. Little need for sleep.'" Billy shot me a significant look over the top of her glasses, and read on, sotto voce. "'Inflated self-esteem. Grandiosity. Recklessness. Excessive talkativeness.'" She sighed. "Sounding familiar yet?"

I grunted, and hunkered down lower over my crossed forearms. We were sitting almost shoulder to shoulder in the reference room of the library, a jumble of books on the table in front of us. Billy poked her glasses closer to the bridge of her nose. They were thick-framed and dowdy, and I adored her in them. Their severity only heightened the feminine softness of her face.

She read on: "'Egocentric. Demanding. Low frustration tolerance . . .'" She looked at me again. "It's *him,* isn't it?"

"It's fucking uncanny," I said, and must have said it too loudly, for the woman at the next table was giving me a murderous stare.

Billy leaned in closer with her book. "Just listen to this," she whispered. "'May display instances of inappropriate wordplay. Such as rhyming, punning, jocular associations.'"

"Oh, brother."

"'Flight of ideas is often indicated—'"

"Flight of ideas?"

"It says here: 'A rapid digression from one idea to another, often tenuously connected, and tending toward incoherence.'"

My back was now a cascade of shivers.

"'Alcohol and drug abuse are often indicated.'" She paused. "'As well as a marked increase in sexual desire and activity.'"

My heart took a bump over that.

"Well, uh, how about that?" I said. "Have you noticed . . . any marked increase?"

Billy sat back in her chair, and her hair, as it brushed past my shoulder, gave off a slight spicy breeze. "There's nothing to compare it to," she said. "He's been like a goat from day one."

I decided not to press that particular point.

"Is that it for the symptoms?" I asked her.

"Basically."

"What does it say about the course of the disease?"

She flipped around through the pages. "Here. Listen to this. 'The age of onset is usually in the twenties.' " Billy shook her head. "Can you *believe* this? It's like they used Redso as their *model* for everything *in* here."

"Go on."

She bent back to the book. " 'At times the mania resembles a normal euphoria. This stage is known as *hypomania*. But eventually it becomes uncontrolled and psychotic. A severe mania may include disorientation, delusions, paranoia and hallucinations, indistinguishable from schizophrenic delirium.' " Billy cleared her throat. " 'The length of episodes may vary widely, from a few days to several years—' "

"Several *years?*"

"That's what it says."

"Jesus."

She read on: " 'Between episodes, some manics are fairly functional, with some residual symptoms of mania, but often enter into depressions as severe as their previous elations, and often more prolonged.' " Billy let the book slide to the table, slipped her fingers under her glasses, and rubbed her eyes.

"What does it say about treatment?"

It took her some time to find what she was looking for.

" 'In more severe episodes, electroconvulsive therapy is indicated.' " She looked at me. "That's shock treatment, right?"

"Yeah, I'm pretty sure."

" 'But lithium carbonate, administered orally, is generally more effective in achieving and maintaining remission.' "

"Lithium carbonate," I said, trying out the words.

"Do you know what it is?"

"Well, I can imagine the chemical composition. It's a salt of some kind. But as to how it could possibly work—no idea."

Billy took off her glasses and stared glumly at the scattered books on the table. "So what do you think?"

I took a while before answering.

"Billy, I don't know what to think."

She scowled at me incredulously. "How can you say that? It's all right here in black and white!"

"Maybe."

"Maybe? These are his symptoms!"

"Look, Billy, these are only his symptoms if you're already convinced he's insane. I mean, for as long as I've known Redso, he's been grandiose, and reckless, and talkative, and full of punning and jokes and inappropriate wordplay. Are you going to tell me Groucho Marx was a manic-depressive just because he cracked a lot of jokes? Where do we draw the line?"

"I don't know," Billy hissed. "But he's *crossed* it!"

"I'm not so sure about that."

"But you've *seen* him. You *know* what he's like. You're just hair-splitting, Arnie!"

"Come on, Billy. You look like you hate me or something."

She turned away. Her shoulders sagged.

"Look," I said. "You may be right. Hell, you probably *are* right. But I just figured one of us should play the devil's advocate, you know?"

"So what do we do?"

"Christ, I don't know."

"You think we can get him to a shrink?"

"Not unless we drag him there kicking and screaming." I pushed back from the table and began to rub at my knees. "And besides, I'm not as convinced about this as you are, Billy. Not yet, anyway. I say we just . . . watch and wait."

Billy blew out an exhausted breath.

"Just what do you think I've been doing for the past eight months?" she said.

I AWOKE the next morning to the pungent smell of frying bacon. The bedroom was still submerged in gloom, the windows faintly aglow with a peach-colored light. I picked up my Rolex from the night table; it was barely six o'clock. What was going on here? My early-morning stiffness usually forced me out of bed before anyone else in the house, Billy rarely staggered upstairs before nine, and with Redso, of course, the question of a normal waking-up time was as moot as that of a regular bedtime. So who was cooking breakfast, and for whom? I growled and winced as I pushed up to my crutches— my arthritis was alive and kicking this morning—and worked on my bathrobe. As I clumped into the kitchen, Billy was emerging from the basement, tugging at the tie of her bathrobe, her hair a gray-streaked mess, her eyes still hooded with sleep. She emitted a soft grunt of surprise.

There at the sink, running water onto a smoking frying pan, stood an impossibly chipper-looking Redso. He wore clean jeans and a fresh black T-shirt; he'd shaved his face, and done a good job of it; his hair was brushed back into a neat orange ball.

"Guten Morgen, guten Morgen," he sang out. "How'd everybody sleep last night? I slept the sleep of the innocent, let me tell you."

Billy and I exchanged looks.

On the table lay an aromatic spread of bacon, scrambled eggs, french toast and syrup. A carton of milk was posted at one end, a carton of orange juice at the other. Redso had set three places, laying the silverware out on paper napkins, folded daintily into triangles. The coffeemaker wheezed and dripped.

Redso loped to the table, crammed several strips of bacon into his mouth, and as he chewed, grinned at us, and said, "I don't know about you people, but I could eat a fucking horse."

Four

IN THE ASTONISHING SPACE of eight days and nights, Redso had polished off *Dutchtown*.

On the morning of his triumph, following the lavish breakfast he'd whipped up, Redso ushered Billy and me into the living room, sat us both down on the sofa, and with a courtly flourish, handed Billy the manila folder containing his two-act play.

She passed me the pages as she finished with them, and in the meantime, Redso paced the room like a condemned prisoner, sucking on his cigarette, flashing us hot interrogatory glances, and demanding that we read back to him whatever lines had made us laugh, or scowl, or sigh, or simply shift our asses on the sofa. Every so often he'd come around behind us, lean down, and breathe heavily through his mouth as he observed us. "Is it moving?" he'd ask. "Is it holding you?" Billy slapped her pages down. "Redso, how do you expect us to concentrate when you keep *hovering* like this? Can't you go play in the yard or something?" But Redso only squatted on his hams in front of the stereo, and eyed us like a panther preparing to pounce. And when we were finished, and had delivered our mutual gushing verdicts, Redso hit the ceiling, literally, with a leap and a slap.

Not even Billy's glowing review of the other night had prepared me for the quality of *Dutchtown*. It was viciously funny, propulsively dramatic, with a tough wise-guy eloquence throughout—and the portraits of his parents, upon which everything depended, were vividly, chillingly alive. Even Redso's stand-in for himself came through as entirely credible. I studied him with awe as Billy passed the final page to me, unable to conceive how such a shapely play could have possibly sprung from such an unhinged and overheated brain.

But then I remembered, with a swarm of butterflies lifting off in my stomach, just a few of those famous artists who had clearly been certifiable—Poe, Hemingway, Swift, van Gogh. The list of madmen-savants could have easily gone on . . . if, in fact, that was what Redso was.

On that question, however, my inner jury was still out. For the next few days I only knew that Redso was a heightened, brightened version of his old compelling self—buoyant as a zeppelin, talkative as a three-year-old, affectionate as a puppy, and, as far as I could see, untouched by any shadow of his recent black mood.

He sent *Dutchtown* off to the Humana playwriting festival in Louisville, Kentucky, a famous old competition that had launched the careers, so Redso kept reminding us, of such luminaries as Sam Shepard and Tennessee Williams. He would receive his reply in two months. And in the meantime, Redso put on his party hat.

He financed his revels by socking me for a loan (or what we diplomatically called a loan) against the future prize money he had no doubt at all he'd be collecting. Much of that, as it turned out, came right back to me, for Redso set about blowing it with his typical rash magnanimity. He restocked my liquor cabinet, and all with premium brands; he insisted on reimbursing me for the basement window he'd shattered. And on the first two nights after finishing his play, Redso took us out on the town, grandly refusing to let Billy or me kick in so much as a nickel. On Friday he treated us to dinner at Balaban's, and then took us dancing (or more rightly, he and Billy went dancing, while I watched) at the Casa Loma Ballroom in South St. Louis. On Saturday night we closed down O'Connell's, and Redso, still percolating with irrepressible high spirits, invited everyone at the bar to follow us back to the house (four or five of them did), where the bleary bacchanalia dragged on until well after daylight.

Redso was so overflowing with jollity and indiscriminate goodwill that he was sometimes hard to take. I was the best pal a guy ever had, Billy was Sarah Bernhardt, Cleopatra, and Eleanor Roosevelt all rolled into one, our martinis were perfect, the steak was impeccable, our waiter was a paragon of the serving profession, and so on and so forth. And hour after hour, drink after drink, Redso's conversation, like a spring that had come unblocked, leapt, flowed and sparkled, washing over a multitude of subjects and making each of them glitter with his cockeyed passionate unfair opinions, his hands slicing the air, his Camels burning down to dangerous nubs between his knuckles, his Asiatic blue eyes infectiously alive.

And Billy—whether or not she still thought he was crazy—was lapping it up. She fell apart at his jokes; she glowed before the crackling bonfires of his monologues; under his stroking and his nuzzling and his gushing compliments, she positively purred. I had no chance to pick her brain about it (Was she humoring him, or was she sincere? Had she abandoned the diagnosis she'd put forth with such ferocity just three days before, or had she amended it somehow?), for during that breathless period I couldn't seem to catch her alone for three minutes at a stretch. When Redso wasn't in her sights, Billy was obsessively hunting him up; and the instant he came within reach again, she was all over him, clinging to him jealously, as if she feared he might go up in smoke at any second. Even when the three of us were out together I felt somehow brushed aside—poking along behind them down the sidewalks of the West End or Soulard, or slumped in the backseat of my Toronado, drenched in self-pity, as they nestled and cooed up front like a pair of blissed-out pigeons.

I supposed, in my more philosophical moments, that the worst they intended was a kind of benign neglect, a way of letting me know that I was no less a part of the intimate goings-on than either one of them, and so required no special treatment. But more often it stung. I remember in particular how, on the night when they danced through song after song on the light-sprinkled floor of the Casa Loma Ballroom (it was Big Band Night, and both Redso and Billy were expert, stage-trained dancers who knew what to do with the old standards, and could actually jitterbug, among other incomprehensible feats), Billy melded to him, and followed with a kind of clairvoyance each unlikely step, turn and dip that Redso so exuberantly improvised. And meanwhile, I waited alone at our rickety, drink-sticky table, grimly checking my watch, switching from single to double scotches, and forcing, like the good sport I was apparently supposed to be, an accommodating smile any time either one of them happened to glance in my direction.

At one point they came back to the table and drunkenly tried to cajole me onto the floor.

"Come on, Arnie," Billy said, her breath sour, bending down to tug at my arm. "Come on and dance with us."

"Billy, I don't dance."

"You mean because of these?" She rattled a crutch. "Oh, screw that, Arnie. Who cares? Come on and dance. It's easy. We'll show you how."

I begged off, finally, with the excuse—which wasn't true— that my arthritis was giving me too much trouble.

So Billy and Redso returned to the dance floor, probably relieved that they'd done their duty by me, and now were free of me again. I watched them move through the whirling scraps of light thrown off by the enormous ball of the cut-glass chandelier, gliding and spinning in their effortless, enviable syncopation—and before long, to my perverse satisfaction, my hips actually did begin to throb.

OF ALL THE WONDERS and surprises Redso sprang on us during that period, none surprised me more than his appearance in the kitchen one morning in a suit and a tie. He must have gone through my closet while I was having my coffee, for it was my blue Armani suit he was wearing, my Christian Dior tie. The coat was a bit loose on him at the shoulders, but otherwise was a passable fit. He was going to start looking for work, Redso announced. First he would try Billy's talent agency, and if that got him nowhere, the other two local agencies, and then he meant to hit up all the advertising firms and production houses in town. He asked if he could borrow my car. Neither Billy nor I had any appointments to get to that day—and she knew as well as I did that I had no good pretext to refuse him. With a twinge of misgiving, I handed him the keys.

Later on that night Redso burst into the house and spirited Billy away for another night of fun and frolic. They did their best to drag me along, but I told them I'd had more than enough of these Dionysian marathons—and stayed home with a book, and a vague sense of grievance.

Billy didn't return until seven the next morning, and when she did, it was alone, and by taxi. I knew, because I had to drag myself out of bed to pay off the cabbie, who waited impatiently outside the door.

"God, I'm a wreck!" Billy said (pretty cheerfully for a wreck, it seemed to me) as she flopped down on the sofa and kicked off her shoes. "Sorry to get you out of bed like this, Arnie. But I was clean out of cash." She smiled at me. "I've been a bad girl, I know. But can you find it in your heart to forgive me?"

I lowered myself stiffly into the reclining chair, and peevishly shrugged. It wasn't easy to show a hard face to Billy, but in this case she'd certainly earned it. I asked her where Redso was.

Billy laughed. "Actually, I don't know."

"What? How can you not know?"

"Well, we went bar-hopping over on the East Side last night. And God, I don't know—we were in one of these funky after-hours places, and Redso hooked up with a bunch of old black blues musicians. You should have seen these guys, Arnie. White hair, gold teeth—I mean, they were straight out of Preservation Hall. Anyway, Redso was in *very* high spirits, right at the top of his form. And these old guys were getting such a big kick out of him, they invited us back to their place after their gig—to smoke pot, or whatever. Of course Redso was raring to go. But I was just too completely wiped out. So I told him to go have fun, and called a cab." Billy slung a forearm across her eyes; her other hand dropped to the carpet. "God, what a night!"

I scowled at her. "You don't seem exactly worried."

"Why should I be?" Billy yawned. "They're not going to leave him stranded on the other side of the Mississippi or anything. They were very sweet old guys. He'll show up sooner or later."

"But how can you be so serene about this? Aren't you at all concerned?"

"About what?"

"What do you mean about what? Redso's state of mind."

Billy slung her arm back over her face. "Not at the moment," she said.

"I don't understand this, Billy. Have you backed off of your diagnosis?"

She limply shrugged.

"But *look* at him. Shit, he's been going like a whirling dervish ever since he finished his play—out partying all night, running his ass off all day, barely eating, not sleeping—and where is he now? Off in East St. Louis, smoking dope with the Temptations! What do you think he *is?* Just a tad overly excited?"

Billy sighed. "Arnie, who was the one telling me just the other day that we shouldn't be jumping to conclusions?"

That confused me for a second. "Wait a minute," I said. "Who was telling *me* he was manic?"

"I'm not saying he *isn't,* all right? I'm just . . . I don't know. Maybe he's in that stage before it gets out of control. Hypomania. Isn't that what it's called? Maybe he's just *hypomanic* right now. But whatever it is, why should I be *dwelling* on it?"

"Because you *care* about him!"

"But just look at the way he's *been.* So charming, and effervescent, and affectionate and funny—just a joy to be around. And it's such a *relief.* Especially after that week of horrors he put us through. He's been happy—for *whatever* reason. And so have I. And if you don't mind my saying so, you've been getting sort of petulant lately, Arnie. Almost like you're *begrudging* us that happiness."

That struck the bull's-eye.

I began to massage the tops of my thighs.

"That's not fair, Billy. I mean, I *have* been in a lot of pain lately."

"Well, so have *I.*" Billy was looking at me now. "And I'm *sick* of it, all right? God, am I sick of it! So will you please not try to spoil this for me now?"

□ □ □ □

"SO IMAGINE," my father was saying, turning his long sagging bloodhound's face to Billy once again, as if her attention were an irresistible magnet. "There's my father, a socialist, blackballed from every clothing manufacturer in St. Louis, and with four children to feed. So what does the poor man do? Well, for the next two decades he *shleps* his family from one tiny hick Missouri town to another—Springfield, Sullivan, Bolivar—anywhere he could manage to find work. And meanwhile, my mother's still learning her English. And where does she pick it up from? From her neighbors, naturally—and all of them Ozark hillbillies! Are you following?" My father popped the last of his eggroll in his mouth. "So for the rest of her life, she'd say things—in her thick Yiddish accent, mind you— things like '*Vay iz mir*, she looks like she's fixing to rain.' Or 'Good *Shabbos*, y'all! *Mazel tov*, y'all!' "

"No!" Billy said.

"Of course, we always used to tease her about it. But I don't think she ever quite understood what the joke was all about."

Billy set down another sparerib on her plate, nibbled and sucked clean to the bone. As usual, she was attacking her *trayf* with depraved relish; her fingers were bloodied with sauce, her plump lips glistened with pork grease. "That's so charming, Mr. Goldman."

"Charming?" Redso said, and slapped the crimson tablecloth. "By God, it's sheer exalted poetry! Good *Shabbos*, y'all! *Mazel tov*, y'all! We're talking Ma and Pa Kettlebaum here. Minnie Pearlmutter! Daisy Mae Yokemstein! Boy, talk about bizarre crosscultural linguistic pollination! Only in America, right?"

My mother showed Redso a thin careful smile. "How are you doing on those martinis, Redso?"

"Fine, fine. Think I'm ready for another, as a matter of fact. How about you, Doris? Can I get you anything? Another cream sherry? Maybe a glass of plum wine? How about another eggroll?"

"I think I'm fine right now."

"Well, you just say the word." Redso craned around and snapped his fingers for the waitress.

I had arranged this dinner at the Lotus Room (a frumpy old Cantonese place in Brentwood that had long been my mother's favorite restaurant) in order to kill several birds with one meal; I was long overdue for a visit with my parents, they hadn't seen Redso since Christmas, and moreover, they had yet to get an eyeful of Billy. And the time was ripe; for all I knew, this window of Redso's relative sanity could slam shut very quickly. So far he'd been cooking along at a fairly low simmer, and if at times he was talking a little too avidly, gesturing a little too frantically, or interrupting a little too often with his outlandish puns and non sequiturs, I figured my mother was ascribing it to all the martinis he'd been tossing down his gullet. My father, meanwhile, was too entranced with Billy to be paying Redso much attention. I didn't think he was actually flirting with her—not consciously, anyway—but clearly her presence had him unusually pumped up. Indeed, between his customary before-dinner manhattan and his egg-rolls, my father had shed so much of his normal self-efface-ment that he was now actually *dominating* the conversation—a novelty that warmed and amused me.

Billy asked me if I remembered that about my grand-mother.

"No," I said. "I'm afraid I don't. She died when I was four or five."

"Which is a pity," my father said. "You would've gotten a kick out of her, Arnie."

"Man, I would've gotten one *hell* of a kick out of her!" Redso drummed his hands on the tabletop. "So? What do you all say? Anybody up for a séance?"

Now both my mother and my father stared at him.

I stepped into that uneasy silence with the subject I'd been waiting to spring all day. I'd received a letter that morning from Desmond Garlick, my old friend and colleague from my graduate school days, who was now in charge of the mineral collection at the National Museum of Wales. He'd invited me —begged me, really—to come to Cardiff and take over the collection in the spring, when he would be called away for a year-long research project in Thailand. The dusty old collec-tion needed a complete revamping, and no one else he knew of on either side of the Atlantic, Garlick wrote to me (laying on the soap pretty thick, I was sure), had both the highly refined eye and the hard-nosed business sense the job required. I hadn't yet made up my mind about it, I told the table, and I wanted to hear their feedback.

There was another sticky silence.

Redso chewed a mouthful of ice, frowning in thought. Billy looked a little dazed.

Then my father, cracking his knuckles, spoke up. "Well, it sounds like a wonderful opportunity, doesn't it? Living and working in a foreign country. What kind of pay are we talking about?"

"The whole project's being financed by the British government," I said. "And it's a very nice stipend, Dad. And the other thing is, I'll be free to do all the dealing I want on the side. And with all those European markets right there across the Channel . . . well, I figure I could come out pretty good." I shrugged. "Not to mention the fun, right?"

"Wales," Redso said. "Think of it! Ancient stronghold of the indomitable Celts! Land of the Bards! Of King Arthur! Dylan Thomas! Tom Jones! Man, can you imagine? Of course, the food stinks, and I hear the place is overrun with Baptists—but what the hell? How 'bout that, Billy? Can you believe this guy's luck?"

Billy forced a smile. But clearly she was worried.

My mother, on the other hand, didn't care to hide her reaction. She scooped some fried rice onto her plate and grimly buckled her mouth at it. "When would you be going if you went?"

"March or April."

"And you'd be gone for how long?"

"A year or so."

"Wales. Doesn't it rain there all the time?"

"Well, I imagine it rains pretty much. It's part of Great Britain. Why?"

My mother shook her head. "It must be the absolute *worst* place on earth for your arthritis, Arnie."

Redso jumped in. "Oh, I wouldn't go that far, Doris. There's the Amazon rain forest, for instance. Or the jungles of New Guinea. Then there's Nicaragua, Borneo, Cambodia. Hell, even Seattle gets an annual rainfall approaching—"

"Redso," Billy said.

"What?"

She held his stare.

"Well, frankly," my mother said, "I don't like it. I just don't think you're up to it, Arnie."

"Oh Jesus, Mom!" She'd just punched one of my sorest buttons. "I'm not an invalid, for godsakes."

"You're not healthy, either. What happens over there if you get a very bad attack? Do you know anything about the English health system? Are you even eligible as an American? The whole idea—it just worries me."

"That's completely ridiculous, Mom."

"What's ridiculous is you pretending that you don't have a handicap to deal with."

"Fine," I said. "So why don't I just check into a nursing home and get the whole thing over with right now?"

"There's no reason to reduce this to absurdity, Arnie. We're talking about some very real problems here."

"Look," my father said. "Can't we leave this discussion for another time? I don't know about the rest of you, but I'd like to enjoy my meal."

"Henry," Redso said, leaning toward him earnestly. "I'm with you. I say, let's have ourselves a *happy* meal, right?"

Once the fortune cookies were gone, and I had defeated my father, as always, in our Oedipal struggle for the check, I accompanied my parents to their car. Billy and Redso, who'd decided to linger for after-dinner drinks, had already said their goodbyes at the table. My mother fussed a little with the collar of my jacket, as my father, standing a few paces off, slowly searched his pockets for his keys.

"I'm glad," she said. "Glad you've got friends living with you now. I think it's going to be much healthier this way, Arnie."

"Yeah, and I'll bet you're glad to be off KP duty, too."

"You know that's got nothing to do with it." She smiled, and let go of my jacket. "Although now that you mention it, it *is* nice, not having to be your maid for once in my life. Anyway, I like her. Billy. She seems very sympathetic. Also intelligent, alert."

"She's all of that," I said, hoping the thickness in my voice hadn't betrayed me.

"But tell me. Is Redso all right?"

I hesitated; I didn't think this was the time to open up that can of worms. "What do you mean?"

"He seems—queer somehow. Off balance."

"Hell, he's just a little drunk, Mom."

"No." She shook her head. "No, it's something else."

Now my father joined us, draping a heavy arm around my shoulders. "That Billy," he said. "She's quite a woman, Arnie. Quite a woman." He raised a cautionary forefinger. "And not only beautiful. Do you read me, sport? Not only beautiful."

Actually, I didn't read him at first. But as my father went on nodding at me—as if we were sharing in some deeply significant males-only understanding—I saw that he'd somehow gotten things mixed up, and was under the misapprehension that Billy was *my* girlfriend.

And yet, not knowing why, I allowed them to get into the car and drive away without bothering to set my father straight.

Redso was off in the men's room when I clanked back to the table.

"I got you a cognac," Billy said.

I thanked her as I took a seat and propped my crutches against the table—but didn't touch it. I'd done more than enough drinking that week.

Billy gazed thoughtfully into her snifter, tracing the ball of her thumb around the rim. "I like your parents, Arnie. They seem very loving. And sane."

"Sane? *My* folks?"

"You know they are. And I especially like your father. He's very soft, isn't he? And kind. You really *like* them both, don't you?"

That surprised me. "Well, sure."

Billy took a sip of the nut-brown liquor, and stared off miserably past the table.

"What is it, Billy?"

"The idea of you going off to Wales. I guess . . . it worries me. Scares me."

That warmed me like a bath of melted butter.

I knit my hands together on the table. "Look," I said. "I haven't come to a decision about it yet. And even if I do go, it won't be until March at the earliest. Things will *have* to be more settled down by then, right?"

Billy took another taste of her cognac, and wrinkled her nose as if it was bitter. "It's something else," she said.

I waited.

She roughly sighed. "I've got to get in touch with my father. I've been putting it off, and putting it off, and . . . I don't know. Maybe seeing your parents tonight made it hit home. But it's been two weeks now. Do you know he still thinks I'm in Pittsburgh?"

"You're kidding."

"He has no *idea* I quit the program. And of course, he doesn't know the first thing about Redso. Which is how I mean to keep it. Anyway. He always called me in Pittsburgh on the last Sunday of the month." She rolled her eyes. "And always before five—you know, when it's the cheapest. And now that Sunday's coming up. So either I move first, and catch him —or he catches me."

"But why did you put it off so long?"

"Just wait till you meet him," Billy said, twisting up a sour little smile. "Then you'll know."

IF BILLY'S CALL came as a shock to her father, he came right back with a shocker of his own. Rabbi Rubin insisted on dropping by the house that Sunday afternoon—and would broach no argument on the subject—to satisfy himself that everything was "right and proper" about his daughter's new living arrangements.

Of course, Billy told us, if her father found out that she was living with a lover, and a gentile lover to boot, there was no telling what kind of shit would hit the fan. So this was her emergency plan. On Sunday morning, Redso would make himself scarce—and keep well away from the house until that evening. Meanwhile, Billy would pass me off as her sole roommate, an old platonic friend from high school or college. Of course her father wouldn't like it that I was male. But the fact that I was Jewish would go a long way toward placating him, and then, of course, my crutches would probably render me all the more harmless in his eyes. Her father had no imagination, she told us; he'd believe whatever he preferred to believe. So we'd have brunch, the whole ordeal would be over in an hour or two, and then the three of us could get on with our lives. Billy understood that it was a lot to ask of the both of us—

"You're damned fucking straight it's a lot to ask!" Redso slammed the refrigerator door, popped open his beer, and kept his slitted blue eyes on Billy as he chugged. He angrily wiped his mouth. "Just where am I supposed to *go* while you're having your bagels and lox?"

"I don't know, Redso. Go to the movies. Go to the zoo. Go over to the East Side and get stoned. You're plenty resourceful."

"Oh yeah? Well, how'm I supposed to get there—fly?"

I had to laugh. *"Can* you, Redso? I've been meaning to ask."

"Would you lend him your car, Arnie?"

I shrugged. "I suppose. That is, if we decide to actually go through with this thing."

"Well, I don't exactly *like* the idea of being vaporized, *verstehen?* Besides, has it occurred to you that I might like to *meet* the Ayatollah Rubin?"

"Redso, you know that's impossible!"

"Why? Am I really that much of an embarrassment to you?"

"It's not you—it's him. And you *know* it!"

"Oh, this is beautiful! This is just fucking beautiful!" Redso was stalking back and forth in front of Billy now. "What the hell century is your father *from,* anyway? Doesn't he realize you've reached puberty?"

"Not really."

"Well, when are you planning on breaking the news? And besides, what's he going to do if he *does* find out you're fucking me? Take away your diaphragm and send you back to Hebrew school? Round up a bunch of zealots and have you *stoned* to death?"

Billy stood her ground with crossed arms. "My father is old," she said, very slowly and distinctly. "And he's rigid, and he's intolerant—and there's nothing I can *do* about that. And I don't want to hurt him. All right? Not if I can help it."

"Oh, sweet Jesus! The all-compassionate Buddha speaks!"

"So in this particular case," Billy went on, her voice as hard as Redso's, "I'm putting his feelings ahead of yours." She shot me a glance where I sat at the table. "Both of yours," she said.

"Well, how about that, Arnie-boy? Do you *mind* being reduced to a harmless Jewish eunuch just to spare her daddy's feelings?"

That hit me hard.

Billy spun at him. "God, Redso! What a shitty thing to say!"

"Hey, it wasn't *my* idea. If you ask me, Arnie's got a perfect *right* to keep his balls."

"You really are a bastard, you know that?"

"*Ach,* just fuck you!" Redso hissed.

Then he stalked out of the kitchen—seeming to purposely collide with Billy's shoulder as he passed her.

I FIGURED there were two ways of looking at it. I could choose to resent Billy's use of me, along with its sorely humiliating implications—but to whose advantage? Or I could ignore the insult, enlist as Billy's confederate, and worm my way still deeper into her gratitude. Besides, this acting assignment of hers held a certain pathetic attraction; the lie I would be colluding in, after all, was one I secretly and ardently longed to be true, the sine qua non of all my abject masturbatory scenarios: to have Billy all to myself, with Redso somehow safely erased from the picture.

I told Billy she could count on me.

On Friday afternoon, before sundown, we drove out to Simon Kohn's Kosher Meats in Creve Coeur to pick up her father's favorite astronomically priced goodies—lox, bagels, cream cheese, a half sheet of kugel, a honeycake, and three fat golden whitefish with their startled-looking heads still attached. I insisted, despite Billy's protests, on paying for it all.

Redso, as it turned out, didn't wait until Sunday to make himself scarce. On Saturday afternoon he snatched some cash off my bureau and roared off in my Toronado—without a word to either one of us about where he was going, or when he intended to come back.

We spent that night in an almost unbroken silence—Billy said she didn't feel like talking—she on the sofa with my hardbound copy of *Rabbit Redux,* me on my bed with a book I'd been trying to plow through for ages, Thomas Mann's *Magic Mountain,* which was soporifically boring, and soon dunked me into sleep.

Early Sunday morning, when I crutched into the kitchen for

my coffee, Billy was already dressed. Aside from that night at the Casa Loma Ballroom, and our dinner with my parents, I'd never seen Billy dressed for anything more formal than a touch-football game. And her attempt at looking smart for her father was so pitifully inept that I wanted, as physically impossible as it was, to crutch over and give her a reassuring hug. She wore her hair back in a ponytail, tied with a bright violet ribbon, along with a screaming fuchsia blouse, a lurid orange skirt, and a pair of open-toed white shoes. Nothing went with anything. She shimmered like a piece of pop art.

I should take a detour here to mention something about Billy's fashion sense—or odd lack of it. Whether because of her sheltered upbringing, an inherent lack of taste, or simple indifference, in the visual arena Billy was as esthetically stunted as I was overdeveloped (she never really did, for example, give my resplendent gems and minerals their due), and when it came to the womanly skills of adorning herself there was something unworldly, almost nunlike, in her helplessness. Her basic daily wardrobe was Pure Unrepentent Slob: jeans, T-shirts, sweatshirts, her favorite beaten-to-hell gray corduroy jacket, tennis shoes, rubber sandals. The only time she ever wore makeup was on stage. And she seemed just as blithely unconcerned about her body. She must have weighed in at a good ten or fifteen pounds above the anorexic ideal of the day; she paid no attention at all to what she ate or drank; and even now, in September, with three months of summer right at our backs, she had the porcelain coloring of a nineteenth-century beauty who never left the house without her parasol. And while that certainly had an allure of its own, I didn't think Billy had calculated the effect. She just didn't seem to *give* a shit if her body was lean or tanned. The one thing that did seem to incite her vanity was her hair, which she brushed assiduously every night, and was forever dousing with the regiments of shampoos, conditioners and rinses that crowded the top of my toilet. And yet, as if to assert her strange detachment even there, she refused to even consider dyeing out the premature gray—never mind how it scotched much of the on-camera television work she might have been getting. On the other hand, of course, as ravishing as she was, Billy could have gone around tarred and feathered and still turned a lot of heads. But that hardly explained why she seemed so perversely determined to devalue her own beauty —which was certainly no less rare and marvelous a gift, if you asked me, than any of the others she possessed.

But as Billy brought my coffee to the table, I made sure to compliment her on her sadly clownish outfit.

WITH JUST MINUTES to go before her father's scheduled arrival, I returned to the kitchen for another cup of coffee, and damn near stuck a crutch into Billy. She was kneeling on the floor before the open refrigerator, a black plastic trash bag at her side. She had the fierce concentrated look on her face I'd come to recognize—the eyes narrowed, the lips pursed, the cheeks indented—which seemed to say, *Don't you dare get in my way*. I stood back and watched her root. She didn't seem to notice, or care, that her skirt was chafing on the floor beneath her knees. She withdrew a log of Genoa salami, scowled at it, then stuffed it in her bag.

"Billy, what are you doing?"

"Getting rid of all the—you know—bacon and stuff."

I stared at her stupidly. "That was a Volpi salami you just threw out. Do you know what that stuff costs a pound?"

Billy sat back on her heels. "I'm going to put it all back. I just need to stick it away in the basement or someplace. You know, until he leaves."

"What makes you think your father's going to be poking around in my refrigerator?"

"He's just like a little boy, Arnie. He can't keep his hands out of anything."

Then the insanity of the whole thing hit me.

"Are you telling me he actually thinks you keep *kosher?*"

Billy defiantly raised her chin. "I lie to him, Arnie. All right? I've been lying to him all my life. If I thought he could handle the truth, I *wouldn't*. But he—"

"Whoa! Just one second here. What's *my* role here? Am *I* supposed to pretend I'm a good Jew?"

She didn't answer.

I was spider-walking around the kitchen now. "Well, you can just forget about that, Billy! I mean, I'm willing to go along with this thing to a point—but I'm just a little out of my *element* here. I don't even know what the rules *are*, much less—"

"Just play it by ear, Arnie. All right?"

She ducked her face, bit her lip.

I stopped crutching. Billy looked so vulnerable at that moment, so small and girlish and wrongheaded, kneeling on the floor in that clashing eyesore of an outfit, that I yearned to fall on my knees beside her—as if I could!—and cover her face and throat with the tenderest of kisses. For once, my desire to touch her had nothing to do with lust. The feeling, in fact, was almost fatherly.

The doorbell rang.

Billy's shoulders jumped.

I volunteered to get the door—to give her time to dispose of her bag of *trayf*—and as I was starting away, Billy stopped me with her voice.

"Arnie?" She was clutching her plastic bag. "I just . . . thanks again for doing this."

WHAT I'D BEEN PICTURING was a man of Old Testament proportions, a towering Jeremiah, a fire-eyed Savonarola, and yet here on my front stoop fidgeted a wiry and plainly uncomfortable little man, a few inches shorter and maybe twenty pounds lighter than his daughter, who seemed unwilling to look me in the face. He stared instead at my crutches.

From the neck up, anyway, Rabbi Rubin appeared sufficiently rabbinical, with a dirty-gray goatee, a bony scholar's nose, and a black fedora, rubbed shiny in spots, tilted back on his close-cropped silver hair. But from the neck down he easily could have passed for a garage mechanic. What I took to be his initials, M.E.R., were stitched onto the breast pocket of his blue denim work shirt, which, like his once white painter's pants, was as densely spattered with paint, grease and dirt as a Jackson Pollock canvas. His gray Chevy pickup in the driveway looked right at home in my proletarian neighborhood; the passenger window was held together by stripes of silver tape, the fenders were battered, the back was overloaded with lumber, paint cans, upright rolls of roofing material.

He looked up from my crutches to my face—his eyes were as black as Billy's, but small and hard-looking, like discs of obsidian—furrowed his brow, then glanced dubiously up and down my street in both directions. He touched the ragged tip of his goatee. "This is 1740 Oxford Street?"

"Yes, sir." I shifted my right crutch into my left hand, and offered my free hand for a shake.

Rabbi Rubin didn't take it.

"I'm uh, Arnie Goldman. Billy's roommate."

"Roommate?" He shook his head. "No. No, that can't be. She didn't mention a roommate."

I laughed. "Well, she's got one. And it's me."

The old man still appeared unconvinced.

Billy joined me in the doorway, standing close enough to grant me a whiff of her spicy hair. "Hello, Daddy." Her smile looked brittle as glass.

"Aha!" the old man yelled, and slapped a thigh. "I knew it! What did I tell you? I *knew* I had the right address!"

"Did you have any trouble finding it?"

"Trouble? You know me, young lady—a sense of direction like a homing pigeon!"

"Well, it's good to see you, Daddy."

She stepped down to the stoop and embraced him. It would have been a strangely cool and uncomfortable embrace between father and daughter, it seemed to me, even if their separation hadn't been a long one. Billy did all the squeezing, while her father, stiff as a golem, got his arms into position around her back, impatiently patted her shoulders a few times, and then broke free and backed off a couple of steps, nodding his ancient black hat.

"So . . ." he said. "Long time no see, as they say."

Billy gave a swing to her ponytail and crossed her arms. She cranked up another smile. "You're looking fit, Daddy."

"Fit?" He laughed. "You'd better believe I'm fit, young lady! Fit as a fiddle, in fact! So, *nu?* Where do you suppose I just came from?"

Billy waited.

"From laying roof at the building on Pennsylvania Avenue! Sixty-four years old next August—and guess what? I laid half the roof in one morning! One morning—half the roof! Hah? Is that unbelievable? And without an assistant yet!" The Rabbi, apparently ready to accept my existence now, threw me a wink. "And she asks her old man if he's fit!"

"That's—remarkable, Daddy."

"Remarkable is right!"

Now the Rabbi's demeanor abruptly switched gears. He knit his hands behind his back, and magisterially raised his eyebrows at his daughter. "So, Billy? How is it that you failed to inform me you had a roommate?"

"I just . . ." Billy shrugged and made a vague gesture.

The Rabbi suspiciously inspected me. "Goldman, did you say your name was?"

"Yes, sir."

"And how is it that you're acquainted with my daughter?"

I readjusted my weight on my crutches. "We're old friends from high school," I told him—and then, remembering that every good lie is twisted out of a foundation of fact, mentioned Billy's alma mater, University City High.

"I see." He kept those hard obsidian eyes on me.

"Well!" Billy said. "What do you say we go inside and eat? We've got lox, whitefish, kugel—all your favorites, Daddy. Are you hungry?"

Now the Rabbi—whose moods seemed as mercurial as Redso's—switched back from somberness to brightness. He grinned and patted his flat stomach. "You know me. Always ready to eat."

"Watch your step, Rabbi," I said, and stiffly led the way inside the house.

The Rabbi's voice boomed heartily behind me. "So the Prodigal Daughter finally returns."

"Oh, come on, Daddy. I don't think I was being all that prodigal."

"Maybe not, maybe not. But now that you've finally taken your master's degree from that school, let's hope you've got this acting *mishegas* out of your system once and for all."

I hesitated in my crutch-walk. Master's degree? Billy must have meant what she'd said in the kitchen—that she habitually fed her father soothing lies.

"Daddy, it's not *mishegas*. It's my career."

"Career, she says! As if she's starring on Broadway! A commercial here, a role in a student production there—that's what you call a career? Nothing but self-indulgent nonsense!"

"I'm *trying*. Besides, what else can I do but act?"

"What else does any sensible woman do at your age? Find a husband, raise a family, fulfill your natural, God-given destiny. After all, you're not getting any younger, young lady. Am I right about that, Mr. Goldman?"

I wasn't sure which idea I was supposed to affirm: that it was high time Billy got cracking on her God-given destiny? Or that she wasn't getting any younger?

Luckily Rabbi Rubin wasn't waiting for my answer.

"Aha!" he shouted. "What have we here?"

We were stopped between the pair of mammoth amethyst geodes that flanked the entrance to the dining room, their hollows packed with sparkling purple ice. The Rabbi stared at them, and then at my glittering spread of rocks behind them, his hands on his skinny hips, his face softened with a look of childlike wonder.

"Will you look at this?" he said. "Why, it's beautiful! Astonishing!"

I smiled at the old man—and then had to wonder why his daughter had never shown half the same enthusiasm for what, after all, was my life's passion.

"These are all yours?" the old man asked me.

"All mine."

"Well, what do you know? This is a hobby of yours?"

"Actually, it's how I make my living. I'm a gem and mineral dealer."

"You mean to say that you buy and sell these things?"

"That's right."

"But who would your customers be?"

"Oh, other dealers and collectors. Rock shops. Museums."

"Museums, you say?"

"There are one or two collections I've worked with."

"Arnie's being much too modest," Billy said. "He's actually one of the top experts in his field, Daddy. He's got clients all around the world. The Chicago Natural History Museum, the Smithsonian, museums in Europe—"

"The Smithsonian? No!"

"Oh yes," Billy said.

The Rabbi scratched at the side of his beard as he peered at me. "And you make money at this? Enough to live?"

"He makes a very nice living," Billy said.

"Very impressive. Very impressive indeed. Do you mind if I take a little look?"

"Heck, I'll give you the nickel tour," I said. "Are you interested in gems and minerals, Rabbi?"

"Interested? Why, naturally, naturally. I find all of the sciences—geology, astronomy, physics, you name it—all of them utterly fascinating. Of course, I'm not what you'd call an expert in any particular field of study. But I read, I dabble, I inquire. And it's not just the sciences we're talking about, young man! History, mathematics, the mechanical arts—if it's a subject of interest, I'm *interested!*" The Rabbi chuckled at that, and pushed up at the brim of his hat. "You might even say that I'm something of a modern-day Renaissance man. Hah? Am I right about that, Billy?"

Billy's smile looked strained enough to crack across her face. "You're a regular Leonardo da Vinci," she told him.

"NOW YOU TAKE THE FISH like so . . . you see? And with your knife, you make an incision here. And then you simply peel the skin away . . . and aha! There you are."

With the tip of his plastic knife, Rabbi Rubin pushed the limp golden skin into a mound at the edge of his paper plate. There was a dainty precision to his operations that I found remarkable, given the massiveness of his hands. They were a peasant's hands, a butcher's hands, huge all out of proportion to his skinny boyish frame, with powerful stubby fingers, and on the backs, a density of wiry black hairs that bristled from the knuckles to the wrist. And although he'd scrubbed them vigorously at the sink (mumbling a Hebrew prayer as he did so) they still looked filthy, the horny nails underscored by scimitars of blue-black grunge.

"So? What are you waiting for?" he asked me. (Billy had already expertly skinned her fish.) "First the skin, and then we continue."

Far less deftly than the Rabbi or his nimble-fingered daughter, I tore the skin away from my whitefish.

"Now, starting on the top of the spine, you just push the

flesh away—you see? You don't cut, you don't scrape, but you *push*. That's right . . . that's right. And now, with the flesh below the bone—just watch how Billy's doing it—you *strip* the flesh away, careful not to catch the bones. Aha! You see? And *voilà!*" The Rabbi dangled his fish skeleton by the tail. "And that, ladies and gentlemen, is how to properly bone a smoked whitefish, according to Master Chef Rubin!"

I was still struggling with my mangled fish.

Billy, meanwhile, had now boned her own fish as swiftly and efficiently as her father, and was already digging in. "Just attack it any old way, Arnie. This is too good to wait for."

"You see how nicely she managed it? Billy's always been very clever with her hands—a genetic trait she didn't inherit from her mother, I can tell you that!" The Rabbi chuckled. "At the age of six, seven, *already* she was boning her own whitefish! Can you imagine?"

"Just think of it," Billy said, with a smirk that I thought was intended for me. "Maybe Mozart was composing symphonies when he was six. But could he bone his own whitefish? Hah!"

The Rabbi laughed appreciatively at that, then aimed his bony nose at his plate and started spearing his fish.

Just why Billy was working so hard to pump up her father's ego was a mystery to me—for by now it was abundantly clear that he could hardly have been more enamored with himself. Of course, I was the one he meant to impress (his daughter, it could be assumed, was already well acquainted with his myriad virtues) and since his arrival at the house he'd been directing most of his booming talk at me. And no matter what the topic, the Rabbi had somehow managed to yank it around to himself and what an admirable fellow he was.

When he'd paused, earlier on, to admire the handmade walnut coffee table in the living room (crafted by the same man who'd done my specimen cabinets), the Rabbi made sure to mention that he, too, had once built a table almost exactly like it—except that his version, he had to admit, seemed a little more solid in the legs. During our tour of my rock shelves, he insisted that I cover with my hand the labels beside certain specimens so that he could take "an educated guess" as to what they were. And the fact that he guessed wrong on everything but some unmistakable clusters of quartz, pyrite and galena, didn't dampen his spirits in the least. "Galena!" he shouted. "You see? What did I tell you? How many other lay-men could spot a crystal of galena just like that?" He even managed to muscle himself onto center stage when the subject of my arthritis came up. Rabbi Rubin informed me that he too had once been forced to use crutches, having broken an ankle in a fall down a staircase—and that his doctors had been abso-lutely dumbfounded at his powers of recovery. "They'd never seen anything like it before! Now, how old was I then? Sixty-one? Sixty-two? And yet within a matter of five weeks—are you listening?—within just five weeks, I'd completely dispensed with the crutches! Now, what do you suppose accounts for that?" I told the Rabbi that he'd have to enlighten me. He tapped at the side of his hat. "Mental attitude! You can talk age, you can talk genetic predisposition—but when all is said and done, it's a positive mental attitude that does more than anything else to heal the body! Now, am I right about that, young man, or am I right?" I answered with a tight smile that if he *were* right, I'd better see about improving my attitude—with which the Rabbi, apparently impervious to irony, cheer-fully agreed.

He had made quick, lip-smacking work of his whitefish, and was now mopping up with a piece of rye bread the last oily flakes on his paper plate. "So," he said. "Now maybe we can get down to our first order of business." He rolled up his rye bread and stuffed it in his mouth.

Billy stood, and carefully took up his plate.

"What business is that, Daddy?"

"What business, she says! The business of how you intend to conduct your life."

Billy turned away, retreated to the garbage can beside the sink, and tossed in the plate. "Do you want some coffee, Daddy?"

"Of course. But not too strong, you hear?" He showed me a candid smile. "Sometimes she brews the coffee like she's out to give me a heart attack." Then his smile died away, and he pressed the palms of his enormous hands together on the ta-bletop, the blunt tips of his fingers pointing at me like the prow of a battleship. "Now, what exactly do we know thus far?"

I shifted in my chair. My right hip had started to throb.

"Know about what, Rabbi?"

"About what! About you, of course."

I glanced at Billy. She was at the coffee machine now, the back of her fuchsia blouse glaring at us, fumbling with a stack of filters.

"Now, you say you're an old friend of Billy's from high school?"

I resisted the impulse to clear my throat. "That's right."

"I see. And how would you characterize that relationship? As merely platonic?"

My left hip began to throb in vicious counterpoint to the right.

"I presume that you're acquainted with the word 'platonic'?"

I instructed myself to keep my temper.

"Sure," I said.

"Daddy, why are you grilling him like this?"

"Grilling? Who's grilling? I'm merely asking your friend a few questions."

"It sounds more like an inquisition."

The Rabbi slapped the table. "Inquisition? *Inquisition?* How dare you use that word with me, young lady—knowing full well the connotations!"

Billy sighed. "Sorry."

"You choose to live in this house, a single young woman, under the very same roof with a single young man—instead of in your own house, where you rightly belong—and you have the temerity to question my right as your father to make a few simple inquiries?"

Billy sucked in her bottom lip, blinked slowly, then let that lip pop free. She weakly shrugged.

"Rabbi," I said, "feel free to ask me anything you like."

He sat back in his chair. "All right. Question number one. How *would* you describe your relations with my daughter?"

"As . . . merely platonic," I managed to say.

"Fine. I'll take your word as a gentleman on that. Now, question number two. Do you consider yourself to be a Jew?"

I risked a smile. "With a name like Goldman?"

"Just answer the question, please."

"Well, sure I'm a Jew."

The Rabbi leaned toward me, a glint in his small black eyes. "Then answer me this. How do you explain the absence of a *mezuza* in your doorway?"

He had me there.

The Rabbi surprised me by laughing. "You see? Maybe you thought it would escape my notice! But you've got to wake up pret-ty early in the morning to fool a sly old fox like me, sonny-boy!" The Rabbi's smile faded, and he was suddenly all grim business again. "You're aware, of course, that every observant Jew—"

"I know what a *mezuza* is, Rabbi."

"Oh? Good, good. So we're not entirely ignorant. Now answer me this, Mr. Goldman. How would you describe yourself? As an observant Jew, or otherwise?"

Again I glanced at Billy. But clearly she wasn't going to be much help. She stood before the wheezing coffee machine, her arms locked tight across her breasts, her eyes averted. I'd never seen her at a loss like this before. Was she afraid of defying her father, or afraid that by defying him, she might hurt him? Or were the two things one and the same in her mind?

"Good morning!" the Rabbi singsonged. "Are we awake over there? I asked you a question, young man. Do you, or do you not, consider yourself to be an observant Jew?"

I wriggled on the hook. "What do you mean, exactly, by observant?"

The Rabbi smiled. "Did you hear that, Billy? He wants me to define my terms! As if there could be any doubt!"

"Rabbi Rubin," I said, "if there weren't any room for doubt, why would there be three branches of Judaism?"

He stroked his beard. "Fair enough," he said. "Then let me alter my question slightly. Which branch would you say that you belong to? Orthodox, Conservative, or Reform?"

I couldn't wriggle any longer. "Actually," I said, "none of them."

"None of the above? Hah! Did you hear that, Billy? None of the above! And yet he calls himself a Jew!"

Billy looked directly at her father now. "Daddy, what's the point of this? All I'm doing is sharing a house with Arnie. You make it sound like we're planning on getting married or something. Arnie's religious ideas are *his* business—"

"Are you defying me, young lady?"

Billy watched her father in silence.

"I'm waiting for an answer. *Are* you defying me?"

"I'm disagreeing with you," she answered in a clotted voice.

He pushed up at the brim of his hat.

The silence thickened dangerously. And then it was broken —by a light insistent rapping at the back door screen.

The inside door was shut, but through the small square pane of translucent glass, I caught a moving flash of vivid orange.

The Rabbi craned around in his chair. "You expecting somebody?"

Billy stared at the door, her jaw open, her teeth partially bared.

Redso rapped on the screen again.

"What's the matter with you?" her father said. "Don't you answer the door when someone knocks?"

Moving robotically, Billy approached the door and swung it open.

Redso lowered his face to the screen, his smile angelic. "Afternoon, everybody. I, uh, didn't come at a bad time, did I?"

Billy stood before him like a pillar of salt.

"So, *nu?*" the Rabbi said to her. "Where did you learn your manners? You've got a guest. Invite him in!"

"Come in," Billy said.

"Thanks, thanks. Don't mind if I do."

Redso stepped into the kitchen as Billy stiffly backed away. He wore a loutish red and yellow checked sport coat that looked one or two sizes too big on him, a wide paisley tie, and on the crown of his frizzed orange hair, floating there like a lily pad, a tiny knit yarmulke of robin's egg blue. I could only guess where he'd picked up that clownish outfit—from Veteran's Village, or Goodwill, with a stop at a Jewish bookstore for the yarmulke—but of course, I knew damned well whose money he'd used to buy it. He was carrying a stack of worn books, four of them, with matching maroon bindings.

"Hello, Billy. Hello, Arnie. How're you both doing? You doing all right? Just happened to be in the neighborhood, and thought I'd drop by and return these books. Thanks for the loan by the way, Arnie. I enjoyed these volumes immensely." Now Redso seemed to notice the Rabbi for the first time. "No! Don't tell me! Billy? Is this your father?"

"Yes," she said.

"Well, speak of the devil!" Redso shrugged his stack of books more securely into the crook of his left arm, and offered his free hand to the Rabbi. The Rabbi hesitated. Then, guardedly, he raised his hand to Redso—who grabbed it, and started pumping enthusiastically away. "I can't tell you what an honor it is to finally meet you, Rabbi Rubin. The truth of the matter is, just yesterday my parents and I were talking about you—"

"I'm sorry—but have we met?"

"Daddy," Billy said, "This is—"

"Arthur Wolff," Redso said, still pumping away. "I don't know if you remember my parents or not, sir, but they used to belong to your congregation. Hermann and Frieda Wolff?"

I caught Redso's eye at that moment, and gave him the most threatening look I thought I could slip past the Rabbi (who was peering off thoughtfully into space) and he winked at me, the son of a bitch.

"Hermann and Frieda Wolff," the Rabbi said. "Yes, yes. Now that you mention it, I do seem to recollect . . ."

"Well, they certainly remember you, Rabbi. Why, do you know what they used to say? They used to say—and I swear I'm not making this up, sir—they used to say that you were such a superior rabbi, in every rabbinical respect, that you spoiled them for every rabbi who came after you! *That's* what they used to say!"

Redso was flying high, all right. He was rocking from foot to foot, like a man on the deck of a tossing ship.

Billy was back at the coffee machine, either busying herself with the coffee, or pretending to. I'm sure I was imagining it, but I thought I could actually feel on the skin of my face the hot static electricity crackling off the back of her neck.

The Rabbi, meanwhile, was digesting Redso's compliment with evident satisfaction. "Well, what do you know about that?" He scratched at his neck, nodded to himself, and then smiled up at Redso. "I'll tell you the truth, young man. Now that you mention it, I wasn't half bad as a rabbi. But the rabbinate turned out not to be my sole calling in life. Of course, I did my utmost to master my duties in those days. But the day finally came when I realized that my interests were a little too—how should I put it? A little too wide, a little too far-ranging, for such a narrow field." The Rabbi laughed. "A little too *catholic*, you might say!"

Redso exploded with laughter. "A little too catholic! Boy, that's a good one, Rabbi! A little too catholic! My parents always *did* say you had a sterling sense of humor!"

The Rabbi was chuckling, too. "And you said your name was what?"

"Arthur Wolff. Son of Hermann and Frieda." So far Redso was impressively under control, staying mostly within the bounds of his role, but I could see by the way his slanted blue eyes were ablaze, and by his steady catatonic rocking, that the pressure was building.

"Do you mind if I set down these books?" he said. "They're getting kind of heavy." Redso placed the stack near the Rabbi's elbow, making sure, it seemed to me, that the spines were facing in his direction. Then he yoked his hands behind his back and grinned at Billy.

She was leaning against the counter, her face drained of expression, her arms hanging inertly at her sides, like soft white sausages.

"Can I get you anything?" she asked him in a monotone.

"Do you have any tea?"

"Tea?"

"Yes. Tea. A nice cup of tea would be nice."

"How about coffee?"

"Coffee? Coffee would be dandy."

"How would you like it?"

"With nondairy creamer, if you've got it. See, I just had a corned beef sandwich before leaving the house—and well, you just can't be too careful nowadays, can you? I mean, with mixing your *milchiks* and your *flayshigs*. Am I right about that, Rabbi?"

"Of course, of course."

"We don't have any nondairy creamer," Billy said. "How about just black?"

"Black? Black is beautiful." Something flickered in Redso's eyes; maybe he sensed that his control was beginning to slip. He readjusted the tiny blue yarmulke floating on his puffball of orange hair. "So, Billy. How was your *Shabbos?*"

Her chest expanded, and her mouth turned downward at the corners just enough to show him her loathing. "Fine," she said. "How was yours?"

"Oh, very restful. Very peaceful. Very restful and peaceful indeed. In fact, I don't *know* when I've felt more rested and peaceful. But of course, that's what the Sabbath is all about, isn't it? A peaceful rest. Rest in peace. And so forth."

Now even the Rabbi gave Redso a curious look.

His rocking cranked up a notch.

"Why don't you take a seat?" Billy said, an edge of command in her voice.

Redso plopped into the chair closest to the Rabbi. He raised a knee and clamped both hands around it, as if to keep it from flying away. Still, it madly jackhammered.

If the Rabbi took any notice of Redso's mounting agitation, he gave no sign of it now. He was frowning intently at the spines of the books. "Well, what do you know?" he said softly, turning to Redso. "Do you read Maimonides?"

"Who doesn't?" Redso said.

The Rabbi contracted his brow.

Redso laughed. "Just a joke, Rabbi. Just a joke. But yes. I *do* read Maimonides. Or, at least, I did my *best* to read Maimonides. But to tell you the absolute truth . . ." Redso unhooked his hands from his knee—which continued to piston—and leaned confidentially toward the Rabbi, tapping the top of the stack with a knuckle. "I didn't quite make it through all these volumes here. Not that I didn't give it the old college try. Or the old *yeshiva* try." He cleared his throat. "Whatever. But Maimonides, as I'm sure you already know, is every bit as challenging and difficult as he is richly rewarding . . ."

"Oh, no doubt, no doubt."

"And frankly, Rabbi, I don't know when I've been so *humbled* as a reader. Maimonides! My goodness! What a brilliant, astonishing, multifaceted mind the man had! A mind for all the ages, and for all mankind—no matter what your religion or creed. The Jewish Aristotle, is how I'd put it."

At that, the Rabbi shot back in his chair and banged his fist on the table. "Yes!" he bellowed. "Exactly!"

Billy dropped a coffee cup. It broke neatly into halves at her feet. She stared down stupidly at the accident for a moment, then bent with a grunt to pick up the pieces.

"The Jewish Aristotle!" the Rabbi crowed. "Of course! Of course! Now, how is it that I never thought to put it quite that way before? But it's true—absolutely apt! Maimonides was the great Jewish—oh, what's the word I'm looking for? Polymath?"

"That's the word, Rabbi. Polymath. Poly from the Greek, meaning many. Math from wherever, meaning whatever it means."

"Not a single subject or discipline then known to the world that Maimonides didn't address himself to! Hah? Am I right about that, Mr. Wolff?"

"Right as rain, Rabbi. Law, ethics, theology, psychology, astronomy, taxonomy, gastronomy, Deuteronomy—why, the list goes on and on! You might say his interests were . . . well, *catholic.*"

The Rabbi barked a laugh at that, and wagged a finger at Redso.

"But I'll tell you where I got stuck, Rabbi."

The old man leaned forward. "And where was that?"

Redso took the uppermost book from the stack and handed it to the Rabbi. "Right in this last volume here. The one that deals with tort law?"

"Aha."

"Of course, I'm sure *you've* read it, Rabbi. But I just found it such hard going . . ."

Rabbi Rubin sagely nodded as he began to flip through the book. "Very technical, of course. Very technical indeed. But brilliant. Indisputably brilliant." He closed the book and smiled at his daughter. "So, *nu,* Billy? How is it you never informed me you had a friend who reads Maimonides?"

"Two friends, Rabbi," Redso said. "Two friends. Don't forget, it was Arnie here who lent me these books. And it was Billy who turned me on to Maimonides in the first place. She loves to tell that story—you know, about how he stood on one foot like a flamingo and recited the Golden Rule?"

The Rabbi touched his goatee. "I believe that was Rabbi Hillel," he said.

"Hillel? Of course! Hillel. How completely imbecilic of me."

The Rabbi turned to me. "These are your books?"

What the hell, I figured. I smiled at the old man and said, with a modest shrug, "To tell you the truth, Rabbi, I found the volume on tort law pretty rough going myself."

The Rabbi's eyebrows lifted. "Well, what do you know?" he said, slowly shaking his head. "Well, what do you know?"

THE TWO-MAN SYMPOSIUM was on. Redso chain-smoked, and Rabbi Rubin put away cup after cup of coffee, slice after slice of honeycake, as their booming, blustering, competitive voices ping-ponged across the table without letup. Billy endured it stoically, bleakly sipping at her coffee—and, judging by the way her jaws kept flickering, grinding her teeth. Every so often I'd wedge in a comment, but for the most part I sat back and listened, both appalled and entertained. They tackled Aristotle, Plato, Heraclitus, they howled in disagreement over what should be done about the hostages in Tehran, they exchanged heated volleys over who was the greatest Civil War general, Grant or Lee, and together they marveled at the shimmering cosmic insights of Newton, Einstein, Hubble, and the mind-boggling phenomenon of an ever expanding universe—the both of them happily hollering, pounding the table, spraying spittle. Redso, unable to remain for very long in one position, paced and sat, paced and sat, and at one point the Rabbi, carried away by the passion of his argument, actually got up and followed Redso around the kitchen like a yammering dog. It was the damnedest thing to see, how the two of them, strangers not fifteen minutes before, had so enthusiastically hit the same voluble groove. Of course, just how much of that was due to Redso's staying in character, and how much to his crazy agitation, was impossible to sort out. Whatever, it was one hell of a shouting match, and I couldn't help feeling, despite my keen awareness of Billy's silent misery, a little disappointed when the Rabbi announced, glancing at his watch, that he'd somehow let the time slip away from him, and was already unconscionably late for an appointment to show one of his apartments.

He didn't know when he'd had such an enjoyable talk, Rabbi Rubin told a beaming Redso, and he hoped to spend some more time with him one of these days, if that could be arranged. But now, alas, he had to be hurrying off.

"Are you sure you have to go?" Billy asked him, a spark of life reentering her voice.

The three of us accompanied the old man to the front stoop. He reminded Billy that they still had to reach an understanding on "certain problematical components" of her new living situation. Then he stiffly withstood her farewell embrace, bade us all goodbye, and hurried off the stoop and across the patchy lawn with a nimbleness that amazed me. He hopped in the cab of his battered gray pickup, backed out of the driveway, and with a gnashing of gears, sputtered off down Oxford Street, trailing plumes of steel-blue exhaust.

Like an indefatigable Queen Elizabeth II, Billy kept up her glassy smile and waved her father on until he grindingly made the turn at the corner. Then she swung around to face Redso —who, a few seconds before, had slipped quietly inside the house. She turned her outraged eyes on me. "Did you see where he went?"

I pointed the way with a crutch.

She tore inside the house. I followed. But Billy was making no allowance for my four-footed pokiness, and I quickly lost sight of her. I crutched through the living room, past my rock shelves, and into the kitchen, where the back door stood wide open. I clumped onto my rotting back porch. There, under the tall oak tree in the center of the yard, sat Redso, his back to the trunk, a bottle of J&B standing upright in the high grass beside him.

Billy stood before him, her feet set wide apart. "You bastard!" she screamed. "You fucker!" She reared back with a foot as if to kick him.

Redso blocked his face. "Hey, what the fuck are you doing?"

Billy's white shoe flashed.

Redso ducked. And then he pulled off a move worthy of Errol Flynn.

He sprang to his feet, jumped into the air, caught hold of a thick limb above his head, and swung himself into the tree. Cackling all the way, he vaulted and swung and scrambled until he found a perch that suited him, twelve or fifteen feet above the ground. Gripping some branches over his head, Redso squatted low on the limb, thrust his grinning face forward, and let out with a powerful, ululating rebel cry that must have echoed all over the neighborhood.

By now I was crutching as fast as I could toward the tree.

"I am the *Ubermensch!*" Redso bellowed. "Eat your heart out, Frederick Nietzsche! I . . . am . . . the motherfucking . . . *Ubermensch!*"

Billy wiped her ponytail out of her face and shielded her reddened eyes as she squinted up at Redso. He grinned down at her like the Cheshire Cat.

"Who are you, little girl?"

"Get out of that tree, Redso!"

"What for? So you can try kicking my face in again?"

"Get *down* here, you shit!"

"Billy, Billy, Billy—why this ugly antagonism? You should be *thanking* me right now! Didn't I see to it that your daddy had a good time? Didn't the old fanatic just go away *happy?*"

Billy crossed her arms, and glared up at him.

"I saved the fucking day—and what thanks do I get? You try to stick a shoe in my brain! *O, monster ingratitude!*" Redso bounced happily on his limb. Then he leaned down, his grin hardening. "I'll tell you what, Miss Rubin. At first, you know, I really did plan on being good. I truly did. But then I thought to myself, Hey! I don't much *like* being Billy's dirty little secret. It hurts my tender *feelings* to be treated like some two-headed monster in the attic who's not good enough to meet her lousy father! Why should I go *along* with this horseshit? Maybe you've got Arnie wrapped around your little finger—but I'm not so easy to pussy-whip, *verstehen?*"

"Redso," I said through my teeth, "do you realize you're out of your mind?"

Clinging one-handed to a branch, Redso hung forward in the air like a tree sloth, and cupped a hand to his ear. "I'm sorry? Come again?"

"You're manic," Billy said, her voice shaky. "You're mentally ill, Redso. You're suffering from manic-depression—"

"Suffering? Hah! Do I look to you like I'm *suffering?*"

"You're sick, and you"—Billy paused to take a breath—"you need help."

Redso gave out a whoop and dipped backward, nearly slipping off his limb. "Oh, sweet Mary, mother of Christ! *I'm* sick? *I'm* manic? You want to know who's manic, sweetheart, just take a look at that *meshugah* father of yours! *He's* the one you'd better hand over to the Brain Police! Talk about megalomania! Talk about a messiah complex! He ought to be wandering the Sinai Desert, preaching to the birds and living off locusts and honey! And you're telling me *I'm* manic?"

"Redso," I said, "will you look at yourself? You're completely out of control. You're not eating, you're not sleeping—"

"*O, beware, my lord, of jealousy,*" he intoned in his best basso profundo voice. "*It is the green-eyed monster which doth mock the meat it feeds on!*" Redso rattled the branches over his head. "You're jealous, Goldman! Admit it! You've been nursing a hard-on for Billy ever since day one—"

"What the hell are you talking about?"

"Oh, please, spare me! You're no actor, Arnie-boy. Take my advice and stick to rock collecting, buddy. I mean, here I am, on the biggest, most amazing tear I've ever been on—and there you are, beating your meat, and hating my guts and just dreaming up ways to undercut me! Don't bother denying it, Goldman. I know you better than you know your own crippled twisted envious self!"

"Just listen to yourself, Redso!" Billy whipped her ponytail across her shoulders. "Can't you *hear* how crazy you sound?"

Redso laughed. "All right, all right, all right." He crouched low on his limb. "Let's just say, for the sake of argument, that I *am* a manic-depressive, as you say. Well? Here's my question. So fucking what if I *am*? Didn't I just write one hell of a terrific play? Well? Come on! You read it, Rubin. Whadja think?"

Billy only stared at him.

"And did I or did I not write that one hell of a terrific play in the record-breaking time of just eight days and nights? Well?"

Still she said nothing.

"Not a bad performance, eh? Even for a guy in the full possession of all his mental faculties—wouldn't you say?"

She looked off into the neighboring backyard.

"And meanwhile, darling Billy, how about you and me? Aren't we having ourselves one hell of a damned fine time? In the sack—and anyplace else we happen to be? Don't you still find me to be an intriguing, fascinating, oh-so-stimulating guy to have around? Don't I still do that voodoo that I do so well?"

Billy looked at him again, her eyes narrowing to slits.

"So what's the goddamned *problem* here?" Redso shot upright, and danced a dangerous little jig on his limb. "You *love* me this way, Billy! Hell, you wouldn't *want* me any other way —and you know it!"

"You're manic," Billy said again, her voice squeezed.

"Okay! Fine! You win! I'm manic! See? Hoo-hah! Yadda yadda ya! Manic as a jaybird! Crazy as a loon! But this is the guy you fell in *love* with, Billy darling! Get it? *This* is your beloved! So why in the name of Christ would you want me to be *cured?*"

Billy crossed her arms again, and turned away. She started walking slowly toward the house. Of course she hadn't been drinking. But she moved with the unsteady, overly dignified gait of a woman bombed out of her skull.

"Admit it!" Redso bellowed after her. "You *know* it's the gospel truth! So if it ain't broke, Billy—why the hell do you want to *fix* it?"

"It's broke," I told him.

Redso showed me a malevolent white grin.

And then, with a ringing shout of triumph, he launched himself into the air.

PART TWO

Five

THE ROAR of the 747 lowered to an ominous hum, the seatbelt signals dinged overhead with a scary finality, and ready or not, like it or not, I was back in St. Louis—haunted St. Louis, where my old abandoned ghosts were about to reach for me again.

A flight attendant, in her strangely flat and nasal American accent, thanked us all for flying TWA (as if, in an airport practically owned by TWA, we'd actually had any choice) and then the whole cabinful of passengers, like worshipers in an absurdly cramped church, arose in itchy unison.

But I kept my seat. It was my practice to let the cabin empty before attempting to disembark, for with my cumbersome backpack, the aisle-hogging contortions it took to work it on, and the nuisance of my two extra aluminum legs, I knew better than to try and fight the crush. Besides, after my long stay in Wales, when even my most homesick thoughts of America had been pierced and soured by dread, I was in no big hurry to confront whatever awaited me at the gate, not even if one of those things was Billy.

When I'd fled St. Louis seventeen months before, I didn't think I was acting mainly out of cowardice. After all, the chance to live in a foreign country, take charge of an entire museum collection, and rebuild that collection from near scratch (and with someone else's money, by God) was one I

would have been a fool to pass up. But now, about to face the
wreckage of what I'd left behind, it seemed clear that what had
really driven me across the Atlantic was nothing but a shame-
ful failure of nerve.

For the truth was, by the spring, when I'd turned tail, I was
desperately sick of it all—sick of what we knew for certain now
was Redso's mental illness, sick of his exhausting euphorias
and outrageous manic stunts, sick of the mental wards, the
police stations, the phone calls in the dead of night, sick of
longing for a woman who seemed perversely bent on forever
squandering her love on a madman—as if Redso, in his fud-
dled frenzy, could even recognize the wonder of that gift,
much less be grateful for it—sick of the whole relentless,
grinding, nerve-jangling roller coaster ride I'd been prisoner
of since Redso first returned from Pittsburgh. And so, when
the time came, I took Desmond Garlick up on his offer, made
my arrangements with Billy, left them my car, my house, and
all the glittering expensive treasures it contained, and bolted
like a terrified rabbit.

And yet, despite my occasional attacks of remorse, I'd had
myself the time of my life in Wales—which, when it wasn't wet
and gray, was just as lovely and otherworldly as I'd hoped,
with its smug cottagelike houses, its romantic outcroppings of
castle ruins, and its hills like softly undulating quilts, dotted
with cows and sheep, and stitched together with snaking
hedges of stone and greenery. To revamp the mineral collection, I met with curators, private collectors and professional
dealers all over Great Britain, from Swansea in the south of
Wales to Snowdonia in the north, from Scotland to London to
Dover, and then across the Channel, to graze among the pick-
ings in such hubs of the international gem trade as Amster-
dam, Brussels and Zurich; and armed as I was with my generous grant from the British government, it all seemed as easy as
picking ripe fruit. Meanwhile, I was amassing my own
splendid catches on the side, and shipping them home in
crates packed full of stale popcorn (which, you may be interested to know, works better than anything else I've discovered
to keep delicate crystals intact during transit). My landlady,
Mrs. Thomas, was a bright-eyed, fussy old thing, who served
me her unforgettable breakfasts in a sunny breakfast nook

adorned with lace doilies and fresh flowers; after work, in the three or four pubs that we frequented, my group of hard-drinking cronies from the museum made for rollicking good company; and then, to top it off, always there was Megan Williams, a skinny, spiky-haired, cheerfully depraved nineteen-year-old assistant in the archeology wing, with whom I carried on a lighthearted and mostly lust-driven affair for the last four months of my stay—and who was apparently no more put off by my physical condition than she was by my American citizenship. And while I'd never felt the pinch of real love for that likable near-teenager, with her boyish figure, bad teeth, and enchanting Welsh singsong of a brogue, I did come to know, for the first time in my life, a new kind of sexual confidence, a sure sense in my bones of my own natural manliness. The lone experience I could measure it against—my short unhappy stint with poor fat Brenda back in graduate school—really bore no comparison at all. This was an affair without angst, and so a revelation to me, all as novel, fresh and exhilarating as Wales itself. I was twenty-seven, but may as well have been sixteen, intoxicated as I was by the newfound wonder of my perfectly ordinary sexuality. There were times, in fact, returning from Megan's "digs" on the south side of town, when I would have been swaggering down the sidewalks like a sailor on my crutches—had that been physically possible. I'd prospered during my time in Wales, all right. But from all indications, things for Redso and Billy had only continued to deteriorate behind me.

The aisles were still clogged with jostling passengers. I gave a careful stretch to my legs—with their three-part headaches pounding in my ankles, knees and hips—sank back against my seat with a groan, and knit my hands over the mound of my substantial new potbelly. It was the price, and probably worth it, of my year-and-a-half-long binge on fried English breakfasts, vinegar-soaked chips, Cornish pasties, those heavenly little Welsh pig-liver balls called faggots, and God only knew how many pints of lukewarm, slightly bitter, easily swallowed English beer. I was dressed as I'd taken to normally dressing in Wales (although to American eyes, I supposed, it might look like a hokey attempt at going native) with a jacket of Scottish tweed over a sweater of lush Irish wool, and a Welsh working-man's pea-cap set jauntily on my head. I'd also grown a beard, trimmed close to the jawline, Robin Hood style, which added some strength to the cortisone puffiness of my face—and gave me the look, I liked to think, of a man who'd actually been somewhere, accomplished something, lived. All of which, in fact, I had. For months now I'd been wondering how Billy would take to my new burly Celtic look . . . as if that could possibly make any practical difference in our relations.

To kill time, and also, maybe, to gird myself for what was coming, I took from my pocket the last of Billy's letters, which Mrs. Thomas had delivered to me (along with her soon-to-be-sorely-missed breakfast of fried eggs, fried bread, thick bacon, and broiled tomatoes) on my final morning in Cardiff. While Billy could be a dazzling correspondent when she was in the mood, lately her letters had turned increasingly brief and opaque—as if the thickening chaos of her life were crowding out the language on the page. This last was hardly longer than a postcard.

Dear Arnie:

You can't *know* how glad I am that you're finally coming home! I've actually been able to breathe a little easier since going to the mailbox this morning and finding your letter there. Your parents, as you probably already know, weren't able to change their bookings on the cruise ship without losing hundreds of dollars—and so they won't be home from the Caribbean in time to meet your plane. But I'll be there, I promise.

I was glad to hear how all of England went ga-ga over your finished collection—and also got a kick out of the newspaper clippings you sent along. But of course I wasn't surprised. You must know how I think you can absolutely do no wrong.

I'm sorry to report that Redso's back in the hospital again. This last episode was just a nightmare, Arnie, probably his worst yet. I won't go into all the grisly details right now—I'll just tell you that he's still in one piece, and leave it at that. You'll get the whole story soon enough. As for me, I suppose I'm holding up all right. My main problem is that I'm just so horribly *exhausted* all the time.

But I'll be doing one hell of a lot better, I know, once
you're home. God, I miss you!
    Much love,
    BILLY

I returned the letter to my pocket, and withstood another
wave of tingling dread. Billy was usually as uncomplaining as a
Hemingway hero; if she'd admitted to exhaustion, exhaustion
was probably the least of her worries.

As for Redso, it was useless to try and imagine what sort of
lunatic hijinks might have landed him back in the hospital
again. As wildly out of control as he was, he had yet to make
the dramatic mistake of repeating himself.

Since that afternoon when he made his crazy leap from the
tree in my backyard, Redso had been falling apart spectacu-
larly, with a kind of pitiful grandeur, like a burning city. His
first manic episode had climaxed on the night of the winter
solstice, when Redso took it into his head to build a bonfire
between the titanic legs of the Arch on the riverfront, strip
down to his jockstrap, and smear his body with blue grease-
paint; he was cavorting around the blaze like a drunken
Apache when a squad car happened to drive by. That resulted
in his first incarceration. In March, roaring along on another
manic tear, Redso had come across an American Express card
on the floor of a National Supermarket, and took off on such
an epic spending spree (a full-length leather coat for Billy, a
Yamaha motorcycle for himself, among a cornucopia of other
senseless purchases) that it had taken the police a mere five
days to track him down and escort him to the loony bin again.
I was already hiding out in Wales when he fucked up for the
third time, and this time, according to Billy, in truly grand
fashion. Redso had sent off a threatening letter to President
Reagan (Billy wasn't sure exactly what he'd threatened to do,
as she never got to see the actual letter), and for once the
federal government proved breathtakingly efficient. Two
agents from the FBI showed up at the door, and in Billy's
dumbfounded presence handcuffed a still happily chattering
Redso (he wanted to know, among other things, their opinion
of J. Edgar Hoover, and especially whether or not they had
him figured for a closet homosexual) and roughly dragged

him away. That last stint on the mental ward had been his longest, stretching through most of the summer. Now it was October, and Redso, back in the nuthouse again, had apparently wasted no time in zooming to another manic zenith.

The only pattern I could discern in any of this was that Redso's shenanigans seemed to be getting meaner—from a harmless hula around a bonfire, to grand larceny, to a presidential assassination threat. So if this latest episode had indeed been Redso's worst, was it possible that he'd actually gone and hurt someone this time? No, I thought, squirming in my seat —that was inconceivable. For all of the variety and flamboyance of Redso's antics, violence had never been his style. I couldn't imagine that he had it in him. But then again, could I have imagined *any* of these grotesque melodramatics just two short years ago?

A flight attendant at the far end of the cabin shot me a questioning look. She was right: the cabin was empty, I had to get going. If I stuck around any longer, I'd be flying on to Salt Lake City. Not that I really would have minded.

APPREHENSION, jet lag, and twelve hours of mostly sitting had all done their job on me. By the time I reached the gate area, my agonized hips were almost completely locked up, my knees were on fire, my heart was hammering, and the shirt beneath my sweater was sticking to my back.

The gate area was nearly empty, and I spotted Billy immediately. She was slumped in a blue vinyl chair, in her favorite scruffy gray corduroy jacket, her legs stretched out in front of her, scowling into a paperback. To my shock, she was smoking a cigarette. She held it down at her side, where it streamed upward; when she brought it to her frowning wine-colored lips, she glanced up from her book and saw me. Quickly, she crushed the butt out in the ashtray beside her, then pushed to her feet and produced a wavery smile. Her hair looked grayer than before—with more salt than pepper in the mix now—and she'd lost weight. Her cheekbones were as sharply cut as a fashion model's; through her rather loose jeans her hipbones were apparent; the sweet womanly bulge of her midriff was gone. Her sleepy black eyes were even bigger, more luminous than before. Beyond just slim, she looked frail, whittled down, as if she were recovering from some long and taxing illness. And yet despite all that, or maybe because of it, Billy was more stunning than ever.

She strode over, swinging her shoulders in her old familiar, forceful way, kissed me quickly on the mouth (I tasted smoke), then carefully looped her arms around me (low at the waist to avoid my small backpack) and squeezed, her loose spill of hair obscuring my vision, tickling my neck, flooding my brain with its maddening spice. She stepped back, swinging her hair behind her shoulders as she inspected me. "My God, Arnie—will you look at you? That beard, and that hat. And *this*." She patted my distended belly and laughed. "I think it suits you. It makes you look so substantial, distinguished. Like an Oxford professor."

"Just look at *you*," I said. "Look at how skinny you are."

I'd meant it as a compliment. But I could see, from the way Billy's smile faltered, that she'd heard something else—dismay at how unhealthy she appeared.

She slipped her book into the long shag purse hanging from her shoulder, and shrugged. "I guess I haven't been too interested in food lately."

"You? Not interested in food?"

"Also, smoking's helped. I guess you noticed?"

"When the hell did you start smoking?"

"Oh, I used to smoke, for years. And it was so easy, starting up again. You know, with Redso constantly puffing away—and without you around to make me feel guilty. I don't know, Arnie. Maybe I just needed an extra crutch."

I passed on the impulse to pull a wisecrack out of that.

"Anyway, I needed to lose the weight."

"No, you didn't. But Jesus, Billy. You're even more beautiful than I remember."

She seemed surprised by that—which made me wonder. Had I contradicted my old style with her? Would I have had the self-assurance, before I left for Wales, to so smoothly deliver the same compliment? The thing was, I couldn't remember. That old self seemed lost to me now.

I readjusted my weight over my crutches. The pain was threatening to overwhelm me again.

"How are you feeling, Arnie?"

"All right, basically. How about you?"

"Oh, not too bad, I guess."

"You know, in Wales, not too bad means pretty good. Is that what you mean?"

Billy showed me a small smile. "I'll be doing a whole lot better," she said, "now that you're home."

We started on the trek to the baggage carousels. But not ten yards from the gate, I suffered a crackling explosion of pain in both hips. I roared and halted, sagging over my crutches.

"Shit!" Billy said. "*Shit,* that sounded horrible! Are you—? Is it really that bad, Arnie?"

I glared at the striped industrial carpet between my crutches, unable to answer.

"Do you think you can make it to the baggage area?"

"I . . . don't know."

"Maybe I can get you a wheelchair."

"No," I said, through my teeth. "No wheelchair."

"But you're in agony. I know they've got wheelchairs available—"

"No wheelchair, all right?"

Billy crossed her arms and glanced worriedly around. "Look. There's a cocktail lounge right over here. Why don't we sit down, have a drink, and take it easy for a while? You must be completely stressed out. How long was your flight, anyway?"

"Twelve hours."

"God, no wonder you're hurting. Do you have any prednisone on you?"

"In my backpack."

"Well, let's get ourselves a table, get that thing off of you, and you can take an extra pill, all right?"

"Fine."

"And meanwhile, I'm buying you a big stiff drink. *Verstehen?*"

I looked at her curiously. It was very odd, after such a long time away from the two of them, to hear one of Redso's pet phrases slip so naturally out of Billy's mouth. It forced me to recognize, all over again, the depth of their alliance, and I felt a sharp inward stab that had nothing to do with arthritis.

"Come on," Billy said, and gave my elbow a gentle nudge.

I poked laboriously alongside her into the bar.

As we got settled (Billy dug my pills out of my backpack; I popped two extra), and the waitress took our orders, we managed to keep warily circling around the subject of Redso. Her money situation was good, Billy told me; they'd renewed her lucrative contract at Southwestern Bell, and she'd also been landing plenty of radio work. She was doing so well, in fact, that she wanted to renegotiate a more realistic rent. I told her we'd discuss that subject later—although, of course, I had no intention of asking for more money. Billy went on to assure me that all of my shipments of rocks had arrived safely; but it was lucky I'd come home when I did, for there were now so many crates stacked up in the dining room that it was virtually impassable. She'd done some improvements around the house while I was gone, she said, but she refused to tell me what. That was meant to be a surprise.

"Sort of a homecoming present," Billy told me as our drinks arrived.

My legs had simmered down somewhat; still, I downed my first big gulp of scotch like it was medicine.

"So tell me about Redso," I said.

Billy carefully balanced her cigarette on the lip of the ashtray. "Do you . . . think you might want to go see him?"

"What? You mean tonight?"

"The thing is, I wasn't able to see him yesterday or today. And I thought we could maybe stop by for a quick visit after this. That is, if you think you're up to it." She paused, glanced away, and bit down on her pouty lower lip. I'd forgotten all about that girlish idiosyncrasy of Billy's. She may as well have pressed her teeth into my heart. *"Are* you up to it, Arnie?"

I was stroking the tops of my thighs now. "Jesus, Billy, I don't know. I mean, this wasn't exactly on my agenda. Which hospital is he at, anyway?"

"Bliss."

Malcolm Bliss (for an institution dedicated to mental anguish, the name couldn't have been more wickedly ironic) was one of two state mental hospitals in the city, and by far the worse—where the city's indigents, howling incorrigibles, and court-referred cases were routinely dumped, for a certain period, before being transferred to the longer-term facility on

Arsenal Street. Redso was already a seasoned veteran of both institutions.

"What kind of shape is he in?" I asked her.

"That's the other thing." Her cheeks hollowed as she pulled on her cigarette. "He's just coming out of ECT."

ECT, as I knew all too well by now, stood for electroconvulsive therapy. Shock treatment.

"Oh, Jesus." I left off massaging my thighs and picked up my drink. "But wait a minute. How long has he been in there?"

"Three weeks."

"But don't they usually use that right at first if they're going to use it at all?"

"Well, sure. But about a week ago, he escaped. And when they picked him up again, they started right in with the shock treatments."

"Redso *escaped*?"

Billy nodded.

"But how the hell did he do it? The whole damned place is a prison."

"Evidently he insinuated himself into a group of visitors. You know, got them to think he was a visitor himself. And then he just rode on down the elevator with them, and waltzed right off of the property. Redso can still be quite an actor, you know, when he puts his mind to it."

"Oh, that's just beautiful! Now he's the fucking Count of Monte Cristo."

"Right. So anyway, the cops found him raising hell in some bar down in Soulard, and they had him back on the ward within hours." Her smile sourly faded. "And then they *really* socked it to him, Arnie. They gave him ECTs for four straight days—which is *much* more than usual. And I just *know* those shits did it partly to punish him."

"Come on, Billy. We're talking about psychiatrists here."

She gave me a sharp look. "When did *you* get so naive about medical people, Arnie? I'd think you'd be the last person to tell me they could do no wrong."

I didn't want to fight her on that. Besides, for all I knew, she was right.

"Anyway, that's why I didn't see him yesterday. He was just

starting to come out of it. Yesterday Redso wouldn't have known who *he* was, much less who was visiting him."

Another thing I'd learned, no thanks to Redso, was that shock treatment was intended to erase—just temporarily, supposedly—the short-term memory, along with whatever recent trauma it contained. But in practice it was a lot more scattershot than that. It was impossible to predict just what portions of the memory would ultimately return—or when, if ever.

I asked Billy what he'd done to land himself at Bliss in the first place.

"He tried to burn down his mother's house," she said.

"Oh Christ."

"I know. Frieda wasn't home at the time, thank God. Which makes you wonder. She was off visiting her sister in San Diego, and of course, Redso knew it. So he was crazy enough to stick all these gasoline-soaked rags around the foundation of the house, and torch it. But evidently he *wasn't* crazy enough to try to kill her. So go figure."

"But what the hell was he trying to prove?"

"God, he gave me sixteen different stories. He was trying to exorcise the house. He wanted to obliterate his childhood. He even claimed it was an *accident* at one point. Anyway, he really didn't do much damage. The whole time he was setting the fire, a neighbor across the street was sitting out on his front porch drinking beer, you know, and listening to the ballgame, and of course he went inside and called the cops. So the fire didn't get very far. And neither did Redso." Billy finished off her drink, and worked her mouth around as she frowned into the glass. She raised her enormous liquid eyes to me. "How are you doing there, anyway?"

"Better."

"You want another drink?"

I nodded. Billy signaled for the waitress. I asked her if she'd spoken to Redso's mother.

"Oh yes. I went and had coffee with her once she got back into town. I swear to God, Arnie—sometimes I think she's even crazier than he is. Do you know what she told me? That his problem is nothing but *insomnia*. That all Redso had to do was *sleep* more regularly, and he'd be perfectly all right. I tried to get her to understand what manic-depression is all about.

But all through my lecture, Frieda just kept showing me this tolerant little smile—like *I* was the one who was crazy—and offering me more coffee and strudel. Can you believe it? God, no wonder he's out of his mind!"

ON THE LOCKED OUTER DOOR of the ward was posted a hand-lettered sign:

TO PREVENT ELOPEMENT, PLEASE CLOSE ALL DOORS BEHIND YOU.

Despite my loathing of euphemisms in general, and in particular those designed to sugarcoat sickness and suffering, this was one piece of doublespeak I'd always found endearing. To elope was to escape from a mental facility. How such a lively term had ever snuck into the dour lexicon of psychiatry—whether it was meant as a kind of wry in-joke, or was used to cloak the news of an escape from highly suggestible inmates—none of the doctors or nurses I'd questioned about it had been able to tell me. Whatever its origin, I couldn't help liking the humor, the color of it. To elope. It made me picture the poor desperate devils as they tried to escape in a whimsical light, like something from a Frank Capra movie—skipping two by two across the lawn of Malcolm Bliss, holding hands, on their rapturous way to the nearest chapel.

Billy clamped beneath one arm the paper sack full of goodies she always brought along for Redso (cigarettes, Snickers bars, sunflower seeds) and pressed the buzzer. "Something funny going on?"

"That word. Elopement. I'd forgotten all about it. Sounds like a hell of a fun thing to do, doesn't it?"

"Yeah, well. Don't forget, Arnie. Everything manics do is for fun."

The lock rattled, the heavy door swung in, and standing before us was a young and very pretty East Indian–looking woman, with a helmet of glossy black hair cut straight across her forehead, and skin the color of lightly creamed coffee. There was a name tag on her starched white blouse that read DR. SHARMA. She showed Billy a tight smile, which struck me as rather sardonic. "Well, hello, Billy. We missed you yesterday."

Billy's smile was just as tight as the doctor's.

"Dr. Sharma, this is Arnie Goldman. An old friend of mine and Redso's."

She eyed my crutches like a medical professional—without a flicker of surprise. "It's nice to meet you," she said.

"Same here."

"I don't believe we've seen you here before, Arnie, or have we?"

"Actually, I haven't been to visit for quite a while."

"Well, Billy's just about our most regular customer here." The doctor chirped a laugh. "Sometimes I think she's on the ward more than *I* am."

Billy crushed, with a crinkle, her paper sack to her chest. "How is he, Dr. Sharma?"

"Oh, he still has some amnesia, and a bit of a headache. But otherwise he's coming along just fine."

"What kind of medication is he on?"

"Lithium, of course. And an antipsychotic."

The doctor turned and led us down a short windowless hallway to the next closed door.

"What kind of antipsychotic, Dr. Sharma?"

She sorted through a jumble of keys on a big bronze ring. "Haldol," the doctor said, and inserted a key in the lock.

"What dosage?"

"I'd have to look at the chart to tell you that, Billy."

"Well, would you mind doing that for me?"

The doctor hesitated. "Why, sure," she said, and shouldered open the ponderous door. "If you'll just follow me to the nurses' station . . ."

"Yo, Billy!" A grinning hill of a black man in an orderly's outfit was strolling by, a thicket of keys jangling on his belt.

"How're you doing there, Earl?"

"Oh, you know. Goin' crazy with the crazies, like always."

"Gee," Billy said. "Me too."

Earl boomed a laugh, wagged a finger at Billy, and strolled on.

As she followed Dr. Sharma to the glassed-in nurses' station, I paused on my crutches to take in the cavernous day room. It was the same as I remembered. The room was a dull institutional green, made all the more oppressive by the sallow neon light from overhead. Compared to the wards on Arsenal

Street, this was a strictly no-frills operation: no Ping-Pong, pool, or fooseball tables, no magazine racks, no potted plants, no couches. A television was perched on a platform high up on the wall, at the same unreachable height as the row of steel-meshed windows, and below, a dozen or so patients, the majority of them black, were scattered among a broken semicircle of hard-looking plastic chairs. Some sat, a few moved listlessly about, and one of them, the inevitable catatonic of the group, a shriveled old pecan-brown woman with hair like an electrified bird's nest, was rhythmically jerking her head and punching her thighs as she furiously paced the outer edges of the day room. Toward the center of the room were two card tables —and at one of them, his hair standing out against the undersea green of the walls like a blob of bright orange paint, sat Redso, utterly still, his back ramrod straight, facing the television. While the inmates around him wore street clothes, Redso was dressed in a pair of faded blue hospital-issue pajamas. It took me a second to remember why: it was standard procedure at Bliss to confiscate the clothes of any patients who tried to elope, and force them to wear instead those POW-like pajamas—partly as a warning to the other patients, but also to make it well-nigh impossible to attempt another escape without being easily spotted. It unnerved me to see Redso sitting so still—in my mind's eye he was forever in frantic motion, zipping and zigzagging around like the Road Runner from the old cartoons. But on closer inspection I saw that he wasn't entirely motionless. Under the table, to the side of his chair, his right knee was madly jackhammering.

I pumped the grips of my crutches, turned away, and clanked into the nurses' station, where Billy stood facing Dr. Sharma. All around the glass walls, above the cluttered desks and gray filing cabinets, hung raggedy old Halloween decorations—black cats, witches on broomsticks, grinning jack-o'-lanterns—which, in their misplaced nursery school cheerfulness, were only woefully depressing. As I joined them, Dr. Sharma picked up from a desk a thick spiral-bound chart, and began flipping through it.

"Here we are," she said. "Haldol. Five milligrams, every hour."

"For how many hours?"

Dr. Sharma leveled a look at Billy, then consulted her chart again. "Not to exceed fifty milligrams every twelve hours."

"Great," Billy said, crossing her arms. "That's *exactly* what you had him on last time around, Dr. Sharma—when he was jumping right out of his skin."

"It's under *control*," the doctor snapped, then shut her chart. Her starched blouse rose and fell. "You know, I don't understand you, Billy. I don't understand why you seem to view the staff here as your enemy."

Billy said nothing. But it wasn't because she was cowed. In fact, she looked indomitable.

"The patient will be much better off," Dr. Sharma continued, "and so will you, I believe—if you'd just let the professionals on this ward do their jobs. Now, we're observing the recommended ceilings—"

"The recommended ceilings are too *much* for him, Doctor! And you already *know* that—or you should. Every single time you've given him Haldol, he's shown signs of akathisia—"

"Well, he's not showing them now."

"Oh yeah? Have you checked? Just take a look through that window. His leg is going up and down like crazy."

"Excuse me," I said, almost afraid to stick my nose in between the two women. "But what's akathisia?"

"It's a side-effect of Haldol," Billy told me. "This terrible restlessness. You can't sit still. You can't control your hands or feet. It's pure torture."

"As I've already explained to you, Billy—we haven't noticed any signs of akathisia."

"What do you call *that?*" Billy said, pointing at Redso through the window.

"He's recovering from a trauma to his system. That's all."

Billy puffed an exasperated breath through her nose. "If you'd just take a look at your chart, Dr. Sharma, you'll see what happened the last time you put him on fifty milligrams of that shit."

The doctor pointedly did not take a look at her chart.

"Billy, I don't wish to be rude, but just which medical school did you attend?"

"This one," Billy told her.

Dr. Sharma's cool smile returned. "Well, I suggest you go

have a look at Redso and make your own diagnosis. It's clear you're not going to believe anything I tell you."

"I will," Billy said, then turned and stalked out of the nurses' station.

I caught up with her as she was getting a cigarette from her purse. She held it to the built-in lighter on the wall and pressed the button beside it; the coil within glowed orange. The gizmo was obviously intended to keep matches and lighters out of the hands of patients—but was also there, I suspected, to spare the staff from being constantly pestered for a light. Billy took a deep drag off her cigarette, blew out a swirling chestful, and squinted angrily through the smoke. "You think I was being too much of a hard-ass?"

"Christ, I don't know, Billy. You were formidable, I can tell you that. Like a lioness protecting her cub."

She seemed to fight down a smile. "Well, I *wasn't* overdoing it. You wouldn't *believe* the pointless suffering they'd put him through, Arnie—if I didn't step in and stop them."

"It sounds like you've been getting quite an education."

"I didn't have any choice. Who else is going to look out for him? Frieda?"

A patient approached us.

"Hey, National Velvet," he said. "Hey, hey, National Velvet."

He was a stringy kid in his late teens or early twenties, with a scraggly growth of yellow hair on his cheeks that was not quite a beard, and his hair in a stiff punk Mohawk. He wore a black T-shirt emblazoned, in neon orange, with a portrait of a pouting Jim Morrison. Maybe I was wrong, but I thought I detected a faint tang of urine coming from him. He scratched at both elbows as he leered at Billy.

"Hello, Carl."

"Hey, hey, National Velvet."

"This is Arnie, Carl. A friend of mine."

He frankly inspected my crutches, scratching still more avidly at his elbows.

"You a friend of Elizabeth Taylor's?" he asked me.

I laughed. "Uh, no. Unfortunately. Are you?"

"Carl seems to think I look like Elizabeth Taylor," Billy explained.

Actually, Carl wasn't so far off.

"Well, shit!" he yelled. "*Look* at her! From *National Velvet!*
That Elizabeth Taylor!" He shrugged his stringy shoulders and
looked at me. "You crippled or something, man?"

"You got it, Carl."

"Huh. With what? Polio?"

"Arthritis."

"Huh. Well, that's cool. And how about those crutches?
What are they, aluminum?"

"They're aluminum, all right."

"Well, those are bitching crutches, man. You mind if I try
'em out?"

"Sorry, Carl," I said. "I sort of depend on these things."

Carl seemed to think deeply about the implications of that,
then left off scratching his elbows and jammed the tips of his
fingers into the tight front pockets of his jeans. "You got a
quarter you can spare?"

Another patient had drifted quietly up to us—an ethereally
thin young black girl, thirteen or fourteen, in a sacklike flow-
ered dress. Her eyes looked full of milk. Without a word, she
held out her hand to Billy and uncurled her fingers. A quarter
lay in her palm. Billy took it, and as she did so, gave the girl a
squeeze around the wrist with both hands.

"How're you doing, Deborah? You doing all right today?"

She slowly nodded.

"You want me to get you a Coke?"

She nodded again and raised her milky eyes to Billy.

Carl spoke up. "Hey, don't forget me, goddammit!"

"Who's forgetting you, Carl? A root beer, right?"

"Shit, yes. A root beer."

"How much money do you owe me at this point, Carl?"

"I don't know."

"Well, you make sure and pay me back whenever your ship
comes in, all right?"

"What ship?"

"Never mind," Billy told him gently, then showed me an
apologetic smile. "Looks like I have to go on a Coke run."

The Coke machine was in the basement, but the patients
weren't allowed to take the elevator down there, not even with
an orderly along. I had yet to visit Bliss when Billy and I

weren't petitioned for soft drinks by some of the inmates. Most often they'd come flocking, like children to Santa Claus, the instant they saw Billy enter the ward.

"You want to come along, Arnie?"

Redso still sat at that card table, his right leg jiggling, but otherwise unnaturally stiff—and for some reason my dread of seeing him, which had followed me all the way across the Atlantic Ocean, was gone. I only felt painfully drawn toward him.

"I think I'll keep Redso company," I said.

I APPROACHED HIS TABLE braced for a shock, expecting a face that was ravaged, cadaverous. But when Redso shifted in his chair at the sound of my crutches, I saw to my relief that he looked pretty good, given the circumstance—a little pale, a little thin, but no thinner or paler than I remembered him. For all he'd been through, Redso was still a handsome man, his fierce hawkish features yoked into balance by his powerful beak of a nose. In his eyes, however, was an unfamiliar weakness, a vacancy. He had the look of a prizefighter who'd just struggled up from the count.

"Hey, stranger," I said.

It seemed to take some effort for Redso to smile—as if he had to think about which facial muscles to tighten. "Hey. Good to see you, man." His voice was faint and raspy.

We shook hands—or more rightly, I shook the weak hand Redso offered. "All right if I sit down?"

"Sure, sure."

I restrained a groan as I sat—my pounding hips were long overdue for a rest—and propped the clamps of my crutches against the edge of the rickety table. A half-smoked cigarette burned in a foil ashtray in front of Redso. As he reached for it and brought it to his mouth, his hand quavered like he was palsied.

"It's been a hell of a long time, Redso."

He nodded vaguely at that, then stared off just as vaguely into the day room.

"How are you feeling?"

"*Ach.* I'm fried."

I shifted my hips on the hard plastic seat. "Well, you don't look so bad to me. Except for those pajamas. Hell, Redso. You look like a prisoner in a Communist re-education camp."

"Yeah," Redso said. "I've been brainwashed, all right."

He turned slightly away, and drew his shaking hands into his lap. To the side of the table his right knee continued to bounce. Redso looked at me again, and now his slanted blue eyes appeared focused. "You grew a beard."

I touched my bristly chin. "Yeah, well. I guess I needed something to keep the chill off back in Wales."

"Wales?"

"I . . . was over there for a year and a half, Redso. I just got back tonight, in fact. You don't remember?"

He shook his head. "Why were you in Wales?"

"I went over there to take charge of a collection. You know, at a museum."

"A rock collection?"

"Right."

Redso scowled at the tip of his cigarette, then crushed it out as if it had somehow offended him. He raked a hand through his bush of frizzed hair. Then he surprised me with a laugh. "Man, you're not going to fucking believe this."

"Believe what?"

"I know you're my best friend. I *know* that. But the thing is . . ."

I waited.

Redso squinted at me. "I can't remember your name."

That knocked the wind out of me. I shuddered and glanced away. That shriveled old woman with the electrified hair was still pacing the perimeter of the day room, knocking the heel of her hand into her forehead with the mechanical persistence of a wind-up toy.

"It's Arnie," I told him.

Redso banged his fist onto the table, which bounced. The foil ashtray leapt; butts and ashes scattered; one of my crutches clattered to the floor. I decided to ignore it.

"Right!" Redso roared. *"Arnie!"* He rolled his eyes and roared again. "Goddammit! God fucking *dammit!*"

"Redso—"

"They've fried me, Arnie! They've made a fucking moron out of me! I can't *think!*"

"Redso, listen to me—"

"First they fucked with my brain, and next they're going to cut off my fucking balls—"

"Redso, will you listen to me? You've had shock treatments. All right? Shock treatments. You understand?"

He glared at the ashy mess on the table, but didn't answer.

"You're suffering from amnesia right now. But it's only temporary. You're going to get your memory back. It might take some time, but you'll get it all back. Now, are you with me?"

"I . . . don't know."

I sank back in my chair. "Well, just take my word for it, Redso."

He was bent forward now, hugging his belly, his face averted—and it came to me, with a sickening plunge of the heart, that over and above his anger, his dullness, and his confusion, Redso was humiliated. He didn't want me to see him in this condition. He wanted me gone.

Then, thank God, Billy was approaching the table with her take-charge, shoulder-swinging walk, carrying a can of Coke in one hand, her paper sack in the other. She looped her arms around Redso's neck, kissed him on the mouth, and dropped into a crouch, so that her bright smile was level with his face.

"Hey, there. How's my lover?"

Redso gripped her upper arm and ducked his face against it, like a child. I had to look away.

"I just . . . love you so fucking much, Billy . . ."

"Well, good," Billy said, her voice thick. "I'm glad to hear that, baby. That means we're even."

When I turned back, Billy was stooped over the table, sweeping the spilled butts into the ashtray with the side of her hand. "Here," she said, moving the Coke can closer to Redso. "I brought you a soda. And all these goodies, too. Cigarettes, Snickers bars, sunflower seeds. The works."

"Great," Redso said, in a watery imitation of enthusiasm. But he neither touched his Coke nor looked inside the sack.

Billy took Redso's hand in both of hers as she sat.

"So? You happy to see Arnie again?"

He considered me, turned back to Billy, and shrugged. "He was in Wales. But I forgot."

"Redso," I said, "it's no big deal."

Billy gave me an inquisitive look. I raised my eyebrows—
what could I say?—and she returned her attention to Redso.
"Your leg's going up and down like gangbusters, Redso. You
feel like you've got akathisia?"

"I don't know. Maybe." He shook his head. "I'm just pissed
off."

"What about?"

"The KGB psychiatrists."

"What about the KGB psychiatrists?"

"They're turning me into a fucking basket case."

"No they're not, Redso. You're just having some problems
with your memory."

"It's fucked."

"I know it's fucked, baby. It's bound to be fucked. You've
just been through a hell of a lot of shock treatments. In fact,
why don't we try some things out, and see how your memory's
doing?"

Redso scratched listlessly at the open neck of his pajamas.
"Whatever," he said.

"Can you tell me what day of the week it is?"

"No."

"Oh, come on, Redso. Just say whatever pops into your
head."

"Wednesday."

"Close, but no cigar. It's Thursday."

Redso looked at her. "So what?"

I laughed. "Maybe he's got something there."

Redso showed me a dim smile.

"What year is it, Redso?"

"1984."

"No, baby. It's 1982."

"It's 1984," Redso said, and jerked his chin in the direction
of the nurses' station. "And Big Brother is watching."

Billy laughed. "Good! You see? You're making connections,
Redso. You're not half the basket case you think you are." She
tightened her double grip on Redso's hand. "Now, how old
are you, Redso?"

He pondered that. "Sixteen?"

She snorted. "Come on, Redso. What would a sixteen-year-
old be doing with a tired old lady like me?"

"Fucking her eyes out, I hope."

"You're twenty-eight, you devil. Does that sound a little more like it?"

"I . . . don't know."

Billy ran the pink tip of her tongue around her lips, and leaned closer. "Can you tell me why you're here, Redso? Do you know what you did?"

He scowled past her for a long while. "Did I . . . write a letter to Reagan?"

"No, baby. That was a long time ago. What you did was, you tried to burn down your mother's house."

He yanked his hand away.

"You took some rags, and you soaked them in gasoline, and put them around the foundation of the house, and set fire to them. It was about three weeks ago."

I wondered why Billy was rehashing this in such detail. Was it some method she'd hit on to jog his memory?

Redso stared at her. "Why would I do that?"

"Your guess is as good as mine, Redso. You were having one hell of a manic episode. And also, you'd taken LSD—"

"He did what?" I said, leaning forward.

"I forgot to tell you about that part of it, Arnie. They found a couple of tabs of acid in his wallet. And you should have seen his eyes when I got down to the police station—nothing but pupil."

Well, I thought, sitting back from the table, that certainly conformed to the pattern. The trouble was that, unlike a depressive or a schizophrenic—who is only terrorized by his symptoms—Redso couldn't have been fonder of his own mental illness. Billy had it right: being a manic, Redso lived for fun. And what, to a manic, was more fun than being manic? He was like a hot-dogging surfer, forever in search of the highest, most dangerous wave. Not only did Redso encourage his manic attacks by refusing to take his lithium, but once the ecstasy was upon him, he'd use whatever he could get ahold of —liquor, pills, marijuana, cocaine—to boost himself into still higher heavens of euphoria. But LSD? I wasn't even aware that the stuff was still available.

"Redso, where the hell did you get LSD?"

He slowly smiled. "Wish I knew," he said.

Something snapped in me then. "You son of a bitch! You *idiot!* Isn't plain old mania *good* enough for you anymore? You've got to juice it up with LSD? I mean, Jesus, Redso! Do you *like* ending up on this ward?"

Billy gave me a fierce warning look.

"Well, I'm sorry, Billy. But it's not like he's totally out of control. He brings half this shit on himself."

Redso bounced his colorless eyebrows at me.

Billy took his hand again. "Anyway," she said, throwing me another warning glance, "your mother's fine, Redso. And so's the house. It turns out you didn't really do much damage."

"Is she . . . angry?"

"No. Not at all. You know your mother."

"Yeah. We're both space cases."

"You're not a space case, Redso. You're just suffering from temporary amnesia. Okay?"

He didn't answer.

I thought I'd try something out. Redso's short-term memory was obviously lost in the fog. But he *had* remembered his letter to President Reagan—and so his long-term memory must have been at least partially intact. But how intact?

"Redso," I said. "Do you remember *Dutchtown?*"

"It's where I grew up."

"I mean the play."

Redso blinked into space. "I wrote it," he said. "Didn't I?"

"You sure did."

"And it was good. Wasn't it?"

"It was damned good, Redso."

He pushed both hands into his bushy orange hair, thunked his elbows on the table, and bowed his head. Then he looked at Billy. "What happened to it?"

"It won a prize," Billy told him. "The playwriting prize at the festival in Louisville. You won two thousand dollars, Redso. Not only that, but the play was staged, and it got absolutely wonderful reviews. It's even been published in an anthology."

Redso's eyes were ablaze now. "It got staged?"

"Yes."

"Did you see it?"

"No, baby. I wanted to—desperately. But that was last fall,

and Arnie was in Wales, and you were in the hospital. And I just . . . didn't think I could leave you at the time."

Redso's breath pumped ferociously through his nostrils.

"I've got the reviews at home, Redso. Every single one of them. And also the anthology. We'll bring them when we visit tomorrow, okay?"

"Have I written anything else?"

Billy was getting a cigarette lit. "Yes," she said, expelling a long stream of smoke. "You've written more plays."

"Are they any good?"

She forced up the corners of her mouth. "Of course they're good, Redso. How could they be anything else, as terrifically talented as you are?"

I averted my face, hoping Redso hadn't caught my shock—for what Billy had just told him was the baldest of lies. I had no idea how else she *could* have answered him. Still, it struck me as not only patronizing, but unwise. What if Redso remembered her saying it? And what if he someday returned, even briefly, to lucidity, and took a look at all the hopelessly senseless drivel he'd churned out in my basement since *Dutchtown*—ream upon heartbreaking ream of it? What then? Would he forgive Billy her clumsy white lie? Or would he hate her for it —and maybe rightfully so?

This was the one point where Redso's downfall, for all of its clownishness, wild slapstick, and low comedy, touched tragedy. There had once been a time when I'd tentatively placed him in that pantheon of genius-madmen—Swift, de Sade, Nietzsche, and so on—whose insanity had seemed to stoke the fires of their art. And certainly Redso himself used to claim, when he was flying high, that deprived of the divine rocket fuel of his mania, his inspiration would sputter out, his muse desert him. Well, he'd been paying the devil's price for more than two years now, and his inspiration had deserted him anyway. *Dutchtown* was apparently an anomaly, a one-shot deal. And the more desperately Redso sought to reach that apogee again, the further away he kept plummeting.

He gripped the edge of the table with both hands—the knuckles bulged yellow—and peered at Billy. "You won't forget it tomorrow, will you? The play? And the reviews?"

I saw her swallow.

"No, baby," she told him. "You know I won't forget."

NOT TWO STEPS out the door of Malcolm Bliss, the pain in my hips exploded lavishly, like two skyrockets bursting in the joints, and I bent over my crutches, teeth clenched, eyes stinging, and silently endured the pounding aftermath.

Billy misinterpreted. "You poor thing," she said. "You still really love him, don't you?"

I grunted in lieu of an answer.

For the truth was, I couldn't say if I still loved Redso. If love was nothing more than an old, deep, irresistible bond, maybe I did. But if it required affection, admiration, a desire to actually *be* with that person . . . Well. Would I have felt anything beyond guilty relief if I never had to set eyes on Redso again?

Billy stuffed her hands into the pockets of her corduroy jacket. "I shouldn't have dragged you here tonight."

"No. It's . . . it doesn't matter."

"Well, let's just get you home."

Once in the car, I felt better—the prednisone had begun to kick in—and as we headed down to Maplewood, I peppered Billy with questions about her life. It turned out that, beyond her work, and beyond caring for Redso, she wasn't living much of one. While she still kept in touch with several old girlfriends from high school, she did so mostly from a sense of obligation. The two friends she saw most often, Myrna Jackoway and Eileen Solomon, had recently been riding her very hard about her relationship with Redso.

"They're both divorced, you know. And so apparently they've earned the right to condemn any man who isn't absolutely perfect to everlasting Feminist Hell. It's become so *fashionable* lately to paint men as the enemy. And it's so easy, so self-serving. So *uninteresting*." Billy shook her head as she swerved for the exit ramp off Highway 44. "Anyway, they're convinced that I'm wasting myself—destroying myself—by staying in this thing with Redso."

I carefully withheld any comment on that.

"I'm not saying that I can't take criticism, Arnie. But I would like just a little bit of sympathy once in a while, you know? Just a little bit of support—even if they disagree with what I'm doing. But all I get is this self-satisfied *sniping*." Billy sighed. "It's just gotten to the point where it's not worth it anymore. It's been over a month since I've seen either one of them."

I had to be very cautious, it seemed to me, with how I conducted my next line of questioning.

"Well, what do you tell them?" I said. "I mean, when Eileen and Myrna start dumping on you? What's your argument?"

"Mostly I just answer them with questions. You know, Jewish style. Like, what would *they* do if they were in my place? If they were in love with a man as sick as Redso? Set some kind of *time* limit on his recovery? Tell him to shape up or ship out? And if he didn't shape up fast enough, or exactly to their liking, then what? I mean, what can I *do*, Arnie? It's . . ." Billy paused and squinted at the road. When she spoke again, the velvet of her voice was especially rich with conviction. "All I know is, I love him. And I want him back—the way he was. And that means I have to *stay* with it, doesn't it? Am I supposed to give up just because it's hard?"

I shifted my aching hips, and didn't answer. The fact was, I had no experience to measure Billy's words by. No lover of mine had ever asked anything significant of me. And that was probably as good a proof as any that I knew nothing of real love. As if I needed any extra proof.

I cleared my gritty throat, and asked Billy about life beyond Eileen and Myrna.

"Oh, I've gone to some parties here and there, through people I've met in the business. But men just won't leave me *alone*, Arnie. Especially if they get wind of the fact that my boyfriend's constantly being institutionalized. *Then* it's open season, right? As if I'm just standing around and *waiting* for some arrogant shithead to show up on a white horse and rescue me! Anyway. I've been pretty much of a hermit lately, if you want to know the truth. Not that it's been any big loss to anybody. I know I'm lousy company these days."

"Not to me you aren't," I said.

"Well, thanks."

"Anyway, I'm sorry to hear all that, Billy."

She reached for her cigarettes on the dashboard.

"What about your work?"

"What about it?"

"Have you been doing anything at all besides commercial stuff?"

She punched in the lighter. "Actually, I did go to this one audition, a couple of weeks ago. At the Actor's Circle Company. It was for the part of Mary in *Long Day's Journey into Night*. It's the best American play ever written, if you ask me. So I figured I'd finally get off my big fat ass and give it a shot. But Arnie, when I got down there and saw the rehearsal schedule . . . well, I just turned right around and walked out."

"Why?"

"Because it would have been six days a week. And there was no *way* I could have done my recording sessions, and my auditions, and visited Redso, and made it to the rehearsals all at once." She glanced at me apprehensively. "I mean, what choice did I have?"

I was silent for a spell, considering the offer I wanted to make.

"Look, Billy, why don't you let me take care of the rent for a while? Then you can drop this commercial garbage—and do what you have to do to stay sane. You're miserable this way. And believe me, the extra hundred bucks a month isn't going to make *me* any happier."

"God, Arnie. That's so sweet of you. I'm almost tempted to say yes."

"Yeah? So just say it."

"I can't. I can't let you support me."

"I'd be helping you out, Billy—just like I am now."

"No, Arnie. All right? I'm already much too indebted to you as it is."

"Well," I said, "I just don't see it that way."

But of course, I did. The more indebted Billy was to me, the better.

We were in Maplewood now, and turning down gloomy, ramshackle Oxford Street.

I was surprised by how large my house looked. To American eyes, certainly, this shabby little bungalow was no big deal. But by Welsh standards it was practically Brobdingnagian. Also, it appeared cleaner, brighter on the outside than I remembered —although that might have been a trick of the moonlight.

"Will you get a load of this place?" I said. "It doesn't look half as crapped-out as it used to."

Billy slowed to a stop on the driveway. "Yeah, great paint job, huh?"

"*You* did that?"

She grinned.

"Well, that's just . . . Jesus. Thanks, Billy." I knew my response was inadequate—but how did you thank somebody for such a favor? "It certainly wasn't necessary, though."

"Hey, I have to live here, too."

Of course, I'd *meant* for the house to look like an impoverished dump—the sort no professional burglar would ever be tempted to burgle. But it would have been gross ingratitude to mention that to Billy now.

Once we were parked in back, and I was up on my crutches, I was in for another pleasant shock. She'd completely rebuilt the once sagging, once rotting back porch. It was now a clean straight sturdy-looking structure, with a triple set of rails all around. I could smell the wood.

"Billy? This is just too much! You built this thing yourself?"

She was opening the trunk now. "Well, sure. With as much help as I could get out of Redso."

"Well, it's just—fantastic."

"Thanks. I thought I did a pretty good job myself."

"What did it cost you?"

"Never mind what it cost me. It's my coming-home present to you."

Promising myself that I'd make sure, somehow, to reimburse her for the outlay, I clumped onto the porch and marveled at it. Flat-footed and grunting, Billy trudged past me with the first of my rock-filled backpacks. When she came laboring up the steps with the next one, I complained that I hated to see her doing this all by herself.

"Don't be ridiculous," she said.

Once Billy had hauled in, like a pack horse, the last of my baggage, I remained on the fresh-smelling porch, staring into the pearly backyard—and was pierced by a sudden sweet hunger. My rocks! Of course! Amid all the miserable distractions that had accosted me between here and the airport, I'd forgotten about them completely. But they were here, all right, just exactly where I'd left them—my shining beauties, my glittering darlings, more colorful than any flower garden in their splendid shimmering rows. I longed to heft them in my hands, run the tips of my fingers down their hard glassy facets, bring them to my nose and sniff their near-imperceptible scent, subtly reminiscent of water and earth. Where my rocks were concerned, at least, I knew precisely what awaited me after such a long time gone. They existed in, and were emblems of, another, far more stable sphere of existence—where nothing ever changed, and there were never any nasty surprises.

Billy, giving a stretch to her back, a twist to her neck, was returning to the kitchen when I crutched in. She showed me a smile (which struck me as rather nervous, with something fishy behind it) and went to the counter, where she cracked the label on a bottle of Glenlivet. "How about a drink?"

"In a minute. I want to check on my rocks. It just occurred to me that I've been missing them."

Billy's smile wavered. "I, um . . . stacked up all your crates along the walls. I hope they're all in good shape. The specimens, I mean. Anyway . . . they're all right in there."

"Well, good. Thanks."

"I'll, uh, have your drink ready for you, all right?"

"Fine," I said, frowning at her strangeness. Then I inwardly shrugged it off, and spider-walked into the dining room.

Even with the dozens of crates stacked two and three high along the walls, the dining room, and the living room beyond it, seemed cavernous. The ceilings could have accommodated a giant. And all along my rock shelves, too, there appeared to be a superfluity of space. The specimens looked scattered, placed too widely apart. Well, that was America, wasn't it? Wide-open spaces, plenty of elbow room. Still, something about those shelves continued to disturb me, and I poked over for a closer inspection.

Billy called out from the kitchen. "Do you want water, Arnie?"

"Just a splash."

"What? I couldn't hear you."

Then I didn't answer her at all.

I should probably explain at this juncture the part that memory—or more exactly, visual memory—plays in what I do. Along with an encyclopedic knowledge of his subject, a highly refined eye, and the haggling skills of a Bedouin, a precise and commodious memory is something no serious collector of anything—whether it's Shaker furniture, pre-Columbian art, or Elvis memorabilia—can afford to be without. In order to know precisely what you're looking at, you must be able to recall precisely what you've seen. One of the smartest things I've ever done was to spend ten days, during a winter vacation back in graduate school, in Washington, D.C., where I basically lived in the gem and mineral collection at the Smithsonian. Each morning I would leave my infinitesimal hotel room armed only with a notebook and some pens, and spend the rest of the day drifting wide-eyed through the stupendous riches of that collection, soaking it up piece by gorgeous piece, and filing away both in my notebook and in my memory the colors, shapes, and artful compositions of those specimens, the other minerals they occurred with, the inclusions and matrixes that added to their splendor, and all the chemical and geographic information provided on the accompanying labels—until, I think it's safe to say, I had a good ninety percent of that vast collection stored away with near-photographic clarity in my brain. That laid the foundation. And now, having studied so many other collections, both public and private, since then, if you were to show me, for example, a pretzel-twist of native copper, a dusky bouquet of petal-shaped wulfenite, or a bubbled hunk of dark green malachite, I could not only rattle off for you its chemical and physical properties, but could most likely tell you the country and state of its origin, the particular mine where it occurred, and whether or not that mine is still producing such material, or has been exhausted—in which case, of course, the price of that specimen could easily triple. So it's no exaggeration to say that I could summon to mind a reliable image of each and every rock in my collection, along with its exact location along my shelves or in my cabinets, with hardly any more mental effort than it takes to count to fifty.

And within seconds I knew, jet-lagged or not, that nearly every third rock on my shelves had been filched.

Ignoring the hot throbbing in my hips, the grinding stiffness in my knees, I moved up and down between the shelves,
taking my horror-struck inventory. The missing specimens,
the tourmalines, the azurites, the hematites, the jade, the perfect fist-sized trilobites, the slices of polished agate whose airy
swirls and layerings of color were as delicately rendered as any
Sung Dynasty landscape—just to scratch the surface of that
nauseating catalogue—intoned in my skull like the names of
loved ones on a casualty list. Those specimens that remained
had been clumsily rearranged (some with the wrong labels in
front of them) to mask the crime. But the spaces between them
yawned like missing teeth.

I received my sole consolation when I unlocked my redwood specimen cabinet and slid out every drawer. There,
thank God, were all of my priciest gems and finest small crystals, lying safe in their appointed cotton-lined boxes. If Redso
had attempted to pick the lock, he'd been stymied.

I dragged myself to the reclining chair, dropped my
crutches to the floor, and not caring if Billy heard me or not,
moaned operatically as I sank into it.

Of course Billy had had nothing to do with the theft. But
when she finally made her appearance in the living room, a
glass of scotch in each hand, her eyes were rounded with guilt.
She came over and handed me my drink. Then she sat on the
sofa, set her glass on the table, and crossed her arms protectively in front of her.

"Arnie?"

I didn't respond.

"I know this has to be horrible for you. I *know*. But will you
—could you try not to be too angry? He was totally out of
control when it happened. He had no *conception* of what he
was doing."

I cranked back the chair, and stared at the ceiling. For once,
I had no desire to look at Billy.

"When did it happen?"

"During this last episode. Before that thing at his mother's
house."

"Where were you?"

"At the recording studio, doing a session. Redso dropped
me off that morning, and was supposed to pick me up that

afternoon. But he never showed. He took your car and was gone for four days. And when he did come back . . . he'd already gotten rid of it all."

"Do you know what he did with it?"

"He—said he'd sold it to some rock shop. Down in the Ozarks."

"Did he tell you which one?"

"No."

"Did you *ask?*"

"Of *course* I asked!"

I heard the ice cubes shift in her glass.

"Any idea how much he made?"

"No. But he'd bought a lot of cocaine with it. And also, the LSD he took that night."

I cranked up the chair—jolting my hips—into a sitting position. Billy had her head bowed, like a penitent.

"Do you have any *idea* how much those rocks were worth?"

"No. How could I?"

"Twelve, fifteen grand. Easy."

"That's—a lot of money."

"You'd better believe that's a lot of money. So just where the hell did all that money *go?*"

"He didn't make anything like that, Arnie. I mean, I would have known. It was more like—hundreds of dollars, or something."

"Oh, Jesus!" I slapped the arm of the chair. "That's just beautiful! First he rips me off, and then he goes and gets ripped off himself! Why didn't he just throw it all down a sewer?"

Billy reached for her drink.

I killed mine off, and kept my eyes on her.

"What are you—? Why are you looking at me like that?"

"Because I don't understand you, Billy. I've just spent the last two hours with you, and didn't hear a *peep* about this. I realize you're one hell of an actress—but how could you have been so fucking *blithe?*"

Her eyes narrowed. "Don't you talk that way to me, Arnie. I didn't take your precious rocks."

I sagged forward in my chair and glared at the carpet.

"Arnie? They're only *rocks.*"

"Is that what you think? Is that really what you think?"

"Yes."

"Then you don't know the first damned thing about me, Billy."

She took up her glass and stood. She considered me, her eyes wet, the slim curves of her delicate underlids pumping. Then she turned and strode out of the living room.

It took some hard effort to work myself out of my chair and retrieve my crutches from the floor, never mind that I could have spared myself the agony by simply calling out for Billy's help. I carried my glass—clamped precariously between my chin and upper chest—into the kitchen, and poured myself another shot. I drank it so fast my eyes watered. Then I clumped out onto the new back porch, and found Billy sitting there, halfway down the steps, the shoulders of her corduroy jacket stiffened against the chill—and, I was sure, against me. Of course she'd heard the noise from my crutches. But she kept facing the backyard. Some of it was splashed with silvery moonlight, the rest was sunk in shadow.

"I'm not done talking," I said.

"So talk."

"I just want you to know that I don't buy this crap about Redso being so helplessly out of control."

"Crap?" Billy swung around to face me. "What are you talking about?"

"I'm talking about letting Redso off the hook for every crazy damned destructive thing he does. He's responsible for his actions just like anybody else."

She wobbled to her feet, spilling some whiskey.

"What's the matter with you? Redso's *sick.*"

"Oh Christ! Who *isn't* sick, one way or another? What does that word *mean?* Redso's *still* a human being, and he's *still* in charge of his free will—and boy, does he exploit it to the maximum! I mean, come on, Billy! Do you see me using *my* illness as an excuse for my lousy behavior?"

"Yes!"

"You—" I tilted forward on my crutches. "When? When have you seen me do that?"

"Arnie, you don't even *know* when you're doing it."

Billy blew out a furious breath and left the porch.

I clumped down after her, shouting at her back. "Redso *chooses* to be manic! He *prefers* to be manic! Shit, you said so yourself! The crazy motherfucker's having *fun!*"

Billy spun around. "You saw him tonight. Did he look to you like he was having fun?"

"All right. So he screwed up, got caught, and had to pay the penalty. But it's a price he's willing to *pay.* You think Redso *cares* that he's ruining his life? Or yours, for that matter?"

"He's *crazy!*"

"He's more than crazy! He's worse than crazy! He's dead set against being *sane!*"

"He doesn't want to be sane because he's crazy!"

A laugh bubbled out of Billy's throat. It seemed to surprise her as much as it did me. "God," she said, rolling her eyes. "Will you listen to us?"

I had to consciously hold on to my anger—for Billy had never been more meltingly appealing than at that lovely moment when she'd laughed.

"The point is," I said, bearing down on my crutches, "it's Redso who refuses to take his lithium, and it's Redso who decides to drop LSD and torch his mother's house—and it's Redso who ripped me off! *Redso.* Not some disembodied list of symptoms. And dammit, Billy, he's *culpable!*"

"What's happened to you, Arnie? When did you get so hard?"

"How long are *you* going to stay so soft? Until he completely eats you alive?"

That sent her striding off toward the oak tree in the center of the yard. I poked right behind her.

"He's just as innocent as the day he was born! Just as long as he's still certifiable, right? And hasn't he done everything in his crazy power to *stay* certifiable for as long as you've known him?"

We were stopped now under the oak tree. Billy's face was darkly spangled with the shadows of the leaves. She didn't answer.

"And why not? It makes him godlike, completely unanswerable to anyone but himself! Which is *exactly* how Redso wants it, Billy. Hell, he *is* the *Ubermensch*—just like he said that day when he was up there raving in this tree. He's getting away with murder, and he *knows* it, and nothing could possibly delight him—"

"Murder? You equate what he did to you with *murder?*"

"He—It was criminal, all right? You think it was some kind of innocent *mistake?* Redso knew what he was doing to me."

"What was he doing to you?"

"The son of a bitch is insatiable! First he takes—"

I caught myself.

Billy tilted her face. "First he takes what?"

Had she guessed which precipice I'd nearly stumbled over?

I gave a roll to my shoulders, and said, "Just look at what he's done to you."

"What has he done to me?"

"Oh, come on, Billy! Who are you trying to kid? *Look* at you. You're a complete nervous wreck. You're not eating, you're smoking, you're losing your old friends. Your whole career, your whole *life* is in shambles, and all because you're so in thrall to that madman—"

"What do you know about it?" she screamed.

That stopped me like a slap.

"Well? What do you know about it, Arnie? About love? Except for what you've read about, or fantasized about? Even with that woman back in Wales, it was nothing but sex—you admitted as much in your letters. My God, you *bragged* about it!" She raised her chin. "And just what right do you have to judge me anyway? I mean, where were *you* for the past year and a half while I've been trying to survive this whole nightmare alone?"

I couldn't look at her now.

"Do you have any *idea* what it's like to have to stand back and watch the person you love in the process of being destroyed? Well? Do you? Do you have any *idea* what that's like?" Billy fiercely tossed her hair. "Don't you dare go condemning me, Arnie. Not until you've been there yourself."

She brushed past me.

I turned stiffly on my crutches to watch her go. She headed for the house, her shoulders swinging, her hips switching, and swept up the porch and through the screen door. When the door banged shut, she was already at the kitchen window, taking up the bottle of scotch.

I stood there for a time, trying to gather myself.

Then I started for the house, in such a fog of generalized pain that I couldn't tell where the arthritis stopped, and the rest of it began.

WHEN BILLY ENTERED my bedroom, I was lying on my back, partly covered by a sheet, and listening, as if to a piece of dull repetitive music, to the pain that rhythmically hammered in my hips.

She'd just come from the shower, and was wearing her thick blue terry-cloth bathrobe. She carried yet another glass of scotch. Her hair was a damp confusion of gray and black tangles. Her heavy-lidded eyes were puffy. Clearly she'd been crying. Swaying slightly, she came to the foot of my bed.

"Arnie? You don't hate me, do you?"

"What? Jesus, Billy. No."

She sipped her drink, gave a twist to her neck. "It's my fault you're hurting like this. I shouldn't have put you through all this shit tonight—the mental hospital and the rest of it. It was too much for you, Arnie. Especially after you just got off the plane. It was selfish of me."

I didn't say anything.

"But the thing is, you seem so *strong* to me, Arnie. Did you know that? Well, you do. I mean, knowing all the suffering you have to constantly put up with . . . I guess it fools me into thinking that you're somehow inured to pain. That you're somehow built to take it better." She paused. "But of course, you're not, are you?"

That did it. All the pent-up exhaustion and misery and humiliation of the past three hours, loaded on top of my pain, burst the dam, and everything, everything, came rushing back at me at once: Billy, looking so reduced and enervated at the airport gate, Redso in his shaky, stupefied, blue-pajamaed ruin, scratchy Carl and milky-eyed Deborah begging us so pathetically for Cokes, and even that wild-haired catatonic woman, madly socking herself in the forehead as she circled the walls of that hellish green day room—and then, of course, me, still made ridiculous, after all this time, by the unfunny joke of my impossible love. All of it washed over me in Technicolor luridness, pummeled me with sadness, and it was my turn to cry. I rolled onto my stomach and buried my face in my pillow. But the pain from that move only forced the sobs more extravagantly out of my throat.

Soon Billy was sitting beside me, her weight slightly rocking the mattress. She set her drink on the night table, and began to stroke the back of my head.

"You poor thing."

I kept bawling.

"That's right," Billy said, still stroking my hair. "Get it out, Arnie. You just go right ahead and get it all out."

The sobs were receding now.

"Better now?"

I sniffed, grunted.

Then, shifting her hips beside me, and leaning down, so that her boozy breath was wafting into my nose, Billy began to expertly massage my neck. She started in at the base of my skull, working her fingertips deep into the muscles flanking my spine, then moved down methodically, with exquisite slowness, centimeter by centimeter, to service each separate vertebra. It was delicious. Currents of heat skittered up and down my back, and colorful fuzzballs exploded, one after the other, in the darkness under my eyelids, like fireworks silently flowering.

"You mind if I do this?"

"God, no."

She continued with her deeply circling, deeply thrilling fingerwork. "You're tense as hell, you know that?"

She dug in harder.

"Ahh!"

"Did that hurt?"

"No. No. Keep going."

"Does anyone ever do this for you, Arnie?"

"My mother. Used to, anyway. But nothing like this."

Her voice was furred with booze. "Well, you should have it done more often."

The mattress rocked again as Billy found a new position, and began to undo, with her magical thumbs and fingers, the knots between my shoulders.

"Arnie?"

"Mm?"

"I hate what we just did to each other. What we said to each other out in the backyard. I just want to reach out and *erase* it all, you know? Every ugly shitty destructive thing we said."

"Maybe . . . some of it had to be said."

"Maybe. I don't know. But let's not ever talk that way to each other again. Not ever. All right?"

"All right."

Her hands became still on my back. "Because . . . I can't afford to lose you, Arnie. Do you know that?"

I stopped breathing.

When I sucked air back into my lungs again, I had somehow twisted around onto my back, and was facing Billy, the pain evaporating before the overwhelming reality of her—here, right here, beside me on my bed. Her eyes were radiant drunken black almonds, her hair was a dark tangled curtain behind her back, her bathrobe, by God, was hanging partway open as she bent forward, and the sight of her partially exposed breasts—those plump, pale, quivering half-moons— made me crazy, knocked all fear and foresight clean out of me, and without another thought, I seized her by the shoulders and pulled her down to me.

And then, damned if I knew why, Billy, as if colluding in my most blatant far-fetched fantasy, allowed me to press her soft lips into mine, and to slip my tongue into the moist velvet hollows of her mouth, and then encouraged me, with a moan deep out of her diaphragm that caused my jaws to tingle, to keep right on with it.

Six

AN EVENING in early December, six weeks later. A gray, cheerless, stagnant time. Redso was still under lock and key, having been transferred from Malcolm Bliss to the longer-term hospital on Arsenal Street, where he continued to languish in a deep and tenacious depression. As for Billy and me (since she'd crushed, back in October, all chance of any love affair developing between us), we'd been like two ships stranded in the doldrums, no wind to blow us anywhere, no hint of any change or any relief on the horizon. This evening, as so often happened nowadays, Billy and I were together, but alone, floating around the house in our separate bubbles of self-absorption—yet each of us acutely aware of the other.

Earlier that evening her brother, Frank, had called from Chicago. I'd gathered by now that Frank—unmarried, under-weight, plagued with colitis and migraines, and barely hanging on with his money-losing bookstore up in Chicago—was the sad case of the family, unequipped with his father's oblivious self-delight or his younger sister's strength, an inveterate *shlemazel* and whiner, who, like everyone else in her life, it seemed, relied on Billy to slap on the emotional balm whenever he needed some nursing. He had called nearly an hour ago, and she was still on the phone with him now, smoking and pacing, tethered in her meanderings by the long white curly cord.

I was in the dining room, cleaning my rocks—a chore I got around to every three or four months, the logistics of which I'd worked out long ago, back when I was a kid in my wheelchair. Seated in a swivel chair that rolled on steel casters, a pile of rags and a bottle of rubbing alcohol on a shelf in front of me, I would stand briefly to pluck down a specimen, resume my seat, lovingly and fastidiously scrub it and buff it to its maximum sheen, then stand again to replace it, and take down another rock; when I'd finished with one section, I'd roll down to the next. For all the pleasure I took from the sight of my beautiful babies gleaming and winking like new, it was a tedious job, and normally I'd have some music on the stereo to keep me company. But of course that was out of the question tonight, with Billy's long-distance powwow going on.

While some crisis on Frank's end had clearly prompted the call, it still struck me as an awfully one-sided conversation. Occasionally Billy would express herself in a burst of complete sentences, but for the most part she kept silent, periodically letting her brother know that she was still listening and still commiserating by the use of grunts (attentive, sympathetic, doubtful, or surprised) and such minimal phrases as "Really?" or "God, Frank!" or her all-purpose "Huh." Mostly she stayed out of view, in the kitchen. But every so often I'd look up from my work to see her pacing in the living room beyond my monumental amethyst geodes, or passing by the doorway to the kitchen, her shoulders hunched with concentration, her brow contracted with sisterly concern, the phone cord bunched in her hand. She wore the same bathrobe she'd worn on that night, six weeks before, when we made love for our first and only time—and each time Billy strolled into view, the sight of her in that thick nubby terry-cloth bathrobe, now supersaturated with so much meaning, would freshly undo me again.

THE MAIN THING to know about our lovemaking that night was that, at first, I failed.

While I'd stolen glimpses of Billy in the nude before—through the crack in my bathroom door on the afternoon when she first broke into my life, or on the night when I spied on her and Redso from the top of the basement stairs, grappling like wrestlers on the rattling brass bed below—nothing could have prepared me for the thumping visual impact when Billy arose from my bed, faced me, and with a toss of her butt-length hair and a double shrug of her shoulders, dropped her sky-blue bathrobe to the floor. Compared to this, the other two women I'd known in the flesh, Megan Williams back in Wales, with her adolescent boniness, Brenda with her stupendous rolls of fat, might as well have been Laurel and Hardy in the buff. I was a man, don't forget, with a sensitivity to beauty that bordered on the morbid, and to actually set my eyes on what I'd yearned so long to see—finally and fully revealed, so freely and incredibly offered—was just too much for me. No physical description could do justice to that blow. I'll only say that I felt like Moses at the burning bush, and wilted before the dazzling sight of her.

Such a failure of the body (and I don't think I'm protesting too much here) must be far more devastating to a healthy man than to a man like me. After all, I'd learned to *expect* trouble from the physical machine, never assumed that it would always do my bidding, and certainly wasn't in the habit of castigating myself for any mechanical breakdowns. Hell, I couldn't even walk. Why should I expect my cock to always obediently snap to attention? So, as bad as the moment was, I managed to keep my humor, cracked a few limp jokes regarding my sorry limp state (I won't oppress you with them here), and Billy, bless her generous heart, came through with the laughs. In fact, she barely seemed upset at all. More than that: the challenge appeared to galvanize her.

For a while, deeply impressing me, if not arousing me, Billy tried some valiant cocksucking, and when that didn't work, got off the bed and led me through a procedure so intuitive, resourceful, and practical that I had to wonder if, at some other unlikely juncture in her life, she hadn't made love to another man with crippling arthritis in his hips.

She took the straight-backed wooden chair from my desk, set it in the center of the floor, got two heavy feather pillows from my bed, and stacked them on the seat. Smiling as she swayed toward me, the flesh of her breasts, belly, hips, and thighs seeming to jiggle my heart, she handed me my crutches, helped me to the chair, and then masterfully took charge of everything else. She covered my face, throat and shoulders with gentle, lamblike, flickering kisses, and as she did, got a good grip on the back of the chair and straddled me, keeping the brunt of her weight on the chair and her spread-apart legs, just above my touchy lap. Then Billy began to rock herself, forward and back, forward and back, her full breasts slapping my chest, her floral-smelling hair falling over us like a cloak, and then she took my hands and placed them, one by one, at the dips of flesh just above the cello-swells of her hips—where I held on and lifted, lending my strength to her rocking. And then Billy dipped, still gliding, until the fringes of her pubic hair were grazing, tickling, my cock and balls. Blood began to gather in my groin. A thick hot urge to bellow filled my throat. She kept on rocking, so weightless she might have been suspended in water, from my knees to my belly and back again, with amazing control and delicacy, as if she were petting me, her kitten, with her pussy, and then she dipped a little lower yet, so that I could feel the swollen stickiness of her nether lips brushing against me, nibbling at me, like a strangely articulated mouth. And then, with a crooked smile of self-congratulation, Billy reached down and guided me in.

I think what astonished me most about that performance, beyond Billy's cunning and her geishalike expertise, was her unexpected physical strength. Maybe I'd been fooled until then by the soft femininity of her looks. Still, I probably should have known that this tower of determination, this succorer of madmen and cripples, this painter of houses, fixer of handrails, and builder of sturdy straight porches, came equipped with deep reserves of secret power. In fact, it was clear to me now that once Billy Rubin put her mind to something, the sheer force of her will was almost frightening.

And soon enough, I ran straight up against it.

When I awoke early the next afternoon, and remembered what had happened—truly happened—the night before, I became so deranged with happiness, so wild with anticipation, that I wondered if even Redso, at the peak of a manic attack, could have felt any higher than this. But just like Redso's raptures, it wasn't made to last.

I found Billy in the kitchen, bent over her coffee, her dark mouth miserably pursed—which didn't put the slightest dent in my euphoria. I poked over to her, and propping my weight on my left crutch, dipped and pressed my mouth to hers. She kept her lips shut tight and tried to pull away from me. But I pulled her close again and this time, with a tremor I could feel in her shoulders, she slowly opened her mouth. She played her tongue ardently against mine. For a spell we were both lost. Then with a moan, she jerked her face away.

"No, Arnie. No. All right?"

I stood up straight, finding my balance on both crutches. Billy turned away.

"Please, Arnie. Please don't get me started again."

I gave her a hollow grin. But already my heart was sinking like a stone. "You mean not before your first cup of coffee?"

"I mean don't get me started at all." Billy encircled her coffee cup with her arms and sagged over it.

I sank into the nearest chair.

"Billy? You don't—don't you want me?"

"I don't want to want you," she said.

The stone in my chest hit bottom.

"I have to ask you . . . not to touch me like that again. Ever."

Then Billy, still staring bleakly into her coffee, talked on.

What had happened the night before, she said, would never happen again. Not that she regretted it. Not that it had been sordid or meaningless. She wanted to make sure that I understood, believed that. But it was over now. She was still in love with Redso, no less than before, and nothing could compel her to abandon him now—not now when he was at his weakest, not now when he needed her most.

Only then did Billy raise her face and show me her bloodshot eyes. Could I understand that? Could I live with that? And most important, could we still be friends like before? Because without my friendship, and the strength she took from it, she might as well have thrown in the towel right then, Billy said, and followed Redso straight into the mental ward.

Shocking as that speech was, deep down I wasn't surprised. This was the sort of disappointment in love that seemed to be my portion in life, the motif around which my story had always been patterned. The bright upheaval was over; the natu-

ral order had reasserted itself. So what else was new? It tasted
as familiar and flat as the spit in my mouth.

And yet, and yet . . . there was always forlorn hope, wasn't
there? The main thing now was not to lose any more ground
than I had. So I managed to master myself (and this, too,
seemed part of the pattern, for no matter how bad things got,
how much pain I was given to bear, I had yet to really lose my
self-control) and told Billy what she wanted to hear. She was
right, I said. We'd been crazy to cross that line; we'd be crazier
still to cross it again, and place everything we had together at
risk; we'd simply have to do our best to put the incident behind us. And like any effective salesman, I half convinced myself of the eminent good sense of that argument even as I
improvised it—never mind that it was pure fakery. I was far
too much in love, my rival was far too weak—and getting
weaker—and Billy was in far too fragile a position, for me to
give up now. I would simply go on biding my time, maintain
strict discipline, and keep vigilant watch, like a sniper, for any
breach in Billy's defenses.

Meanwhile I had my tactics for psychic survival. At night, to
staunch my howling and dangerous lust, I fell back into my
old sad habit of yanking what cold comfort I could from the
pages of my skin magazines. During the days I buried myself
in my work. And luckily, there was plenty of it, for I still had
that pirate's hoard of treasure I'd amassed in Europe to sell or
trade. Over the next six weeks I took one extended business
trip after another, to Chicago, Denver, and Santa Fe, some
towns around the Grand Canyon and the Painted Desert. But
my house in Maplewood couldn't be avoided forever. And
while Billy and I usually got along fairly well when we were
trapped there together, at other times we were so stiffly and
inauthentically pleasant, solicitous, correct, and polite, we
might have been plotting each other's murder.

"I'LL BE THERE on Friday," Billy was telling her brother.
"But don't you *dare* get in after sundown—you understand?"
She rolled her eyes at the ceiling as she paced behind my
geodes. "Dammit, Frank! You think Daddy doesn't *know* how
you feel? What are you going to do, enlighten him? Just don't
force me to drive you home from the airport on *Shabbos,* all

right? Well, of *course* there must be a morning flight." She clamped the receiver between her shoulder and her cheek and dug a pack of cigarettes from her bathrobe pocket. "Fine," she said. "You call with the flight number tomorrow. And I'll see you on Friday. And oh—congratulations, too. What? No, I *don't* think it's too precipitate. My God, Frank, you're thirty-eight years old." She laughed at something. "Yes. And will you tell Khadija hello for me? No, really. I couldn't be happier. Okay, Frank. *Okay*. Love you, too. Bye now."

Billy strode into the kitchen and slammed down the phone. Then she drifted right into the living room, dumped herself onto the sofa, and simply stared.

I set down my rag, my rubbing alcohol, and the twinned cube of pyrite I'd just burnished to a glowing finish, and swiveled in my chair. "So how's Frank?"

"Just when you thought you'd heard everything . . ."

I waited.

"You know that Pakistani woman he's been seeing?"

"Sure. The first *real* woman he's ever dated, right? The one who actually knows how to treat a man?"

"Right. Well, break out the champagne. They're getting married."

"You're kidding."

"Oh no I'm not." Billy sighed out a cloud of smoke. "I'm not saying this woman won't be good for him, Arnie. For all I know, she's just as wonderful as he claims. But it's just so *Frank*. I mean, he's waited until he's practically forty to get married, and who does he pick? A Moslem! The one choice most likely in the world to give my father an aneurysm."

I laughed. "Well, it could have been worse. He could have held out for a Palestinian."

"Believe me—Pakistani is bad enough. Anyway, the wedding's scheduled for the week before Christmas. And Frank's only known her for five *months*. But that's not the topper, Arnie. Oh no. Get this. He wants my father's *blessing*, for some damned crazy reason. And worse, he's insisting that he come to the wedding."

"I thought Frank hated your father."

"Well, he does, and he doesn't. Sometimes my brother gets weirdly sentimental about things. And besides, what a triumph for the forces of racial and religious toleration, right? To put my father through the torture of having to *be* there when Frank marries his infidel! I swear, Arnie, it's almost like he's marrying this woman just to teach my father a lesson. Anyway. Frank called him today with the news—four times. And each time, my father hung up on him. So now Frank's flying in on Friday. You know, for a showdown. And of course, *I've* got to be there the whole time—to make sure they don't end up killing each other." Billy snorted. "God, save me from people with principles!"

AFTER WEEKS of my hectoring, Billy had finally broken down in November and allowed me to buy her a car—but only on the condition that it set me back no more than five hundred dollars. We took what we could get for the price: a beat-up, canary yellow '76 Plymouth Horizon, with ripped upholstery, a trunk that wouldn't stay shut, and a host of engine problems which even Billy, who was pretty handy with cars, couldn't plumb the mystery of. On Thursday it was back in the shop again. And on Friday afternoon, serving once again as her chauffeur, I drove Billy to her childhood home in University City—where I would return on Saturday afternoon, at the close of *Shabbos,* to pick her up.

I was used to that routine. For the past two years Billy had made a habit of spending most Sabbaths at her father's house, playing the Good Pious Daughter, for his sake, from sundown on Friday until sundown on Saturday. Like Dracula, she'd once said. And Dracula was right. There was something downright gothic in the image I had of Billy, holed up all Sabbath long with her fanatical tyrant of a father, as morbidly obedient, prim, and depressed as a Jewish Emily Dickinson—and in a house which I imagined, until I actually saw it, to be a witchy old Victorian, replete with gables and spires and bats in the attic, like something from a Charles Addams cartoon. More than once I'd let Billy know exactly what I thought of her demeaning and hypocritical masquerade. But I might as well have been talking to myself.

The Rabbi lived in a tiny pocket of conspicuous Jewishness on the south end of University City (the north end was now mostly black) not far from the Orthodox cemetery. I drove up snow-flanked North and South Road, past Petrovsky's Bakery, Diamond's Kosher Meats, and the squat-domed Chesid Shel Emeth synagogue where Rabbi Rubin walked to worship every morning, then up the ice-patched slope of Gannon Street, and saw that his battered Chevy pickup was still taking up the driveway. Usually the Rabbi zoomed off for his apartments the moment the sun went down. But dusk was already settling in, and the old man—who was the last person on earth I wanted to see—was still in the house. Well, at least I'd get to finally meet Frank. I had a positive hunger to set eyes on anyone who shared even a small portion of Billy's genes.

I parked at the edge of the snow-covered lawn, took up my crutches, and left the car.

The Rubin residence was nothing like the spooky old Victorian I'd once imagined. In fact it was a rather cozy-looking place, a snug two-story with an ample front porch, a wooden swing, and a fleur-de-lis of stained glass set into the heavy arched door. Aside from what I'd glimpsed through that door (a dark hallway, a hat rack, a swath of grim gray wallpaper) I didn't know what the interior was like, for now that Rabbi Rubin had me pegged for what I was—a nonreligious Jew, barely a notch above the *goyim* on Yahweh's fiery shitlist—I had yet to be invited inside.

I was nearly to the porch when the front door flew open and Rabbi Rubin charged out in his inevitable black fedora and a loose gray ankle-length overcoat that billowed and flapped behind him. He stomped to the edge of the porch, halted, spun on his heels, and stomped right back to the door.

"You are out of my life!" the Rabbi bellowed. "Do you hear? Gone! Banished! From here on out—a persona non grata!"

"Hah! Why don't you excommunicate me while you're at it? Just like they did to Spinoza! You hateful, bigoted old fuck!"

"What? What was that word you just used?"

"Fuck! Fuck, fuck, fuck!"

The door banged shut in the old man's face.

He raised a tremulous fist, then, seeming to have second thoughts about striking the door, thrust both hands in his coat pockets and came down off the porch, his enraged face bent to the snow. He unwittingly made a beeline to where I was standing.

"Evening, Rabbi."

The old man drew up short, and took me in with those gleaming obsidian eyes. "You," he said, and poked up at the brim of his hat. "Billy's not here, if that's who you're looking for."

"She's not? Well, do you—"

"Gone for a walk."

"Well, then, is Frank—?"

"Who? There's nobody here by that name. In fact, there's no one in the house at all."

The Rabbi strode past me in his billowing overcoat.

I crutched slowly up the porch, wondering at, among other things, the old man's relative verbosity. The most I'd come to expect from the Rabbi during our *Shabbos* encounters was a reluctant nod, or maybe, if he was feeling particularly sociable that evening, a grunt. Evidently his battle with Frank had thrown him out of whack.

The Rabbi's ancient pickup sputtered off behind me. I rapped on the door with the clamp of a crutch. It took some time before Frank answered.

He was a gaunt, gangly, delicate-looking man, with moist black soulful eyes that appeared a little bruised around the sockets. His shoulders were narrow and inward-curling; beneath his fuzzy brown button-down sweater there was no sign of a chest or a belly. His thinning black hair was touched with gray (but nowhere near as much as his sister's) and started up high on his forehead. Stripes of pink scalp showed between the locks. As Frank stared at me, without smiling, he kept one arm clamped to his side by the elbow—as if that arm, or the ribs under it, were broken. That, as I'd soon learn, was a characteristic stance of Frank's, and a telling one: it seemed contrived to let you know that he was one of the walking wounded. Frank tightened his grip on his elbow.

I took my right crutch into my left hand, and held the free hand out for a shake. "Frank? How do you do? I'm Arnie Goldman."

He still said nothing.

"I've . . . sure been looking forward to meeting you," I said.

Frank seemed to weigh his decision. Then he let go of his

elbow and limply accepted my handshake. "Arnie. Of course."
He came up with a wan smile. His lips were plump, like Billy's,
but on his drawn and unshaven face they looked swollen,
overripe. "Well, come in, come in. You must be freezing."

I stepped into the hallway, which smelled of paint.

"Welcome to our unhappy little home," Frank said, and began to massage his left temple. "Billy's told me all about you—
thinks the world of you, apparently. Anyway, hail fellow and
well met, and all of that . . ." He kept rubbing at his temple.
"Sorry if I seem distracted. You must have heard what was
going on with me and my father."

"Some of it."

"Also, I'm afraid I feel a headache coming on. I suppose
Billy told you about my migraines."

I couldn't tell if that was a statement or a question. But
Frank appeared to be waiting for some confirmation.

"Yes," I said. "She did."

Apparently, he was waiting for something more.

"I uh, understand they can be pretty agonizing. Migraines."

"Agonizing's close. But actually, there's no good word in
English to describe it. Maybe in Russian. They're very big on
words to denote states of misery, you know. Like Eskimos,
with their hundreds of words for snow?" Frank soundlessly
laughed. "Anyway, let's hope it's just a false alarm. I've had
enough Sturm und Drang for one day, let me tell you." He
shut the door behind me and stared openly and thoughtfully
at my crutches. "Would you . . . do you need any help getting your coat off?"

"Actually, it's an easier operation if I do it sitting down."

"Ah. Yes, I can see how that would work. Must be a hell of a
life, always futzing around with those crutches, eh?"

I forced a smile.

"God, the things we put up with! Anyway, Billy's not here
right now, I'm sorry to report. Right when things were getting
hot and heavy with my father—poof. She disappeared. And I
have no idea where she went. But of course, she can't be gone
for very long. Not out in this cold. Do you . . . would you
like some tea while you wait?"

"Sure. Thanks."

"Ginseng all right?" Frank began to massage his temple

again. "I find that ginseng can sometimes help stave off a headache."

"Ginseng's just dandy."

"Not that I usually go in for those kooky herbal cures. But nothing the so-called modern medical establishment has to offer seems any more effective. Besides, a billion Chinamen can hardly be wrong, right?" Frank's swollen-looking lips turned up at the corners. "So it's teatime, then, apparently. Right this way."

He turned and led the way down the long gloomy hall, narrow and stooped, his bald spot shining like a pink embedded halo, oppressed-looking even from the back.

I crutched slowly behind him, wanting to take in what I could of the house. From what I saw—three rooms—the place had an odd double sense to it. It looked both long lived-in, and not yet ready for occupancy. The Rabbi's small study was as full as the back of a moving van, containing an enormous oak desk, two overstuffed chairs, a worn crimson loveseat, magazines and newspapers stacked around the floor, and bookshelves built along every available inch of wall space—one whole wall packed tight with *Reader's Digest*s and *National Geographic*s, probably going all the way back to their maiden issues. And yet in what I took to be the living room, there wasn't a stick of furniture—just several paint-spattered sheets on the floor, paint cans and brushes, piles of rags, a ladder, some left-about tools. The chandeliered dining room was just as hollow, just as cluttered. In the high-ceilinged kitchen, once I'd taken a seat at the battered wooden table, worked off my coat, and hung it on the back of my chair, I asked Frank what sort of fix-up projects his father was working on. He turned the fire up under the teapot and rolled his eyes.

"Painting, replastering, who knows? This house was in *exactly* the same shape the last time I was fool enough to come down here—and that was over a year ago. Maybe you don't know it, Arnie, but my father's a classic manic. Starts a million projects, never gets around to finishing one of them."

I hesitated—for after all, I'd only just met the man—then decided to give Frank my opinion. "Come on, Frank. Your father may be crazy, but he's no mental case, believe me."

"You've *met* the man, haven't you?"

"Well, sure. But I know what mental illness is. And believe me, your father doesn't qualify."

"Ah. You must be thinking of your friend—Kedso, Fredso, whatever his name is. It's the name of a clown, I know that."

"It's Redso," I said.

Frank grunted.

I was well aware—as Billy had written to me about it while I was in Wales—that during his last visit to St. Louis, Frank had had the dubious pleasure of meeting Redso. And they'd taken such an instant and intense dislike to each other, Billy reported, that they'd practically come to blows in the middle of a restaurant.

"Anyway," Frank went on, "maybe my father hasn't been officially certified like this lunatic boyfriend of Billy's. But *look* at the man. His compulsiveness, his constant running on at the mouth, his insane egoism, his grandiose opinion of himself. How he's been managing to pass for all these years is beyond me."

I decided it might be wiser to just let the subject go. Obviously nothing I said was going to move Frank from his diagnosis.

As he waited for the water to boil, Frank rather distractedly roamed the kitchen, knitting his hands behind his back or clamping an elbow to his side, and started in on a line of speculation that surprised me. It didn't exactly come out of the blue; but nothing had prompted it, either. Maybe it had something to do with the fact that Frank ran a bookstore—an environment, I'd noticed, where people tended to speak easily to strangers, skipping right past the pleasantries and going straight for the throat of an author or an idea. The subject was pain. And once Frank had ascertained (to his melancholy satisfaction, it seemed to me) that I was usually in plenty of it, he floated off into airy abstraction.

"Of course, I suppose it finally all comes down to the ancient dispute between the Epicureans and the Stoics," Frank was saying. "The Stoics maintaining that pain is the best moral teacher, the prerequisite for wisdom and good character—while the Epicureans would describe pain only as a negative to avoid, the opposite of the one true good, which in this case would be the Pleasure Principle. I don't know. Maybe I'm bringing it up because I don't often get a chance to hear from a person like you. You know. Someone else who has to live with chronic pain." Frank leaned against a counter, cradling an elbow, and studied me. "So I'm wondering what your thoughts might be—if I'm not being too intrusive. *Has* living with pain made you a better person in any way, do you think?"

"It's uh, kind of hard to say, Frank. I mean, the last time I wasn't in this condition, I was eight years old."

"Ah. Well, that adds a different wrinkle, doesn't it? In terms of your ability to judge."

"Actually, it's not something I talk about much."

Frank smiled. "Then you must cast your lot with the Stoics."

I smiled back noncommittally. "How about you?"

"Oh, I suppose I'm of two minds about it. Of course, I like to *think* that my pain has made me a more sensitive, more compassionate person. But then I get a headache, or an attack of colitis, and suddenly I couldn't give a shit about the possible spiritual benefits."

I laughed—partly because of Frank's absolute earnestness as he said that. "Yeah, well. I'm with you, Frank. I'm a Stoic when it suits me, and an Epicurean when it doesn't. And it never seems to affect my arthritis either way."

Frank took that in thoughtfully. "Do you often use irony as a defense?" he asked me.

In a funny way, I was beginning to like this sad peculiar man. "All the time," I told him.

"Of course, you're still being ironic, aren't you?" He sighed. "The truth is, I've never really been much of one for irony . . ."

The kettle whistled. Frank jerked away from the counter and hurried to the stove.

Once he had me set up with my ginseng tea, and joined me at the table, Frank watched with deep interest as I took my first sip. "Is it all right?"

"Not bad," I politely told him. Actually, it tasted like hot water brewed with dirt.

"Really? I think it's awful. But like I said, it appears to help, for some reason. Of course, that might be purely due to the placebo effect. Which in itself is a very interesting phenomenon, don't you think? How the expectation generated by one portion of the brain can act to override—"

"Sure," I said. "It *is* interesting." Then, switching gears before Frank could soar off on another philosophical riff, I congratulated him on his upcoming marriage. I was surprised to see him flush.

"Well, thank you," Frank said, and rubbed at his sunken chest. "I realize it may not appear that way, but I'm actually very happy."

Then, all shy smiles and throat-clearings, Frank got out his raggedy black wallet and passed across the table a much handled snapshot of his fiancée. For some reason, when I'd thought of Frank's Pakistani bride-to-be, I'd pictured Dr. Sharma back at Bliss—a lithe little copper-colored beauty with flashing black Scheherazade eyes. But in the photo was a drab, round-faced, unsmiling woman, whose eyes, like lumps of coal, were almost lost behind the porky hillocks of her cheeks. She looked about as friendly as one of those grim stone heads on Easter Island. It was both sad and poignantly reassuring, it seemed to me, that such an uninviting woman could apparently make Frank so happy; there was someone for everyone, I supposed. And certainly a guy like Frank would do better to lower his expectations.

Then I took a bad jolt—for who, after all, wouldn't say the very same thing about me?

"She's lovely," I told him, handing the photo back.

"No, she's not," Frank said, with a small smile. He delicately replaced the picture in his wallet. "But that's all right. Khadija is simply the kindest, the finest . . . Well. Just wait until you meet her, Arnie."

He sipped his tea. I left mine alone.

Then Frank, slumping forward on his crossed arms, suddenly looked capable of murder. "And when I stop to *think* that my own father refuses to even recognize her humanity! A woman whose goodness and inner radiance make that man look like a *baboon* by comparison! Do you see why I hate him? Can you blame me? And the joke is his so-called Jewishness! His piety!" Frank's hands fisted on the table. Then he pushed back against his chair, blew out a breath, and wagged his head.

"Anyway . . . I really should let that subject go, shouldn't I?" He started rubbing at his temple again.

I had no idea where to take the talk from there. Also, I began to fear, like Frank, that a full-blown migraine headache was about to strike.

But now Frank brightened up—a little. While Khadija had their apartment plastered with photos of her relatives back in Islamabad, he told me, she had yet to see any pictures of Billy, or of himself when he was a child—and he'd promised to bring some back with him to Chicago. Upstairs in a closet was a boxful of old snapshots that Frank hadn't looked at in years. Did I want to accompany him upstairs while he sorted through them?

"You bet I do," I told him.

Now that he'd brought it up, I was dying to see some pictures of Billy when she was younger—I knew perfectly well they'd only make me crazy with longing and regret.

As Frank led the way, stooped, bony, breakable-looking, I poked down the paint-smelling hallway, up the dusty un-carpeted stairs, and into the room that, Frank informed me, had been Billy's as a child. I felt very strange as I entered—tingling on the outside, hushed within; if I hadn't exactly stepped into her childhood, I was certainly standing here among some of its props. It looked as if nothing had been disturbed since Billy was twelve. There were some paintings of horses on the walls, and also some old black and white publicity photos of actresses: Katharine Hepburn, Marlene Dietrich, Vivian Leigh. All damned *good* actresses, I noted. The furniture was in that frilly, blue and white and gold French Provincial style which seemed only to exist in the bedrooms of middle-class American girls. I lowered myself to the edge of the bed where Billy, with her flawless young skin and developing breasts, had lain so many nights . . . But here I ruthlessly cut off my thoughts.

Frank had already taken from the closet the cardboard box full of snapshots, and was on his knees and rooting. "Some of these will absolutely break your heart," he said.

I didn't doubt that at all.

Frank kept digging.

Then I noticed something else. On the floor beside the desk

was what appeared to be a big elaborate doll house—but not exactly. I crutched over for a better look, and when I realized what it was, lowered myself carefully, with a few winces, to my butt in front of it, and laid down my crutches on the floor.

It wasn't a doll house, but a doll-size wooden theater. I'd never seen anything like it. Funny, but the words that came to mind were out of my own childhood: keen, neato, cool. And so it was. The thing stood about waist high, and was tightly carpentered, meticulously painted, ingeniously conceived. A round stage, still shiny with shellac, extended out a couple of feet or so, and was ringed with tiny wooden carvings, shaped like scallop shells, to represent footlights. The back was deep enough to hold three different stage flats—painted slats of wood that could be slid in and out. While the painting was pretty crude, it was clearly the work of an adult. One flat showed the entry hall of a mansion or a palace, with a swooping staircase, a chandelier, a suit of armor, and a rather botched attempt at rendering a checkered floor in perspective; the next was an exterior view of a plantation-style mansion set back on a lush green hill, with a gnarled black tree in front, like Tara in *Gone With the Wind;* the last, oddly enough, was a village of crooked wooden shacks, with a well in the foreground and a dirt road running past, dotted here and there with cartoony chickens and cows, that might have been a *shtetl* in Russia—and sure enough, there on the peaked roof of one of the shacks was the silhouette of a dancing fiddler. How you could get a story line to run from the antebellum South to Sholom Aleichem seemed pretty problematical to me; but then again, I wasn't a kid with a kid's imagination. The stage curtain was made of a spangly blue chintzlike material, and on the side of the theater was a tiny copper crank, which either unfurled the curtain or drew it up into glittering puckered folds. The most exacting woodworking had been lavished on the proscenium arch, its outlines fantastically curlicued. And on the front of that arch, carved in relief and painted gold, were the words THE BILLY RUBIN THEATER.

Beside the doll theater, in a redwood box, I found the actors in the company: two Barbies and two Kens, sans costumes.

"Frank? What's the story behind this?"

"Behind what?"

I smiled when I said it. "The Billy Rubin Theater."

Frank craned around. "Oh, that. You know, I can't believe it's still in one piece? Billy used to practically *live* in that thing. And who could blame her? It was her one good escape from our father." He sat back on his heels. "You wouldn't believe the demands he used to make on her, Arnie. Especially after our mother died. They were like Siamese twins. My father used to drag her around practically everywhere he went—the store, the synagogue, his horrible slum apartments. He was even jealous of her friends—never wanted them around the house, you know, where they would steal her attention away from him. It was all extremely sick. But for some reason he used to leave her alone when she was playing with that thing. As if it were somehow off-limits. And Billy would lose herself in it for hours on end—making up her little plays, doing all the voices—probably just so she could *breathe*."

I was frowning at Frank, who was rooting again through his box full of photographs. Then I turned back to the theater. "This is really some piece of work."

"Isn't it? But I'll tell you the truth. I used to resent Billy for it. Never mind that I was a teenager by the time my father built it for her—or that boys don't play with dolls, supposedly. But never in a hundred years would my father ever have done anything *approaching* that for me. I used to tell myself that it was fine with me if Billy was his favorite—so long as it kept him out of my hair. But of course, that was just a pathetically transparent rationalization." Frank sighed. "Isn't it ridiculous? What still hurts?"

"Your father *built* this?"

"Oh yes. For her tenth birthday, I think. It took him nearly a year to finish it. I remember he used to keep it covered with a sheet down in his workshop—and absolutely forbade Billy to go near that end of the basement. It was all so hush-hush, you would have thought he was down there developing the atom bomb."

I went on inspecting that marvelous toy.

"So he really loved her," I said, almost to myself.

"Or so she thinks. I suppose you could say that my father *coveted* Billy—still covets her—which is about the most he's capable of. But not love. Oh no. Not when it's his *own* welfare that's always come first. And yet Billy still refuses to see that. Which is the whole crux of her problem, isn't it?"

"I'm not sure I'm following, Frank."

"Why else do you think Billy still insists on playing the good little dutiful daughter after all these years? She's still desperately trying to win the love our father never gave her—and this from a man who's never loved anyone but himself! All her life she's been doing *back-flips* trying to please that man—in whatever form he happens to take. This Redso lunatic, and before him, that alcoholic coach. What was his name? Larry?"

"Yeah, I think. But she never told me he was an alcoholic."

Frank ruefully smiled. "Well, ask her about it again. And don't be fooled if Billy denies it. The point is, it's all the same pattern—the same sick, utterly self-absorbed, emotionally unavailable man. Redso for instance. Do you imagine it's some kind of *accident* that he's a maniac exactly like my father? Hah! And if Billy can save Redso from himself, make him over into a sane and caring human being who would actually know how to love her—well, *voilà*. She's resolved her ancient problem with Daddy, hasn't she? By proxy." Frank slowly shook his head. "I'm sad to say it, Arnie. But in many ways my sister is a textbook case. Billy Rubin—forever to the rescue. And of course, if she doesn't turn herself around pretty soon—first by dropping that madman, and then by getting to a good reliable therapist—I'm afraid she's going to need some rescuing herself."

That dissertation seemed to take a lot out of Frank. He sank back weakly onto an elbow, sighed extravagantly, shut his eyes, and began to massage the bridge of his nose.

Maybe, just maybe, I thought, there were some nuggets of truth buried somewhere in Frank's analysis. But overall it struck me as awfully darned neat, and, given his hatred of his father, pretty self-serving as well. There were several points in particular I wanted to dispute—that Billy was a textbook case of anything, for example, or that Redso could possibly be taken as some kind of mirror image of Rabbi Rubin. But the poor man looked so enervated at that moment, slumped there on the floor, massaging his nose, that I didn't have the heart to lay into him.

I turned back to the theater, and started fooling again with the crank of the spangly blue curtain.

Frank resumed his rustlings in the cardboard box behind me. Then, for the first time since I'd entered the house, he actually raised his voice. "Here it is!" he cried. "I *knew* it had to be here!" Frank scrambled across the floor, all elbows and knees, and handed me the picture. "Now, just get a load of this!"

In the snapshot—the corners curled, the colors faded—Frank and his sister were sitting together on the front porch steps. Frank sat a step or two lower than Billy, who had her arms yoked around his narrow shoulders and sunken chest. I guessed she was thirteen or fourteen—and thought of scratchy Carl on the ward at Malcolm Bliss, for this was indeed Billy at her *National Velvet* stage: long-necked, huge-eyed, her bare arms in her sleeveless summer dress so graceful and slim they might have been done by Degas. Frank was somewhere in his twenties, with a much fuller head of hair. But he was still Frank. He scowled reluctantly as he smiled, looking every bit as put-upon as now. Despite her age and her coltlike skinniness, Billy seemed the older and the stronger of the pair. In fact, in the way she had her arms wrapped so tight around Frank's chest, and was pressing her cheek to his, coaxing her peevish older brother to smile for the camera, there was something precociously protective, maternal. So even at that age, Billy was what she was.

It pained me to look.

But of course, Stoic that I was, I kept on looking.

"ON THE OTHER HAND," Frank was saying from the backseat of my Toronado, "it still might be possible to get a flight out tonight. If I went standby, or something."

"Frank," Billy said, "you just accepted our offer. So that's the end of it, okay? You'll sleep at our place tonight."

"Well, if it's not too much trouble . . ."

"Believe me," I told him. "It's not."

Frank sighed. "I do appreciate it," he said. "The truth is, I don't know how I could have stood another night in that torture chamber of a house."

"Well, now you won't have to." Billy got a cigarette lit, and then, probably recalling that Frank couldn't stand tobacco smoke, took one final puff, lowered her window, and flicked it out.

"Thank you," Frank said.

"You're welcome."

We were headed to the hospital on Arsenal Street. On the seat next to Frank was the army surplus duffel bag he was traveling with; between Billy and me sat her inevitable sack of supplies for Redso: cigarettes, toothpaste, shampoo, Snickers bars.

"So . . ." Frank said. "After all the blood and thunder, it seems that all I really did was waste the price of an airplane ticket."

"Oh, I don't know, Frank. You got to tell Daddy off to his face, didn't you? Wasn't that the whole point?"

"Of course not! And besides, if it *did* come down to that, well, it certainly wasn't due to *my* insanity." Frank steamed in silence for a spell. "So it looks like the wedding will just have to go on without him."

Billy craned around. "Frank, it's no big loss. I still can't understand why you'd even *want* him there."

"Why? Because he's my *father*."

"Yeah, well. If you really want him at your wedding, try marrying someone named Goldberg the next time around."

"You don't actually think there'll be a next time around, do you?"

Billy faced forward again, and sighed. "No, Frank. It was just a joke. Anyway, Khadija's parents won't be at the wedding, either. So there's a nice kind of symmetry to it, don't you think?"

"With Khadija's parents it's not a matter of a *boycott*. My God, they live in Islamabad."

"And Daddy lives in a medieval Jewish ghetto. So what are you going to do? Arnie and I will be there, and so will Khadija's friends, and the people from the bookstore—and we'll all have ourselves a grand old time, I promise you."

"Maybe you're right. But just don't expect me to forgive him. Some things are beyond forgiveness."

I could sense Billy's struggle not to respond to that.

"And have you thought about this, Billy? What happens if

we have a baby? We *are* planning on it, you know. What then? Is he going to pretend it doesn't *exist* because it's half Indian? My God! That man—do you realize what he is? Nothing but a twisted Jewish version of a *Nazi,* with his insane fixation on racial purity! But of course, try getting him to understand *that!* God, if I could only get that man to see his own face!"

"Frank, please. It's over now. Can't you just let it drop?"

By then I was pulling up before the entrance to the state mental hospital. This place on Arsenal Street was a much grander—and creepier—affair than Malcolm Bliss: a collection of old brick buildings which in the daylight were the color of dried blood, all ponderously domed and turreted, like a grim sprawling castle.

"This is it?" Frank said.

"This is it," Billy answered.

"Scary-looking place for a mental hospital, isn't it? You'd think they'd try and make these places look as innocuous as possible. For the patients' sake, if nothing else."

"You think *this* is scary," Billy said, "wait'll you see what's inside."

"Oh no," Frank said. "You're not getting *me* to go in there. Not after all I've already been through today."

"Fair enough," Billy said, and turned to me.

I only tightened my grip on the steering wheel.

"Arnie?"

"I uh, think I'll stick around here with Frank."

Billy seemed a little disappointed by that—although on what grounds, I had no idea. Obviously we couldn't just leave Frank stranded out here in the car. And besides, she knew perfectly well what my position was on visiting Redso nowadays.

"Could you pick me up in about an hour?" she asked.

I glanced at my Rolex. "How's a quarter after nine?"

"Fine," Billy said, then took up her sack and left the car. She moved swiftly up the steps to the high gothic doors of the hospital.

"This seems strange to me," Frank said.

"What's that?"

"Don't you ever visit him?"

I expelled a breath. "Not anymore."

"But I thought Redso was your best friend."

"That's right," I said. "He was."

"But not any longer?"

"No."

"Do you mind if I ask why?"

"It's just . . . something that happened between us a while back." I didn't want to start in with Frank about that episode when Redso had ripped off my rocks.

"Ah," Frank said. "So what do you want to do while we wait?"

"We could go get some coffee or a beer."

"I could use a beer," Frank said, surprising me a little. He didn't strike me as the type who would drink.

I looked into the rearview. "Why don't you join me up front, Frank?"

He did, settling in beside me with his arms crossed, and an elbow protectively cradled in each hand.

"Just how often does Billy visit him, anyway?"

"Every day," I told him, starting us away from the hospital entrance.

"What? You're joking. Every *day?*"

"Unless something extraordinary comes up."

"My God, it's worse than I thought." Frank slowly wagged his head. "It's beyond belief, isn't it?"

"What?"

"Well, *look* at her. Running off to minister to that madman every single day of her life! When all the while she's got a good, sane, decent man like you, just waiting there in the wings for her."

I kept my face carefully to the road—for I was unable to find an expression to mask my consternation.

"I don't know," Frank went on. "Is it supposed to be some deep dark secret that you're in love with my sister? Because if so, it's certainly not *my* place to blow the whistle. That is, if Billy doesn't already know. But I don't see how she couldn't. It's been written all over your face since the moment she showed up at the house. Your *voice* even changes when you talk to her, Arnie. Did you know that? It gets deeper, more resonant."

I licked my lips, which had gone dry as paper.

"Anyway, don't think I don't empathize with what you're going through. It took me *months* to find the nerve to tell Khadija how I really felt. It's frightening, isn't it? That sense of naked exposure, of complete powerlessness? But of course, it all turned out to be in my head. That was the joke. When I finally did confess to her, do you know what Khadija did? She laughed—and asked me why in the world it had taken me so long."

At this point, of course, if I didn't strenuously deny Frank's allegation, my silence would confirm it. But all I seemed to be able to do was swallow.

"Well, you just hang in there, Arnie. Don't give up the ship. One of these days—and I really do have a gut feeling about this for some reason—Billy's going to wake up and see what she already has in you. My God, you're certainly a better deal than that lunatic of hers! And then, of course, with your condition . . . well. My sister won't have to *completely* abandon her calling, will she?"

Frank slid a little lower in his seat with a satisfied sigh. "But will you promise me one thing? When it happens, will you make sure to let me know? I'm serious. Call me collect, if you have to. Because, believe me, I'll be absolutely ecstatic for *both* of you."

ON THE NEXT NIGHT, when I pulled up once again in front of the state hospital on Arsenal Street (alone this time, as Frank had gone his melancholy way back to Chicago that morning), I could tell from the way Billy beamed when she spotted me, and came tripping down the double set of stairs, that something funny was going on; lately her visits with Redso had been leaving her drained and morose. As she approached the car she stopped, tossed her hair behind her shoulders, and broke into a brief, lovely, expert little tap dance on the sidewalk—her sneakers flying and kicking, her arms rowing charmingly through the air in front of her, Shirley Temple style. Then she gave out a hoot, whipped open the door, plunged across the front seat, and supporting herself on her knuckles, kissed me sloppily on the side of the mouth.

I touched my lips as if she'd stung me there. "What's going on, Billy?"

"He's better," she said, flashing me a grin as she slammed the door. "They're doing an evaluation tomorrow—but that doesn't matter, Arnie. He's *better*. I mean, he's still pretty down, but nothing, nothing like he was just *yesterday*. Do you know what he did? He asked me to bring some fresh pens and legal pads tomorrow—because he's got some ideas for a new play he's itching to write down! Hah! Can you believe it?" Her wet smile was stretched about as far as it would go. "I mean, my God, is that wonderful, or what?"

Seven

IN THE DAYS leading up to Redso's release Billy was dizzy
with anticipation—so dizzy, in fact, that despite her usual sensitivity to my moods, she seemed utterly oblivious to my glum
preoccupation, my ever mounting dread. Flushed, fluttery,
full of blissful plans, she flitted around the house like Cinder-
ella getting ready for the Prince's ball; and if I was slouching
behind her in a guilty nervous funk—like a jealous stepsister,
foreseeing the bad end of the tale—well, that was no concern
of Billy's. Nothing, apparently, was going to stand in the way
of her hard-earned happiness.

More than once I considered bolting. Clearly the only ra-
tional course of action, before Redso rammed his way back
into my existence, was to move out, get my own place, my own
life, and leave the two of them to their mutual clinging crazy
impossible fates. Just what did I owe them, anyway? Especially
after so much generosity? My case against Redso, of course,
was open and shut. He was the one who owed me. And where
Billy was concerned, what was either one of us getting out of
this vague gray no-man's land where our relationship had
drifted—somewhere between friendship and romance, which
was worse than nowhere at all? This unrequited longing at
such close quarters was slowly killing me. And to imagine that
Billy might be devastated by my going (in any other way, that
is, than financially) was pure vanity, wishful thinking. The sit-

uation called for that toughness of mind that had once been one of my cardinal strengths. It was time to shake off this unmanly torpor, this spineless Hamlet routine, and become Arnie Goldman again. Step one was to dislodge Billy from my heart—and only another woman could do that. Hell, there were other females in St. Louis, weren't there? I hadn't even *checked* on that proposition in more than two years! All I had to do was to start limping around in singles bars . . . or run an ad in the Personals section of the *Riverfront Times* . . . or finally swallow my self-respect, make my mother happy, and show my mortified red face in whatever crowded, sweaty, malodorous church basement where the next Funfest for the Physically Challenged was scheduled to be held.

And here, of course, my inner argument would stop cold, turn tail, and drag me right back to the beginning again.

The truth was, I was paralyzed.

And on the afternoon when Redso returned, I was waiting right there in the house I couldn't escape to pretend to welcome him home.

Billy had gone all-out for the occasion. Before taking off in her Plymouth that afternoon, she made sure the house was absolutely spotless (as if Redso would give a damn); there was a vase of yellow roses on the coffee table in the living room; on a counter in the kitchen sat a rack of lamb, ready to roast; in the refrigerator lay two bottles of Moët Chandon—which I'd gone ahead and popped for, not wanting to appear the bad sport that I was. And on the wall above the stereo Billy had tacked up a banner, cut from a sheet, and trumpeting in purple Magic Marker a quote from Dr. King:

FREE AT LAST! FREE AT LAST!
THANK GOD ALMIGHTY, I'M FREE AT LAST!

That was pretty good, I had to admit, and would probably hand Redso a laugh—that is, if he were capable of laughing.

But as I stood at the window and watched him stiffly emerge from Billy's car, Redso hardly looked capable of smiling. He wore his bulky blue overcoat with its almond-shaped buttons down the front, a scarlet scarf around his neck, and a tricolored, pointy-headed stocking cap, its brightness only accentuating the pallor of his face. Billy held him by the elbow as they

picked their way across the snow, Redso taking tiny halting
steps, like a frail old man. When he saw me watching through
the window, he tried on a slow-forming smile. My heart contracted. I didn't want to pity him, not now. But I couldn't help
remembering the Redso he'd once been—so vital and vivid
and boomingly self-confident. The cliché was horribly apt: he
was indeed a mere shadow of his former self. Redso stumbled.
Billy smiled, said something to him, and gently led him on.

For the next two days, despite Billy's tireless efforts to cheer
him up—with jokes, with caresses, with his favorite foods on
the table and his favorite albums on the stereo—Redso remained as quiet and lethargic as a dying cat. Mostly he slept.
Otherwise, when Billy wasn't around and trying to entertain
him, Redso divided his inertia between the television—not
seeming to care which moronic program happened to be on—
or the typewriter in the basement, where, having some chore
to attend to down there, I saw him several times, slumped
over my old Royal, pecking listlessly at the keys, sifting
through a pile of senseless manuscript papers, or simply immobilized there, his elbows on the desk, his skull in his hands,
his knuckles pumping and pumping away at the crown of his
frizzed orange hair, like he was struggling to massage his
ruined brain into action. If I crutched past him in the living
room, slumped in front of the TV, or observed him at the
dinner table, getting down one of Billy's fabulous dishes with
no more apparent relish than a cow chewing cud, or noted his
lightless eyes, his lackluster voice, as he tried his damnedest to
respond to Billy's efforts to charm him out of it, Redso's suffering took all the sting out of whatever anger or resentment I
still harbored for him. How could you actively dislike a man in
such a state? Even *I* was impatient for Redso to snap out of it.
After all, I only wanted him out of my life. I'd never wished
him as good as dead.

But on Redso's third night home, to my dismay, he finally
did seem to snap out of it—and with bells on.

It woke me up, and then wouldn't let me sleep. He and Billy
were fucking like demons down in the basement. As far as I
knew, this was the first time in three months that they'd managed to reunite their starving genitals. And by the sound of it,
they were making up for lost time. Well, I thought, three

cheers for them—and sank back into my pillows. While I happened to know that their bed was located almost directly below the sofa in the living room, the drumlike resonance of the basement made it sound like they were humping right under my box springs.

And if Redso's puppylike yips, Doberman barks, and deep-chested leonine growls were any indication, his depression was already history.

"YOU'RE SURE Frank wants him at the wedding?"

"Arnie, I discussed it with him just this morning. I told him how much better Redso's been doing—and Frank said, fine then, bring him along."

"But he can't stand Redso."

"Maybe he figures the more the merrier. Who knows what goes on in Frank's mind? Anyway, I pretty much insisted on Redso coming. If *anybody* ever needed a little vacation, it's Redso, right? After the hell he's been through."

I bore down on my crutches through my calfskin gloves.

Billy stooped with her shovel and flung, with a grunt, another load of powdery snow to the side of the driveway. Three inches of the stuff had fallen overnight; more was expected tomorrow. This was a chore, it seemed to me, that Redso should have volunteered for. But he was off in Billy's car this afternoon, ostensibly looking for work. Well, maybe he was and maybe he wasn't; I was taking everything Redso said and did these days with a careful grain of salt. He was alive again, no doubt about that—sprung from his depression like Lazarus from his tomb—and doing a fairly good job of acting the part of a fairly sane man. Just yesterday Redso had practically gone down on his knees in apology for ripping me off. He couldn't remember, he claimed, just which rock shop he'd taken the stolen goods to—his memory was riddled with blank spots—but he swore up and down that he would somehow make it up to me. He even suggested that, as soon as he got a job, I could start garnishing part of his wages, if that seemed fair to me. Well, what more could I ask for? And what better proof could there be than this unprecedented show of remorse that Redso was indeed on the road back to sanity? And yet I wasn't convinced. These past couple of days there had been an edginess, a restlessness, a hint of potential explosiveness about Redso that was impossible to ignore—never mind that it seemed to be slipping right past Billy's radar undetected. But maybe that radar of hers wasn't operating at all. Maybe, in her desperate need to believe that Redso was going to finally be all right, Billy had unconsciously switched it off.

"You should've waited for Redso to do this," I told her.

"Oh, I don't mind." A bloom of condensed breath puffed from Billy's smile. "I've got so much extra energy these days, I don't know where to *put* it all. Who knows? Maybe it's like *The Picture of Dorian Gray*. You know: the calmer Redso becomes, the more manic *I* seem to be getting."

Billy laughed, stooped, and flung away more snow. She was wearing, along with Redso's goofy pointy-headed stocking cap, a pair of sunglasses. As odd as they appeared in this setting, they served a purpose. The sun was high in the cloudless blue sky, and the glare from the glittering snow—like a plain of crushed diamonds all around us—was blinding.

I poked a hole in the snow with the blunt rubber tip of a crutch.

"You think he'll behave himself up in Chicago?" I said.

"Well, sure. To a point. I mean, we wouldn't want him to *completely* behave, would we? Then he wouldn't be Redso."

I deepened the hole until I saw some brown grass. "I don't know, Billy. The thing is, Redso's so damned *volatile*. Aren't you worried at *all* that he might make some kind of scene up there?"

"No. Are you?"

I had to be careful how I answered. It was almost certainly a doomed hope, but nothing could have been sweeter, or more rife with possibility, than to somehow shunt Redso aside, and make this weekend trip to Chicago with Billy all to myself.

"Maybe I'm just being suspicious," I said. "But he *has* seemed a little more worked up since yesterday. Haven't you noticed?"

She aimed those sunglasses at me. "No. I haven't. What's he been doing, specifically?"

"For one thing, his talk has been getting wilder, more grandiose. Hell, last night at dinner you would have thought he was Napoleon, plotting out the conquest of Europe."

Billy leaned on the butt of her snow shovel. "Arnie, he just got out of a three-month stint in the mental hospital—not to mention a terrible depression. *Naturally* he's bubbling over with plans and enthusiasm. My God, if you were in his shoes wouldn't *you* be feeling pretty effervescent?"

"I suppose so," I said with a shrug. "But it's not easy knowing exactly what's going on with Redso. I mean, does he really appear entirely normal to you?"

"What's entirely normal? Especially for Redso? All I know is, he's *living* again. And if you want to stand there and analyze it to death, you go right ahead. But I'm just not in the mood to look that gift horse in the mouth, all right?"

I stood uselessly by for a spell as Billy shoveled clear another patch of the driveway.

"So do you figure he's been taking his lithium?"

"Yes," Billy said, plainly aggravated now. "He's been taking it religiously."

"How do you know?"

"Because I've been checking the bottle every morning. And the pills are disappearing like clockwork."

"But how do you know they're disappearing down his throat?"

Billy stood up straight and regarded me through those opaque sunglasses; it bothered me that I couldn't see her eyes.

"What are you doing, Arnie?"

"I . . . nothing. Hell, I'm just . . ." I squeezed my crutch grips, gave a roll to my shoulders. "I just want to make sure that everything's going to be copasetic tomorrow, that's all."

"Everything *will* be copasetic, all right? And if not . . . well, you can just hold me personally responsible."

I wasn't sure what Billy meant by that, exactly—what sort of promise was actually contained there—but made sure to make a mental note of it anyway.

Then I told Billy that I needed to get some things in order before we took off on our trip tomorrow, and left her puffing and grunting in the snow.

BY THE TIME we reached Litchfield, Illinois, barely a quarter of the way to Chicago, the blizzard was raging full force. The world had contracted to a malevolent tunnel; our side of

Highway 55 was nothing but a treacherous shifting alleyway of white; snow wasn't so much falling as exploding against the windshield; and it had begun to feel to me like a daredevil risk to push the speedometer much past twenty. Most of the road signs were completely bearded over, and the only suggestions of a landscape were the lonely humps of snow-shrouded cars abandoned on both sides of the highway. We might have been anywhere or nowhere at all, and there was nothing to be done —despite the wicked pounding in my knees and hips—but to keep on driving.

Redso, utterly unfazed by the crisis, continued to belt out song after song from the backseat in his lusty trained baritone. Having first regaled us with a medley of old show tunes from *South Pacific, Oklahoma!, Carousel,* and *My Fair Lady,* he'd then taken us on a musical tour of America. Starting with "New York, New York," "I'll Take Manhattan," and "Give My Regards to Broadway," he veered down the eastern seaboard with "Carry Me Back to Old Virginny," "Nothing Could Be Finer Than to Be in Carolina," and "Georgia on My Mind," turned west with "My Old Kentucky Home" and "The Tennessee Waltz," stopped off at home for the obligatory "Meet Me in St. Louis" and "The St. Louis Blues," and having sojourned briefly on the West Coast with "California, Here I Come" and "I Left My Heart in San Francisco," swung back east again by way of "Route 66," and headed south to "Dixie," where he segued, quite naturally, into a selection of Civil War songs. Billy and I, transfixed by the danger we were in, had long since stopped singing along. And now, midway through Redso's booming rendition of "Rally 'Round the Flag, Boys," I asked him if he couldn't please can it for a while.

"Would you prefer I sang a Confederate song?"

"I'd prefer you shut the hell up and let me concentrate."

"Ooh! That hurts, Arnie. That really does hurt. I was hoping my little concert was affording you some pleasant distraction."

I glanced into the rearview. Redso's silhouette, in that peaked stocking cap, had a sinister, gnomelike look.

"Redso," I said, "the last thing I need right now is distraction."

"Aw, come on, Goldman. You're not afraid of a little blizzard, are you?"

"You'd better believe I'm afraid."

"Well," Redso said, and began to sing again: " 'Whenever I feel afraid, I whistle a happy tune—' "

"Redso, please," Billy said, getting her umpteenth cigarette lit. Between the two of them the car was as smoky as a battlefield. "Will you just do as Arnie says? He's having a hard enough time as it is."

"Oh yeah? Sorry to hear that, Arnie. And I'll bet your legs are just killing you, aren't they? The way you've been sitting, all clenched up like a fist over that wheel."

"They're fine," I lied.

"Are they?" Billy asked me.

I shrugged, and kept my eyes on what I could make out through the furious heavings and swirlings of snow against the windshield. Beyond the reach of the headlights, the highway simply vanished.

"So what is it now?" Redso asked. "Three hours?"

"More like four."

"And we're how far?"

"We just passed Litchfield. Not that I saw it."

"Just Litchfield? Jesus, Arnie—why don't you step on it a little? How much are you doing up there, anyway?"

"Twenty."

"Oh, brother! What time's the wedding tomorrow?"

"Ten," Billy said.

"Shit. We'll be lucky if there's any wedding cake left."

"We'll be lucky if we get there at all," I said, and then the car began a dreamlike slide. There was a low *whoosh*, a sickening sense of release, and the Toronado was floating down the highway sideways. I reared up in my seat, jiggled the brake-accelerator rod with my right hand, and with my left rolled the steering knob in contradictory directions—until the hood of the car, like the back of a reluctant whale, finally righted itself. I sank back behind the wheel, unable to suppress a groan. Pain hammered in my hips. I let the speedometer dip to ten.

"Having problems up there?" Redso asked me.

"Redso, why don't you just fucking cram it for a while?"

Redso yelped. "Oh, mercy! Did you hear that, Billy? The vitriol? The poison? I think our boy's just a wee bit uptight. Maybe you oughta give him a little neck massage or something. Would you like that, Arnie? The touch of those amazing magic fingers? Or would that blow your concentration entirely?"

Again I glanced into the rearview. Redso's pointy-headed shadow looked positively demonic.

Billy fired smoke out her nose, and craned around to glare at Redso. "You stop aggravating him," she said. "Do you hear me?" She turned around to me. "And you need a break. Even *my* legs are stiff. Also, I'm just about out of cigarettes. We should turn off at the next exit."

"Fine," I said.

"And then it's my turn to drive," Redso singsonged.

Now he wasn't in the rearview at all. That threw me for a loop—as if Redso's disembodied voice had been coming out of nowhere—until I realized that he must have been lying on the seat.

"Forget it, Redso," I said. "I don't trust you to drive."

"What? Oh, for chrissakes, Goldman! I'm *fine*. Perfectly fine. Why the fuck can't you lighten up on me a little? Even when I'm *sane* you treat me like I'm crazy! And it's not fair, pal. It's not fair at all—*verstehen?*"

Maybe it wasn't fair. But this was certainly no time to start handing Redso the benefit of the doubt.

"*You're* the one we ought to be worried about, Goldman. A cripple like you, trying to pilot us through this soup. And don't hand me that crap about your legs not hurting you, either. You're hurting like hell, I know it. I can hear it in the oh-so-labored way you're breathing up there."

"Is he right?" Billy asked me.

"Maybe you should drive," I said.

Billy shook her head. "I'm just too completely wiped out. In fact, I need to sleep for a while after this stop."

"You're really that tired?"

She nodded. "Redso? You think you're all right to drive?"

Redso's silhouette shot upright into the rearview. "Well, I'll put it this way. I'm not tired, and my legs aren't stiff, and I'm sure as hell not a gimp. I'd say that puts me in better shape than either one of you." He drummed a tattoo on the back of my seat. "So? What do you say, Cap'n Ahab? Do I spell you, or do you keep on doing your macho routine and drive us straight into a ditch?"

I asked Billy if she'd hand me an extra prednisone.

She dug around in her shapeless cloth purse.

Redso sprang forward, his pale hawkish grinning face jutting between Billy's shoulder and mine. "Why don't you take some of my lithium, while you're at it? Might smooth out some of those nasty sharp edges, Arnie-boy."

"Maybe *you* should take some extra lithium," I said.

"Me? No. No, thanks. I've had my lithium for the day."

"Have you?"

Redso flopped back into his seat. *"Gott in Himmel!* Do you doubt me, *mein Führer?"*

I set my jaws together. Billy handed me a pill. I worked up some spit and popped it. Then, spotting a snowed-over highway sign, I took a chance, and signaled for the exit.

But there was no exit ramp to be seen—just an endlessness of white in every direction, interrupted only by the dim ghost of an overpass, a hazy pearl-string of streetlights, and a vague yellow glow to the right, on what might or might not have been the horizon. We lucked out. There, riding toward us through the murk like a gaily lit ocean liner, was a Fina station, apparently open for business. I coaxed the Toronado down into that oasis of brightness and stability, and pulled up under a neon overhang, beside a bank of gas pumps. The fluttering in my belly died down—even as the pain in my hips kicked up.

"Ich muss pissen!" Redso hollered. *"Ich muss pissen!"*

He flew into the storm, banging the door shut behind him.

Billy watched him go, her lips warily pursed. Then she roused herself, tugged her stocking cap down over her ears, left the car, and slogged to the gas pumps. I needed badly to give my screaming legs a stretch—but she'd forgotten to hand me my crutches from the back. I waited until she'd filled the tank, then lowered my window and shouted out my request.

We headed together across the parking lot, bent against the whipping wind, our boots squeaking like mice on the fresh-fallen snow.

Once inside, Billy insisted that I let Redso drive.

"Billy, he's acting up. Can't you hear it? Jesus, now he's speaking *German!*"

"It's you I'm worried about." Billy pushed her hands deeper in her coat pockets. There was a fine dusting of snow in her eyebrows; specks of it glinted on her eyelashes—and even now, in the middle of all this shit, I couldn't help envisioning how sweet it would be to lick those eyebrows, those eyelashes, clean.

"Redso's right," she said. "You're in much too much pain to drive. *Look* at you, Arnie. You can barely even stand up."

I glowered at the filthy tiled floor between my crutches. The pain in my legs was like a thick burning fluid pumping up and down between my ankles and my hips; I doubted I could stand another two minutes behind the wheel. But I wasn't about to tell Billy that.

"Please, Arnie. You've got to be reasonable. It's scary enough out there without you going paranoid on us. I mean, what's Redso going to do? He'll be in the car just like us. And one thing he's *not* is suicidal."

I kept scowling at the floor.

"Arnie, will you look at me?" Her cheeks were wet with melted snow. "I'm pleading with you, all right?"

SO NOW it was Redso behind the wheel. Jumbled on the seat between us was the haul he'd come away with at the gas station —with my money, of course: three packages of Twinkies, several Snickers bars, a bag of pork rinds, some Cokes, and a dozen or so Tootsie-Roll Pops, which Redso claimed were even better than cigarettes as aids to concentration. Back at the station, he'd also bellied up nonchalantly to the counter with a six-pack of malt liquor; but Billy and I put up such a stink about it that he finally relented, and returned it to the cooler at the back. In my lap I held a Styrofoam cup of black coffee. A Tootsie-Roll Pop bulged like a goiter in Redso's right cheek; every few seconds, with a slosh of saliva, he'd roll it to the other side of his face. He was handling the wheel (and sometimes, just for kicks, I supposed, the extra steering knob) with the aplomb of a teenager at the controls of a video game. His back was straight. His breath pumped audibly through his big eagle nose. His eyes were narrowed and aggressively bright. He was enjoying himself, the idiot, relishing his mastery—so far—over the challenge the blizzard offered. Behind us, beneath a blanket, Billy was asleep, her breath coming and going in a slow untroubled rhythm.

"Goddammit," Redso said. "Will you knock it off?"

He looked both dopey and dangerous in that peaked stocking cap, his face a sickly blue in the reflected light of the snow.

"Knock what off?"

He plucked the sucker from his mouth. "Grinding your teeth like that."

"What do you—? I'm not grinding my teeth."

"Oh yes you are. It's like nails on a fucking blackboard. And it's distracting the hell out of me, *verstehen?* Why don't you chew on a Twinkie or something?"

I kept a clamp on my anger and stared into the storm. The sucking convolutions of the snow made it seem like we were barreling straight into the sky.

"And you can knock *that* off, too, while you're at it."

"What the hell are you talking about, Redso?"

"Pumping that imaginary brake on the floor. Maybe you don't fully realize it, Goldman, but this is a life-and-death situation we're dealing with here. I mean, are you *trying* to blow my concentration, or what?"

"Redso," I said, through rigid jaws. "I don't even *use* my foot when I drive. What do you think that rod on the steering column is for?"

Redso widened his eyes cartoonishly at the brake-accelerator. "Hmmm . . ." he said. "What *is* this contraption for?" He seized the rod, goosed the engine, and we lurched into a nauseating skid. Redso let us drift—the Toronado woozily fishtailing, the white world veering dizzily around us—and when he figured I'd had enough, stuck his Tootsie Pop back in his mouth and smartly swung us out of it. "See? You're doing it right now, *putz.* You've practically got your foot shoved right through the floorboard."

"Listen to me, Redso—"

He whipped his Tootsie Pop out of his mouth. "Don't bother protesting your innocence, Goldman! I know what goes on. There's not a thing under the sun that escapes my omni-

science, Arnie-boy. Not even the fall of the lowliest sparrow.
Not even the grubbiest machinations of the lousiest envy-eaten
cripple. So you just watch yourself, pal. You just watch yourself. Because you're not quite as smooth as you think, slick."
He stuffed his cheek full of candy again.

I looked at him closely. His blue Tartar eyes, narrowed at
the blizzard, were crazily incandescent.

"You son of a bitch," I said.

"Moi? But what could you possibly mean, kind sir?"

"When was the last time you actually took your lithium?"

He effeminately tapped a palm to the side of his face. "Oh
deah me, now let me think! Whah, it must have been the
spring, for Ah do seem to recall that the calla lilies were in
bloom . . ."

"You haven't been taking it at all, have you, Redso? What've
you been doing with it? Flushing it down the toilet?"

Redso slapped the steering wheel. *"Ach,* for chrissakes,
Goldman! Why don't *you* go volunteer for a mental castration?
You know what that shit does to you? You ever *been* on brain
medication? Haldol? Thorazine? Not to mention lithium carbonate? Well, let me just enlighten you, pal—" Redso caught
himself, and shrugged. The car slowed a little. He crunched
down viciously on his sucker, chewed, drew the white stick
from his mouth, and flipped it over his shoulder—never mind
that Billy was sleeping back there. "So, anyway. Tell me all
about it, Goldman. All those months when my brains were
leaking out of my ears—how come I never saw you? How
come you never visited me in the loony bin? I've been wondering about that quite a lot, you know."

My guts knotted.

"So, all right. Let's face it. We're not exactly Damon and
Pythias anymore, are we? But you'd think you could at least
fake it once or twice during the three months I was rotting
there in the nuthouse—for old time's sake, if nothing else. But
then again, well, you never *have* been the sentimental type,
have you?"

The terrible thing was, Redso sounded genuinely hurt.

"I did go to visit you," I said weakly.

"Yeah, once. Once!" Redso looked at me. "Well, fuck. Who
could blame you, right? There wasn't much of anything to

visit, was there? Hell, it's *boring* to have to sit there and watch some poor depressed shmuck eating his heart out, right? Like news footage of people starving in Ethiopia. Well-meaning and compassionate as you are, you can only take so much."

"Look, Redso, I'm sorry about that—"

"Oh? Sorry about that, are you? Well, that helps, let me tell you. That helps tremendously. My erstwhile best friend. A guy I loved—actually and truly loved. And who I thought loved me." Redso tightened his mouth bitterly as he squinted at the storm. "And now he's sorry."

I sat in pained silence, gazing into the sucking, swirling chaos all around us—where, crazily enough, I would have much preferred to be.

And then Redso, skipping into a different groove, started whistling. It was Brahms' Lullaby.

"Ah, listen to it!" he said, cupping a hand to the side of his stocking cap. "The sound of a wood nymph, gently snoozing in her bower! Funny thing is, though, Billy usually snores like a steam shovel. Especially after she's been drinking. But of course, I guess you must already know that." Redso smiled at me. "Of course, I'm using the verb 'to know' both in the cognitive and the biblical sense. Or am I wrong?"

I stopped breathing.

"Something the matter, Goldman? You're suddenly so quiet."

It was the last thing I would have expected, but now that the dreaded monster had finally reared its head, I felt no panic at all. I felt, in fact, quite clearheaded, ready and willing to spar. Even if Billy *had* told him the truth—and why on earth would she do that?—it would simply be her word against mine. I readjusted my aching legs and settled back against the seat. Redso would get nothing more out of me than my rank and serial number.

"Just what are you driving at, Redso?"

"How about some of that coffee?"

I handed it to him. He took a swallow and passed back the cup.

"Allow me to set the scene for you," he said. "There I am, locked up in the nuthouse for three straight months—and there you are, holed up with Billy for all those long lonely nights in that claustrophobic little house. Now, people being what they are, and the flesh being weak, and given the fact that you apparently no longer feel bound by the traditional loyalties and duties of friendship—"

"You really *are* out of your goddamned mind, Redso, you know that?"

Redso laughed. "Boy, talk about ad hominem remarks! And so what if I *am* out of my goddamned mind? Aren't you begging the fucking question?"

"You haven't *asked* the fucking question!"

"Oh really, Goldman. Do I have to paint you a pornographic postcard?"

I finished off the coffee and dropped the cup to the floor.

"This is completely pathetic, Redso. If you really want to be jealous, can't you at least come up with a plausible suspect? I mean, Jesus! You think Billy would even consider a thing like that with me?"

"Why? Because you're a gimp?"

"Yeah. There's one good reason. Because I'm a gimp."

"I'm surprised at you, Arnold. I had you pegged for a lot more arrogant than that. I mean, just look at your credentials. A fine, upstanding, nonviolent Jewish boy, with no criminal record, no psychiatric record, money coming out of his ass, and a nice rosy no-risk future spreading out before him just like Disneyland! None of which you can exactly say about me, can you? Hell, why *shouldn't* Billy go for you? Besides, you think she's actually *repelled* by a little chronic illness? I'd say it was more like some kind of sick *attraction*, wouldn't you?" Redso laughed. "Christ, take you and me out of the picture, and she'd probably be out trolling for ass at the nearest VA hospital."

I winced at the meanness of that—vicious even by Redso's standards.

More snowed-over humps of abandoned cars slid past us. The attrition rate seemed to be climbing.

Redso punched the radio on. A shrieky blast of heavy-metal music ripped through the car.

I punched the radio off. "Billy's trying to sleep."

"Shit," Redso said. "If she can sleep through that last little donnybrook, she's out for the count."

He punched the radio on again.

I punched it off.

We locked eyes.

"Don't you think you ought to watch the road?" I said.

Redso grinned at me. And then, like a bratty child, he reached for the radio again. I grabbed his wrist and gave it a mean squeeze, a violent twist. Redso yelped. But I held on, still bending his wrist the wrong way.

"Are you going to cut that out?" I said.

"Jesus—will you let up? You're breaking my fucking arm."

"Are you going to cut that out?"

"Yeah, yeah. I swear."

I let go.

"Jesus," Redso said, petulantly rubbing at his wrist. "Where'd you get all the upper-body strength, anyway? From all the marathon jerking off you do?"

"Just drive," I told him—and realized then what a mindless move that had been on my part, given the perilous mess he was trying to steer us through.

We picked up speed. Redso hunkered down over the wheel. His breath sawed furiously through his nostrils. "I'm telling you one thing, *putz*. I've had it with this fucked-up little threesome of ours. I don't *like* the idea of you slinking around behind my back, like some lousy Iago—no, make that Richard the Third—hatching your cruddy little schemes. I'm telling you, Goldman, once this trip is over, and we're back in St. Louis, something's got to give."

I grunted.

"Yeah, something's got to give, all right."

What was giving way at the moment, however, was my bladder. I pressed my thighs together and cursed myself for all the coffee I'd drunk. It irked me to have to ask a favor of Redso now—but of course, I had no choice.

"Redso, could you take the next exit?"

He didn't reply.

"Redso."

He looked at me, all innocence. "Sorry. Were you speaking to me?"

"Will you take the next exit? I have to pee."

He threw his hands up over the wheel. "Oh no! Say it ain't

so, Joe! That's just so damned *inconvenient,* Arnie. The thing is, we're making such good time right now, I'd hate like hell to have to slow us up. Wedding's at ten tomorrow, don't forget. Tell you what. Why don't you just whip out that diminutive little thing of yours and pee into that coffee cup down there?"

"I'm not pissing into any goddamned coffee cup."

"No? Well, suit yourself. It's a free country, isn't it? But *damn.* I'd sure hate to see you spring a leak all over the fine upholstery in this car. This stuff *is* genuine leather, isn't it? Nothing but the best—right, Mr. Goldbucks?"

"Just do it, you fuck."

Redso shrugged.

We drove on through the raging white formlessness. But there was no highway sign of any kind to be seen.

Now I was squirming. "Redso, just pull over."

He listed toward me. "Come again? I can barely hear through this stocking cap."

"Pull over, dammit. I can't hold it anymore."

Redso smiled serenely. "Anything you say, Arnie-boy. Anything you say."

He jerked the car to the right, hit the brakes, and then we were stopped. The blizzard took on a thunderous hush. The wildly whipping sheets of snow seemed to thicken, tighten around the car.

Redso raised his colorless eyebrows. "What are you waiting for?"

"I need my crutches."

"Well, heck! Why didn't you just say so?"

He craned over the seat, puffed as he paddled around, then slid back down, crutches in hand, and passed them to me.

"Thanks."

"Hey, don't mention it. You know me, pal. Always ready to lend a hand to the handicapped. Even when I'm terribly busy, or preoccupied with my own little problems—so trivial, really, compared to what people in your condition have to so hero-ically put up with every day—I try to lend what small assis-tance I can to those less fortunate than myself. I help blind people across the street. I give piggyback rides to quadriple-gics. I buy pencils from the hearing-impaired. And sometimes,

if I'm feeling especially altruistic, I might even ask a legless or
armless girl out for a date—"

I slammed the door on that manic blathering.

I should have thought to put on my hat. But too late for
that. The wind, tearing in from all directions, maliciously bit at
my face, ears, neck. I hobbled a few steps from the car, faced
the snow-drifted shoulder, pulled a glove off with my teeth,
and managed, with fingers already going numb, to work down
my fly. I hunched my shoulders and let it loose.

As I was zipping up, Redso revved the engine.

I didn't think anything of it.

But when I got myself turned around on my crutches, the
ruby taillights of the Toronado, retreating down the highway
ten or fifteen yards away, were already going dim, and soon
were blotted out completely by the blizzard.

"MR. GOLDMAN? You awake back there?"

The voice, deep and gentle, was coming out of the blizzard.

"Mr. Goldman? You're going to have to wake up. I need
some help with the directions right about now."

I opened my eyes, and through the haze that filmed my
vision, struggled to locate myself. I was not, as it had seemed,
still standing hunched by the side of the highway, my face
frozen in a gargoyle's grimace, my teeth uncontrollably chattering, squinting and squinting into that merciless stinging on-
rush of white, and wondering, now panicked, now enraged, if
I could actually be allowed to die in such an unjust, pointless,
and just plain ridiculous way. No: I'd been saved, evidently. I
was slumped in the back of a car, in a pool of thick golden
light, the rumble of an engine all around me, breathing a stink
of old leather marinated in stale cigars. It was a taxicab. There
was the cabbie ahead of me. A dark blue cap sat on his woolly
white head; his neck was fat, honey brown, deeply corrugated,
and dotted with large black freckles—details my dreaming self
couldn't possibly have invented. Moreover, my knees and hips
were banging brutally, insistently, as if to assure me that this,
indeed, was reality.

Pieces of my ordeal returned to me. Standing in that raging
white formlessness, both numb and aching from the crown of
my bare head to the soles of my feet, my crutch sticking out

into the narrow drifting road like a hitchhiker's exaggerated thumb. A ride in a different car than this, a man and a woman up front, country music on the radio, through still more whirling, unending blizzard. The hard clanging light of a truck stop. A bank of pay phones. The worried face of a waitress who plucked a pencil from the depths of her layered, lacquered hair. Coffee in a white porcelain cup. A big elderly black man in a dark blue uniform, shaking my shoulder where I sat in a booth.

"Mr. Goldman? You gotta wake up."

"I'm up," I managed to croak.

Now I remembered the cabbie's name (Mr. Hamilton) and the sum we'd agreed on for the ride to St. Louis (a hundred and twenty-five dollars) and, don't ask me why, the fact that he was a die-hard White Sox fan. I clenched my teeth and pushed up higher against the deep spongy seat. The cabbie peered at me in the rearview. Those moist sad yellowish eyes seemed at that moment the kindliest pair of human eyes I'd ever seen.

"You holdin' up all right?" he asked me.

"Yes."

"Well, good. We're on Big Bend Boulevard now, like you said. But I'm going to need some help on where to turn."

"At Oxford. Half a mile or so. On the left. Near a Vicker's station." That catalogue of details wore me out.

"Gotcha."

I must have dozed off again, for now, without any sense of transition, I was lying on the seat of the stopped taxi. The door was open. The cabbie's broad back was blocking the sun as he hovered in front of me.

"We're here," Mr. Hamilton said. "1740 Oxford. You need any help?"

I shook my head, groaned as I pushed myself upright, and still groaning, scooted to the door. I set my crutches out in front of me, and somehow struggled to my feet. I hung over my crutches, breathing hard.

"You sure you don't need some kind of help?"

I nodded.

The cabbie inspected me with such genuine concern that I wondered just how bad-off I really looked. His face was all burnished brown folds and bulges spotted with dime-size black freckles.

"I'm uh . . . going to have some trouble getting my wallet out," I said. "Could you get it? The left hip pocket."

Mr. Hamilton pursed his lips. Then, very delicately, he extracted my wallet.

"What did we agree on?"

"One hundred and twenty-five. That's all the way from Springfield, now. Plus taking the weather into account." He looked uncomfortable with that plump wallet in his hands. "I'd charge you less. But you know, with nobody to carry on the way back . . ."

"What've I got there?"

He frowned as he counted. "One sixty," he said. "Exact."

"Take it," I told him.

"You mean all of it?"

I nodded.

"You sure about this?"

"Yes."

"Well, now. That's one hell of a tip, Mr. Goldman."

"You did me one hell of a favor."

Once inside the house I popped two prednisones and several aspirins. Then I carried the phone on its long white cord, clamped under an arm, to the living room, dropped it on the carpet in front of the sofa, then lowered myself to my back, clenching my teeth against the pain. Still, this arrangement had a purpose: I was afraid that if I crashed out in my bedroom, and Billy called, I'd be unable to hobble to the phone in time.

I shut my eyes. I was back in the rumbling Toronado, trapped in the malevolent blue light of the blizzard. Redso was at the wheel, grinning at me demonically under his pointy-headed stocking cap, his face distorted like a Goya grotesque by the bulge of that Tootsie-Roll Pop in his cheek—and until the moment I finally slid off into a black and dreamless sleep, what kept me awake was the longing for murder in my heart.

I GRABBED THE PHONE on the second ring.

"Yeah."

"Arnie? Is that you?"

I made a noise deep in my throat.

"God! Thank God you're home! When—how did you get there? Are you all right?"

"I've . . . felt better."

"What? I can barely hear you."

"I'm all right."

"You sound awful."

"I'll . . . be fine."

Billy's tongue made a gluey click against her palate. She wetly sniffed. "I've just been sitting here, driving myself crazy, imagining the most horrible things . . ."

"Where are you?"

"Some motel room. In Peoria."

"Peoria?"

"Never mind about that right now. Tell me how you got home."

My hips suddenly seized up. My pelvis wrenched, my back arched, and I shouted, dropping the phone.

When I finally got the receiver back to my ear, Billy was still talking.

". . . don't even try if you can't. All right? Arnie? Are you there?"

"Yes."

"It's really bad, isn't it?"

"Mm."

"That son of a bitch! That fucking *bastard!* He—my God, you could have died!"

"Come on, Billy . . ."

"Come on what? You don't think so? You don't think people can freeze to death in blizzards?"

I let that ride.

"How did you get home?" she said.

I told Billy what had happened, although not in much detail.

"Shit," she said. *"Shit!* What if those people hadn't picked you up?"

"I guess it's pretty hard . . . to pass up a cripple in a blizzard."

Her feathery breath pumped into the phone. "When did the cab get you home?"

"Not long ago."

"Did you take some extra prednisone?"

"Yes."

"Has it helped?"

"Not yet."

Billy was intensely silent.

"Billy? What the hell are you doing in Peoria? And where's Redso?"

"Orbiting the moon, for all I know. Or care."

I frowned at that, but said nothing.

"He drove us here," she went on, "after he ditched you out in the snowstorm. And don't ask me why. And I must've really been out like a light. Because when I woke up, here I was, in this damned Red Roof Inn. And there Redso was, manic as all hell, chugging on this bottle of Mad Dog wine, walking all over the furniture, practically foaming at the mouth . . ." She paused, and stickily swallowed. "And of course, you were missing. And when I asked him where you were, what'd happened, he just kept handing me all this *bullshit*. You jumped out of the car for no reason, you insisted he drop you off at some truck stop—his story kept changing, and of course, none of it made any sense. And then, when I realized what Redso had actually done to you . . ."

I waited.

"I don't remember what I said to him, Arnie. But it must've been pretty good. Because then he started getting rough with me."

"Oh no . . ."

"Did you tell him? You know. About us?"

"Of course not."

"Well, he seemed to know. Somehow."

"What do you mean, he got rough with you?"

"He didn't actually hit me. He just kept pushing me—you know, very threatening, shoving me around the room while he ranted and raved. But it scared me, Arnie. I mean, it really scared me. Because I *know* he wanted to let loose and actually hurt me. I could see it in his eyes—" Billy's voice broke. Again I heard that gluey click. "Anyway. I started fighting back. You know, scratching and kicking like a wildcat. And he finally backed off. And then I told him to get out—to just get the fuck out of my life."

"What?"

"I told him I'd had it. That I couldn't stand it anymore. That he could just go ahead and *drown* in his insanity, if that was what he wanted, but I'd be damned if he was going to drag me down with him—" Billy clammed up. For a moment she was silent, maybe forcing back the impulse to cry. Then she went on, in a low roughened voice. "So then he left. Just like that. He just turned around and left the room. And that was hours ago, Arnie. I've been calling you ever since. And now . . . I don't think he's coming back."

Prickles of dangerous hope scuttled up and down my spine.

"Do you *want* him back, Billy?"

"No. *No.* I meant what I told him, Arnie. This was it. I just can't *take* it anymore. He's been wrecking my life, tearing me to pieces, fucking me up for long enough—" She fiercely sniffed. "Anyway . . . this was it."

I kept carefully silent.

There was a sucking sound, a harsh release of breath. She must have lit a cigarette. "So he's taken your car."

I closed my eyes as I absorbed that piece of news. "Any idea where?"

"No. But Arnie? What do we do about it? Should we . . . do you want to call the police?"

I had to think about that. On the one hand, it wouldn't be a bad trade at all: my Toronado for Redso's absence from my life. But on the other hand, if Redso was still in possession of my car, what was to prevent him from roaring straight back to St. Louis?

"Christ, I don't know, Billy. What do *you* want to do?"

"He's dangerous," she said. "He's as manic as I've ever seen him, Arnie. He could easily hurt himself—or someone else. Also, he was drunk. I . . . it doesn't look like we have any choice."

"No," I said. "It doesn't."

"Then it's settled. I'm calling the police as soon as we're done talking. What's the license number?"

I gave it to her.

"Then it's settled," she said again.

My hips were throbbing a little less viciously now; I was no longer a mass of tensed muscles.

"Arnie? I'm just so sorry. God, I'm so sorry! It was all my stupid, blind, idiotic fault. You warned me, and I wouldn't listen. And I should have *known*. But . . . I guess I wanted so *desperately* to believe he was really getting better—" She roughly cleared her throat. "And what happened? He ended up almost killing you because of it."

"Billy, cut it out. It wasn't your fault."

Her breath kept beating into the receiver.

"So what next?" I said. "What are you going to do?"

"I don't know. Try to get to the wedding, somehow. It's only seven o'clock. Maybe I've still got time. I'll find out if there's a bus, or maybe a train—"

"That Visa card I lent you for the gift? Do you still have it?"

"Yes."

"Well, use it. Take a cab."

"But it'd be so expensive. There must be a bus—"

"Take a cab, Billy. It's the quickest way there. For godsakes, don't worry about the money."

Billy tremulously sighed. "All right." She sighed again. "And . . . just thank you, Arnie."

I wasn't sure what exactly she was thanking me for—my generosity, my refusal to blame her for what had happened, or something more. But I narrowed my eyes at the ceiling, filled now with a mounting, almost giddy sense of triumph.

"And after the wedding?" I dared to ask her. "What's going to happen then?"

Billy didn't answer right away.

"Well, what do you think?" she finally said. "I'm coming home."

PART THREE

Eight

ON THE NIGHT she returned from Chicago, very late, as I lay awake in bed with my pounding arthritis, Billy entered my room, and without a word to me, dropped her bathrobe to the floor, slid beneath the covers, and pressed her trembling body into mine—less like a woman making a sexual advance, it seemed to me, than like a child, terrorized by a nightmare, seeking the mute bodily comfort of a parent.

The great transition took place as quietly as that. Afterward there were no agonized soul-searching sessions, no operatic vows of undying love, no tears. Instead we eased into our new roles with such a comfortable, friendly, matter-of-fact simplicity, we might have been an old married couple merely getting past some initial awkwardness following a long separation. In the mornings we'd have our coffee, share a newspaper, and then Billy would drive off to her auditions and recording sessions, and I would be left to my rocks; in the evenings she'd whip up one of her spectacular meals, and afterward we'd settle down to an old movie on the VCR, an amiable fight across a Scrabble or Monopoly board, or a couple of good books against a bank of pillows on my bed—and except, maybe, for the frequency of our careful and delicate lovemaking, no outside observer could have guessed that we were on a kind of honeymoon. There was no big mystery in that. After all, we'd been sharing the same roof, the same scarifying problems, and much of our intimate lives, for years now. And right from the start Billy and I had been friends.

It was sweet beyond description, all right, and gratifying to the bone. But on the other hand, it wasn't exactly *Wuthering Heights*. Did I feel at all cheated by the lack of violent passion? Maybe. And maybe, too, I was jealous of the wild romantic tempests that had been Redso's stock in trade—for what man wouldn't secretly prefer to think of himself, in the sexual arena, anyway, as some primitive Heathcliff type? But that kind of madness, I knew, was the last thing Billy needed now. And besides, could I help it if I happened to be a mostly decent guy? Caring, thoughtful, reliable, sane? Weren't those the very aspects of me, dull and stolid as they were, that kept Billy, like a freshly reissued miracle, returning to my bed every night? Didn't she require from me precisely those things she could never get from Redso—not the least of them being a warm safe island of stability where she could finally get herself some peace of mind? *Of course,* I kept trying to assure myself. *Of course.*

But underneath the placid surface of it all, I was boiling. How I did it, I don't know, but mostly I managed to keep my delirious joy, my ceaseless amazement, my abject gratitude, and my superstitious terror of seeing it all evaporate at any instant, like a mirage, to myself. For in the weeks that followed that fateful and fortunate blizzard, Billy remained in such a precarious emotional state that I was afraid of rocking her too far in one direction or the other.

Of course her fragility was easy to account for. Actually, I was surprised that she seemed as put together as she did. Not only had Billy been brutally traumatized by her abduction to Peoria, and all that followed, but she was now caught up in the difficult twin struggle to evict Redso from her heart, and fill that wounded space with me. All the same, her mood swings worried me. It was almost as if, in a kind of unconscious penance for throwing him to the wolves, she'd taken on some aspects of Redso's manic-depression.

Often throughout the day, even several times an hour, Billy would veer between a glum impenetrable silence and an almost hysterical talkativeness—jabbering on and on about such irrelevancies as the peccadilloes of her clients from Southwestern Bell, the latest romantic fuck-ups suffered by Eileen Solomon or Myrna Jackoway, or what she was planning on cooking for dinner that night—anything at all, in fact, except for what was really spreading its dark wings over her mind. One minute she would be all over me, following me around the house like an affection-starved puppy, or mussing my hair and nuzzling my neck as I tried to hold up my end of a haggling session with a client on the phone—and the next thing I knew, she would be flat on her back on the sofa, a forearm slung across her eyes, her tense purple mouth twisted downward, as stonily forbidding as a sphinx. Just as worrisome, while Billy had always liked her liquor, lately she'd been drinking like a drunk. Most nights, between getting dinner started and coming unsteadily to bed, she would put away three or four stiff drinks of scotch; and more than once she'd stumbled through the door after a night out with her girlfriends, so slurrily bombed that it was impossible to carry on a sensible conversation with her. And yet despite all the heavy sedation, she could barely sleep. Under normal circumstances my stiff knees and hips would force me awake every few hours or so; but now, more often than not, it was Billy's moans, thrashings, intense somnambulistic mutterings and sudden jerky departures from the bed—to pace, or pee, or smoke a cigarette—that were jolting me awake. Of course I didn't have to ask her what was robbing her of sleep. But we seldom mentioned Redso unless Billy broached the subject, and even then, she refused to go very deeply into her feelings. And if I persisted in digging, she would put me off with her old line—now pretty suspect, I thought—about the stupidity of talking things to death.

By late winter she was becoming paranoid. She was jittery, hypersensitive; her whole system seemed to be on red alert. The ringing of the telephone made her flinch; if the mailman started clanking in the mailbox outside the door, she'd jump like she'd heard gunfire; the sounds of children playing harmlessly in the street set her strangely on edge. Also, she'd developed an obsession with the answering machine. First thing upon entering the house, Billy would fling her purse and coat to the sofa, drop to her knees beside the machine on the floor, and play back the latest messages; then she would back up the tape to listen, and listen again, to the parade of obsolete messages she'd been listening to for days. And if I asked her what she was doing, she would disingenuously reply that she was simply afraid of missing something important—and I would carefully leave it at that. But of course I knew as well as she did just whose voice she was anxious both to hear and not to hear. Several times, late at night as we lay reading, Billy insisted that she heard suspicious noises—rustlings, footsteps, scratchings—and despite my assurances that I'd heard nothing, would spring out of bed, throw on her robe, and grab a flashlight and a crutch (not much of a weapon, I'd point out to her) to investigate the backyard or the basement. And again, when she came back to bed, chastened and embarrassed, I'd sit on the impulse to ask her (not wanting to tease her, or upset her any further) just who she suspected might be haunting our house.

Things came to an unexpected head in early March. I was poking down the basement stairs with a backpack full of second-rate specimens I meant to put into storage, when I found Billy on her knees in front of Redso's writing desk. She was surrounded by maybe a dozen slanted stacks of his abandoned manuscript papers; a cardboard box beside her was already packed half full of them. A tumbler of scotch sat on the gray concrete in front of her. I could see that she'd been crying. Her face was puffy and hot-looking, and when she finally raised her face, her eyes were as pink as a rabbit's.

I crutched closer, and asked her what she was up to.

"It's been bothering me. The idea of all this stuff just sitting down here, rotting away, gathering dust . . ." She shrugged. "So I just thought I'd pack it up."

Redso's mocking presence seemed to fill the basement like a gas.

"Have you been reading any of it?" I asked her.

Billy nodded. And then a fresh fit of crying overtook her. It was a soft cry, however, a worn-out residual cry, and she managed, sniffling and swallowing, to keep talking right through it. "It's just so horribly *sad,* Arnie. Most of it's nothing but nonsense—crazy wordplay, manic raving. And what I *can* make out of it is so ugly, so mean-spirited and vicious . . . I never *knew* he had all that hate inside of him." She impatiently wiped at her eyes with her knuckles. "I shouldn't have looked at it. I should've just put it all away, without even reading a page of it—or else burned it. Except that he might show up again someday, you know, and want it all back . . ." She took a drink from her tumbler; her shoulders sagged. "I guess this looks crazy, doesn't it?"

I said nothing.

"Well, I *feel* crazy. Sometimes it's like there's someone *else* in my head, blabbering away about the same useless sickening shit, over and over again—and I can't *stop* it. And I'm drinking too much—I know that. And I can't sleep, and I can't concentrate . . ." She looked up at me then with her pink swollen eyes. "I just have to get *rid* of him somehow, you know? Just put him the fuck out of my life, once and for all. Slam the door and keep it shut. But the thing is, I don't know *how* . . ."

"Come here," I said.

Billy obediently wobbled to her feet, swayed toward me, and leaned against me, her arms hanging limp at her sides. I kissed her slippery hot cheeks, the sticky side of her mouth, the moist tip of her nose, and she wrapped her arms around both me and my lumpy backpack, and buried her face in my neck.

"Arnie?" Her voice was clotted. "Maybe this is crazy. Maybe this is the craziest thing that's ever occurred to me—I don't know. But I don't think it is."

"What's that?"

She pulled away and showed me a wan, uncertain smile.

"What would you say if we just got married?"

Nine

I'D RESOLVED to go through the ceremony on my own two feet.

Less than an hour before the wedding, in a Sunday school classroom in the basement of Temple Israel (which boasted St. Louis's oldest and largest Reform congregation), I stood without my crutches, gripping the back of a steel folding chair for support, and readied myself for another practice run.

My hips were thumping with pain, my heart was still hammering from the last excruciating attempt, and my soaked tuxedo shirt, probably ruined for the day, was sticking unpleasantly to my back—but I wasn't about to surrender now. From here to the map of ancient Israel that hung from an easel at the far end of the room, was about half the distance I'd have to go (using Billy for support) down the tabernacle aisle at the conclusion of the service. My personal best so far was once to the easel, and three shaky steps back. But hey, that wasn't exactly chopped liver. Not so long ago I couldn't have made it five paces without my crutches.

Along with all the other happy astonishments I'd been hit with recently, my arthritis had taken a breathtaking turn for the better—although just why, as always with that capricious disease, was impossible to say. Maybe my joy, my anticipation, and my general superfluity of well-being had somehow spilled over into my immune system—who knew? The fact was, I was in better shape now than I'd been since I was nine. The inflammation in my knees, which had once pumped them up like melons, had gone down to a mere sore puffiness, and even better, my hip joints had loosened up marvelously. Of course I knew that this remission, like a stretch of balmy weather in the dead of winter, couldn't be trusted to last; I meant to savor it, milk it, while I could. And what better venue for strutting my stuff than at my own wedding ceremony?

I gave the top of the chair a parting squeeze, filled my lungs with air, and as I set my right foot forward, was stopped by my mother's sharp voice.

"This is killing me," she said. "It's absolutely killing me, to have to watch this!"

"So don't watch," my father told her.

"I've got a terrific idea, Henry. Why don't you just go over there and kick him in the knees?"

"Oh, for godsakes, Doris—"

"It's just the same as encouraging him like this! Just the same!"

"Would anyone care to hear what *I* have to say?"

Both my parents turned to me. My mother, wearing a sunny floral dress and a wide-brimmed white straw hat, was ensconced in one of the child-size wooden desks that had been pushed to the side of this Sunday school classroom—so the janitor could mop the floor, I supposed. She was tiny enough to make the fit. My father stood beside her, looking—despite the elation I knew he was feeling, the sheen of Brylcream slicking down his hair, and the tuxedo he wore, which he himself had altered and pressed at the tailor shop just yesterday—as rumpled and baleful as ever. Over one arm he'd draped my meticulously folded morning coat; in the other he held the shafts of both my crutches.

I readjusted my grip on the back of the chair. "Look," I said. "Why don't you both go upstairs for a while—"

"Not until you've heard me out," my mother said, and leaned down to yank at a stocking.

I sighed.

"For twenty minutes of pure torture I had to watch this on Thursday night, Arnie—and now it's the very same thing!

What makes you think you're going to do any better this morning than you did at the rehearsal the other night?"

"Well, you know what they say in show biz, Mom. Lousy rehearsal, great performance."

"Go ahead and joke—but I'm not laughing. Why do you imagine people are coming to your wedding? To see you make a public spectacle out of your suffering? They're here to share in your happiness, Arnie—not to watch you act out the Stations of the Cross!"

I couldn't help smiling at that.

"Now, what shame could there possibly be—"

"Mom, you know how my arthritis has been improving. Why shouldn't I try and push the envelope a little?"

"Because you're just begging for a catastrophe, that's why. What happens if you fall flat on your face in front of the entire congregation? Have you thought about that? And what about Billy? Have you taken her feelings into account? This is her wedding day as much as yours—"

"Mom, Billy and I have discussed this, and it's fine with her. And if she doesn't have any objections, why should you?"

"Well, she *should* be objecting—and strenuously." My mother shifted around morosely behind her desk. "Maybe I shouldn't say this, Arnie, but it seems to me that she isn't taking this wedding very *seriously*."

That was true enough. All the fussy elaborate prenuptial planning that was supposed to make brides giddy with bliss left Billy utterly cold. In fact, the selection of the gown, the floral arrangements, the menu, and most of the rest of the conventional trappings had been largely overseen by her stalwart girlfriends, Eileen and Myrna—while Billy stood by, flipping through the catalogues or nodding at their suggestions, with a humorous detachment. She'd only been submitting to all this frilly, silly stuff for my sake.

"It's not that I don't like her, Arnie. You know I do. But she's far too soft with you. She spoils you. Anything you want to do is fine with Billy. If you told her you wanted to go jump off the Eads Bridge tomorrow morning—"

"Doris," my father said, "will you just let it drop? It's the kid's wedding day, for chrissakes."

"That's just the *point*, Henry!"

"Look," I said, and glanced at my Rolex. "It's nine-thirty now. Let's say I meet you upstairs at ten. That still gives us half an hour to get panicky together before the wedding, all right? Now, is that fair?"

"Fair enough," my father said.

"Then will you please both do me a favor and get the hell out of here?"

My mother arose from the desk. "Just where you get your bullheadedness from is a mystery to me," she said, and came over and started messing with the collar of my shirt. "Oy, God, will you look at this? It's ruined—completely soaked through with sweat."

"Where do you want your coat and crutches?" my father asked.

"Over there on the teacher's desk is just fine."

He shambled over to it, then hesitated. "You sure you can get to this stuff over here?"

"Yeah, Dad. Thanks. I'm sure."

"Well, just promise me one thing," my mother said. "Promise me that if it's too painful, you won't push it."

I promised.

My mother smiled. "Well, I don't believe you," she said.

My father took my mother by the elbow and half escorted her, half dragged her to the door.

"We'll see you upstairs at ten o'clock," my mother said. "And don't you be late."

"I won't."

"You take it easy, sport," my father told me.

And then I was alone.

The air smelled of chalk. The map of Israel hung before me like a taunt. Ringing the walls of the classroom were the letters of the Hebrew alphabet, printed on big white placards. Beyond Aleph and Beth, it occurred to me, I had no idea what those other cryptic symbols stood for; I was that unschooled in Judaism.

And yet it had been me who'd insisted on a Jewish ceremony—never mind that Billy would have much preferred a small and painless quickie with a justice of the peace. I admitted to her openly my shallow reason for it: I longed for all the ritual pomp and circumstance.

After all, hadn't I achieved the near-impossible in winning
Billy's hand? Well, by God, I wanted the world to witness it!
Like a middle-aged, balding, and epileptic Julius Caesar
marching back to Rome with his knockout teenage Egyptian
queen in tow, I wanted a big, expensive, gaudy, vainglorious,
and very public display of my triumph. So much so, that I was
the one popping for the temple fee, the reception hall, the
caterers, the musicians—the whole absurdly pricy ball of wax.
Concerning his traditional obligations on that score, by the
way, Rabbi Rubin had been uncharacteristically silent. But that
was more than fine with me. The less money the old zealot
kicked in, the less he could have to say about the proceedings.

In fact, I'd used Billy's father as my main tool in extracting
her compliance with my plans. If we weren't going to have an
Orthodox wedding (and that was certainly a moot point)
wouldn't a Reform service be vastly preferable, as far as her
father was concerned, than no Jewish service at all? Did she
really want to cause her father all the hurt, the resentment, the
conniptions he would certainly suffer if the wedding were entirely secular?

Of course not.

And so here we were at Temple Israel, where a *chuppa*, an
officiating rabbi, and a wineglass there for the smashing were
all quite properly awaiting us—not that it had mollified the
Rabbi in the least. For one thing, I wasn't exactly his first
choice for a son-in-law, as he'd made very clear to us on the
night when we'd joined him in his study to break the news.
But as he was a fair-minded and flexible man, Rabbi Rubin
explained, he was willing to overlook, for the sake of his
daughter's happiness, certain glaring deficiencies in me—my
medical condition, for one thing, which would have been a
heavy burden to place on any wife, not to mention my shameless apostasy. What he was not willing to overlook, however,
was our decision to have the wedding performed in a Reform
temple, which, as far as the Rabbi was concerned, was no more
a legitimate house of Jewish worship than a mosque, a cathe-
dral, or the stinking mud hut of a witch doctor.

In keeping with that theological viewpoint, Rabbi Rubin had
announced at first that he would have nothing to do with the
wedding at all. But after several heated interviews with Billy,

and yet another interminable meeting between the three of us in his cramped and airless study, the old man finally bent—somewhat. He told us that while he could not in good conscience attend the ceremony per se, he would be agreeable to joining us at the reception afterward (so long as it was held at the airport Marriott, which offered a kosher kitchen) and there, following the wedding supper, he would be more than willing to deliver a few short informal remarks reflecting his thoughts upon the happy occasion.

And that was how it stood.

So apparently I wouldn't have to set eyes on Rabbi Rubin until, whether he liked it or not, the *fait* was *accompli*, and I was already Billy's lawfully wedded husband. No arrangement could have been more to my liking—except, of course, not to have to deal with the old bigot on my wedding day at all.

Now I eyed the map of Israel, clenched my teeth, and gave a careful preparatory swivel to my hips—and then, wouldn't you know it, someone was rapping lightly at the door.

I expelled a furious breath. "Who is it?"

"Your father. All right if I come in for just a second?"

I gave up, came around, and lowered myself to the chair; my knees and hips were so shot at this point, I probably couldn't have made to the easel anyway. "Come on in," I told him.

So here he was again, my stoop-shouldered, baggy-faced father, shuffling through the door with a sly little smile.

"Where's Mom?"

"I gave her the slip," he said, and winked. He picked up another folding chair, brought it over and took a seat. Then, with another wink, he produced from his tuxedo pocket a half-pint bottle of Wild Turkey.

"What is this, Dad?"

"I thought maybe you could use a little nip."

"You want to get me drunk?"

"Not drunk. Just a little loosened up. You must be nervous."

Actually, I wasn't. I was plenty excited, all right, thrumming with anticipation, but no more nervous than a general surveying a battlefield where his troops already had the enemy on the run. But I didn't want to disappoint my father by admitting that. We grooms had a certain comical obligation to be nervous.

I shrugged. "I could use a drink, sure."

"Also, it couldn't hurt with your legs, am I right?"

"Right."

He uncapped the bottle, handed it to me, set an ankle across a knee, and started plucking at the sharp crease in his pant leg. "Actually, this is something sentimental on my part. Maybe I never told you this, Arnie. But on the day I married your mother, before the ceremony, your grandfather took me aside and made me drink a little whiskey—just like we're doing now. *Brumfen,* he used to call it. You never knew your grandfather, but in some ways he was a very cold fish. Very stern, very proper. And it wasn't like him—you know, a gesture like that. And I was so touched . . . well, I just never forgot it." My father smiled and rubbed at the deeply lined side of his mouth. "So, anyway, drink up. *L'chayim.*"

"Cheers," I said, and took a slug.

"Go on. Have another."

I did, and handed it back. The booze burned nicely in my belly.

"Aren't you going to join me, Dad?"

"Me? Well, why not?" He took a drink, recapped the bottle, and slipped it back into his pocket. Then he began to slowly nod to himself, as if in deep agreement with something voicing in his head. "That Billy," he said.

"What about her?"

"I just hope you appreciate how lucky you are."

"I appreciate," I said, and was surprised as my eyes misted over. Well, what the hell? I'd probably be going around with maudlin red eyes for the rest of the day—yet another comical prerogative of grooms.

"Maybe this might sound crazy," my father said, plucking again at his pant leg. "But sometimes I wish I had just a little bit of your kind of luck." He laughed and sawed a hand across his forehead like he'd caught himself at something foolish. "Will you listen to me? As if you haven't had more than your share of *tsooris* in your life. But on the other hand, you have to admit, you *have* had a certain kind of luck. The kind of luck in business I've never had, certainly. And now with you marrying

Billy . . . well, who knows? Maybe with all the rotten luck you've accumulated to your credit, it's only fair you should have a woman like Billy coming to you now."

My face warmed—for more than once during these past few months I'd succumbed to the same superstitious, infantile idea: Billy as the late consolation prize for all my unjust early sufferings. As if there were a God who kept track of such things. As if He would owe you a fair shake if there were. But I wasn't about to come clean on that.

"I don't know, Dad. You really think there's any kind of justice in any of this?"

"No. I suppose not. I suppose I'm too old to think that." He stared past me for a spell, lost in thought. Then he slapped both knees and stood up. "Well, I'll just get out of your way now . . ."

He patted me on the shoulder, and before I could draw him down into an embrace, shuffled away, plucked out the whiskey bottle, and set it on the teacher's desk. "I'll just leave this here —you know, in case you need some extra courage later on."

"Thanks, Dad."

When he opened the classroom door, there stood Frank in the hallway, his shoulders apologetically hunched, his elbow tightly clamped to the side of his tuxedo coat. Together with my father, who was my best man, Frank completed my half of the wedding party. To keep things symmetrical, Billy had recruited only two bridesmaids—the inevitable Eileen and Myrna, who'd certainly earned the honor with all the tactical assistance they'd given to the bride. It wasn't a big wedding— just sixty guests in all, mostly my relatives, along with several of my clients and their wives, a few of Billy's friends from Carnegie Mellon, and a smattering of uncles, aunts, and cousins representing the Rubin side—but there would be audience enough to confer the glory I was after.

"Am I intruding?" Frank asked.

"No, no," my father told him. "I was just leaving, as a matter of fact. We'll see you later on, all right, sport?"

My father slipped out. Frank came in, still gripping his elbow as if he were applying a compress to it. "So, how are you holding up?" he asked me—and in a tone so concerned he might have been approaching me where I lay in a hospital bed.

"Just dandy, Frank."

He frowned quizzically at that. "Really? I know how *I* felt right before I married Khadija. I'd think you'd be a quivering mass of nerves at this point."

I smiled. "What can I do for you, Frank?"

"I was wondering if we could talk for just a minute."

I sighed, and got more comfortable in my chair. Evidently the gods had put the kibosh on my workout session. I told Frank to take a seat. He did, in the chair facing me, and finally let go of his elbow.

"Where's Khadija?"

"Oh, buzzing around Billy with the rest of the women."

"Yeah? And how's Billy?"

He wagged his head. "You should see her, Arnie. She's doing her Bette Davis routine—you know, chain-smoking, wisecracking, throwing her shoulders around, putting on a very brave show. Of course she's terribly nervous. But I think she's also quite elated."

My throat filled with emotion.

"Well, that's good," I said, and swallowed.

Now Frank leaned forward, peering at me with intensity. "Arnie? I just want you to know how very happy I am."

As usual with Frank, you had to take his word for it when he told you he felt good. He looked as oppressed and dyspeptic as ever.

"Since Khadija and I got to St. Louis—well, the change in Billy has just been remarkable. And a lot of that is due to you. The way you've encouraged her to get back to her acting, for one thing. After her performance in that play the other night —Well, you saw how she looked. She positively *glowed* with self-esteem. Never mind that the director had no idea of how to do Chekhov—Billy was marvelous in her role, and she knew it, and that's exactly the sort of healthy affirmation she's been so desperately in need of. And you made that possible, Arnie. If you hadn't stepped in when you did . . . well, there's no telling how much further she would have sunk." Frank scratched thoughtfully at his Adam's apple. "Anyway. I just wanted to make sure that I thanked you properly. You know. For marrying my sister."

I laughed. "Hell, Frank. That's nothing to thank me for. This isn't exactly an act of altruism."

He remained entirely earnest. "Nevertheless, I can't help feeling a certain gratitude . . ." He pursed his fat lips and shrugged. "So? What about this Redso lunatic?"

Just the sound of Redso's name gave me a jolt. I shifted uncomfortably in my chair. It was unrealistic, I knew, but I'd been hoping to get through this day without so much as a whiff of a reminder of Redso's existence intruding to stink up the show.

"Have you heard anything at all from him?"

"No," I said, rubbing at the tops of my thighs now. "Nothing."

"Not even a phone call? Or a letter?"

I shook my head.

"Well, what have you heard from the police"

"Zip," I told him. "In fact, they finally asked Billy to stop bugging them. They promised to get back with us the minute they had some information. But so far we haven't heard a thing."

"So apparently he's just vanished?"

"Apparently."

"Huh. But it doesn't make sense, does it? Not with a maniac like that. You wouldn't think he'd give up so easily—that he'd be waging some crazy campaign of manic harassment against you by now."

"You're right. It doesn't make sense."

"Unless, of course, he's incommunicado in some mental ward or jail. Or else very sick. Or else dead. Not that I mean to be morbid. But it *is* a possibility, isn't it? As insane and reckless as he is . . ."

I grunted—and decided not to mention that the same depressing thought, along with its attendant grisly images, had been plaguing me for months: Redso's unidentified and unmourned body cooling in some city morgue, or lying in a ditch beside a highway, picked to the bone by carnivorous birds and stray dogs. Frank was right; it wasn't so far-fetched at all.

"Well, let's just hope you're finally rid of him," Frank said, and he roused himself and stood, clamping hold of his elbow again. "I'm glad we could have this talk, Arnie. I feel quite a bit better now, actually. You know. Hearing that that madman is out of the picture." He smiled. "So, I'll see you at the moment of truth. And meanwhile, you keep a tight asshole, all right?"

"I'll try," I told him, a little surprised by Frank's use of such macho barracks language. But there was no guessing what this sad peculiar man was likely to say—which was one reason, maybe, that I rather liked having Frank around.

Once he'd moseyed off, I stood behind my chair again, and tried to steel myself for another painful stagger across the room. But my heart was no longer in it. Redso had trespassed too far into my thoughts. Suddenly I was uncomfortable being alone.

I wobbled to the teacher's desk and treated myself to a final swig of whiskey. Then I slipped on my tuxedo coat, took up my crutches, and left the classroom to confront—as corny as it sounded as it voiced inside my head—my destiny.

RINGED, PROMISED, wedded and blessed, then kissed, kidded, mazel-toved and back-slapped to near exhaustion, I sat at the head table, finishing off my plate of kosher chicken, content for the moment to be basking alone in my glory amid a patch of empty chairs. Billy, who should have been seated to my right, was down below in the clamorous reception hall, working the tables like a hyperkinetic social director, while Rabbi Rubin, who should have been seated on my left, was off somewhere in the hotel, putting the finishing touches on his after-dinner remarks. My parents were off in a huddle with my Uncle Duke and Aunt Sunny down by the bandstand, where the four elderly musicians were wheezing their way through an instrumental version of "We've Only Just Begun." The very awfulness of the music had me smiling; my mood was that expansive, that benign.

My performance at the ceremony had gone off without a hitch—which is to say, I hadn't fallen flat on my face. There were a couple of times, however, when I did come close—such as the moment when I arrived beneath the tentlike *chuppa*, passed my crutches to my father, and took my first close look

at my breath-stopping bride. The sight of Billy in that simple
silver sheath of a gown, with her head adorned only by a small
white lace tiara and some artfully scattered sprigs of baby's
breath, and that novel touch of mascara that so dramatically
accentuated her dark flashing Nefertiti eyes, all fell like a sweet
stunning blow on my solar plexus—and I weaved. But watchful Billy discreetly grasped my upper arm, steadied me, and
kept me propped up that way against her shoulder for the rest
of the ceremony. Then, at its conclusion, when it came time
for me to smash the wineglass under my heel, I damned near
toppled again. Like an idiot, I'd forgotten to practice that part
of the ritual—and now I could only wing it. I raised my right
foot as high as it would go, brought it down, and when I did,
such a white-hot bolt of pain roared into my head that I tee-
tered backward, almost spilling, until Billy firmly caught me
around the waist. The congregation drew in a sharp collective
breath. I glanced down, and saw to my embarrassment that
I'd completely missed the glass. Then Billy did something surprising; she threw me a sidelong smirk, and stomped on the
wineglass with her own silvery heel. There was a short shocked
silence in the tabernacle. Then some wise guest decided to
applaud and whistle, and soon the whole congregation joined
in—apparently no more worried than Billy about her violation
of the ancient routine. (I was just glad Rabbi Rubin wasn't in
attendance.) We were pronounced man and wife, we kissed—
maybe a little more lingeringly than was proper—and then I
was limping crutchless down the aisle alongside Billy, leaning
into her like a blissed-out sloppy drunk, too afloat on a cloud
of euphoria to even mind my pain, and then we passed
through the sunstruck door at the back of the tabernacle, and
lo and behold, believe it or not, the incredible coup was accomplished.

Now, watching Billy circulate through the hall, I swelled
with the pride of proprietorship. Fluttering as she did from
table to table in that elegant shoulderless gown, she might
have been an anthropomorphized tulip, animated by Disney,
paying her regal respects to all the lesser flowers below. All
along Billy had chafed, albeit mostly with good humor, against
the whole idea of this conventional extravaganza—and in that
sense she was here under protest, however ironic or mild. And

yet she had risen splendidly to the occasion, was playing her role to the hilt, and, from all appearances, was having herself one hell of a good time. Just look at her now! Pausing to shmooze with every guest like a smooth politician, smiling nicely for each compliment, sweeping her hair behind her shoulders and tossing back her head to laugh at every no-doubt corny joke—my glowing, hard-working bride—my radiant silver tulip! And she was mine, all mine. My woman, my wedded wife.

I was touched by the cold hand of terror.

Billy was my wife, all right. But suddenly the word was drained of meaning. What did it actually insure? How was she any more fundamentally my own than she'd been two hours ago? All she'd really given up was her single state; her free will was still her own. I squirmed behind the table and watched Billy, with a kind of horror, as she floated so freely from table to table, from bouquet to bouquet of seated admiring guests; she could just as easily be floating out the door. What I really wanted, I realized, was something far more binding than a mere marriage contract—something closer, really, to a life sentence without parole. And even then, would I have felt safe?

I filled my champagne glass and drank half of it away.

Oddly enough, that one swallow seemed to work. A mass of shivers migrated to my tailbone, dispersed, and all of my terror was gone. Hmmm. Maybe that was only par for the course; maybe every groom on his wedding day had at least one jolt of pure panic coming to him. The band had started in with "Sunrise, Sunset." I smiled at the selection, wondering how many more times this afternoon they would regale us with that creaky Jewish crowd-pleaser—and was utterly serene again.

But then, like an assassin dispatched to do away with that serenity, here came Rabbi Rubin, hurrying along behind the head table, pointedly ignoring Frank and Khadija where they sat (since arriving at the reception, he'd been giving both Frank and his wife the widest of berths), then took the chair beside me, nodding as he sat, and slapped a manila folder onto the tablecloth between us.

"So?" my new father-in-law said. "Tell me. How does it feel to be an old married man?"

"Just great, Rabbi. How does it feel to be the father of the bride?"

"Oh, not bad, not bad . . ." he answered vaguely. Then he patted twice, with meaningful emphasis, the top of his manila folder with those enormous thick-fingered hands.

I would have assumed that the father of the bride had thought to bathe today; yet the evidence pointed against it. His pawlike hands looked as filthy as ever, the nails still underscored with blue-black grunge. Also, the old man gave off a musty odor, like an unaired library. In accordance, I supposed, with his general protest against today's heretical proceedings, the Rabbi was not wearing a tuxedo. But at least he'd put on a suit. It was a dark blue pinstriped *shmata,* as ancient and worn as the black fedora on his head. And for once his cheeks, where his ragged goatee didn't show, were cleanly shaven.

"Sorry I'm so late," he said, patting his folder again. "But I needed to add some last-minute corrections to my text. What is it they say? A true writer never finishes his work, but merely *abandons* it. Hah? Am I right about that, Mr. Goldman?"

"Sounds right to me," I said, now staring at his folder. The Rabbi had promised to deliver "just a few brief informal remarks." But judging by the thickness of his folder, those remarks were running to twenty or thirty pages.

"That's your speech, Rabbi?"

"Of course. What else?"

"Well, uh, just about how long do you expect it to run?"

"How long? Why, the right length! Which is to say, long enough for the purpose—and yet with nothing in it that's *not* to the purpose. Not a bad definition for the proper length of any piece of writing! You agree?"

I smiled as agreeably as I could and killed off my champagne. "You hungry yet, Rabbi? I asked the waiter to keep a plate warm in the kitchen."

"The truth is, I don't seem to have much of an appetite. Who knows?" The Rabbi laughed. "Maybe I'm as nervous as the bride today! Also, I'd rather not deliver my remarks on a full stomach. You know, the blood goes to the belly, leaves the brain . . ."

I showed the old man a smile full of teeth. Was this perfect?

Did this take the fucking cake? Here I'd rented out this hall at the airport Marriott and paid the whopping premium for the use of their kosher kitchen, and all for the sake of Rabbi Rubin —surely the only guest at this affair who gave a shit if his food was kosher—who apparently wouldn't be eating.

I refilled my glass with champagne.

"You know," the Rabbi said, "I've been anxiously looking forward to this occasion on a number of scores."

He couldn't have meant my marriage to Billy—or could he?

"Looking forward to what, Rabbi?"

"To what, he says! To delivering my remarks, of course. It's been what? Nearly two decades since I last had a congregation? And without tooting my horn too loudly about it, I have to admit that I was quite the public speaker in my day. In fact, of all my rabbinical duties, I think that was the one most clearly suited to my natural strengths. Rhetoric, logic, the turning of a phrase . . ." Rabbi Rubin paused and took a sip of water. "Now, the last time Billy heard me speak from the pulpit, she must have been what? Twelve, thirteen? And in those days she was plenty impressed with my oratorical abilities, let me assure you! And guess what? Today she's going to see that her old man *still* hasn't lost his touch—not by a long shot, sonny-boy!" The Rabbi cheerfully wagged a finger at me. "You just wait and see, young man. You just wait and see." He sat back, smiling with immense satisfaction, and glanced around the hall. "So, *nu?* How did the ceremony go, by the way?"

"Fine," I answered in a gravelly voice.

"I see, I see. And the officiating rabbi? What's his name? Blum? Bloom?"

"Bloom."

"And this Bloom, he did all right?"

"He did just fine."

"And the cantor? Did you notice?"

"Notice what?"

The Rabbi laughed and shook his head. "You didn't notice? The blond hair? The blue eyes? You actually mean to say that you don't know?" He slapped the table. "Why, the man's an Irish Catholic! Hah? Have you ever heard of such a thing? Incredible—scandalous—but true! His name is Morrison,

Harrison, something like that. He makes his real living by singing in *nightclubs*, would you believe! And yet for years he's been moonlighting as a cantor at Temple Israel. *Impersonating a cantor is more like it!*" The Rabbi waited for that to sink in. "You look shocked."

"I . . . had no idea, Rabbi."

"Of course not. How could you? What do you know about what goes on in the St. Louis Jewish community? So tell me this, young man. At any point in the proceedings, did he happen to break into a rendition of 'Danny Boy'?"

I laughed.

"And yet you can sit there and claim you were just married in a Jewish ceremony?"

Oh boy. I took in a careful breath. I had to keep in mind that I was now the Rabbi's son-in-law, however bizarre and indigestible that concept was. I was going to have to coexist with him one way or another—and who could say for how long? I could easily imagine Rabbi Rubin, with his robust constitution, boyish spryness, and unsinkable self-delight, hanging on past the age of Methuselah. Wherever our future relationship was headed (most likely even further down the drain) this certainly wasn't the time to reopen hostilities.

Now Billy, thank goodness, appeared, smiling radiantly, her long shining tresses of flower-decked hair straight out of a Pre-Raphaelite painting. Her face, throat and bare shoulders were all rosily flushed—not unlike the dermatological reaction she sometimes got, I couldn't help remembering, in the throes of her sexual climaxes.

"Hey, you two," she said, and bumped my shoulder with a satiny hip. "How're you boys getting along?"

The Rabbi's face had softened in an unfamiliar way. He almost looked kindly. *"Gottenyu!"* he said. "Just look at you, Billy. You're simply—I've never in my life seen you looking half so beautiful."

Billy's smile wavered oddly. "Well, thanks, Daddy. What a terribly sweet thing to say."

The old man seemed a bit embarrassed by his outburst. He cleared his throat, nodded his hat, patted the table. "So? Have a seat, have a seat . . ."

I poured Billy some champagne, which she went for immediately. She was in a frisky mood, all right; even as she smiled benignly at her father, she surreptitiously reached below the skirting of the table, and gave my crotch a jiggle and a squeeze.

"So, *nu?* Have you eaten?"

"Not a bite," Billy said. She gave my nuts a valedictory pat, then smoothly returned her hand to the table. "I haven't had any appetite at all."

"Hah? How do you like that? Neither have I!"

"Why's that, Daddy? Did you also get married today?"

He laughed and wagged a finger at her. "No, no. The truth is, I'm just a little bit nervous about my speech."

"Oh, you'll do wonderfully, I'm sure."

"Well, probably you're right. But what is it they say? A little stagefright is good for a performance?"

"That's right," Billy told him. "You put those butterflies to work for you. Anyway, Daddy, it's too bad you missed it."

"What's that?"

"The ceremony."

"Ah."

Billy nicked her bottom lip with her teeth. "You especially should have seen Arnie, Daddy. He was so splendid and brave. Do you know he made it all the way down the tabernacle aisle without his crutches?"

"So I heard, so I heard."

"Well, don't you think that's just terrific?"

"Of course. Naturally." The Rabbi scratched at the side of his goatee. "Such a show of courage is very commendable. Very commendable indeed."

"His arthritis has been getting so much better—I'm telling you, Daddy, one of these days he's going to get off those crutches completely." Billy slung an arm around my shoulders, and took up her champagne again. "Although why Arnie's so reluctant to admit he's improving is a mystery to me."

"Well, let's not go counting our chickens," I said.

The Rabbi cast his eyes uneasily around the room. The fact that he was not the center of attention—and that my disease and I were—was clearly not to his liking. "So, Billy," he said, toying with his folder on the table. "When exactly was the last time you heard your old man make a speech?"

"Probably the last time we talked, Daddy."

Her father gave her a curious look—then seemed to decide that she'd just made a joke. He smiled. "Very good, Billy. Very good indeed. You got me there, didn't you?" He turned his smile to me. "You watch out for this woman, young man. She's nobody's fool, you know."

"I'm well aware of that, Rabbi."

Now Rabbi Bloom showed up behind us. He was a corpulent, fierce-eyed, full-bearded man who bore a disconcerting resemblance, I'd been thinking all day long, to Karl Marx. He smiled at Billy, then at me, and set a plump hand on Rabbi Rubin's shoulder—who visibly stiffened.

"Everyone enjoying themselves?" he asked us.

"We're all just ducky," Billy told him.

"Well, good. So, Rabbi Rubin? You about ready for your speech? You said when the dinner plates were cleared."

"Of course, of course. The microphone's all hooked up?"

"All hooked up."

"Well, then . . ."

"You get up there and break a leg, Daddy."

Rabbi Rubin nodded seriously at that, sighed, picked up his folder, arose from his chair, and carefully maneuvered around the bulk of Rabbi Bloom as if the man had leprosy. Then he snapped his fingers, ducked under the table, emerged with the brown paper sack he'd stashed there earlier (top secret, he'd informed me, when I'd asked him what it contained), and followed Rabbi Bloom to the podium. It was set up in the center of the table, to Billy's right. Rabbi Bloom tapped the microphone a few times, then leaned into it.

"Ladies and gentleman. If I could have your attention, please. It is now my distinct honor and great pleasure to introduce to you the proud father of the bride, Rabbi Mordecai Rubin, who's prepared some special words for this occasion." Rabbi Bloom smiled down at the guests, most of whom were up on their feet, milling about and talking. "So if we could have your undivided attention, please—and if Rabbi Rubin could stop *kvelling* long enough to find his notes—I now present to you Rabbi Rubin."

There was some applause, but it was by no means universal. The Rabbi shuffled his papers behind the microphone. He coughed significantly into a fist. But much of the crowd was still wandering and buzzing around.

Billy came to the rescue. She picked up a fork and started tapping at the side of her champagne glass. I followed suit, as did the rest of the wedding party along the head table, and before long nearly all our guests were seated at their tables and tapping at their glasses, and the reception hall was filled with a sound like a hundred wind chimes.

Rabbi Rubin smiled at the crowd. He rustled his papers. He coughed again. Then he turned his bright black eyes to the musicians on the bandstand and fixed them with a long expectant stare. Nothing happened. The Rabbi pushed up at the brim of his hat. "Gentlemen," he said. "If we could have our music, please."

The musicians stopped cold in the middle of a treacly bossa nova, conferred for a moment, and then started in, the violinist taking the lead, with the melancholy strains of the "Hatikvah," the Israeli national anthem.

THE "HATIKVAH" played on. By now the four oppressed musicians, shifting wearily in their chairs, must have slogged through more than fifty bars of it. Except for that, and the rise and fall of the Rabbi's droning voice, the hall was as silent as a morgue. Sometime back, the once-chattering, joking, gesticulating guests had finished their desserts, drunk the last dregs of their coffee, and been beaten into numb submission. This must have been something close, I thought, to what the miserable Russian masses endured each May Day, crammed into Red Square with no means of escape, during one of Stalin's notoriously endless harangues. I checked my watch for the umpteenth time. We were eighteen minutes into it, with no peroration in sight. Beside me, Billy was putting up a valiant show of strict attention, but she was fading. Several times a minute now, she would give her stiff neck a twist and reposition her butt on her chair; she was blinking so often she might have crawled out of a cave; her ashtray was mounded with butts.

Now Rabbi Rubin paused, looked up from his text, and indicated Billy with an outstretched hand.

She managed to dredge up a smile.

"When you, my daughter, were all of one year old, your dearly departed mother and I—*avra-shalom*—took it upon ourselves to prepare well in advance for this day of all days." With this, the Rabbi reached inside the podium, produced his paper sack, and drew out a crusty-looking bottle of red wine. He held it aloft. The "Hatikvah" dragged mournfully on. "At that time we had prepared for us this very bottle of wine that I now hold before you. Our plans, our fondest hopes, were that it would someday be used to sanctify your future marriage. The wine was duly ordered and duly prepared, with grapes full and bursting with sunshine from the garden, duly cleansed, and duly blessed. And just as you, my beloved daughter, grew and matured and ripened with the years, so too, did the wine within this bottle." The Rabbi stroked his goatee. "And yet, due to certain circumstances wholly unforeseen at the time—circumstances, I am sure, which do not require reiteration at the moment—the wine I now hold before you, I am sorry to say, was not the wine employed to sanctify your marriage."

"Oh Jesus," I muttered.

Billy threw me a warning look.

"Well, what do you want me to say?" I whispered. "Hooray? Thanks for the kick in the groin?"

"Just *control* yourself," she whispered, and turned back resolutely to her father.

". . . and thus I thought it better, in my fatherly concern, to withhold this bottle of wine from use in that said ceremony. That the marriage took place where it did, and in the manner that it did, has now become, as they say in the common parlance, water under the bridge, a dead horse not worth beating." The Rabbi touched a finger to his tongue, and turned a page. "And yet . . . today joy reigns supreme. And so, in that spirit of goodwill and generous reconciliation that such an occasion calls forth, we have decided to make the very best of a less than optimum situation." The Rabbi pulled the cork. Then, appearing confused, he glanced all around the podium.

"Here, Daddy," Billy said, holding out her empty champagne glass.

Her father solemnly nodded his thanks as he leaned down to take it, then poured it half full of wine, and held it aloft.

"I now propose a toast," the Rabbi said.

Our moribund guests stirred, widened their eyes, and picked up whatever lukewarm drinks were still standing around on their tables.

"To my beloved daughter, Billy, to my new son-in-law, Arnie, and to all the joy, prosperity and fruitfulness we fervently pray await them in their coming life together. *B'ruch atah adonai, elohainu melach ho'olom, br'ai pri hagofen.* May the Lord bless you and keep you. *L'chayim.*"

The crowd desperately and hoarsely seconded that *l'chayim*, drank, and burst into relieved applause. More than a few guests began getting stiffly to their feet.

The Rabbi smiled tolerantly at his restless audience. Then he set down his wineglass, licked a forefinger, flipped a page, and continued with his speech.

A few people stood and gaped. Others sank back with heavy defeat into their chairs. There were some groans, a few incredulous guffaws, and all throughout the hall, a general mutinous undertone of murmuring.

If the Rabbi noticed, he gave no indication.

"It strikes me now," he went on, "that perhaps I have not spent adequate time reflecting upon the qualities of the groom, Arnie Goldman."

"I don't fucking believe this," I said, not bothering to whisper.

"Shhh!"

I whispered now, however, leaning into Billy's ear. "You know what this is? It's the Revenge of Rabbi Rubin. First we get married against his wishes, then we have a pagan ceremony, and now he's going to extract every last drop of blood—"

Billy jammed me sharply in the shoulder with her elbow.

"Hey! That *hurt.*"

"It was supposed to hurt. Now will you please shut *up?*"

I leaned back in my chair, rubbing at my shoulder—I was

pretty sure she'd bruised it—and decided I'd be smarter not to tangle with her now.

Rabbi Rubin droned on.

"And in choosing this young man, Billy has no doubt displayed both the tenderness of heart and the perspicacity of mind with which all of you, I'm sure, along with her doting father, have long been well acquainted. True—and we won't mince words here—it is undeniably true that Arnie suffers from a painful physical handicap. But what, we are behooved to ask ourselves, *is* a handicap? What is the true meaning of the word?"

I chugged some champagne.

"We now turn to Webster's Unabridged, where the first given definition is this: 'Handicap. Any disadvantage that makes success more difficult.' " The Rabbi glanced up from his text to allow that to sink in. "And yet, ladies and gentlemen, here before you sits a young man who is without question a success, both in terms of financial remuneration, and in terms of his high reputation in his field, that field being the study and the trade of precious stones and minerals. Surely that road to success must have been more difficult for Arnie Goldman to walk than other young men who are free of any such so-called handicap. And yet . . . and yet! Despite his handicap, Arnie has refused to let that handicap *remain* a handicap. Which is to say, that through his own intrepid efforts, this young man has vanquished the very meaning of the word!" The Rabbi turned a page. "Yes, he walks about on crutches. This much is incontestable. But who among us honestly can say—"

The Rabbi froze in midsentence. He licked his lips, touched the brim of his hat. His obsidian eyes were fixed on something at the back of the hall.

Bare-chested, grinning, swinging a bottle of champagne at his side, and wearing nothing but frayed cut-offs, sneakers, and a fat yellow polka-dotted tie around his naked neck, Redso came loping toward the podium, vivid as a nightmare.

He crisply saluted the Rabbi, flashed his grin at Billy and me, grabbed a chair from the table directly across from the podium (where my Aunt Sophie, my Uncle Ned, and their three daughters sat, their eyes round as poker chips), and plunked himself down, setting a skinny sunburned calf across a bony sunburned knee. The knee began to bounce; the mud-caked sneaker atop it jiggled. Redso took a swig from his champagne bottle, wiped his mouth, and smiled at the Rabbi, all eager and respectful expectation—as if he'd simply arrived late in a lecture hall where a speaker he admired was holding forth.

Billy let out a grunt, a breath. I sought her eyes, but she turned away, shifting in her seat, and resolutely kept her gaze on her father. I turned back to Redso. The son of a bitch gave me a wink. Then he raucously coughed, cleared his throat, and tapped the front of his fist politely to his mouth. He resumed that angelic shit-eating smile. His sneaker was a blur.

The old man bent back down to his speech. "And now," he continued, his voice aggressively loud, "the bride and groom make ready to take their rightful places in society as Jewish husband, Jewish wife, and future Jewish—"

"Tell it!" Redso hollered. "Thass right, Rabbi! Uh-huh. *Good* God! Tell the truth!"

Rabbi Rubin slowly raised his face, and pushed up at the brim of his fedora.

Now Redso was rocking rhythmically in his chair, throwing his arms around, extravagantly nodding.

"Preach it, Rabbi! Oh, sweet Lawd A'mighty! *Tell* the truth!"

The Rabbi stared, yanking at the point of his goatee.

There was some consternation, and some laughter now, rippling through the hall.

Then Redso was undone by a violent coughing fit. He hacked, wheezed, and bent over double, hanging his bush of wild orange hair between his knees. I didn't think he was pumping it for effect; the coughing was too desperate, too harsh; it sounded like rotten cloth ripping apart in his chest. After a spell, he quieted down, flopped upright against his chair, and roaringly brought up some phlegm. He spat into the palm of a hand (I shuddered at that) and wiped it on the tablecloth behind him. He took a long chugging swig of champagne. Then he slumped lower in his chair, his bony chest still heaving, and smiled up weakly at the Rabbi.

"If I may continue now . . ." The Rabbi glared down from the podium—although surprisingly, not at Redso. Instead he was scanning his audience, which, for the first time since he'd gotten up to speak, had finally come alive. There was an unrestrained excited buzz from one end of the hall to the other. The old man looked positively murderous. He boomed on: "For what, after all, constitutes a Jewish marriage? Is it enough, I ask you, that we keep a kosher home, observe the Sabbath laws, and oversee our children's religious education?"

"Oh, mercy hallelujah!"

"Is it enough—"

"Mine eyes have *seen* the glory!"

"I say, is it enough—"

"Thank you Jesus, thank you Jesus!"

"Who is this man?" the Rabbi thundered.

"A voice crying out in the wilderness!" Redso bellowed—and was cut short by another onslaught of coughing. He hunched forward so sharply the champagne bottle flew from his hand, and rolled under the skirting of the head table.

Now the hall was in an uproar.

I caught Billy by the elbow as she attempted to bolt from her chair. She swung around. "Let me go, Arnie."

"To do what?"

"I'm going to handle this."

I stared dumbly at that, and tightened my hold on her arm.

The Rabbi slapped the podium. "Who is this man? Who *is* he? Who allowed this derelict in here?"

Billy jerked away so hard she broke my grip. Then she was sweeping down behind the head table, actually shouldering people out of her way—Frank, my mother, even rotund Rabbi Bloom—who were attempting a well-meaning roadblock.

"Out of my way," she was shouting. "I mean it, people! Out of my way right now!"

I pushed up onto my crutches and scrambled after her.

"Is there a security guard in the house?" The Rabbi rapped on the microphone. "Hello? Is anybody out there? Is anybody listening? Is there a security guard somewhere to escort this bum from the premises?"

Redso was on his feet now, doing an exuberant high-stepping cakewalk sort of dance in the moat of empty space before the podium.

"Don't you fret none, Rabbi! I'm on my way! Thass right!

Praise Jesus, I'm on my way! Good golly, Miss Molly—I'm headed for that Promised Land!"

He high-stepped his way swiftly through the tables—as dozens of guests turned in their chairs, many of them broadly smiling, to watch him go—and headed out the way he'd come in, banging through the double swinging doors.

Billy, unsteady on her heels, was plugging along a few yards behind him. But I was moving at a pretty good clip myself, and caught up with her just as those swinging doors swung shut.

I summoned all my self-control, and asked her what she intended to do.

"Right now I'd like to kill him! Of all the crazy shitty things he's ever done—"

"What are we going to *do*, Billy?"

She stared past me, tears in her eyes. "First we have to keep him away from this reception," she said. "That's number one. And then we've got to—I don't know—get him into bed somehow. He's sick, Arnie. He might be terribly sick. You heard that coughing."

"What bed?"

"Our bed. Here in the hotel."

I pumped the grips of my crutches. "Our wedding bed? Is this insanity *catching* or something? What are we going to do— have a nice little pajama party before we leave on our honeymoon? Our plane's at eight o'clock tomorrow morning!"

"What else can we do, Arnie? Just let him roam around the hotel?"

I didn't answer.

"Look," Billy said. "I'll just get him up to the room somehow—and then I'll need a few minutes alone with him."

"To do what?"

"To calm him down, make sure he's all right. I don't *know!*"

I bore down harder on my crutches.

"Arnie, please. No one else but me can take care of this right now. I know it's a lot to ask—"

"You're damn straight it's a lot to ask!"

Billy raised her chin. "Well, I'm asking it."

□   □   □   □

I HAD NO INTENTION of cooling my heels in that reception hall; the last thing I needed now was to field all the shocked, or solicitous, or wisecracking inquiries that would surely be thrown at me from every direction. I briefly considered, as I passed it, ducking into the hotel bar for a drink—but no: that would be the first place any search party would look. Instead I took the elevator down, and wandered around in some unlikely areas; the dirty-sock-smelling corridor in front of the glass-walled health club, where several brutes were struggling on their backs against what looked like gigantic metal insects intent on devouring them, and then down the humid Astroturfed walkway alongside the swimming pool, where several screaming children were trying to drown each other, and then outside to the parking lot which, to my distracted and guilty eyes, seemed filled exclusively with cars belonging to my rudely abandoned wedding guests.

I checked my watch obsessively.

Finally, figuring I'd given Billy more than enough time, I went back inside the hotel, and glancing all around me like a jewel thief as I slinked down the quiet corridors, grabbed the elevator up to our floor.

I entered the room without knocking.

The first thing to hit me was Redso's body odor—so rank and powerful it was like stepping into a barn. I turned the corner past the bathroom, and saw that Billy had indeed gotten him into bed. He was propped up against a hill of golden pillows, a golden sheet drawn up to his middle, his face, throat, and naked torso as red as a boiled lobster; everywhere his skin was peeling. He smiled at me dreamily. So there he was, I thought, stinking up the very sheets upon which my marriage was supposed to have been consummated. If the same thought had occurred to Redso, he must have been relishing it. His shorts and tie lay neatly folded on a dresser; below them, side by side, sat his mud-caked sneakers. There was a box of Kleenex and a glass of water on the night stand beside him. And beside it sat Billy, bent forward in an armchair, looking so stricken and inconsolable that even her silver gown, her lace tiara, and those sprigs of baby's breath adorning her hair had a faded, forlorn quality, as if she were Miss

Havisham from *Great Expectations,* still mourning the cobwebby ruins of her spoiled wedding.

Redso began to sing in a weak cracked voice: " 'Another bride, another June, another sunny honeymoon—' " A fit of coughing cut him short. His hacking was as violent as it had been at the reception, maybe worse; he jangled like a puppet; the whole king-size mattress shook.

Billy watched him closely until his hacking had mostly subsided, then handed him a wad of Kleenex. Panting now, Redso put it to his mouth, and with a series of grating juicy tubercular noises, brought up and spat out some phlegm, eyed the Kleenex, and passed it back. She dropped it in the wastepaper basket beside her.

"See how nicely Nurse Rubin's taking care of me? Just like old times, huh, Arnie-boy?" He turned his grin to Billy. "Say, Nurse, how about a cigarette?"

"Forget it, Redso."

"See what I mean? She really does care, the dear thing."

If I hadn't been looking at Redso, I might not have known it was his voice. It was that raspy and frayed.

Billy pressed a palm to his forehead. "God, he's burning up! He's even hotter than he was two minutes ago, Arnie. We've got to—I don't know. Get him to a hospital somehow—"

"In just a minute," I told her.

"What?"

"First I'm going to find out what the hell's going on."

Billy sat back in her chair, and stared at me.

"Fire away, Torquemada," Redso rasped. "Anything at all you want to know . . ."

I readjusted my sweaty grip on my crutch handles. "Where've you been?"

"Here . . . there . . . everywhere . . ."

"He was in Mexico," Billy said.

"Mexico? Oh Jesus! For how long?"

"That's where he drove—you know, after the blizzard."

"Figured you might get the cops out after me," Redso told me with a smile. "Not that I'd blame you, Goldman. Hell, a man's gotta do what a man's—"

"Where's my car?"

"Well, the last I knew, it was in a car lot in Tijuana, being driven away by a particularly unsavory-looking Pancho Villa type . . ."

"You sold it?"

"So sorry, señor. But you see, I needed the *dinero* . . ."

"What did you get for it?"

"Oh, enough for the necessities of life. You know. Tacos . . . tequila . . . *las putanas* . . . peyote buttons. Things are quite affordable in downtrodden Mexico, you know. And of course, with the way the peso's been falling . . ."

"How long have you been sick?"

"Hard to say. Wasn't feeling too hot back in Mexico City. And then, what with sleeping in ditches and living on Twinkies in the four weeks it took me to hitchhike here . . ."

"Four *weeks?*"

"Four days. Four years. Whatever. Time, as Einstein informs us, is a concept wholly meaningless outside the context of any particular closed system. Consider, for example, a man pacing at five miles an hour aboard a speeding train, which itself—"

"Dammit, Redso! Will you just answer Arnie's questions?"

Redso made goggle-eyes at her. "Yes ma'am," he said, and saluted. He started hacking again. Billy watched him with a hollow expression. When he'd mostly hacked himself out, he hung forward, accepted more Kleenex from Billy, and flopped back against his pillows, wiping his mouth.

I was pacing in front of the bed now. "How did you find out about the wedding?"

Redso lobbed the Kleenex onto the floor. "A little bridey told me."

I stopped crutching. Billy was staring intently at the floor. "Billy?"

She raised her face. There wasn't a trace of denial or apology in her stony expression. "He called the house. About a week ago."

I pivoted to Redso. "How the hell did you get our number? It's not listed."

"Piece of cake. Piece of *wedding* cake, if you will." He was picking at some peeling white skin on his sunburned forearm. "Called the Rabbi. Told him I was your old friend Arthur. You remember Arthur, don't you? And he graciously coughed up the number. Hell of a guy, old Mordecai. Always had a soft spot in my heart for the Ayatollah Rubin. And hey—was that a speech or was that a speech? A tad flowery, I'll grant you, but otherwise right up there with the Gettysburg—" Redso choked on a cough.

Billy kept her stricken eyes on me.

"It just slipped out," she said.

"You told him about the wedding?"

She nodded.

"How could you possibly *do* an imbecilic thing like that?"

"I just couldn't lie to him, all right?"

"Why the fuck not? You lied to me, didn't you?"

"When?"

"This whole past week—by not telling me!"

"What *good* would it have done? My God, you would have been a nervous wreck all week—and then right through the wedding! Besides . . ." She shrugged. "It never *occurred* to me that he might actually make it here in time. Not without money or transportation . . ."

"Well, it looks like you figured wrong, doesn't it?"

"Yes! I figured wrong! Now what do you want me to *do* about it, Arnie?"

"Lovebirds, lovebirds, lovebirds! Married just two hours, and already bickering! Hate to think what this augurs for the future. By the way, have I tendered my heartfelt congratulations to the bride and groom yet? Shit, that's the whole reason I came down here! Just wanted you to know there are no hard feelings, kids. Of course, you both treacherously stabbed me in the back—but hey, who's keeping score? You know me. The soul of Christian forgiveness. So let me be the very last to congratulate—"

"Shut up!" Billy screamed, and lunged from her chair.

Redso opened his mouth in mock astonishment.

She hugged herself, hunching her bare shoulders as if she was chilled, and strode over to stand at the window.

"Jeez," Redso said. "Such hostility!" Then he smiled at me serenely, and patted with childishly splayed fingers the mattress on either side of him. "Boy, will you look at this hotel room? Plush, plush, plush. Must've cost a pretty penny, Mr. Goldbucks. And hey, what about this e-nor-mous bed? Not a bad place to croak in at all. Plenty of room to spread out and really do a bang-up swan song, wouldn't you say?" He growlingly shifted some sludge in the pit of his throat. Now his playfulness was gone. And without the smoke and mirrors of his bitter manic humor, Redso only looked like what he was: a sick, crazy, wasted human ruin. "Because that's what I feel like doing, you know. Dying."

She spun around. "Don't, Redso! Don't you even *start* talking that way!"

"Only being honest. Hell, let's face it. I'm fucked. I'm officially a nutcase. My talent's down the toilet. No money, no friends, no prospects. The whole degrading, oh-so-tragic nine yards. And now, with you hooked up with that insufferable self-righteous gimp over there—Christ! You tell me what I've got to live for, Miss Rubin!"

"Don't you do this, Redso! Don't you pull this shit on me!"

He laughed. "Billy, Billy, Billy. The lady doth protest too much, methinks. Did I punch a button maybe? Did I activate a little remorse? No? Not a whit? Well, maybe you should contemplate your sins a little more *studiously,* young lady . . ." He coughed, swallowed. "Hell, even *Judas* had enough good taste to go and find himself some rope—"

"Shut up!"

". . . and do the honorable thing in the end." Redso came forward off his pillows. "So how come *you're* still in such radiant good health, darling Billy? Well? What's the answer, you back-stabbing cunt?"

Billy stared at him for a beat. Then she turned and headed for the door, and as she passed me, said in a faint voice: "Meet me in the hallway."

I took one last look at Redso. He smiled, lifted a hand, twiddled the fingers. As I crutched out of the room I heard him raspily singing behind me: " 'But don't forget, folks, that's what you get, folks, for making whoopee . . .' "

Billy shut the door and thumped her back against it. She already had a cigarette lit. "All right. What do we do?"

I scowled at the gray and maroon striped carpet between my crutches.

"What do we *do,* Arnie?"

"How should *I* know, Billy? It was your brilliant idea to drag him up here."

"Are you *blaming* me for this?"

I sighed. "No," I said. "Of course not. But can you blame *me* if I'm not exactly being a good *sport* about this, Billy?"

She drew hard on her cigarette "We've got to get him to a hospital," she said. "We should call an ambulance right now."

"Okay, fine."

"Okay, fine—and then what?"

"What do you mean, and then what? Then we call in the maids to change the sheets and fumigate the room. And then we do our damnedest to put this entire insane episode out of our minds and enjoy our honeymoon!"

"We can't just stick him in the hospital, and then run off to Wales for three weeks."

"Why not?"

"What happens when they release him? What's he going to do then?"

"He can go to his mother's, can't he?"

"His mother's as crazy as he is—totally useless! He could be *extremely* ill, Arnie. He's going to need someplace to recuperate. And where's he going to do that if we're in Wales? On the street?"

"I don't care if it's in a fucking ditch! Goddammit, Billy! Why is this *our* problem?"

I saw that I'd gone too far. There was genuine loathing in her eyes, and it terrified me.

I dug my nails into the waxy plastic coating of my crutch-grips, and desperately sought a way out.

And then, with appalling ease, the solution came to me—and all of a piece, like a neatly wrapped package. I only hoped it didn't contain a silently ticking bomb. I gave a roll to my shoulders, and looked at Billy again. "Look," I said. "First we'll call an ambulance."

"What if no hospital will take him? He's not insured—"

"I'll give him a credit card, all right? We can even follow him to the hospital, and make some kind of arrangement for him there. How's that?"

"That's . . . fine," Billy said, frowning at me dubiously. "Then what?"

"Then we'll give him the keys to the house. Have you got your extra set on you?"

"Yes."

"Good. So he'll have the keys to the house, and also to your car. Then, when he gets out of the hospital, he can go there and recuperate until we get back."

Billy crossed her arms. "You'd really do that, Arnie?"

I shrugged.

"But aren't you—I mean, do you really trust him alone in our house for three weeks?"

"It doesn't look like we have any choice, does it?"

Billy observed me for much longer than I would have liked, gnawing worriedly on her pouty bottom lip. Then she came away from the door, embraced me, and fervently kissed me on the mouth. Her breath was sour, metallic; it seemed to somehow embody her misery. She finally pulled away. "Arnie, I know how horrible this is for you. It's just as horrible for me. And . . ." She limply shrugged. "Just thank you."

I stiffened up over my crutches.

"Could you do me one favor?" I asked her.

She waited.

"Could you give me a couple of minutes alone with him?"

"Well, sure. I guess. But why?"

"That's just the way I want to handle it right now. Please, Billy. You owe me one."

"All right," she said carefully.

Then she opened the door to let me in, and closed it softly behind me.

I paused, hit once again by Redso's gritty stink. Then, my guts twisting with misgiving, I approached him where he lay on the bed—gaunt, lobster red, and grinning like the lunatic he was—and presented Redso with an entirely different proposal.

Ten

IT'S NOT TRUE, I've discovered, that you can't run away from your problems, at least temporarily. And throughout our three-week honeymoon in Wales, just knowing that the entire Atlantic Ocean was standing between Redso and me had worked like magic. I won't bore you with a lot of pretty post-cards of our trip, except to say that the misty green gorgeousness of the country, the gregarious good company (Desmond Garlick had been a tireless and entertaining host), and the thrill of having my wonder-struck bride at my side, knocking the socks off every envious Welshman we met, had been enough to keep at bay all but the faintest nagging memory of what awaited me back home. But now, headed back from Lambert Airport in St. Louis, I was feeling like Faust as the dark finale approached—cringing in the inescapable cage of my own making, and not at all ready to pay the devil his due.

Billy, smiling serenely behind her sunglasses, seemed utterly unaware of my mounting apprehension. "It's weird," she said. "But you know what I'm already missing? Those fabulous Welsh breakfasts. I could go for one right now, in fact—just exactly like dotty old Mrs. Thomas used to make. Eggs fried in bacon fat. That scrumptious fried bread. Lamb kidneys. Broiled tomatoes. Heinz beans. God, I'm actually drooling! Even those horrible squishy pink sausages—what did they call them, Arnie?"

"Bangers," I said.

"That's right," Billy said. "Bangers. Well, who knows? Maybe I'm only craving it because I know I can't have it anymore. Or maybe it's actually time for breakfast."

"Billy, the sun's going down."

"By my body clock, I mean."

We were driving west on Highway 40, straight into the glowering sunset, and caught in the thick of the homecoming traffic; aggravating America had lost no time in swallowing us up again. I was at the wheel of my Lincoln Continental—which I'd had custom-equipped, just like my long-lost Toronado, with another Rube Goldbergian complex of hand controls on the steering column. I sometimes thought of that Mexican, whoever he was, who'd bought my car from Redso—and what in the world he must have made of all that inexplicable extra hardware. Of course I'd never know.

Now Billy snuggled up against me, trapping a clump of her loose sunstruck hair between our shoulders. "I know I've said this sixteen times already, Arnie. But I'll just say it again, for good measure. This wasn't just the best honeymoon I've ever had . . ."

I came up with the requisite smile for that.

"It was the best trip I've ever taken *anywhere*. Thanks again, baby. It was just swell."

"You're welcome," I told her in a low constricted voice.

She scooted away to light a cigarette, sighed out a mist of smoke, and cracked her window.

"God," she said, "I hope he's taken care of himself!"

The air went out of me. I took the exit for Highway 270, and clenched my teeth as I braked for the stalled mass of cars. "Come on, Billy. When have you ever known Redso to take care of himself?"

She glanced at me, almost shyly. "But what do you think? You think he's all right?"

"How in the world should I know?"

"Just take a guess. I mean, what's your gut feeling?"

"I don't have a gut feeling," I told her, which wasn't exactly true. My guts were in knots.

"I'll tell you what worries me. How he never answered when we called."

"Hell, he was probably out tearing up the town every night. I gave him a fat enough bankroll for it."

"But what about when we called in the morning? And besides, what makes you think he was out drinking, as sick as he was?"

"Christ, Billy. Who knows what Redso's capable of?"

She shrugged. "Anyway, we left the number on the answering machine. He could have called us in Wales."

"Well, you know manics. They're extremely busy people."

She inspected me. "Arnie, what's going on with you?"

"Nothing."

"Don't give me that. What is it?"

"What did you expect, Billy? That I'd be jumping for joy right now?"

"Listen," she said, crushing out her cigarette. "We'll get him out of there just as fast as we can. We'll call a cab and send him straight to a motel—so he won't even have to spend the night with us, all right? Now, is that fair?"

I shrugged.

"And until we do get him out of there, will you at least make an attempt to be nice?"

"Nice?"

"Okay. How about just decent?"

"That's a pretty tall order, Billy."

"Well, just *try.*"

We were driving down Olive Street Road now, the fever-dream of gaily colored postmodern shopping centers crowding both sides of the street. Billy slumped against her door.

We made the turn into Tempo Drive, and headed into that valley of boxlike pastel ranch homes where I'd grown up, the pinks and turquoises and pale yellows all dimming toward gray in the dusklight.

When I pulled up in front of the carport of my old childhood home, where Billy's Plymouth sat, she said, "Will you look at this? Miracle of miracles. My car's still in one piece."

I switched off the ignition.

"Arnie? Are you going to be okay?"

"I just . . . need a second to psych myself up for this."

"All right." She took the keys from my hand. "I'll just go on ahead."

"What about the luggage?"

"I'll get it later. I want to check on Redso first."

I watched her hurry across the darkening lawn, her hips anxiously switching. She opened the door, slipped inside, and in her haste forgot to shut it; it hung open like an evil black fissure.

Maybe it seems strange that I'd choose to start my married life in the house where I'd grown up. But I had my practical reasons for it. First and foremost, there had been the pressing need to simply move—it didn't matter where—to put Redso off our scent. Also, it was time for a modest step up in the world, and this modest little bungalow, I figured, would be no more alluring to a professional burglar than our ramshackle dump back in Maplewood. There was some sentiment involved, too. In usurping my parents' house, and insisting on my inflated purchase price, I'd made it possible for them to take a much nicer place for their retirement years, which wouldn't be long in coming; they were now set up in a very nice condominium ten miles to the west of here, in fashionable Chesterfield. And then, to bring my dazzling bride across the threshold of my childhood home—where for so many years I'd wondered, and for good reason, if I'd ever marry at all, or live anything like a normal existence—was still more sweet icing on the wedding cake.

Inside the house, I shut the door and switched off the burglar alarm on the wall; in another thirty seconds the Creve Coeur police would have been alerted. Billy, meanwhile, was moving through the house, banging doors, calling out for Redso.

As swiftly as I could, I scrambled down the hallway, through the kitchen, clanked down the swooping concrete ramp and into the newly refinished basement, which was now a combination office, storage area, and, if I said so myself, quite impressive rock museum. I'd junked my old steel shelves; now my glittering beauties were displayed on shelf after shelf of white ash, on half a dozen polished, island-shaped pedestals crafted from the stumps of redwood trees, and in four long track-lit glass cases reserved for my most resplendent and expensive specimens. It was to those cases that I plugged—compelled, however irrationally, to assure myself that Redso hadn't gotten to them somehow, despite all my careful and ruthless precautions.

I snapped the switch on the first display case. The light stuttered on. A glowing garden of gorgeous minerals winked into view; of course none of them were missing. Yet I kept on with my compulsive inventory until, as I approached the fourth and final case, Billy appeared at the top of the ramp.

"Anything missing?" she asked me.

I didn't answer.

"I asked you a question, Arnie."

"No. There's nothing missing."

"Well. That's not exactly surprising, is it? Seeing as how nobody's been in this house since we've been gone."

I went on staring into the case, as if those stones lined up in their brilliant rows possessed the alchemical power to clear my mind, give me strength—or even to get me out of this, somehow.

I turned away, and feeling Billy's eyes on my back as I crutched, went to the swivel chair in front of my desk and stiffly sat. Billy came down the ramp, halted in front of my desk, and regarded me with unnervingly clear and dispassionate eyes.

"So? Where is he?"

"I have no idea," I said.

She kept on studying me. "Of course this is your doing, isn't it?"

"Yes."

She waited.

I set my elbows on my deskpad, and started rubbing at my eyes. "I made him a deal. You know. When you left us alone in the hotel room."

"Oh God! I should have known!"

I looked up at her then. Her eyes were narrowed with disgust.

"So tell me all about it, Arnie. It must have been a very sharp deal, whatever it was. I mean, that's your great forte, isn't it? Making very sharp deals?"

I filled my lungs with air, and, almost relieved to finally be making my confession, let it all go.

I'd given Redso my credit card, all right, just as I'd promised Billy at the hotel—but only with the understanding that I'd be calling the Creve Coeur police, and asking them to keep an eye on our house while we were gone, and especially, to keep an eye out for Redso. If they wanted proof that he was a menace, they only had to call up his record. Then, once we were in Wales, I'd periodically check in with the police. And if, I told Redso, I found out he'd been spotted in the neighborhood—or that anyone at all had been spotted lurking around our house—I'd put an immediate stop on the credit card. On the other hand, if Redso decided to be a good boy, and steered clear of our neighborhood, he could do whatever the hell he liked with the five-thousand-dollar limit. So if Redso had any sense left at all, he'd take the money and run. And that was the deal we'd agreed to.

"And apparently," I said, "Redso's been as good as his word. For once in his life."

"You don't even sound *guilty.*"

"Why should I feel guilty?"

"You don't even *know?*"

"Let me guess," I said. "For putting you, and me, and our marriage, and this house, and everything we have together ahead of some fucking maniac who's just itching to destroy it all? Is that what I'm supposed to feel guilty about?"

"He was sick!"

"Oh Christ! There's that sacred word again!"

"What do you mean, sacred? What's that got to do with anything? You heard what they said at the hospital when we called. He had *pneumonia.*"

"Billy, you'd let Adolf Hitler off the hook if you thought he was running a temperature!"

"Don't you even know what you did? You threw a sick, crazy, helpless human being right out into the street. Like he was nothing—like he was garbage!"

"Come on, Billy! He was cured already, or the hospital wouldn't have released him."

"He needed to recuperate! I mean, just where do you think he went?"

"I don't *know.* And hey, guess what else? I don't *care!*"

"No? Well, just what *do* you care about, Arnie? Besides all these fucking rocks?"

I pushed away from the desk and jerked toward her in my swivel chair; the pain that tore through my hips was nothing next to my rage. "All these fucking rocks, for your information, are going to send our kids to college someday—not to mention all the other good things all these fucking rocks are going to do for us! What do you think this is, Billy? Playtime? Never Never Land? The Billy Rubin Theater? This is the real world, in case you didn't know, and it's *not* always nice, and some people *do* happen to be dangerous, and goddammit, we've got certain things worth protecting! I mean, there he was—raving and stinking, right in the middle of our marriage bed—our marriage bed! And all you could think about was *him*. *His* welfare. Well, let me ask you something, Billy. Just how is it that Redso's welfare has always come before mine?"

Her mouth fell open. "You're jealous."

"I . . ." I averted my face. "Come on, Billy. That's crazy. I'm not jealous."

"I can't believe I've never seen it before. But you are. You're scared to death of him."

I said nothing.

"You really think he's still a threat to you? Can you actually still see him as a *rival*? My God, Arnie! I had no idea you were this insecure."

Still I didn't speak.

"And just what do you think *I* am, while we're at it? Where does that put me? Do you actually think I've been lying to you ever since I got back from Chicago? Do you think I haven't *meant* the things I've said? The things I've done? Don't you even know me at *all*?"

I couldn't answer.

Billy blinked at me for a spell.

"You know what?" Her voice was low and soft now. "I really don't think you do."

Without another glance at me, she turned away and headed for the ramp.

My anger was gone now. All I felt was humiliation, and fear. "Billy?"

She kept moving slowly up the curved white concrete slope. "Billy? Please. Will you come back here?"

Now she halted, but didn't turn around.

"For what?"

"So we can talk."

"We've already talked," she said.

"Well, where are you going?"

"To the spare bedroom."

"To do what?"

"To go to bed."

"Why can't you do that in our room?"

"Because I don't think I want to sleep with you," she said.

That struck like a physical blow. "You mean tonight?"

Billy sent a shiver through her hair. "I don't know what I mean," she said, then continued up the ramp and out of sight.

PART FOUR

Eleven

MY WALKING CANE was an elegant piece of work, as fine, in its way, as the most superlative of my crystal specimens. In the year since I'd been using it, in fact, I'd come to cherish it as soulfully as all my mineral treasures lumped together—not only for what it was, but for the new life, the new and still amazing incarnation of myself, that it had naturally come to stand for. The shaft was solid ebony, black in some lights, a rich chocolate brown in others, and so dense, hard and heavy it might have been composed of an alloy of wood and stone; the T-shaped handle, waxy to the touch but providing a good gritty grip in the fist, was carved from an amber-colored staghorn; a band of antique silver joined the handle to the shaft, and engraved there was the date of our second wedding anniversary, when Billy had made me a gift of this cane. Another anniversary had come and gone since then. And lately when I took hold of that staghorn handle, it often hit me— sometimes with a sting of remorse, but more often with a mere dull throb of resignation—that this cane was maybe the sole thing in our marriage that had survived completely unscarred and intact.

On a late afternoon in March, in the fourth year of my foundering marriage, I stood leaning on that cane, taking in through the window of a twelfth-story bedroom the dazzling view of downtown St. Louis below. The skyline was steeped in the syrupy light of sunset. The Arch was planted grandly on the horizon, like a gleaming croquet wicket set up for the gods. Naked, sated, and gazing down upon the world with immense self-satisfaction, I was feeling at that moment pretty Olympian myself—and about as remorseful as incorrigible Zeus, following yet another of his adulterous escapades.

"No. Don't you move a muscle, Arnie. You just keep leaning on that cane—just like that—while I lie here and eat you with my eyes, all right?" The speaker, speaking from her canopied bed, was Claire Johnson—a highly paid anesthesiologist, an avid collector of fine and expensive things, a valued client for much of this past year, and for the past ten days, a lover of mine as well. "God, I'm wild about that cane! Did you know that, Arnie? It makes you look so gallant, so old-fashioned and European. Like that handsome English poet with the clubfoot. What was his name?"

"Byron," I said, tightly smiling to myself.

"That's right. Lord Byron. The one who was supposed to be such a lady-killer."

I pumped the head of my cane, and kept my eyes on the shimmering Arch. Behind me there was languorous slithering of limbs among sheets.

"Isn't it nice," Claire said, "that we're not in love? And that we don't pretend to be? No muss, no fuss. Just two consenting adults who both know what they want. Isn't it really much better this way, Arnie? Think of all the time and energy we save, just for starters."

"Yeah," I said. "Ain't it the life?"

Yet I felt just a little uneasy. I'd heard something like that same speech from Claire Johnson before, and in almost the very same words—which made me wonder if maybe she wasn't protesting too much. Still, there was no good reason not to take her at her word. Claire was right. We weren't in love, or even pretending to be (just coming off a bitter divorce, Claire kept insisting that she was out for nothing more than some hard-earned, long-deferred fun), and that was more than fine with me.

Now I pivoted on my cane, and Claire quickly drew her sheet up to her collarbone. For a woman who worked so hard to keep herself in shape (four nights a week at Vic Tanny, a

punishing regimen of running, cycling and swimming in between), Claire had a funny kind of modesty. It might have had
something to do with her age (she'd just turned thirty-five,
and could hardly stop talking about it) but with that lean,
supple, still girlish body, Claire certainly had nothing to be
ashamed of. Yet after sex she would wrap herself up in a towel
or a sheet, she insisted on showering alone, and when she
peed, she always kept the door primly shut. In that she was
the polar opposite of Billy, who wandered naked around the
house with the insouciance of a savage, not even caring if the
blinds were up or down—never mind that in the past couple
of years she'd begun, perversely, to let her once spectacular
figure go to hell.

"Claire, why do you cover yourself up like that?"

"I'm just—a little shy."

"Just a little shy, huh?" I was poking over to the bed now.
"Well, maybe this calls for some therapy." With a swift thrust
and parry of my cane, I flipped Claire's sheet away. She
shrieked and curled up like a bug. And then I was upon her,
growling, snorting, pinning her arms to her sides, and sloppily
kissing her throat, her small firm breasts, the taut jumping
slope of her giggling belly, and the rough reddish fringes of
her pubic delta, which still smelled grittily of sex—until Claire
sat up, took firm hold of my head, and made me look at her.

"Hey," she said. "Do you realize you're nothing but an overgrown teenager?"

I grinned and bounced my eyebrows—Redso-style—and
wondered if Claire knew how right she was. If there was such
a thing as a second adolescence, I was in it.

"Not that I'm trying to get rid of you, Arnie. But didn't you
just say you were running late?"

I glanced at the clock on her night table. "Oh Christ, I completely lost track."

I pushed up from the bed and started caning around the
room in search of my underwear. "Sorry, Claire. But the thing
is, we're having an early dinner tonight. There's this party at
Dr. Krause's–"

"I know, sweetheart. I'm invited."

This came as no surprise, for Claire and I tended to haunt
the same social circles—made up largely of doctors, shrinks,

hospital administrators and the like. In recent years I'd added
a new and very lucrative angle to my business; I now made a
good portion of my sales to clients in the medical profession,
who were in the market for fine collectibles as well as inflation-
proof investments. I'd met Claire at just such a gathering of
prospective buyers, in fact, where I'd gotten her started on her
collection of very nice midlevel fluorites, beryls, and tourmalines that now shared space in her lavishly appointed apartment with her Baccarat crystal, her Dutch porcelain, her num-
bered prints, her sleek Italian furniture. What Claire and I
had in common, beyond our lust, was our love for lovely objects—one of those areas, by the way, where Billy and I would
always remain as far apart as planets.

By now I'd found my jockey shorts and was pulling them
on, savoring, as I still did these days, the ease with which I was
able to perform that once excruciating operation. The prick-
ling in my hips was so minimal, so feeble, such a pale reminder
of the fires that used to rage there, that in an odd way I actually enjoyed it. I took my pants from the back of a chair, and
asked Claire if she was planning on showing up at the party
tonight.

"I'm not sure, Arnie. You want me to? I'll bet your wife
doesn't."

"Claire, how many times do I have to tell you? Billy doesn't
have a jealous bone in her body."

"I'm not even talking about that. She just—doesn't seem to
like me for some reason."

That seemed to me a peculiar thing for Claire to be worried
about. "Well, who says you have to be pals with her?"

"Maybe it's strange. But actually, I like Billy. She seems so
spirited and intelligent—with a nice keen edge to her, you
know? The kind I like to see in a woman."

I scowled as I tugged up my pants. Reminders of Billy's
good points only pained me nowadays.

"And then, she's such an absolute living doll . . . I don't
know, Arnie. It makes me wonder sometimes what in the
world you'd want with me."

"Claire, are you nuts? Don't you know you're a beautiful
woman?"

She shrugged, and tugged her sheet a little higher.

"Just take it from a professional connoisseur, all right? You're exquisite."

Claire eyed me carefully, brushed some fallen strands of wheat-colored hair from her forehead, and finally smiled. "Hey," she said. "Could you do me one last favor before you go?"

"Well, sure."

"Why don't you come over here, like a good little Lord Byron, and let me check out that lovely cane of yours again?"

Needless to say, I didn't leave Claire's apartment until a good while later. I figured I'd just tell Billy that my business meeting had dragged on longer than I'd expected—and almost certainly she would swallow that tired excuse without question. What I'd said to Claire was true; Billy seemed constitutionally incapable of jealousy.

Long leaded mirrors lined the hallway of this swank apartment house, and I observed myself with pleasure as I caned through them—reminded once again of the striking visual contrast between a man who walked on two sticks and a man who walked with one. On crutches you were a pitiable hulk, a hunched and crooked thing. But with a cane flashing smartly at your side, your limp took on a certain air of rakish glamour, as if, like a dueling scar, you'd acquired it in some manly test of courage. And the image you evoked was no longer that of Tiny Tim, but of some paragon of virility, self-reliance and dash. A young Winston Churchill, maybe. Or even better (as Claire would have it), a Lord Byron.

I was prone to such preening in those days, all right. But I felt no pressing need to correct it. After all, an enormous and shocking change, through no fault of my own, had been rudely thrust upon me. And if I was reacting in ways I would have thought impossible just one short year ago, if my ego had gone a little inflated around the edges, if I'd turned rather vain and self-centered—all right then, if I was acting like an absolute prick—I figured I'd suffered long enough for the temporary privilege. Because I *saw* it as a temporary condition. And that, it seemed to me, was the rub, the crux, the special mitigating factor that allowed me to plead for leniency at the court of my own conscience. One of these days, no doubt, I would come to take my new lack of pain, my new freedom of movement, and the sweet secret knowledge that I no longer cut a ridiculous or pathetic figure for granted—and then, no doubt, I'd shrink right back into my usual moral proportions. But until that time, I was in my glory days. And dammit, I meant to mine them for all they were worth.

OVERALL, my improvement these past few years had been nothing short of jaw-dropping. My knees were no longer blotched with red, or hot to the touch, or even noticeably swollen; in my ankles the disease seemed to have packed up and left entirely. It was only in my hips that I still had occasional attacks—but so mild and so short-lived, they barely slowed me down at all.

And as always, there was no one, medical professional or otherwise, who could begin to explain what was happening inside my body.

That included my rheumatologist, Dr. Finkle, a kindly, owl-faced, soft-spoken old gentleman who was himself so badly gnarled with arthritis in the neck, back and shoulders (he suffered from osteoarthritis, the far more common kind) that he had to stiffly swivel from the waist, like a mannequin, in order to turn to you. He'd been my doctor since I was nine, and while I had no doubt that he was fully competent, about the most Dr. Finkle had been able to do for me—aside from keeping me stocked with prednisone—was to offer the kind of sympathy that maybe only a rheumatologist who was himself ravaged by arthritis could provide.

During a checkup about a year and half earlier, I'd pressed Dr. Finkle (and you had to press that cautious man pretty hard for anything more than careful equivocation) for the reason behind my unexpected recovery.

As usual, he carefully equivocated. "Arnie, I'm afraid the best explanation I can give you is really no explanation at all."

"Just try me, Doctor."

"Well, all right," Dr. Finkle said, and stiffly took a seat in the chair beside the examining table. "It's something I call my one-third dictum. Now, it doesn't hold the weight of clinical evidence, mind you. It's just something I've taken notice of over the years."

According to Dr. Finkle, it seemed that approximately one

third of all rheumatoid arthritis sufferers tended to show general improvement with time; another third or so held fairly steady, with periodic ups and downs—which, until recently, had been the case with me; and the remainder, suffering a progressive deterioration of the joints, could be expected to end up as invalids.

"So which third do you figure I fall into?"

"Well, it's clear that you've been improving—and to a remarkable degree. But will you continue to improve?" Here Dr. Finkle smiled, and slowly shook his stiff old head. "Don't let this get around, Arnie—it could ruin my reputation. But frankly, your guess is every bit as good as mine."

One tangible good thing did emerge from that visit, however. As Dr. Finkle was getting up to leave, he wondered aloud if the prednisone was even doing me any good at this point—for while my inflammation had dramatically receded, my dosage hadn't changed at all.

Naturally that electrified me—and I immediately insisted on doing whatever we could to find out.

We agreed on a plan to reduce my cortisone dependence, and if possible, get me off the poison altogether. Of course going cold turkey was out of the question. Instead I would begin that month by cutting back by half a pill, and if my adrenal glands didn't go so utterly haywire that I was unable to function at all, press on with further reductions. At my current level of twenty milligrams a day—four pills—the entire ordeal, if I was lucky, would only last eight months.

I pressed on, all right. But I hadn't known what I was in for.

Each time I reduced my dosage by another half a pill, I would plummet, for the next three weeks or so, into a deep tenacious funk that was every bit as emotional as it was physical. Worse than my intense debilitating fatigue, I declined into a mean-spirited caricature of myself at my most petulant and crabby. Nothing was right, nothing my poor put-upon wife could do was enough for me, nothing could distract me from my sour incessant complaints. Food had lost its savor; I couldn't concentrate enough to read a book; I had no interest in making conversation, or even getting up from the sofa unless I had to. If Billy was listening to music, or talking on the phone, or trying to memorize her lines, I would banish her to another room where I didn't have to hear it. And if, in a conciliatory moment, she made the smallest hesitant attempt at cuddling with me on the sofa, I would meanly brush her away. Even sleep, which had become my main occupation, was spoiled by intense, repetitive, nauseating dreams (I might be searching for a pair of matching socks in a drawer where a multitude of unmatched socks kept horribly increasing—that sort of thing) so that when I awoke, I was just as exhausted and testy as before. How Billy could bear to be around me during those periods, I had no idea. But then again, had I *ever* understood her saintlike forbearance—not only with me, but with those two other insufferables in her life, Redso and her father? Monumental as Billy's patience was, I chipped away at it, I know, and maybe at last I eroded certain spots in her affection that could never be fully restored. There were other things, certainly, and bigger things, that sickened the roots of our marriage. But all those long hellish months it took to kick my cortisone habit had doubtlessly contributed their poisons.

It was over, just as I'd planned, in eight months. I was now free of steroids; and better yet, my arthritis had only continued to improve. And I'd also been hit by another transformation, this one entirely unanticipated.

I'd become, to my surprise, a handsome man.

The face I'd carried into adulthood, remember, was the typical face of a prednisone addict—flushed and puffy as a cherub's. Why I never stopped to think that those distortions would disappear along with the medication that produced them, I'm not sure. Maybe I just had bigger things to worry about. But at the end of those eight months, the redness and the roundness had melted away like last year's snows, revealing a set of cheekbones, a chin, and a jawline underneath that I'd had no idea were lurking down there. I'd gone from looking like a pink and bubble-cheeked choirboy to the sort of manly chiseled character you might see slinging a saddle over his shoulder in an ad for Ralph Lauren. Moreover, thanks to all those years of plugging around on crutches, my back was just as broad as ever, my chest just as massive, my shoulders just as rocky and intimidating. And while I'd added some new meat and muscle, thanks to my cane, to the lower half of my body, my hips were still matador-thin.

And now, by God, the women were coming around.

It's important, I think, to put this in perspective. All my life I'd been consigned to the sidelines of the sexual game, and was used to being ignored or condescended to by desirable women—Billy being the one remarkable and inexplicable exception. Yet suddenly here they all were—doctor's wives, bank tellers, waitresses, you name it—giving me the eye, sidling up to me at parties, handing me their business cards, barking extravagantly at my lamest witticisms, and much much more than that—and if I was reacting like a fat kid in the proverbial candy store, wouldn't it have been far stranger if I'd managed to resist?

My problem was that I didn't know where to stop. Claire Johnson wasn't the first of my adulterous entanglements, nor, as I'd made clear to her, was she the only woman I was currently carrying on with. That was apparently just fine with Claire, who, like me, was indulging in a period of reckless sexual gorging. Yet even I had to admit, in my greedy satyriasis, that things were starting to get out of hand. Along with Claire, there was June, an impressively well-preserved woman of forty-two (married to a client of mine, an ear-nose-and-throat man), who was a hyperactive organizer of charity balls and other such events, and just as hyperactive in the exorbitant hotel rooms where we met for our afternoon trysts; and there was also Colleen, a smashingly beautiful young waitress who'd slipped me her number one night on a napkin, and whose airy head was filled with lots of silly New Age nonsense, including a belief in the healing powers of plain old dime-a-dozen quartz crystals, with which I kept her bountifully supplied. It was June every other Tuesday, and Colleen any day before five, when she had to show up for the dinner shift, and Claire on either Wednesdays or Fridays, and recently there had been nights when I couldn't sleep for all the complicated schedules and tactics I had to keep straight in my head while juggling three women at once. Not to mention, of course, the fourth and the trickiest ball to keep up in the air, my wife, who lay snoring beside me night after night while I squirmed in my horny insomnia, just as trusting and ignorant as ever.

□ □ □ □

I ARRIVED HOME half an hour late—breaking the speed limit all the way—and by the time I showered, dressed, and fixed myself a salami sandwich, there was still no sign of Billy. Usually, if she knew she was going to be late, she'd tape a note to the door or leave a message on the answering machine. But not tonight.

I poured a scotch and paced the house like a three-legged panther in my sleek Armani suit, obsessively checking my watch, the light on the answering machine, and the driveway through the window—half convinced, in my furious impatience, that this was a game she was intentionally playing, that by keeping me waiting like this, Billy was passively-aggressively twisting the knife. For she made it no secret that she loathed these parties we now so frequently attended (medical people bored her silly, Billy complained), never mind that she knew perfectly well that such affairs were now crucial to my business.

Around the time of our marriage, I'd realized that I could only move ahead so far by dealing strictly with other collectors. For one thing, true museum-quality pieces were getting harder and harder to come by; there were only so many mineral masterpieces still left in the crust of the earth (which wouldn't be producing any more for quite a few million years) and most of the finest pockets around the globe had long since been mined out. Also, knowledgeable rock aficionados were naturally the wiliest of bargainers. So I'd begun cultivating other, less finicky, and far more cash-rich customers—almost exclusively medical people, who were so flooded with liquidity and so strapped for time that they were more than happy to rely on the investment advice of a bona-fide expert like me. I'd begun by selling a few pieces to Dr. Finkle, who'd then put me on to several of his associates, and things had quickly expanded from there. I'd even run a few ads in the local medical journals. All in all, it was one of the smartest moves I'd ever made. And there was a nice poetic justice to it, too. All my life I'd been filling the pockets of doctors—now, by God, they were filling mine. And such affairs as tonight's party—hosted by one of my happy customers, a kidney specialist, who'd invited some other likely suspects—had become my main venue for peddling my goods. But more and more, Billy had been chafing at my dragging her along. All right, so she might find the company a little less than enthralling—unlike the egomaniacs, poseurs, sexual deviants and high-strung neurotics who flitted around Billy's theater parties. But was a little social tedium such a high price to pay for the kind of life I was able to give her?

I kept pacing and fuming (we were already more than an hour late) until the telephone rang.

That it wasn't Billy was aggravation enough. But it seemed the Furies really had it in for me tonight—for the reedy voice on the other end was Rabbi Rubin's. I sat on the sofa, stretching the cord, and somehow remembered in my consternation to ask the old man how he was feeling.

About four months before, he'd broken a hip in a fall from a ladder, and was still only partially up and about. Of course, there would be nothing at all unexpected in that for a normal human being of seventy-three. But in Rabbi Rubin's case, it was peculiarly disturbing; until now, I'd never known that incredible old dynamo to be slowed down by so much as a cold.

"Well," the Rabbi said. "I'm still on these cockamamie crutches. Which can get rather frustrating—" He laughed. "Hah? Will you listen? How's that for irony? Look who's explaining to who about crutches! But anyway, anyway . . . I suppose there's no point in complaining."

On this one score, at least, I had to hand it to Billy's father: he was one sick old man who wasn't interested in milking you for sympathy.

"So, *nu?* Is Billy there?"

"No, Rabbi. She sure isn't."

"Aha. So I suppose she's already left for my apartments?"

Now the light bulb snapped on. I settled back slowly against the sofa, and warned myself that it would only be self-defeating to lose my temper. "Rabbi," I said, keeping my voice on a tight leash, "I thought we'd already discussed this particular issue."

"Oh? Which particular issue is that?"

"You know perfectly well which issue. About using Billy as your all-purpose"—I nearly said "slave," but decided to amend it—"handyman."

"Well, all right. We discussed it. But you have to admit, the situation has altered considerably since then. Obviously, in my present state of incapacitation—"

"Just what've you got her doing tonight, Rabbi?"

"You make it sound like I *ordered* her to help me. Billy *volunteered* for this, I'll have you know."

Of course, in Billy's dealings with her father, the word "volunteer" was hardly applicable. She was simply helpless to refuse the old man anything—despite the howls I'd been raising for years over his shameless exploitation of her good giving nature. Even now, she still spent at least one *Shabbos* a month at his house, playing sweet Cordelia to his Lear, not to mention all the plumbing, painting and general fix-up work she'd taken on since he'd broken his hip.

"Rabbi, I swear to God, if you've sent her up onto one of those roofs again—"

"Roof? Who said anything about a roof? After that last little conniption fit you threw, didn't I say I'd subcontract for a roofer? Well? Didn't I say I'd do that?"

"Did you?"

"Well, no. Not yet. But on the other hand, no roofing problem has recently come up." The Rabbi cleared his throat. "Now, it so happens that today is the fifteenth of the month. And so naturally—"

"You've got her out collecting *rents?*"

"Yes. And why not? I can't see—"

"Which apartment house?"

"What's the matter with you tonight, anyway? You've been hostile since the moment—"

"Which apartment house, Rabbi?"

"The one at Page and Pennsylvania."

I hunched forward and smacked my forehead. "Oh Christ! I don't *believe* this! I must be *dreaming* this! Are you telling me you actually sent her all alone into a neighborhood like that?"

"A neighborhood like what? We're not talking East St. Louis here. We're talking North St. Louis County. All right, so I'll grant you it's mostly *shvartzer,* and that maybe it's not the safest—"

"It's a slum!"

"It is *not* a slum! I've had that property since 1953, and I can emphatically assure you—"

"Do you realize it's after dark? And that Billy's still *out* there? Alone? For godsakes, Rabbi! Don't you even *care* about your own daughter's safety?"

"What? Not care? How dare you imply such a thing! Now just you listen to me, mister! First of all, I don't appreciate your choice of language—or your lack of due respect! And secondly, the rent has to be collected. That's fact one. And fact two is, who else is going to collect it? You, maybe?"

"So hire somebody! Pay somebody!"

"You know perfectly well I haven't got that kind of—"

"Then *I'll* pay somebody! Or have your tenants *send* you the goddamned money like any *sane* landlord would do! Don't you think that'd be a little *wiser* than putting Billy's *life* at risk for your lousy fucking rent?"

There was a poisonous silence on the Rabbi's end.

"You just tell her I called," the old man said, and cracked down the phone.

"ARNIE, it was no big *deal.* I mean, really. You're actually sounding like some kind of racist."

"Come on, Billy—that's not fair. This has nothing to do with race, and you know it. A dangerous neighborhood is a dangerous—"

"It's *over* now. I'm back, and I'm fine, and nobody robbed me, and nobody raped me, and nobody even looked at me sideways. My God, the only people I even *saw* tonight were some poor intimidated women, children and old men. If anything, *I* was the one doing the mugging. All right? So will you please just calm down?"

I decided to try. The last thing I needed was to further blacken my mood before the party—for peddling fine minerals was like peddling anything else: no upbeat enthusiasm, no sale.

Billy, looking especially dowdy tonight in her shapeless gray corduroy jacket and baggy white painter's pants, swayed over to the kitchen counter for another handful of Doritos.

"There'll be food at the party," I said.

"I'm hungry now. Do you mind?"

I consciously relaxed my stomach muscles. "Could you at least do me one favor, Billy?"

"What?"

"Could we please just put an end to this insanity? Will you just tell your father that it's over—that you're through with being his lackey? Because I'm telling you, Billy, it just scared the living shit out of me tonight—"

"I'm not his lackey," she said. "I'm his daughter."

I blew out a breath. "Look, I told him I'd *pay* for someone to help him out until he's back on his feet. And I will. But I've got to have your cooperation on this, Billy. I mean, what could you possibly have left to prove? What haven't you done for that man already?"

"It's irrational, Arnie. There's no reason—"

"All right, fine. Let's say it *is* irrational. Let's say I'm completely out of line about this. Can't you just indulge me here anyway?"

She peevishly shrugged.

Now the dam burst. "Goddammit! How is it that your father can make you jump through hoops anytime he likes, but when *I* ask one simple important favor out of you—"

"He's an *invalid* now! Do I have to *explain* that to you? And anyway, you know he doesn't have the money to hire a man. And he's got too much pride to let you—"

"You know what this is, Billy? It's *triage.*"

"It's what?"

"Triage—you know, the method they use to rank injuries in the emergency room. If they decide you're deathly sick enough, well, lucky you—they'll take you in for treatment. But if it looks like you just might possibly *survive* for another ten minutes, you can just sit out there and *bleed* for all they—"

"What exactly are you saying?"

"First it was Redso, and now it's your father. Don't ask me how it happens, but it seems there's *always* some victim of one fucking thing or another in line ahead of me! Well, just when do *I* get in, Billy? What do *I* have to do to get your undivided attention? Put a shotgun to my head? Get back on my fucking crutches?"

She looked at me steadily. "I think you'd better have another drink," she said. "Otherwise you'll be a complete nervous wreck at your party." She turned away. "Meanwhile, I'm taking a shower."

□ □ □ □

I WAS SITTING at the coffee table and sorting through the small, near-perfect sample specimens in my compartmented hard-shell valise, when Billy, wrapped from chest to thigh in a bathtowel, padded vaguely into the living room. I reminded her, in a tone as neutral as I could manage, that we were already very late.

Billy frowned at the case. "Do you really have to bring that stuff along tonight?" she said.

I fingered the topaz in my hand. "Maybe I'm missing something here, Billy—but how am I supposed to sell my merchandise if I don't show it?"

"Couldn't you just tell them about your rocks at the party, and then make appointments to show them later? Wouldn't that be the more tasteful approach? There's just something so *tacky* about it, Arnie. Every time we go to one of these things, I feel like I'm showing up with the Tupperware representative."

I heroically kept my temper. "Could you please just get dressed?" I said, my voice scraping bottom.

Instead Billy picked up her pack of cigarettes from the coffee table and lit one; as she stooped, her towel rode up in back, exposing the heavy undercurves of her rather mealy-looking buttocks. Sad to say, the pellucid yellow depths of the topaz I was handling was the more heart-quickening sight.

Billy was nearly thirty-eight now. And yet, far from making any special effort to conserve her beauty, she seemed just as blithely indifferent as ever to the threats of time and gravity. She ate and drank exactly what she wanted. Aside from her warming-up routines before a performance, she never exercised at all. Unsurprisingly, then, she was softening up, spreading out—in the thighs, the rump, the belly. The gray in her hair had almost completely overtaken the black. And on her face—always devoid of makeup, unless she was on stage— the wrinkles at the corners of her mouth, the puffy half-moons under her eyes, were steadily becoming more marked. Was it a failing of mine—the dark underside of my connoisseurship— that I expected the beautiful woman I'd married to stay that way? Was that really so indefensible? I didn't think so. The inescapable fact was, you had to *look* at your spouse, day in and day out, to the point of visual saturation and beyond—and while Billy was still undeniably attractive, she was just as undeniably slipping. Yet try suggesting to her that she slow down with the booze or the Doritos, or that she experiment with a little hair color, or that she put on some makeup once in every blue moon, or even, God forbid, that she go out and buy herself something decent at Saks or Neiman-Marcus—and see how far you got. I'd even pointed out, to no avail, that her slovenliness was affecting her work. Once she used to land the ingenue roles fairly often; but now she was mostly relegated to the matron, the maiden aunt, the comical sidekick, the spurned wife.

I went on inspecting Billy—that incipient double chin spoiling the curve of her neck was especially depressing—and swallowed the mean impulse to insult her.

"So who's going to be there tonight?" she asked. "Aside from the entire cast of 'General Hospital'?"

"You just might surprise yourself and have a good time tonight, Billy."

She fired smoke out her nose. "What about that anesthesiologist? Will she be there?"

I very carefully set the topaz back into the case.

"You know, the one who looks like an aging pom-pom girl? The one who's always so *brisk*? What's her name?"

"Claire Johnson," I said. "And I have no idea if she's going to be there or not."

"But she seems to follow you around to these things, doesn't she?"

"She's a collector, Billy. Not to mention a doctor. She happens to know the same people I know."

Billy gave a twist to her neck, and stared off bitterly toward the hallway.

The silence took on a threatening pressure.

Finally she moved out of the living room—not in the direction of the bedroom, as I'd hoped, but into the kitchen. She soon came back with a drink in her hand (a few fingers of straight scotch is what it looked like), wandered over to the reclining chair, and, like a pouty loose-limbed teenager, plopped herself down.

"Billy, I hate to keep harping on this, but it's already nine o'clock—"

"Just let me drink my drink, all right?"

I sat there, controlling myself.

She pushed all the way back in her chair. The wrinkled soles of her feet rose into view. "I'll tell you what would make these damned medical conventions easier to take," she said. "If these doctors would just talk about what they *do* for once—instead of what they *own*. I mean, that really would be a relief."

"Come on, Billy. Don't you think it's only natural they'd rather not dwell on their jobs? Hell, most of these people work twelve-hour days."

"Well, if you want to own a lot of vacation homes and Jaguars and so forth, I guess you'd better expect to put in some extra hours, huh?"

I couldn't resist making a dig. "Not everybody's like your theater buddies, you know."

"Meaning what?"

"When *don't* they get tired of talking about their work? Even after a performance? *Especially* after a performance? Hell, what do they ever talk about at these parties except their own fascinating careers—or else the Crisis of the Theater in America? I mean, really, Billy. Doesn't that relentless self-absorption get a little tiring after a while? Even for you?"

"I see. So prattling on all night about your limited edition bronzes and your no-load mutual funds *isn't* self-absorption?"

At that point, I didn't know why, my anger melted into regret.

"Terrific," I said, and sighed. "So either I'm getting stuck with your phony theater pals, or you're getting stuck with my shallow materialistic clients. What's happened to us, Billy? We used to have a pretty good time, didn't we? We used to enjoy each other."

"I still enjoy you," Billy said, but added, "sometimes."

I didn't want to rise to that bait. "Well, what about other people? Hell, don't we know anybody else? Don't we have any mutual friends anymore?"

"Come on, Arnie. We've only had one mutual friend. And for all we know, he's dead."

That landed like a punch to the throat. Which, of course, was exactly what Billy had intended.

Abruptly, with a thunk, her chair came upright. She pushed to her feet, took a swallow of her scotch, and headed off, shoulders swinging, down the hallway.

I sagged forward on the sofa and stared at nothing.

So, once again, we'd slammed right up against the most massive and immovable of all the stone walls between us. Billy would never let me live down, much less forget, what I'd done to Redso so long ago on our wedding day. If our marriage had fallen sick, so her unspoken accusation went, then it was *my* original sin, *my* unforgivable breach of trust, *my* monstrous selfishness, that had introduced the virus. Sometimes, in moments of weakness or confusion, I actually thought she was right. Then I'd have to remind myself that it was only the *health* of our marriage I'd been trying to protect, and that if anyone had wanted to throw open the doors and welcome in the plague, it was Billy—willfully blind to the very real threat that Redso posed. But try telling that to her now. I'd been branded a criminal, I was the Judas-goat, and the stigma was there to stay no matter what I said or did.

Well, fuck her, I thought. Just fuck her! I'd been more than reasonable up until now, had tried my damnedest not to let things get too far out of hand, had patiently absorbed her repeated blows—and in return Billy had hit me full force below the belt. Well, now I was coming at her with my gloves off.

I caned into the bedroom.

As if I needed any more fuel for my rage, Billy had decided, in her fathomless perversity, to come up with an outfit no self-respecting woman would have worn to a bowling alley. Her blouse was a loose Russian-peasant sort of thing that billowed frowsily over the waist of her frumpy black skirt, and had gone through so many washings there was no telling if it had originally been yellow or white. Her clunky brown shoes looked orthopedic. Around her head, God knew why, she'd wound a headscarf of purple and orange and black. The ugliness struck me as intentional. If I insisted on going to this party as a Tupperware salesman, Billy seemed to be letting me know, then she was going to show up as some threadbare gypsy clown.

"What the hell is that?" I said.

She continued to adjust her headscarf as she frowned into the mirror above the dresser. "What's what?"

"What you're wearing."

"You don't like it?"

"Billy, don't you have eyes? For godsakes—you look like the gypsy in a grade-B werewolf movie."

She pretended to give herself a serious appraisal in the mirror. "You really don't like it, huh?" Swiftly she crossed her arms at her waist and yanked the blouse off over her head. Her brown-nippled breasts wobbled heavily into sight. She stooped and pushed her skirt down to her ankles. "To tell you the truth," she said, stepping away from her clothes, "I wasn't in love with that outfit, either." She headed over to the closet door, and took her bathrobe down from a hook.

"Now what are you doing?"

"Getting comfortable."

"For what?"

"For the nice quiet evening I'm going to spend here all alone." She yoked her bathrobe tight around her waist, then sat on the edge of the bed and started unlacing her hideous brown shoes. "I'm not going to your party," she said.

"Billy, what is this?"

"You'll have a much better time there without me, I'm sure."

"What the fuck are you *talking* about?"

"Go and have fun. Sell lots of rocks. Make lots of money. Show everyone your handsome new profile. And while you're at it, go find some other woman to drag around as your trophy. I've had it with being your Barbie doll."

I only gaped at her.

"Just find some other woman. Buddy up to your pom-pom girl, for instance. Spend the night with her, for all I care. You must be getting pretty tired of all these secret afternoon rendezvous, right? Well, I'm giving you free leave. Come back whenever you feel like it. Or don't come back at all. Frankly, I'm just too sick and tired of it all to really *give* a shit what you do." Billy let her shoe drop to the floor. "The main thing is, I don't want to fight about it. It'd just be too exhausting—and too boring. I mean, there are only so many ways you can play the wronged wife—" Billy paused. "And I guess this is one of them, right?"

"Billy, for godsakes . . ."

"What? Do you want to stand there and plead innocent?"

I only sagged over my cane.

"I'm not sure I even *needed* any proof, you know. There's just been this air of falsehood around you—this inauthenticity. But then your mother called the other day to invite us to dinner, and so I went down and looked at your appointment book—and I couldn't believe it. Are you dumb or just incredibly arrogant? I mean, really, Arnie—if you're meeting with this woman three times a week, why on earth would you keep a written record where I could find it? Did you want to get caught?"

Nothing I could say would extricate me. I just went on stupidly standing there, squeezing the head of my cane.

"Are you in love with this woman?"

"No."

Billy took that in. "Well, is there anyone else?"

"Yes."

"Who?" she said. But then she roughly shook her head. "No. Never mind. Why the fuck would I want to know that?" She stared off past me, her eyes appearing to lose focus. Then they fixed on me again. "So here's the million-dollar question. Are you still in love with me?"

I didn't—couldn't—answer.

"Well," she said. "I guess that just about covers it, doesn't it?"

Billy arose from the bed, walked up to me, and halted.

"Do you mind?" she said. "You're blocking the door."

I moved my cane and stepped aside for her.

Twelve

"WELL, YOU'RE LOOKING GOOD," my mother said, inspecting me with her slightly bulging, shrewd gray eyes. "So trim and healthy and handsome. Walking along on that cane with barely a limp. And yet I'll bet you've never felt quite this awful, have you?"

I grunted.

"Or this guilty?"

"Jesus, Mom. You sure don't believe in coddling me, do you?"

"I don't think you want to be coddled," she said.

Most likely she was right. Most likely I was in need of a strong tonic dose of Doris Goldman's special brand of acerbic mother-love; otherwise, why would I have invited her out on this picnic today? We were walking—my mother swinging her picnic basket, me swinging my cane—through Laumeier Sculpture Park in South St. Louis County, one of my mother's favorite spots. When I was a kid she used to sometimes bring me out here in my wheelchair, and drag me up and down these mild but still considerable hills, as backbreaking as that labor must have been for her. The park was as weird as it was lovely, its neat green meadows and small stands of trees studded here and there, like some Stone Age ceremonial site, with sudden and indecipherable outcroppings of burnished steel, painted wood, plastic tubing, strangely gesturing hulks of bronze and stone. Since April (when Billy had moved out, and taken her own apartment) I'd been mostly ducking my mother, wriggling out of her weekly dinner invitations when I could, sticking to safe banalities at the table when I couldn't, and turning slippery as a government official when she tried, over the phone, to pry some genuine responses out of me. But now it was late June, and as we strolled through this odd green landscape, I was finally fessing up. I'd hoped it would be a relief to purge myself. But my mother's sharp probing, compounded by the intense noonday sun above our heads, had me feeling as if a third-degree lamp was aimed right at my face.

"So, Arnie? Tell me this. Do you ever wish you had it to do all over again?"

I sighed heavily. "You want to know the truth, Mom? I'm not sure I'd act any differently if I did."

"Oh?"

"Most of the time, sure, I feel culpable as hell. But at other times . . . well, it just doesn't look like I had much choice in the matter."

"You're saying you were an innocent victim of circumstance?"

I glanced at her. She had her mouth carefully pursed.

"Well, yes," I said. "In a way, I *was*. I didn't ask for my arthritis to improve."

"Now wait a minute, Arnie. Your *arthritis* was responsible for breaking up your marriage? You can't really mean that, can you?"

"I'm just saying that something cataclysmic happened to me. I mean, there I was, thirty-two years old, all ready to settle down into a nice dull predictable middle age—and *wham*. Suddenly I had a whole new face, a whole new body. Women were starting to act very funny around me, I was acting funny around women . . . the whole thing was totally *unprecedented*. How could *anyone* know how to behave in a situation like that? Hell, I was fourteen again."

"Except, of course, that you weren't fourteen again."

"Mom, I wasn't even fourteen when I was fourteen. I never had a real adolescence, you know."

"Why, sure you did, Arnie. Believe me, I was there."

"You know what I'm talking about. While all the other kids my age were out there exploring the brave new world of sex—what was I doing? Sitting at home, fondling my rocks. Do you know I didn't even lose my virginity until I was twenty-three?"

My mother grunted, and trudged on. "So what are you saying, Arnie? That cheating on Billy was just a matter of reclaiming your lost youth? What is that? Sort of a boys-will-be-boys defense?"

"It's not a defense. It's a partial explanation."

My mother pointedly said nothing.

"I'll tell you what, Mom. As strange as it might sound, I think that getting healthy was just as much of a disaster for me as being sick."

My mother considered that. "Actually," she said, "that doesn't sound so strange to me at all."

She sharply increased her pace; I had to work to keep up.

"I suppose I can't blame you for how you felt, Arnie. But that's not at all the same as exonerating you for what you did."

"Shit, Mom. You think I don't feel the same way?"

"Well, let's hope you do. Maybe it's old-fashioned of me, but I'm a big believer in guilt—where it's appropriate. And never mind all this silly self-esteem nonsense that's going around. There's nothing like a healthy sense of remorse for whipping your character into shape."

"Yeah, well. You'll be glad to know that I despise myself plenty right now."

"That's not exactly what I was driving at, Arnie."

We walked on.

"Why don't we take a look at that strange white thing over there?" my mother said. "I don't recognize it. I think it must be new."

I followed her to a whale-sized heap of madly twisted white plastic tubing. She set down her picnic basket, and sucked in her cheeks as she considered it.

"Doesn't do much for me," she said.

"Me neither."

"Arnie? You mind if I bring up a touchy subject?"

"Shoot."

"I don't imagine your sex life with Billy was going very well?"

I smirked at her—what other guy had a mother who talked to him like this?—and said: "Actually, it wasn't bad. In fact, it didn't have much to do with Billy at all—my catting around. It was more a matter of . . . I don't know, Mom. Curiosity, I suppose. That, and ego."

"But you're still catting around, aren't you?"

I didn't answer.

My mother turned back to the sculpture. After a while, she said, "Do you miss her, Arnie?"

"Yes," I said. "I miss her."

I was alarmed at how despairingly thick my voice sounded.

"Then why in the world don't you just *drop* these other women?"

"Billy and I are *separated*. What am I supposed to do? Sit home at night and knit?"

"I just wonder how long you can expect Billy to wait."

"Don't assume she's waiting for me, Mom. It was her decision to leave, remember. And besides, Billy seems perfectly happy in her new place—with her one plate, her one fork, and no furniture. Happier than me, anyway."

"Is she seeing anyone else?"

"Not that she's told me about."

"So you do still talk?"

"Sure. In fact, we seem to be getting along much better, now that she's moved out. It's almost like we're a couple of old war buddies—you know, who've been through the worst together."

"Well, you and Billy always were friends, weren't you? Right from the start. That's one advantage you've got over most other couples, you know." My mother's thin shoulders lifted and fell. Then she stooped and retrieved her picnic basket. "Why don't we head for that battleship thing over there?"

What she was referring to, at the far end of the long meadow, was a jumble of titanic scarlet tubes that indeed looked something like a battleship—albeit one hit by a torpedo, with the cylinders, like gun turrets, sticking out wildly in every direction.

It was a long walk. Halfway across the meadow, my mother stopped and turned to me.

"Arnie, can't you just swallow your pride, go crawling back

to Billy, promise to act like a responsible and honorable adult, and beg her forgiveness? Believe me, please. You won't have a *chance* at happiness until you do that."

I stood very still over my cane, my heart knocking.

"It's not that simple, Mom."

"Maybe you're just overcomplicating it."

"Maybe," I said. "Or maybe not." I looked up at that enormous, insecure-looking pile of gigantic red cylinders. "Or maybe I'm just not ready."

"How many more women do you have to sleep with before you *are* ready, Arnie?"

I winced at that, and turned to her.

But my mother wasn't looking at me now.

She was peering at something at the far edge of the meadow. I looked where she was looking, and thought, at first, that what had seized her attention was just another abstract metal sculpture jutting from the crest of the hill. But no.

It was a man slumped in a wheelchair, facing the intense blue screen of the sky. He and his chair cast a netted shadow, like a ship. The wheels glinted spikily in the sunlight. His large dark head rested heavily on a shoulder; his right arm hung down from the side of the chair at an unnatural, broken-looking angle, with both the elbow and the wrist turned out. He remained absolutely still. He might have been asleep, or dead drunk, or—who knew?—overcome by some rapturous vision taking shape in the sky before him.

We watched him without speaking. Then my mother took hold of my arm.

"Come on," she said gently. "What do you say we go eat?"

Thirteen

ON A SATURDAY EVENING in August, I drove to Billy's childhood home in University City, and parked behind her father's junk-filled pickup in the driveway. Just moments before, the sun had gone down, and Rabbi Rubin, punctual vampire that he was, was already out and about.

He was perched near the top of a ladder (his difficult recuperation from that broken hip had apparently taught him nothing) and was energetically clawing through the gutter, flinging clod after clod of black gunk to the ground. At the sound of my idling engine he turned to glare at me, then poked up at the brim of his fedora, and resumed his rooting. The old man still hadn't forgiven me for our last little tussle on the phone—five months earlier—and lately when I showed up at the house, I no longer even received his customary gruff nod.

That I was here at all at the end of *Shabbos* was, of course, Billy's doing. While in the context of our marriage I'd been the deceiver and Billy the deceived, in her relations with her father she was the same bold and systematic liar she'd always been. The ethical difference, I supposed, was that I'd been lying in order to spare my own hide, while Billy only lied to spare her father's feelings—assuming, that is, that the old fanatic had any.

And since our separation, Billy had been deceiving her fa-

ther in yet another way: she still had him thinking that our
marriage was in one piece. Why needlessly upset her father,
Billy argued, when things were still so unsettled between us—
when, for all we knew, we might still get back together, when
neither one of us was even thinking yet of filing for divorce?
And while I failed to see how my loss as a son-in-law would
break the Rabbi's heart, I saw no reason to blow Billy's story.
What did I care if the old man was as deluded by his daughter
as he was by himself? And anyway, it was easy enough to keep
up appearances. If the Rabbi called for Billy, I'd simply make
up some excuse, and then relay the message to her apartment.
And there was little chance he'd pop up without warning at
the house in Creve Coeur; in all the years of our marriage the
grand total of his visits could probably be counted on one
hand.

So while Billy and I now lived apart, we came together on
these *Shabbos* evenings when I served as her chauffeur—dropping her off on Friday afternoon, driving her back to her
apartment on Saturday—for Billy feared that if we broke our
old pattern, and she began to drive herself, her father might
have cause to get suspicious. As absurd as the whole routine
was, I'd been looking forward more and more to these brief
and poignant reunions in the twilight—for more and more,
I'd been missing Billy painfully. I was still seeing other
women, all right, but my heart was no longer in it. I was following my dick around mostly out of habit—and was beginning to lament the blind egoistic stupidity that had rendered
my life so empty.

Billy came sashaying across the lawn in the gray grainy light,
her overnight bag swinging at her side. She paused at the
ladder and said something to her father; he nodded, waved,
and plunged his hands back into the gutter. When she got
inside the Lincoln and shut the door, I was stung by the familiar floral fragrance of her just-washed hair, and could have
kicked myself as I looked at her.

While Billy insisted that she hadn't been dieting, she'd still
dropped a good ten or fifteen pounds since moving out; probably, she'd said, because she was no longer preparing three
meals a day for me. Maybe my regret, my shame, my longing,
and the indigestible fact that my wife was actually off-limits to

me now, all added a certain luster to her looks—but Billy was once again as maddeningly desirable as when I'd first laid eyes on her. And her physical beauty was the least of it. Nowhere else in the company of other women had I found anything approaching Billy's intelligence, her gift of empathy, her peculiar solidity of being. Other women were as light as air.

I was in love, and wretchedly, all over again.

She set her overnight bag on the floor and sighed.

"How're you doing, Arnie?" She sounded tired.

I shrugged, sadly—wanted her to get the message that I was miserable without suffering the indignity of telling her so.

"Did you have another thrill-a-minute *Shabbos*?" I asked her.

She grunted.

I pulled out of the driveway, and then we were moving down the slope of Gannon Street, past the Chesid Shel-Emeth synagogue, past Diamond's Kosher Meats, past Petrofsky's Bakery. When I looked at Billy again, she was intently gnawing on her fat lower lip.

"Billy, are you okay?"

"Actually," she said, "I'm not okay at all."

Hope flickered dangerously in my chest. Could she be having second thoughts? Was it possible that these four months of separation had finally worked their magic—and left her just as desolate as me?

"I'll tell you the truth," I said, my voice full of gravel. "It's been lousy lately, Billy. *I've* been lousy."

She stared out her window. "Well, I'm sorry to hear that, Arnie. You know I don't want you to be unhappy."

"Do you . . . have you been missing me at all?"

Billy looked at me then. "Arnie, do we really have to talk about this now?"

"What else is there to talk about?"

"Redso," she said, and dropped her head back to her seat.

We came to a red light. I very cautiously applied the brakes, amazed at how violently my heart had started to pound.

"You've heard from him?"

"Yes."

"When? How? Did he call?"

"He wrote me a letter."

The light changed. I reached for the acceleration rod at the side of the steering column—which, of course, was no longer there. It had been a long time now since I'd driven a car rigged up for a cripple. Back around Christmas, I'd gladly had the whole complicated jumble of rods and wires stripped from the steering column—a move both practical and symbolic, and nearly as sweet as the act of finally sticking my crutches away in the closet. I instructed myself to use my foot, and started us forward.

"When did you get the letter?"

"Thursday."

"But I saw you on Friday. Why didn't you say anything?"

"I needed time to think."

"About what?"

"I've got the letter at my apartment. Just come up and read it, Arnie. Then you'll see what I've got to think about."

BACK IN APRIL, when we'd thrashed out Billy's new (and I'd hoped temporary) living arrangements, I'd tried to be as generous and flexible as possible. I told her I didn't give a damn what the place cost, or what we paid for her new furniture; I wasn't out to punish her by depriving her of anything. But naturally Billy didn't want much. She took an efficiency apartment in the De Mun area of Clayton—a leafy old neighborhood of red brick apartment houses, populated mostly by young professionals and some well-heeled college students from nearby Washington University—and the bill for her new furniture had barely exceeded one month's rent.

Billy led the way up the three flights of stairs—making no concession, in her haste, to my limp—and left me alone in the living room as she went to fetch a couple of beers. I was already jittery with dread, and the sere white emptiness of her living room only added somehow to my consternation. As if to prove some point, Billy had furnished it with a grand total of six objects: a dining room table of unpainted pine, two chairs to go with it, a crammed bookshelf against an otherwise empty wall, a futon that served as a sofa, bent at the middle on a wooden frame, and before it a low table, hardly bigger than a chessboard, that held her cigarettes, a butt-filled ashtray, and the book she was currently reading, *Middlemarch*, of all things,

with a bookmark stuck in the middle of that massive novel—
which suggested to me that she wasn't having much of a social
life. All in all, it seemed to me, Billy had finally gotten her
dream apartment. Gandhi would have been right at home in
this monastic white cell of a room.

Billy returned, handed me my beer, lit a cigarette, then un-
folded the letter and took a seat on the futon. I remained
standing, grinding a thumbnail into the waxy head of my
cane. She put her thick-rimmed reading glasses on—which, as
always, only accentuated the feminine softness of her face—
and began to read aloud.

"Dear Billy:

"Yes, it's really me. I'm sure you're not exactly overjoyed
to hear from me after all this time, and all that's happened.
But please, don't tear this letter up or throw it away. Please
just keep reading.

"I'm back in St. Louis. I've been back since around
Christmas, when, I'm sorry to report, my mother passed
away of a brain tumor. I'm now living in her house in South
St. Louis, and believe it or not, I'm all right. I won't go into
all that's happened over these past four years right now—it's
much too complicated. But I would like to see you again, if
that's possible, and fill you in then. Maybe that's about as
appealing to you as a case of the flu. But please, Billy—I
wish very much that we could talk again, for old times' sake
if nothing else. So I'm inviting you here for dinner on
Friday night, September 5th, at eight o'clock. (I'll be making
my famous barbecued ribs.) That gives you two weeks to
think about it. If you decide you want to come, please call
me at 481-9263. And if you don't, I'll completely
understand.

"As always,
"REDSO

"And that's it," Billy said, setting the letter down. She took
off her glasses and stared at nothing.

I only squeezed the head of my cane.

"Do you know," she said, "the first time I read it, I actually
kept thinking it was some kind of *forgery?* Just that phrase
'passed away,' for instance. Redso *never* would have used a

namby-pamby word like that. But of course, who'd bother pretending they were Redso?" Billy slowly wagged her head. "Anyway, it's not him. I don't know who it is, Arnie. But it's not *him*."

"All right if I sit down?"

"Of course."

I joined her on the sofa, taking the letter from the table. The second time through, now that I could see the actual text, it was even more bizarre. It was surrealistically neat, without an x-out, smudge or typo to be found in it anywhere.

"This is beyond belief," I said. "You remember how sloppy his typing used to be? You could barely read his manuscripts. But *look* at this, Billy. It's like the work of some executive secretary."

"I know. And what about that ending? He didn't even say 'Love' . . ."

"He certainly doesn't sound manic."

"He doesn't sound manic. He doesn't sound depressed. He doesn't sound like anything at *all*."

"But what do you think? You think it's possible he's actually straightened up?"

She didn't answer right off. "I suppose anything's possible," she said. "Or maybe when he sat down to write that letter, he was just having a lucid moment—who knows? God, I don't know what the fuck to think!"

We sat there quietly for a spell, as the import of my question crept up on me. What if Redso *had* straightened up? What if the inconceivable had actually happened, and Redso had somehow seen the light, begun to take his lithium, and reformed himself into a sane, civilized, perfectly acceptable human being? What then?

I pushed up to my cane, and began some agitated three-legged pacing around the room.

"Of course I'm going," Billy said.

I stopped and turned. Slumped there on the sofa, her arms akimbo, her tennis shoes splayed, she looked as limp and empty as a rag doll.

"I mean, how could I *not* go? Just for the sake of curiosity, if nothing else?" She blinked at me. "But Arnie?"

I knew that look in her shining eyes. She was about to plead for something.

"Would you come with me?"

"What? Oh Jesus . . ."

"Maybe I'm afraid to go alone. I don't know. But I just— don't think I can handle this all by myself."

"Billy, I'm not even invited."

"You're my husband, aren't you? And it's not like you're some innocent bystander in all of this. Redso would *expect* you to come. Anyway, I'll make sure it's okay when I talk to him. I'm positive he'll want to see you, too."

"Oh, brother, I don't know about this . . ."

"Well, just think about it, all right? And Arnie? One other thing. That is, if you do decide to come." Billy weakly shrugged. "Could we maybe not tell him that we're separated?"

I scowled at her.

"I mean, right now he doesn't know. He *can't* know. And I just . . . think it would be much better if we kept it that way."

"Billy, how is it that I'm always colluding in your lies?"

"There's a *reason* for this."

"Sure. You want me there as a buffer. In case things get a little too dangerously emotional, right?"

She looked at me evenly. "Right."

"But it's still a lie, isn't it?"

Her eyes became half hooded. "Please don't talk to me about lies, Arnie."

Of course that shut me up.

"I know I'm in no position to ask this kind of favor from you now. But if you just did this one thing for me . . . well. You can't know how grateful I'll be."

I stared at the frozen swirls in her hardwood floor. Just how grateful *would* she be, I wondered?

Then I looked up into Billy's imploring eyes, and realized I'd be a damned fool not to find out.

STILL ABSORBING THE BLOW, Claire Johnson slowly set her wineglass on the coffee table—between the two stunning clusters of rod-shaped violet tourmaline, streaked with inclusions of golden calcite, that I'd sold to her earlier this spring—

and sat back against the sofa, crossing her finely muscled arms. "I guess I should thank you for breaking the news in person," she said. "I mean, some men would just leave it at a phone call. Or else not bother telling me at all—" Her voice quavered. She squeezed her forearms. "But you're not like that, are you, Arnie? You've got manners."

I bore that in silence, holding my cane across my lap, as if to protect my testicles—which probably wasn't such a bad idea.

"So what about those two other women you were seeing? I suppose you paid them both courtesy calls, too?"

"I wish you wouldn't do this, Claire . . ."

"What? Oh, I forgot. We're supposed to be sophisticated adults about this, aren't we? Well, you're right. I mean, what's the point in getting ugly? You want another glass of wine?"

"No thanks."

"And what about dinner? No. Forget *that*. It would just be too horrible if you stuck around, wouldn't it? And that's too bad. Because it really was one hell of a dinner I was going to make for you, Arnie. I went all the way down to Soulard to get the red snapper—" Claire's mouth buckled. "God, will you listen to me? As if it matters where I bought the fucking fish!"

I pushed up heavily to my cane.

"It's actually sort of heartwarming, though, isn't it? Like the ending of a lousy movie. You know, the wayward husband finally returning to the bosom of his faithful wife . . ."

"Claire, I'm sorry. But I really do have to go."

"Of course you do. But first just answer me this. How could you not *know* you were still in love with Billy? Are you some kind of imbecile?"

At this juncture of my life, I had no doubt that I was some kind of imbecile. Certainly I'd been mindlessly unprepared for Claire's depth of emotion, her vehemence. I'd expected her to maintain her pose of devil-may-care breeziness.

"I'll just ask you again, Arnie. How could you not know you were in love with your wife?"

I sagged over my cane, and fixed my gaze on a cluster of tourmaline. The colors looked garish, overdone. "Christ, I don't know, Claire. Maybe . . . I just had to go out and learn it all over again."

"You had go out and *learn* it?"

"Well . . . yes."

"By fucking *me?*"

She'd practically screamed it. For an instant her hot eyes burned into mine. Then she picked up her glass, killed off the wine, and turned away.

"Claire, you're really not being fair about this."

"I'm not being fair?"

"Weren't you always claiming you had no real emotional investment in this thing? Wasn't that the official line?"

Claire harshly sniffed, rubbed at her nose, and raised her chin. Her mouth indented at one corner, but it wasn't a smile.

"And you believed me, didn't you?" she said.

I LIMPED for the last time down that hallway lined with mirrors, but this time without a glance at my caning reflection. I was no longer much enamored of my Byronic good looks, which had caused me so much trouble—and even less so of that liar behind the mask. My preening days were over.

But I was still in the business of pruning the truth to suit my ends. What I hadn't revealed to Claire (or to hyperkinetic June, or to starry-eyed Colleen, during similar awful scenes with both of them this week) was that, in truth, Billy and I hadn't come to any agreement at all about patching up our marriage. I'd used that line because I'd thought it would be the simplest, the most decisive, the kindest way of letting those women down—not that I could see how it had softened the blow in any of those three cases.

And what I hadn't told Billy (not yet, anyway, with our dinner at Redso's still looming, with everything still hanging in the balance) was that I'd finally taken my mother's stern advice, and radically changed my act.

Throughout these last two weeks, I'd been unable to shake the fear, however groundless, that Redso had indeed straightened up—that he'd begun to take his lithium, that his mood swings were under control, that whatever portions of his mind, his personality, had been scattered in the whirlwinds of his mania were now fully and brilliantly restored—and that a healthy Redso would prove so formidable a rival that I would barely stand a chance against his charms. Not that I was without a few advantages, of course. After all, I was hardly the same callow moon-faced cripple I'd been when Billy first entered my life. And the private history we now shared (which certainly hadn't been *all* bad) could only strengthen my hand with a woman like Billy, who placed so much value on loyalty. Still, when I imagined a new and improved Redso Wolff—every bit as charismatic as before, but with all the defects of his madness expunged—hope shriveled. What woman could resist a package like that? Especially one who had loved him so long and so strenuously, in spite of his appalling negatives?

I now believed that I had the fight of my life on my hands. But before making my abject overture to Billy, I needed to do all I could to buttress my position. And my first order of business was to put a screeching halt to my adulteries. I'd be a fool as well as a hypocrite to beg Billy's forgiveness while still carrying on with other women—which would have rendered the promises I meant to make, and meant to keep, a joke. But there was also a superstitious impulse at work. I felt I had to somehow make myself worthy of Billy (or worthier, at least, than I'd been), that some ritual sacrifice was required of me, and that by washing my hands of these women, by casting out the devils of my lust, I might throw myself at her feet as a purer penitent.

And so, my penance done, I caned away from Claire's apartment—shaken, shamed, and about as ready as I'd ever be, I supposed, to face whatever awaited me at Redso's place to morrow night.

Fourteen

I DOUBLE-PARKED in front of Billy's apartment house, honked once, and waited for her appearance in the vague sad light of dusk.

It seemed that nowadays we only came together in this gray uncertain light, that we didn't exist as a couple at any other time of day—and that seemed to me bitterly appropriate. Our marriage itself was in some iffy twilight stage, not quite alive, not quite dead, and it would be impossible to know until tonight's ordeal was over just which way the vital signs were tending.

Billy walked slowly to the car. For once her outfit had been smartly thought through. Her black slacks went nicely with her butter-colored blouse; she'd tied around her waist a tasteful sash of cream and crimson; and unless the fading light had me fooled, she'd even gone so far as to put on some eyeliner and lipstick. My heart rose—then sank. For after all, she'd done this for Redso. For *Redso*. Then why had she so seldom, and almost always under protest, done as much for me?

Billy took a last pull off her cigarette, dropped it to the sidewalk, mashed it with the toe of her shoe, and got into the car. The *chunk* of the slamming door carried an ominous finality.

I told her how lovely she looked.

"Thanks. I feel like hell."

"Nervous?"

"Scared sick is more like it."

I didn't mention that I was scared sick, too. I started us down the street.

"I really don't feel like talking, Arnie. If that's all right with you."

"Fine," I said.

Billy fished around in the box of cassettes on the seat between us. "All right if I play some music?"

I forget what she picked out. But she cranked up the volume, relieving us of the duty to talk until we were down on South Hampton, and Billy, spotting a liquor store, reminded me that we had to pick up a bottle of wine.

SOON AFTER THE DEATH of her husband, Frieda Wolff had pulled up stakes in suburban Creve Coeur—where she'd never really felt at home—and returned to the old German-Catholic neighborhood of her roots. She'd chosen the house on Sunshine Street, I'd always thought, as much for the sticky-sweet sound of its name as for anything else. What better street than Sunshine Street in which to hunker down, snug among your comforters, sentimental samplers and Lawrence Welk albums, as you mistily waited for death? The houses on this Dutchtown street were nearly identical: gingerbready one-story red brick bungalows, each with a tiny front porch, a door outlined in rough chunks of limestone, and a lawn so minimal it was barely lawn at all—just a mere grassy hump above the sidewalk. On both sides of the street, the chimneys marched in lock step to the horizon. We had some trouble locating Frieda's house (the numbers were stenciled on the sidewalks, as if no one in this sleepy neighborhood ever expected any visitors after dark) until we spotted the untended garden covering most of the lawn, and at the back of it, Frieda's dead-giveaway concrete Madonna, her hooded face sadly inclined, her palms lifted in a gesture of melancholy invitation.

"Will you get a load of that?" I said, pulling up to the curb. "He's still got his mother's Virgin Mary out front."

Billy looked at it, but said nothing.

"You'd think he would have gotten rid of it by now," I went

on. "Or else given it a pair of Groucho Marx glasses—*some-thing.*"

"It *is* strange," Billy said, in a weak voice.

I looked at her. "You ready?"

She nodded and pushed open her door.

We moved together up the steep hump of the lawn and to the tiny front porch, where the yellow porchlight was on to greet us. On the door was another of Frieda's leftover decorative touches—a flat wooden duck with a blue ribbon around its neck and a banner at its webbed feet, entangled with pink and blue flowers, that read WELCOME, FRIENDS. With a crackle, Billy pressed her sack to her chest (I'd sprung, pretty generously, I thought, for a bottle of Châteauneuf du Pape) and rapped hard on the brass knocker. I watched her as she waited in the lurid yellow light, her eyes narrowed resolutely at the door, her plump lips parted with suspense, and then I took another look at that wooden duck, at that syrupy and yet weirdly appropriate message, WELCOME FRIENDS, and then the knob rattled, a whiter light lit Billy's face, and Redso was filling the door.

I say filling the door because he had gone that thick, that paunchy. He wore a black turtleneck shirt, which sloped down from his chest and spilled over his belt like it was poured full of pancake batter. His once lean and hawkish face had filled out, puffed up, the cheekbones and the jawline blurred with fat. Only in his big sharp nose was there any hint of the ferocity I remembered. His hair was no longer a frizzed electric bush, but had been cut back, tamed, into a close-hugging carpet of rusty curls. I realized that I'd never seen the shape of Redso's skull before—and something about the sunken areas at his temples, described by delicate ridges of bone, suggested fragility, mortality. Maybe I should have been relieved to see his good looks gone; on that score, anyway, he no longer posed a threat. But what I felt was shock, and then a melting, spreading sadness. I had to remind myself that Redso was just about my age—for that plump, pale, worn-out-looking stranger, nervously shifting his bulk on the doorstep, could have easily passed for forty.

Redso flashed me a brief uncertain smile. But of course his real interest was in Billy. He stepped down rather awkwardly to the porch—as if he weren't quite sure how to carry his extra weight—and into Billy's waiting arms. She locked him in a tight embrace, her eyes shut, her face pressed to his neck, and crushed her paper sack against his back. "Oh, Redso . . ."

"Billy . . ."

I tightened my grip on my cane.

Then Billy stepped back, swung her hair behind her shoulders, and smiled at Redso, hard. "God, Redso. Just look at you."

He touched the sloppy spill of his gut. "What?"

She laughed. "Well, for starters, you're alive."

Redso tried on a grin. But it was a far cry from the confident powerhouse grin that had once been his trademark. It looked, in fact, a little pained. "Billy," he said, "you look fantastic. Just fantastic."

"Yeah? Well, thanks. So do you."

"I've put on a lot of weight, I know . . ."

"Oh, come on, Redso. At least you're not all skin and bones like you used to be." She hugged her sack tighter. "Anyway, I'm just . . . awfully glad to see you."

They went on desperately smiling at each other.

Then Redso turned to me. "Hey, Arnie."

"Hey, stranger."

I took my cane into my left hand, and we shook. Redso's grip was viselike—as if he hoped, by crushing my fingers, to counter his softened, almost feminized appearance.

"How the hell are you doing, Redso?"

"Oh, not too bad. Pretty good, as a matter of fact."

"Yeah? Well, terrific."

Redso finally released my hand. I had to pump the head of my cane to get the blood moving again.

"I was awfully sorry to hear about your mother," I said.

Redso nodded, sighed. "Thanks, Arnie. It was—well, it all happened pretty fast. I mean, she didn't suffer much."

I made a noise of commiseration in my throat.

Redso licked his lips. Then he grinned that uncertain grin again. "And look at *you*, Arnie. Just look at you on that cane. Fucking A, man. Congratulations. It's just . . . fantastic to see you like this."

I wondered at the flatness of Redso's delivery, the missing

music. Despite the ostensible exclamations in that speech, he'd barely strayed from a low careful monotone.

"Billy told me you were using a cane these days. But shit, man. I never thought I'd see you off your crutches."

"Well, that makes two of us," I said.

"Three," Billy chimed in.

"And your *face* looks good. Different somehow."

"Yeah, well, I kicked the steroids a while back."

"Did you? Well, shit. That's just fantastic."

That must have been the fourth or fifth time Redso had already used the word "fantastic"—as if his once-rich vocabulary had gone as impoverished as a teenager's. Or maybe I was jumping the gun. Maybe he was just nervous, tongue-tied. Hell, weren't we all pretty tongue-tied?

As if to confirm that, nothing happened. For a bad distended moment we all just stood there in the gelid yellow porchlight, not speaking, not moving.

"Well, here we all are," Billy said, in a too-bright singsong. "The three of us, together again."

That fell with a complicated thud.

I thought I'd try joggling things loose with some teasing.

"So, Redso, what's the deal? What the hell is that Madonna still doing in your yard?"

He looked puzzled. "The what?"

"The Virgin Mary. You know, the mother of Jesus? Shit, Redso—I couldn't believe my eyes when we drove up here. Why would you still have it around—an old iconoclast like you?"

Redso peered at the statue.

"It was my mother's," he said.

I laughed uneasily. "I think we're aware of that, Redso. But what's it still doing there? And while we're at it, what about *this* piece of frightening sentimentality?" I tapped the wooden duck on the door. "What's happened to you, pal? Have you turned into a sappy old Bavarian grandmother, or what?"

Redso shrugged. "I just . . . haven't gotten around to fixing things up yet, I guess."

Billy's sack crackled. "Well, what are we all doing, just standing around like this? I don't know about you guys, but I sure could use a drink."

"Right," Redso said. But he didn't make a move. He was searching Billy's face. He seemed lost.

"Well, you could serve us out here," Billy said, hiking up another bright stage-smile. "Or you could invite us inside. It really doesn't matter much to me."

Redso softly laughed. "Sorry. It's just so completely strange. You know. Seeing the two of you again." He cleared his throat. "But good, too."

"It *is* good," Billy said, with too much force.

"Anyway. Come in, come in . . ."

We followed him into the living room. It was the same overstuffed, kitschy mausoleum I remembered. Everything here was Frieda's; nothing, from what I could see, had been added or subtracted by Redso's living here at all. There was even the same familiar cloying smell—part cabbage, part roses, part stale cigarettes (Frieda used to chain-smoke Lucky Strikes). Maybe it was the thought of smoke that triggered it, but suddenly I recalled Redso's manic attempt, so long ago, at torching this little house. I scanned the room, the plump faded sofa and armchairs, the wallpaper with its oppressive green and pink floral pattern, the dark oval rug, the glassed-in cabinets and knickknack shelves filled almost to overflowing with souvenir ashtrays, artificial flowers, framed photographs, colored glass balls, and scores of sugary ceramic figurines—puppies, rabbits, ducks, big-headed children, twirling ballerinas, sad-eyed clowns, not to mention several additional Virgin Marys—but saw no signs of any scorch marks, or burned areas, or whatever the hell I thought I was looking for.

"Well, here we are," Redso said. "Home sweet home."

The dullness of that remark gave me a shiver.

"Redso," I said. "How can you live with all this icky-sweet stuff? I mean, Jesus. Doesn't this place screw up your blood-sugar levels?"

Redso glanced around the room as if he hadn't taken a good look at it until now. "I should probably get rid of some of this junk, shouldn't I? I don't know why I haven't yet. I guess . . . I just don't notice my surroundings very much."

I heard Billy exhale.

"Well, heck, Redso," she said. "It's not like interior decoration was ever tops on your priority list, right?"

Redso smiled. Then he turned and loped to the ornate coffee table (his old jittery wolfish stride was gone; now he moved more like a heavy shambling bear) and picked up his drink. It looked like a Coke—rum and Coke, I figured, although I'd never known Redso to go for sweet drinks. He hesitated as he brought it to his mouth. "Sorry," he said, shaking his head. "I'm not thinking straight at all. What can I get you two to drink?"

"We brought wine," I told him, and gently pried Billy's sack away (she resisted at first, automatically, like a tense child clinging to a teddy bear). I thought I might actually faint if I didn't escape this suffocating room for just a breather. "I'll just uh, take this into the kitchen," I said. "Have you got a wine-opener, Redso?"

"The drawer under the sink. But hell, I'll do that for you, Arnie."

"No, no. That's fine. I'll find my way around."

"Well, there's a bottle of Glenlivet on the counter."

"Fantastic," I heard myself say.

"Just a little bit of water in mine," Billy said. "Redso?"

He dug his hands into the tight front pockets of his jeans. "Actually," he said, and licked his lips, "maybe you ought to be sitting down to hear this. But I've stopped drinking."

I was sure, when Billy looked at me, that my mouth was hanging open just as stupidly as hers.

"You have?" she said.

"I haven't had a drink for . . . well, let's see. It's going on a year and a half now."

Billy rather shakily got a cigarette lit.

"Well, Jesus Christ," I said. "That's just—really? You really quit drinking?"

"Scout's honor," Redso answered, with a smile.

"Well, congratulations, Redso. I'm glad as hell to hear that."

"Me too," Billy said, without conviction.

"But how did you manage it? It couldn't have been easy."

"Actually, I didn't have much choice. I was killing myself, to put it mildly." Redso rasped a laugh. "That's funny, right? Killing myself, to put it mildly."

"It *is* funny," Billy said. But she hardly looked amused.

"The thing that finally broke the camel's back—" Redso

stopped in midsentence. He plucked his hands from his pockets, and crossed his arms above that landslide of a gut. "You're
not going to believe this, I know. But what happened was, I
had a heart attack."

It took me a second to process that sentence—and then my
own heart took an erratic leap. I glanced at Billy. Her cheeks
looked slapped.

"I know. It's completely unbelievable, right? Hell, I was only
thirty-three when it happened. But with the way I'd been going . . . well. You two know all about it. The fact is, I'm lucky
to be alive at all." Redso shrugged. "So, anyway, for once in
my life I've been following doctor's orders. No booze, no cigarettes. And naturally, no more drugs. I'm just about as clean as
they come nowadays. Shit, the only thing I do anymore is
lithium."

I tilted forward over my cane. "You've been taking your
lithium?"

"Well, sure, Arnie. That's sort of a given. I mean, if I were
still crazy, there's not much doubt I'd be dead by now. Also,
I'm taking these." Redso tapped a pocket of his jeans. "Nitroglycerin tablets. I'm supposed to carry them with me at all
times. Even when I'm in the house." He smiled rather bash-
fully. "Hell of an exciting life, huh?"

Neither Billy nor I said a word.

"You uh, sure you don't want me to take care of that wine
for you, Arnie?"

"I'm sure," I said. "But you don't mind if we drink?"

"Christ, no. Why do you think I bought the Glenlivet?"

Billy was kneeling at the coffee table now, and crushing out
her cigarette in one of Frieda's crazy ashtrays; a green ceramic
dolphin leapt from the center of it.

"Billy, you can smoke. It's fine with me."

"No, that's . . ." She squinted at that dolphin, then shifted
on her knees and looked at Redso. "You had a *heart attack?*"

Redso readjusted his crossed arms.

"But when?" she said. "What happened? Where *were* you
when it happened? This is just—" She shook her head. "I'm
sorry, Redso. I'm just—having a very hard time absorbing all
of this."

"Hey, that's only natural, Billy. I mean, I had a pretty hard time absorbing it myself."

"But what happened?"

"Maybe we should save that for later. You know, once you've gotten your drinks, and we're all a little more comfortable. It's a pretty long and involved story. That is . . . if you're really sure you want to hear it."

"Of course I want to hear it."

Redso blinked at her intently.

She dropped her stare back to that dolphin.

"Well," I said, "I guess I'll go fix those drinks."

Billy twisted around to look at me. Her eyes were darkly shining. "Arnie? Just a little bit of water in mine, all right?"

IN A VOICE that rarely rose above a grave cautious monotone, plump Redso fidgeted on his mother's plump sofa, and told us his story. He did so without veering off into his old beloved tangents, allusions or asides, and in a style unenlivened by puns, jokes, rhetorical playfulness or any obvious exaggeration; his narrative was as straightforward and unadorned as a newspaper article. I remembered what Billy had said about the first time she'd read his letter, and there were moments during his story when I couldn't help wondering if she'd been right—if Redso hadn't somehow traded places with an impostor. There had once been a man who'd suffered the things I was hearing about, but this mild, bloated, prematurely middle-aged stranger before me seemed no more intimately connected to that hellbent Dionysian maniac than some distant surviving relative. And yet, as I had to keep reminding myself, Redso *had* survived, hadn't he? That should have been a cause for celebration. Instead the atmosphere in the room— as I listened from my armchair, and Billy, sitting cross-legged on the rug, watched Redso with glassy stricken eyes—was practically funereal.

It didn't take Redso very long to cover the four years of his brain-blasted wanderings, for there were vast blank stretches of time, he said, that were simply lost—to his drinking, his drugs, his black depressions, and whatever violence all those years of shock treatments and antipsychotics had done to his memory.

Basically Redso had drifted, mostly by thumb, around the southwestern part of the country, and also Mexico, for as long as the five grand I'd handed him on my wedding day held out. When that was gone, he'd survived on handouts, petty drug deals, garbage from dumpsters, leftover scraps on the tables of fast-food restaurants, soup kitchens. He slept in abandoned buildings, or shelters for the homeless, or city parks, or on the streets, or once in a while, if he got lucky, under the roof of some not-too-particular woman he'd managed to hook up with.

"Once in a while I'd still get a manic attack, you know, and have myself a pretty good time." Redso smiled—rather wistfully, I thought—as he scratched at his fat chin. "But those were coming fewer and farther between. Mostly I was depressed—and *so* depressed, well, there were times when I'd wake up in some alley, or under some bridge, half-starved and covered in filth, and not even remember what city I was in. Much less how I'd gotten there. I mean, I was that completely obliterated."

He'd suffered his heart attack—and this detail, for some reason, particularly chilled me—halfway through a plate of red beans and rice in a diner in New Orleans's French Quarter. "Luckily," he said, "the place was run by this kindly old Creole woman, whose husband had evidently died of a heart attack a few years back. Anyway, she recognized the symptoms—"

"What symptoms?" Billy said.

"You know. Chest pains. Nausea. Sweating. She said I was actually turning blue." Redso carefully reached down for his Coke. "Anyway, if she hadn't been there and called for an ambulance, I easily could have died. Right there on the sawdust floor of that restaurant." He paused. "So that's what finally turned me around. I mean, after all those years of toying around with death, I'd finally stuck my head right in its jaws. And I'll tell you what. It didn't look so good at such close quarters."

On his release from the hospital, Redso went on to tell us, he'd applied to a state-run psychiatric clinic and gotten started on his lithium treatment. Soon after that, he managed to find work as a janitor in an office building (as far as I knew, and as

bizarre as it seemed, the first real job he'd ever had) and existed for some months in a cheap furnished room, blurred,
friendless, and still only half sane—until he called his mother
one evening in November of last year, and got the news about
her condition.

"And that's when I came back," Redso said, letting go a long
sigh. He shifted his hips now, dug into his pocket, produced a
small vial, and popped a pill so tiny I couldn't see it. He raked
a hand back through his brushy hair, and sighed again. "It's
weird. But I think that's what brought me back down to earth
more than anything else—having to take care of my mother
while she was dying. Being forced to deal with all of that. I
mean, the heart attack was one thing. But this was the
clincher. For once in my life, I didn't have any *choice* but to
stay sane. There was just no one else around for my mother.
And I mean no one." Redso narrowed his slanted blue eyes at
Billy where she sat, her arms wrapped tight around her middle. "I guess you must know what I'm talking about," he said.

She bit her lip and slowly nodded.

Redso kept observing her—until she finally ducked her face
—then sank back against the sofa. "So anyway. I guess that
about brings us up to date."

I squirmed in my deep mushy armchair. "Christ, Redso. I
don't know what to say. Except that it's practically a miracle
you're still alive. Not to mention all right."

Billy straightened her back.

"*Are* you all right, Redso?"

"Well, sure, Billy. As all right as I've ever been, anyway. I
mean, don't I . . . ? Isn't that pretty apparent to you?"

She only stared at him. Then the air went out of her lungs,
and she sagged forward as if she'd been punctured. I pushed
up out of my armchair, and went over to her, stooping for her
empty glass. "You want this freshened?"

She nodded.

I was in the kitchen, pouring her drink, when a sudden
surge of raw emotion overcame me. I set the bottle down,
leaned on my cane with one hand, and steadied myself on the
counter with the other. My eyes clouded and stung. I drank
away the whiskey in Billy's glass, waited for the burning to die
down, then fixed her drink a second time, and caned back to

the living room. As I handed Billy her glass, I realized that she and Redso hadn't exchanged a word since I'd ducked into the kitchen. And now they still weren't speaking. Redso was staring at the knickknack shelves beside the sofa. Billy was staring at him.

Apparently I would have to keep things going.

"So, Redso," I said, sinking back into my chair. "You came back to St. Louis in November?"

"Right."

"And your mother—when did she die?"

"It was at the end of January."

"Huh. So you've been back in town for almost ten months?"

"That's about right."

"But why did it take you so long to get in touch with us?"

He furrowed his brow as he reached down for his Coke. "It's hard to say, Arnie. But I guess I just—wasn't ready until now."

I looked at Billy. She was holding herself unnaturally still, as if she was fending off an attack of dizziness. I turned back to Redso. "So what've you been doing all this time?"

"Not a whole heck of a lot, really. It's been a sort of recuperative period for me. I've been reading a lot. Walking a lot. Mostly I've just been taking stock."

"Well, what about now? What are your plans?"

Redso leaned forward and clasped his hands between his knees. There was finally a spark of genuine eagerness in his eyes. "Actually, I'll be starting school again in the fall."

"You mean college?"

"No," he said, with a crooked smile. "I mean kindergarten."

I gave that a much bigger laugh than it deserved; maybe because I was that relieved to hear Redso even attempt to crack a joke.

"Going to school for what?" Billy said. Her voice was high and tight.

"My teaching certificate. At Webster University. I've been thinking I'd like to teach high school English. That, or maybe drama. It all depends on what the job market looks like."

"You want to be a teacher?" I said.

Redso nodded.

I had to smile at the image that evoked—Redso in all his

anarchic glory, running amok, and at the mouth, among his adoring and impressionable students. But then I realized I was way off track; I'd been thinking of a Redso who, as far as I could tell, no longer existed.

Billy managed to drum up a smile. "I think that's a fine idea, Redso. I think you'd be a damned good teacher."

"Do you?"

"Yes. I really do."

"Well, to tell you the truth, so do I."

Billy gave a shake to her hair, and raised her glass.

"And what about money?" I asked. "Are you doing all right?"

"Oh, I'm holding out fine. My mother had some savings in the bank. And this house is practically paid for. Also, my college is being taken care of through Disability. It's completely absurd. But all you have to do is fuck up your life big-time, and the government rewards you with a free ride. Go figure, right?"

"Hell," I said, "just take the money and run."

"That's what I plan on doing."

The ice cubes clinked in Billy's glass.

"What about writing?" she said.

Redso stretched his arms along the top of the sofa, and gripped the upholstery. "What about it?"

"Are you writing anything? Have you written anything?"

"Billy, I haven't written anything for years."

"But you . . . don't you miss it? You must."

He didn't reply.

"I mean, just think of it, Redso. My god, you've got the kind of material now that any other playwright would *kill* for. You must be champing at the bit to start working again."

"To tell you the truth, Billy, I just don't feel the urge. The writing . . . well, that was in another life."

She stared at him. "How can you say that?"

"It's the truth."

She took a swallow of whiskey. "Well, what about acting?"

"Billy, I'm finished with that, too."

"But *why?*" She pressed her knuckles into the rug on either side of her, and craned forward; the tendons in her neck stood out. "I'm not understanding you, Redso. You say you're all right. And I believe that. And your mind *does* seem clear. So how can you—? My God, after all the shit you've been through, and after all the time you've lost, you've finally got the *chance* to work again. And now you tell me you're not interested? In writing *or* acting?"

"Billy, what do you want me to say?"

"Don't you *know* how gifted you are, Redso? Don't you remember? Are you—?" She violently shook her head. "How can you just sit there and blithely tell me you want to throw it all *away?*"

Redso bent forward, set his elbows on his knees, and made a steeple of his hands—a gesture that struck me as oddly sanctimonious. "Billy, my number-one concern right now is staying sane. Staying sane, and staying sober. And it's probably not a great idea to start thinking of myself as an artist again. Not with all the crazy romantic bullshit that goes with it. The ego trips, the self-absorption . . . well, you know what I'm talking about." Redso showed her a small conciliatory smile. "What's that line from *Lear? That way madness lies.*"

"But you *are* an artist, Redso! It's not like you have any *choice!*"

Redso sat back, gripped the sofa again, and regarded her carefully. "Well, of course I do, Billy. I mean, in a way that's been the story of my life. Even with my insanity. Don't you see? I've always had the choice."

NOW REDSO AND I were alone (Billy was detained in the bathroom) in the corner of the fenced and floodlit backyard where he'd set up the barbecue grill. On a TV tray beside it were a pair of tongs, a carving fork, a brush, a bowl of sauce, a box of kitchen matches, a platter piled with pork ribs, and a spritzer bottle, all arranged with such persnickety tidiness— the tongs, fork and brush laid parallel to the tray, the matches, sauce bowl and spritzer bottle lined up in a strict plumb row— that it gave me the willies. Some anxious devil of control had taken possession of Redso. It was as apparent in his stiff, cautious, flattened way of moving and speaking as in this compulsive arrangement of objects. I thought then that I saw into it. Crazed for so long, bound for so many years to the terrible turning wheel of his moods, how could Redso ever really trust this fragile sanity? He must have sensed potential slippage in every emotional bump; in every shifting shadow he must have glimpsed another attack of mania or depression, coiled to spring. He was keeping this rigid grip on himself in the terror of flying apart.

He dropped a match onto the neatly mounded coals. They whooshed into flame. Redso folded his arms against his chest. "I don't know, Arnie. Ever since you got here tonight, all I've been doing is going on and on about myself—" He showed me a half smile. "Just like when I was manic, right?"

"Not exactly," I said.

"But anyway, how are you two really doing? You and Billy?"

Constrained by the promise I'd made to Billy—and not exactly eager to broach the subject of my failing marriage, my failed character—I lied. "Oh, we're doing all right. Of course we have our ups and downs, like in any marriage . . ." My voice trailed off.

Redso seemed content with that nonanswer. "And how's business? Still raking in the bucks?"

"You could put it that way."

"You always did have the Midas touch, didn't you?"

"I just hustle a lot, Redso."

He tightened his crossed arms. "And Billy? How's she doing? She mentioned on the phone that she's been doing some stage acting again. So does she—is she happy with that?"

"Billy can probably fill you in on that better than me, Redso."

He nodded vaguely. "Well, she looks just fantastic, Arnie."

I said nothing.

"Except . . . she does seem sort of uptight tonight, doesn't she?"

That struck me as an interesting observation—considering the source. "Hell, Redso. I'd say we were all pretty uptight tonight. Wouldn't you?"

"Right," he said.

We went on staring at the coals.

I thought I'd better nudge the conversation, such as it was, as far away from Billy as I could get it. "Anyhow, I'm sure looking forward to your barbecued ribs, Redso. How long has it been since I had them? Seven or eight years?"

"At least. But . . . was I doing any cooking those last couple of years? You know, at the house in Maplewood?"

"Redso, you weren't even eating."

He heaved a sigh. "I've got to tell you, man. My memory's shot so full of fucking holes—I don't know. The truth is, I was hoping that maybe you and Billy could help, you know, fill in some blank spots tonight. Connect the dots. Or at least set me straight on a couple of things."

That surprised me. "You mean sit around the dinner table and reminisce?"

"Well, yes. Sort of." He shot me a sidelong glance. "Or do you think that's a lousy idea?"

"Jesus, Redso—are you really sure you want to hear about that stuff? It won't be pleasant. I mean, you pulled off some pretty wild shit."

"Hell, I know that, Arnie. It's like I don't remember anything. I know what I did to you in that blizzard, for instance. And that scene I made at your wedding. But I just . . . feel like I need a more complete tally of my sins."

"Your sins?"

"My crimes. My fuck-ups. Whatever. You're talking to a lapsed Catholic here, don't forget."

"But why? What possible good could it do?"

"Arnie, don't you get it?" Redso looked me full in the eyes then. "I'm trying to figure out just who the hell I am."

That undid me. I pumped the head of my cane and stared off into the glaring backyard. I had the strong urge to put an arm around Redso's fleshy shoulders and give him a reassuring squeeze. But something stopped me.

"And the other thing is, if I don't really *know* all of what I did to you . . . how can I ask you and Billy to forgive me?"

It was my turn to sigh heavily. "Redso, you don't need to ask for our forgiveness."

"No. You're wrong about that. I do."

I wanted to simply say, *All right, then—you're forgiven.* But that proved as impossible—and again, I couldn't say why—as placing my arm around Redso's shoulders.

"Well, anyway," he said. "One good thing. You don't seem to hate me."

"Don't think I didn't hate you, Redso."

He took that in. "But not now?"

"Redso, I wouldn't know who I was hating. Just look at you. You don't need me to tell you that you've changed."

"That's—awfully generous of you, Arnie."

"No. It's not. As a matter of fact"—I had to stop and gather myself—"I've never been particularly generous to you."

Redso frowned at me.

"I was always ready to believe the worst about you, Redso. Maybe I even hoped for the worst—I don't know. But don't forget how crazed with jealousy I was over you and Billy." I averted my face. I'd made it sound like my jealousy belonged to the distant past—when, in fact, it had still been corrosively alive until the moment I'd set eyes on his bloated face tonight. I went on with my confession. "Once in every blue moon, I could have given you the benefit of the doubt. Hell, you certainly overlooked *my* glaring defects. Especially in the beginning. But I never was very generous to you, Redso. Not like you were to me."

"Shit, Arnie. You would have been a fool if you were."

"That's not the point," I told him, my voice turning dangerously thick. "The point is, you were my friend."

We both did the safest thing then, which was to keep our eyes fixed on those smoldering coals.

The screen door rattled and banged. We both flinched and turned. Billy, drink in hand, was coming across the lawn, her shoulders working, her smile so wide and stiff that it was practically a grimace.

ACCORDING TO MY ROLEX, the entire ordeal had lasted less than four hours. But at the end of what felt like the longest evening of my life, I waited alone in my Lincoln as Billy, who'd asked for a moment alone with Redso, stood talking with him in the sad yellow porchlight. Redso bent toward her earnestly as he spoke, his hands in his jeans pockets, his shoulders hunched. Billy kept her head bowed. Then she swept her hair behind her shoulders, hiked up on her tiptoes, and kissed him on the cheek. As he raised his arms for a parting embrace, she pivoted evasively, scurried off the porch, and came down the steep hump of the lawn in such a hurry that I thought she was going to lose her balance.

Redso watched her go, stuffing his hands back into his pockets. My heart felt squeezed for him.

Billy got in and slammed the door. Redso offered us a hesitant limp wave. I limply waved back.

Then we were driving.

Billy lit a cigarette, and with a groan, dropped her head against the seat. "God," she said. "I thought we'd never get out of there."

I made the turn onto Hampton, and for several blocks we were silent. Billy finally spoke up. "You were good," she said.

"What do you mean?"

"You were good, that's all. The whole evening. You were nice to him, and you were full of the right questions, and you never let on that you were horrified—and meanwhile, I was a complete fucking *mess*." She let out a shuddery sigh. "And the worst part was, I couldn't *hide* it from him, Arnie. A few times I actually told myself to just approach it like an *acting* exercise, you know? But even *that* didn't work. I know I was a bitch to him, Arnie. I *know*. And I was *hating* myself for it. But no matter how hard I tried—"

"Billy, for godsakes—you don't have to beat yourself up about it."

"But why I couldn't I act right?"

"You were upset, all right? And a lot more upset than I was. Hell, it was easier for me to put up a good front."

"Don't tell me you weren't upset, Arnie."

I looked at her. "That isn't what I said."

She turned her face to her window. "Oh, don't even listen to me," she said. "I'm half out of my mind right now."

We drove on quietly. I was very careful how I phrased what I said next.

"I don't know, Billy. In certain ways I'm *glad* to see what's happened to him. All right, so maybe he's not exactly a scintillating personality anymore—"

"Not scintillating—" She jerked around to stare at me. "He's a *zombie*, Arnie! Like one of those expressionless people tottering around in the *Night of the Living Dead!* He's flat, and he's dull, and he's not even *funny* anymore. He doesn't seem to have an *opinion* about anything—"

"Jesus, Billy. You don't need to exaggerate it."

"I'm *not* exaggerating it. God, I wish I were!"

"Look, the point is, Redso's alive, isn't he? And as far as I can tell, he *is* sane. And he *does* seem to have his life back on track. I mean, come on, Billy. Who'd want that other Redso back?"

I glanced at her. She did.

I squirmed behind the wheel, trying to beat down a rising dislike for her. "You're just not being reasonable, Billy. Or even kind. And it's not like you at all. Hell, isn't there at least *some* part of you that's happy for him?"

She crushed out her cigarette, knocked the ashtray shut with the heel of her hand, and didn't answer.

I took the ramp for Highway 40.

Then she spoke up in a high strained voice. "Why did he have to keep doing that at dinner? Insisting that we keep digging up the past like that and throwing it in his face?"

"You know why. His memory's shot. The poor guy's trying to reconstruct his life."

"But it was more than that. There was this element of *punishment* in it. Like we were supposed to help *flagellate* him or something. It was just torture. The whole night. You remember when I got up from the table? Well, it wasn't to pee. I threw up."

I looked at her.

Billy was sawing her teeth into her lip. "And then, of course, I had to waltz right back into the dining room, all smiles, and dig right back into my barbecued ribs again . . . God! It was just pure torture!"

We were silent. Billy's breathing was sounding increasingly feathery, labored.

Then she shocked me by barking out a laugh.

"What an *idiot* I was!" She slapped the seat between us. "Do you know—? Shit! Are you ready for this, Arnie?"

I waited, squinting at the highway.

"I may as well come right out and tell you. I mean, why not? No point in keeping secrets now, is there?" A residual laugh bubbled out of her throat. "It's humiliating, the things you can talk yourself into. But do you know that I actually had myself all worked up into a lather for tonight? Oh, yes. You should have seen me these past two weeks, Arnie. I was like some airheaded debutante, getting ready for her coming-out ball! All nervous and hopeful and completely idiotic . . ." She slid down lower in her seat, thunking her knees against the glove compartment. "I mean, with our marriage down the tubes like it is—and with you turning out to be such a shit—and with me pushing forty, and my life just as fantastically screwed up as ever—well, what do you think I was thinking?" She shrugged. "That Redso was going to be the answer. Yep. That he was going to be better—but not all the *way* better. That he was going to have just enough of his craziness left, just enough dangerous sexy edge . . . well, I think you know what I'm talking about. That he was going to swoop down from the sky like some shining Greek god in his chariot, and carry me away from all this . . ." She made a loose sweeping gesture, and let her hand flop onto the seat between us. "Pretty hilarious, huh? Not that I really thought it consciously. Not that I would've *allowed* myself to think it consciously. But I was feeling it, all right. Because I sure as hell came crashing down from *something* when we got there tonight, and I saw what was actually left of him."

I drove on, feeling sick, feeling like the car was going to escape my control at any moment.

"Do you remember what he used to say when he was manic? Why he wouldn't take his lithium? God, he laid it all out, point by point! He said it would lobotomize him, emasculate him. Flatten him out like a two-by-four. He said that if he ever started taking it, he'd never act or write again—that his talent would just go up in smoke. And . . . he said that I'd stop loving him. That it'd kill everything about him that I found so utterly damned charming and enthralling. You remember him saying that, Arnie?" Billy sniffed, and brushed impatiently at her eyes with her knuckles.

I was surprised; I hadn't even known that she was crying.

"Well," she said. "Guess what?"

By the time we were headed down De Mun Avenue in Billy's neighborhood, I could no longer keep it contained. It seemed to me that the whole mad, ever-shifting, hopelessly muddled mix of our three-way love affair, after seven long overheated years, had finally reached critical mass—and that once I allowed the chain reaction to start, there would be no controlling it. Deciding it would be smarter not to drive, I pulled over in front of the parklike grounds of Concordia Seminary, and switched off the engine. Billy eyed me suspiciously in the gloom.

"We need to talk," I said.

"About what?"

"Us."

She closed her eyes. "Oh, God, don't do this, Arnie . . ."

I found that I couldn't look at her. I focused instead on the seminary bell tower, jutting black and somber against the lead gray of the sky.

"Billy, will you please come back?"

She sighed, but didn't answer.

"I know I've been a shit, a fool, an egoistic bastard. I know that, Billy. But I can change. And I *will* change, I swear it—if you'd just give me another chance." I looked at her then. She evidently wasn't going to offer any help. She still had her face averted. I slumped forward and hugged the steering wheel. "I've got to tell you, Billy. I'm scared. And I mean really scared. These past months—" I had to stop and swallow. "The thing is . . . when I try to imagine what my life would be like if you never did come back . . . all I can see is this empty pointless silly repetitive *nothing*. And it just scares the living shit out of me, Billy. Don't you know you're the only woman I've ever really loved—ever really trusted?" The words, falling so flatly, so feebly in my ears, simply ran out. I flopped back against my seat and smacked the steering wheel. "*Christ*, I don't know how to do this!"

"Arnie—"

"Boy, you should have heard me during rehearsals! I was convincing as hell. A regular Cyrano de Bergerac. You were supposed to be swooning at my feet by this point."

"I'm asking you, Arnie—please don't do this now."

"Hell, why not now? Isn't everything in shambles? Aren't we sitting here among the smoking ruins? Don't you think this is a pretty *good* time to talk?"

"It's the worst *possible* time. Can't you see that? Too damned much has already happened tonight, Arnie. I'm sorry. But I just don't have anything *left* for this right now."

She opened her door.

I lunged sideways and grabbed her wrist.

"What is it?" I said. "Is it Redso?"

She stared at me in amazement. "Weren't you *there* tonight, Arnie? Didn't you hear a single thing I said? My God, don't you *get* it? It's finished. Forever. With *both* of you."

I was speechless.

"Please let go of my wrist," she said.

I did, and Billy pushed out of the car.

I took up my cane and went after her.

She was striding, arms crossed, up the sparsely wooded slope of the seminary grounds. I had to poke furiously to catch up with her.

"You can't just walk away from this, Billy!"

She halted and spun at me. "Have you lost your brains or something? I walked away from this a long time ago! It's *over*, Arnie, all right? There isn't going to *be* any happy reunion. So will you please just drop it? And also, will you please just go? I can't *take* any more melodrama tonight. Please—just get in your car and go. I'll walk home by myself."

I bore down hard on my cane. There was a hot thick swarming in my chest that felt like actual hatred.

"You can't forgive either one of us, can you?"

She looked genuinely puzzled. "Forgive you for what?"

"For recovering."

"Am I supposed to understand what that means?"

"Oh Jesus! Are you really going to play innocent with me? Look at what just happened tonight. Look at what's *been* happening for the past seven years! As long as Redso and I were sick and needy, boy, you couldn't get enough of either one of us, could you?"

Billy only narrowed her eyes.

"But then something happened, didn't it, Billy? Something you never planned on. We got *healthy*. I got back on my feet, and Redso got sane—and what did *you* do? You lost interest! Well, shit, it's only *understandable*. We deprived you of your one great role in life!"

"What role?"

"Oh, come on, Billy! The one you first perfected with your lunatic fucking father—playing nursemaid to sick crazy men!"

She studied me intently before she spoke, and when she did,

the softness of her voice unnerved me. "Is that what you think, Arnie? Is that really what you think this has all been about?"

"What am I *supposed* to think? I mean, Christ—just take a look at your record!"

"You don't believe I ever loved you? You and Redso both? Simply for who you *were?*"

I found that I couldn't answer. The sweet reasonableness of Billy's reply had undone me. All my rage had simply blown away and I was no longer sure of a single thing I'd said. The ground felt watery under my feet. My cane wobbled.

But it was Billy's legs that seemed to give out. She sank, with a despairing grunt, cross-legged to the ground. She drew up her knees, wrapped her arms around them, and stared dully into the darkness. She didn't move a muscle, not even her eyes.

"Billy? What are you doing?"

She didn't respond.

"Billy, for godsakes—will you please get up?"

Now she flashed her wet eyes at me. "Just leave me alone," she said, in a far-off-sounding voice.

"Just leave you sitting on the ground like this?"

Again, she didn't answer.

"Well, will you—? Jesus, Billy. Are you going to be all right?"

"How should *I* know? Just leave!"

I watched her for a moment, my heart as heavy and jagged as a rock inside my chest. And then, too drained of hope to push the damned thing any further, I finally turned away, and started slowly caning down the hill.

Fifteen

"I'M AWFULLY GLAD to see you, Arnie. And I mean that. Actually . . . well, this might sound crazy after that last terrible scene we had. But I've been missing you."

"I wish you wouldn't say that, Billy."

"But it's true."

"Especially if it's true."

Billy took a taste of her beer, settled back against her side of the booth, and inspected me sympathetically. "Has it really been that awful for you, Arnie?"

I shrugged. "What do you want me to tell you, Billy?"

"Whatever you feel like telling me."

"Well," I said, "it hasn't been a picnic."

She took that in. "You never were much for talking about your pain, were you?"

"It's a pretty boring topic, don't you think? Pain is pain. I've never found a particularly original way to talk about it."

Billy frowned at her beer mug as she fingered it. Then she looked up at me, almost shyly. "Could you at least tell me what you've been doing these past few weeks?"

Something finally gave way inside of me—and I was glad of it.

"I'm sorry, Billy. I don't mean to give you a hard time. It's just . . . this isn't easy for me."

"I know that, baby."

Her use of the word "baby" unhinged me. I reached for my beer. I didn't want to be reminded now of Billy's gift for empathy—or any of her other gifts, for that matter. This might have been more bearable, I thought, if we'd both been simply and purely out for blood, like any normal couple in the throes of a divorce. But of course, what was there about us that had ever been remotely normal?

"So what *have* you been doing?" Billy asked again.

"Not a whole lot, really. Working too hard. Thinking too hard."

"Coming to any conclusions?"

"That's the problem," I said.

Billy showed me a small smile. "Well, you really don't look so bad to me, Arnie. You don't have that hollow-eyed, desperate look at all."

"No?"

"No."

"I'll probably survive."

"I know you will. You're actually built very tough, you know. Just like your mother."

I grunted ambivalently at that.

For a spell we both sipped quietly at our beers.

Three weeks had passed since that catastrophic evening at Redso's house. Just how I'd been managing to limp on from day to day doesn't really bear detailing. What I'd said about pain to Billy, I'd meant: unless you're a real connoisseur of the stuff—a Dostoevsky, maybe, or a Sylvia Plath (both, unless I'm mistaken, manic-depressives)—it makes for a pretty deadening subject. So I'll just say that even at the nadir of my despair and deep confusion, I hadn't missed an appointment with a client, or forgotten to tie my shoes, or drunk myself into a stupor, or given any serious thought to driving on the wrong side of the road, or even, as desperate as I got, succumbed to the urge to throw myself on Billy's mercy once again. One thing I did have left was my old obstinate pride. And I'd already done my stint as a beggar.

More than once, however, I did come close to calling her. But each time I replaced the receiver after only one ring. It was Billy who had broken things off, so my thinking went—

and therefore it was Billy who would have to renew the connection.

And she finally did, in the first week of September, by inviting me to lunch here at O'Connell's—one of our favorite haunts back in the bad old days (which almost looked good to me now) when we'd all three been helpless prisoners on the runaway carnival ride of Redso's jolting mood swings.

Billy looked as splendid this afternoon as I'd ever seen her, never mind the grubby outfit she had on: ratty old jeans, her now–ancient Carnegie Mellon T-shirt, that faded gypsy headscarf, and as usual, no makeup, no jewelry. While I'd been hanging on by my fingernails, Billy, it was clear, had been gaining life and strength. It was all shining forth in her face, her eyes. And while I didn't think that I truly begrudged her any happiness, that didn't mean I had to sit here and enjoy it. After all, what was causing her to glow like this, if not my final exit as her husband?

"I may as well drop the bomb right now," she said, lighting a cigarette. She blew smoke out her nose. "I saw Redso."

"Oh Jesus." I thunked back against the booth. Not that I was really surprised. Somewhere inside I must have known that Redso wasn't so easily gotten rid of. "When?"

"About two weeks ago. You remember at his house, when you were waiting in the car, and Redso and I were talking on the porch? Well, he asked me out." Billy balanced her cigarette on the lip of the ashtray, then took a long swallow of beer. "He said he knew the evening hadn't gone very well. And of course, I was feeling like that was all *my* fault. So when he asked if just the two of us could get together—you know, and see if things didn't go a little better the second time around—Arnie, I just didn't know how to say no. And then, I don't know *what* came over me. But like a fool, I told him we were separated. I don't know. Maybe somewhere in the back of my idiotic brain I was still hoping against hope . . ." Billy picked up her cigarette, stared off glumly into the jammed and noisy dining room, shrugged one shoulder, and looked at me again. "But of course, he would have found out anyway, right? When I told him where to come and pick me up. So anyway, we went out. The next Wednesday night, when I didn't have a rehearsal. Dinner, dancing, the whole *shmeer*.

And Arnie, he was no different than when you saw him. He was so *flat*. So rigid and brittle. So terribly overcautious. And he *still* didn't have a sense of humor. I mean, the little jokes he kept making . . . he was about as funny as Bob Hope."

"So what happened?"

"Well, first we had dinner at Dominic's—and don't ask me how Redso could afford it. And then we went dancing at the Casa Loma Ballroom. They were having another one of those special Big Band Nights. You remember that time all three of us went there?"

I remembered, all right, and the memory pained me. I nodded.

"It was like he planned the whole night as some trip down Memory Lane—so he could use the nostalgia angle to soften me up, you know? Anyway . . . it was all just a nightmare." Billy scowled as she stubbed out her cigarette. "Do you remember what a terrific dancer Redso used to be? God, he was so graceful—so inventive, so *witty* on his feet. I think he was the only man I ever met under sixty who actually knew how to jitterbug. Well, he's *not* anymore—" Her voice snagged. She seemed to have to force herself to go on. "That night, he was so klutzy and stiff . . . I swear to God, it was just like dragging a wooden Indian around the floor. Half the time I actually had to *lead*. And all through it, all I could think about was what a wonderful dancer Redso *used* to be. And then this terrible, crazy thing happened. Maybe I'd been drinking too much, I don't know. But all of a sudden I started crying. And I mean big-time—bawling like a baby. So there we were, standing right in the middle of that dance floor, with that big crystal ball spinning over our heads—and me leaning into Redso's shoulder and just sobbing and sobbing my head off. People actually stopped dancing and stared at us. And Arnie, Redso just took it all *wrong*. He thought that I was crying . . . you know, because I still loved him."

"Oh Christ," I said softly.

"So then he started in with this whole pathetic pitch, you know, about how he still loved me, and how he'd never stopped loving me—" Billy seemed to catch herself. Did she realize she was describing just what *I'd* done three weeks before, as we'd driven home from Redso's? If so, I decided to ignore that inadvertent slap.

"And then what?" I said.

"And then I just had to put a *stop* to it. I mean, right then and there—and in no uncertain terms. Otherwise it just would have gone *on*." Billy looked at me imploringly, as if she feared I was going to condemn her. "I mean, to give him the slightest reason to hope would have been *twice* as cruel. Don't you think?"

I didn't answer.

"So what I did was . . . I told him you and I were getting back together."

"Oh shit!"

"What?"

"Nothing. Never mind. Go on."

"I just figured it would be the best way to let him down. So that maybe he wouldn't take it so personally." Billy took a drink of beer, and licked the foam from her upper lip. "But of course, he did."

I waited for her to elaborate. But she only stared miserably at the table, rubbing her thumb up and down the side of the mug.

"What did he do, exactly?"

"I'd really . . . rather not go into the details, Arnie."

That made me shudder.

"Did he put up any kind of fight at all?" I asked.

"No. He just took it. And I think that was the worst part of all. He just sort of hung his head . . . you know . . . and took it."

Billy drained away her beer.

"You ready for another?"

She nodded.

I signaled for the waitress, and within a minute (the service at O'Connell's was almost intimidatingly efficient) we both had fresh mugs of Watney's ale in front of us.

I asked if Redso had tried to get in touch with her since then.

"No. But the thing is . . ." Billy roughly shook her head, roughly sighed. "These past two weeks, every time the phone rings, or a kid yells in the street, or a neighbor slams a door—

well, I practically jump right out of my skin. You remember
that period when we first became lovers? When I was so paranoid? Always thinking that Redso was prowling around in the
backyard, or skulking around in the basement? Well, it's been
the same *thing*, Arnie. I'm constantly dreading that Redso's
going to call, or suddenly show up at the door, or come crawling up the fire escape—it's like I'm a spooked little girl, convinced there's a monster under the bed. And of course, it's not
Redso that's the problem. It's me. I need to wake *up* from all
this craziness, Arnie. I need to be *free* of it—finally and completely. And that's . . . really what I wanted to tell you about
today."

Billy bent down for a sip of her beer, then sat back with a
smile I had some trouble deciphering. It was a little sad, a little
shy—and also a little bit mischievous.

"I'm running away from home," she said.

"You're what?"

"I'm leaving."

I leaned forward. "You mean you're leaving St. Louis?"

"Yep."

I stared at her, open-mouthed. "Jesus, Billy. Are you serious? Where the hell would you go?"

"Pittsburgh," she said.

My mind must have skipped a groove—for at first I thought
she was kidding. People ran away to places like French Alge-
ria, or Timbuktu. But Pittsburgh? Then I remembered the
connection.

"You mean back to Carnegie Mellon?"

"Well, sure. I figure I'll finally finish my degree. I checked
up on it, and apparently the statute of limitations hasn't run
out on me yet. Of course I'll be the oldest student in the program. But hey, that was the case seven years ago, right?" Billy
was smiling easily now, all aglow again. "And then I'm thinking about going for my Ph.D. You know, and teach. I mean,
I've long since given up on the idea of earning my living as an
actress. And I figure teaching is the next best thing. And not
only that, Arnie. I think I'd really *like* it. I don't know what in
the world it means that both Redso and I want to be teachers
—maybe nothing. But anyway, there you are." Billy picked up

her beer, gave a wiggle to her shoulders. "So? What do you think?"

"I . . . just give me a second here, Billy."

I peered intently into space.

"Also—are you with me, Arnie?"

"Yes."

"It'll be the best thing for *you* if I go. The *last* thing you need is to have me still hanging around in the background, casting doubt on everything, dragging you down. You have to get your life *moving* again. I just think we'd all be much better off if I simply took a hike, you know?"

I squinted at her now. "But what about your father?"

"What about him? He's like you, Arnie. He's actually a very tough old bird, you know. He'll survive."

"Billy, what the hell are you saying? Are you telling me you could just up and abandon your father like that? After all these years of being his caretaker?"

She took some time to consider her reply. "It's not like I haven't agonized over it, Arnie. But yes. I really do think it'll be all right."

"But who's going to collect his rents when he's under the weather? Who's going to tear his *Shabbos* toilet paper? Who's going to be around to reassure the old crackpot that he really is God's gift to mankind? I don't *understand* this, Billy. How could you do such a complete about-face?"

Billy encircled her beer mug with both hands, and frowned into it. She remained silent for so long that I started to fidget. Finally she looked up. "I've been thinking about what you said to me that night—you know, at Concordia Seminary. What you said was pretty cruel, Arnie."

"I know that."

"But the truth is, from a certain angle . . . well, it's pretty hard to dispute, isn't it? That all my life, I've had some kind of sick desperate need to take care of sick men. I mean, just like you said—all you have to do is take a look at my record. Right?"

"Listen, Billy, I was half out of my mind when I told you that stuff."

"But did you believe it?"

I sighed extravagantly, and shook my head. "Christ, I don't

know, Billy. I don't trust myself to believe anything these days."

"Well, I don't know if you were right or not, Arnie. But I'm going to *act* as if you weren't. I mean, enough is enough. I've spent my whole life trying to fix things up for other people, trying to make everything all better—and all I've really succeeded in doing is making everyone more miserable. Especially myself." Billy paused. "So now it's time to try something else. And if it turns out when I get to Pittsburgh that I can't take the worry or the guilt . . . well, then we'll just have to see what happens. But meanwhile, my father isn't going to shrivel up and blow away. He's not helpless. Far from it. I've just tricked myself into believing it all these years."

I understood completely everything Billy had said. Nevertheless, I stared at her, dumbfounded.

Billy narrowed her eyes as she smiled. "And guess what else? Even if I *did* have some sick compulsion to play nursemaid to the men in my life—well, I don't even care *why* at this point. Maybe it was all just a series of suspicious-looking accidents. Or maybe it *was* all due to some deep dark neurosis of mine. But I'm through with *worrying* about it. Screw psychology, you know? I'm just getting out of here, Arnie. And that's all."

Sixteen

BILLY GOT OUT OF TOWN in a breathless hurry. Within ten days of our meeting at O'Connell's, she'd made her arrangements with her landlord, the post office, the utility companies, and so forth, broken the news to her theater group, had her painful talk with her father, celebrated her escape with Myrna and Eileen, sold her furniture, packed her beat-up Plymouth to the roof, and by the first Saturday in October, was all set to make her exodus to Pittsburgh. I insisted on giving her a few thousand to get her started (and practically had to break her kneecaps to get her to take it) and we also agreed to wait until she was well settled in before putting our no-fault divorce into motion. Billy did leave one piece of unfinished business behind her, however. She hadn't breathed a word of her departure to Redso. She knew she was being a despicable coward, she said, but the plain truth was, she was tired of being brave, and couldn't bear the thought of facing him again, or even of talking to him over the phone. Of course I understood her failure of nerve. Still, it struck me as not only weak, but uncharacteristically cold—and on the Saturday morning I came by to see her off, I couldn't resist nudging her about it one last time.

Billy set down the heavy suitcase she was *shlepping* to the car. "Arnie, what am I going to tell him? The truth?"

"Why not?"

"Are you serious? My God, don't you know it would absolutely devastate him?"

I suggested that she didn't need to employ the whole truth.
She could tell him, for example, that it was only *me* she was so
desperate to get away from—which was certainly part of the
truth. After all, wasn't something, even a lame white lie, better
than nothing? Could she really just leave him hanging like
that?

"I'll write to him when I get to Pittsburgh," she finally said.

"Will you really?"

"Arnie, what is this? Since when have you been so concerned about Redso's welfare?"

I shrugged morosely over my cane. "I don't know, Billy.
Maybe I just . . . can't help identifying with him right now."

Billy crumpled her mouth. "Hey," she said. "Will you
promise me something?"

I waited.

"Will you get over me just as fast as you possibly can?"

"Sure," I said. "You bet. Will do."

"And meanwhile, I *will* write to him, okay? You have my
word on that, Arnie."

We exchanged our thick-throated goodbyes. Then Billy
kissed me, fiercely hugged me, took up her suitcase, climbed
into her old yellow junker, and without a wave or a backward
glance, sputtered out of my life.

And that was the conclusion of the matter—from Billy's end
of things, anyway. But I couldn't shake the feeling that Redso
deserved something better, more substantial, than a Dear
John letter. That, and a sharpening curiosity to see him once
again, kept eating at me. And so, in early October, I arranged
to come see him at the house on Sunshine Street.

It was a crystalline late afternoon when I arrived, the air
tinged with silver, the sky a brilliant sapphire blue. Frieda's
concrete Virgin Mary was still out front, performing her per-
petual benediction over the tangled little garden. And Redso
was out front as well, perched on the edge of the tiny front
porch in a bulky red-checked sweater, and hunched intently
over a paperback. I noticed something different about his face
—he'd grown a beard. Even from the car I could see that it
was neatly trimmed, and had come in partly reddish, partly

gray. Then I recalled, with a melancholy stab, the one beard I'd grown in my life—back in my stint as a museum curator in Wales—and surely for the same self-conscious reason as Redso: to mask the unmanly cherubic roundness of my face.

I caned up slowly and uneasily to the porch, feeling something like a military officer during wartime, saddled with the duty of bearing bad news.

Redso, on the other hand, seemed purely glad to see me. We shook hands (much more vigorously than the last time around) and exchanged some mild pleasantries (I teased about the gray in his beard) and then, scratching at the sagging bulk of his red-checked belly, he asked if I wanted something to drink. What was he having? Root beer, he said. Root beer was fine with me.

As Redso lumbered into the house, I sat on the cool cement, set down my cane, and absently picked up the book he'd been reading. I received a queer jolt. It was, of all things, *Slaughterhouse Five*—the very same novel I'd been reading on that watershed afternoon, so long ago, when Redso first bounded up those stands overlooking the high school football field and into my friendless life. When he came back to the porch, a glass of root beer in each hand, I was still getting goosebumps about it.

"Jesus, Redso. Will you take a look at this?"

"At what?"

"What do you mean, what? Hell, it's *Slaughterhouse Five*."

He touched his beard, furrowed his high pale forehead. "We're, uh, studying it in my methods class at Webster University," he said. "You know, to see how we'd teach it. Apparently it's used quite a lot in high schools—never mind how subversive it actually is. You ever read it, Arnie?"

I rode silently over the hard bump of that. As Redso leaned down to hand me my root beer, I took a close look at his light blue, slightly Asiatic, utterly placid blue eyes. Evidently he didn't have a clue. And I didn't have the heart to enlighten him.

"Sure I've read it," I said. "Back in high school, as a matter of fact."

Redso smiled. "You see? What did I tell you? Actually, though, it's mostly wasted on high school students. The structure of the thing—well, it just absolutely shimmers. You really ought to read it again sometime, Arnie. You'll probably be surprised at how well it holds up."

I reverted to my old nervous habit of stroking the tops of my thighs. "Maybe I will," I said.

"Something the matter, Arnie?"

"No. Or yes. Christ, I don't know. Just have a seat, Redso. We need to talk."

I soft-soaped my story the best I could, making sure to over-emphasize—just as I'd recommended to Billy—that *I'd* been the hairy problem that had finally sent her packing. But I had the feeling that Redso didn't quite buy it. When I was through talking, and fiddling nervously with my cane, Redso sipped at his root beer and stared off at the row of near-identical red brick houses across the street, above which the sun was beginning to fatten and sink.

Finally he sighed, his huge gut ballooning and shrinking, and said, "Nice try, Goldman."

"What do you mean?"

"I know damned well I scared Billy off."

I set my cane aside, and stuck my hands in the pockets of my leather jacket. It was my turn to sigh. "Well, shit, Redso," I said. "Don't give yourself too much credit. I scared her off, too."

Redso faced back into the sun. "Well, it sure was one hell of a roller coaster ride, wasn't it?"

"It sure was."

"Anyway," Redso said, "here we are."

I wasn't quite sure what he meant by that. Yet it had the ring about it of deep truth. Here we were, all right. But of course, the real question, still remaining—and just as muddy and bottomless as ever—was how we'd gotten here.

"I guess Billy told you what happened that night at the Casa Loma Ballroom?"

I nodded.

"Well, I'll be honest with you, Arnie. I can't really blame her for turning tail and running. I mean, shit, just look at me."

I had to swallow. "What's that supposed to mean?"

"I'm not exactly the same guy she fell in love with, am I?"

That pierced me. I couldn't think of anything to say that wasn't false or patronizing.

"I don't know, Arnie. Maybe I gave you the wrong impression the other night, when the two of you came over. That I was so completely satisfied with my wonderful newfound sanity." Redso wrapped his arms around his middle, bent forward, and squinted into the dazzling sun. "But I'll tell you the absolute truth, man. It's *boring. I'm* boring. Shit, I bore *myself*. Not all the time, all right. But enough of the time . . ." He tightened his grip on himself. "Some of it's the lithium, I know. But also some of it's just *me*. I think I'm afraid, down deep, that if I give myself an inch emotionally—well, that I'll end up taking a mile, you know, and go rocketing right off into orbit again. Do you know what I'm talking about?"

"Yes. I think so."

"So I know why Billy reacted the way she did—why she was so horrified. Hell, I'm about as exciting as an evening in a Christian Science reading room. I realize that." Redso shrugged. "But I'll be straight with you, Arnie. Sometimes I wonder if I wouldn't be better off if my memory were *entirely* shot. You know. So I wouldn't have any basis of comparison."

"Jesus Christ, Redso. I had no idea you felt this way."

"You ever heard about these Vietnam veterans who served in combat, and then had all kinds of trouble afterwards adjusting to the letdown of civilian life? Well, it's been something like that for me. Because nothing can ever *touch* that life-or-death feeling again. That feeling of being *more* than alive. Of being *super* alive . . ." He paused. "I know mental illness is nothing to get nostalgic about. But all the same, I can't seem to help . . . getting these moments."

I didn't say anything.

Then Redso surprised me with a smile. "But hey, don't worry, man. I don't have any plans to try it out again. I just needed to tell someone, I guess. And who am I going to tell, if not you?"

Redso finished off his root beer and settled back onto his elbows, his stomach spreading out like a red-checked woolen landscape. For a while we sat there, drenched in the thickening sunlight, and didn't speak. Then Redso asked me what my plans were.

I blew out a breath. "Shit, you're the one with the plans

now, Redso. I'm just trying to make it from one day to the next."

"Oh, you'll be just fine, Arnie, believe me. *I'm* the one who's got to figure out how to live—and practically from scratch. But you had your life figured out a long time ago. You've always known exactly what you wanted. You just . . . sort of got sidetracked for the past decade or so."

"That's an interesting way of putting it."

"What did you ever want, except to be John Doe Normal American? A wife, some kids, a house in West County, a terrific credit rating—the whole bourgeois ball of wax. And you'll get it, too. Especially now that this insanity is over."

I didn't know what had gotten under Redso's skin—maybe the tonic of his bitter confession—but he was sounding awfully close to his sardonic, bristly old self.

"And the joke is," Redso continued, "I'll probably end up getting it, too. A normal life." He twisted up his mouth. "Whether I actually want it or not."

I shifted around to face him. "For godsakes, Redso. Why would you settle for the kind of life you despise?"

"Because it's better than no life at all."

Again I had no idea how to respond.

"Oh, don't get me wrong, Arnie. Most of the time, the future looks perfectly all right to me. So I'll become a teacher, and go on living in this house, and get a steady paycheck, and meet a nice woman somewhere along the way, and stay about as sane as the next guy, et cetera, et cetera. There are worse fates. Christ, I've already suffered about a dozen of them. It's just that . . . well, like I said. Sometimes I get these moments."

I did then what I'd been unable to do a month earlier, when we were talking in his backyard. I reached over and gave Redso's shoulder a firm squeeze.

He nodded, maybe in response to that. "Anyway," he said, "I'll survive, which is the main thing. But you'll do better than that, Goldman. You'll get over Billy soon enough—" Redso paused. "Sooner than I will, anyway. And then everything else will snap right into place, and you'll be right up there where you've always belonged—in conventional American nirvana.

I've got you pegged, Goldman. Shit, I've always had you pegged. Even back when I was crazy."

I didn't respond to that. But I was thinking that maybe he was right.

"And another thing, Arnie. Don't ask me how I know it. I just see it coming, that's all. Your arthritis is going to keep right on improving. And one of these days, pretty soon now, you're going to toss that cane away forever."

I shaded my eyes as I looked at him. The sunlight was very intense now.

"Yeah?" I said. "And then what?"

Redso also shaded his eyes. "What do you mean, and then what? Then you'll be healthy."

I sank back onto my elbows with a sigh.

"Whatever that means," I said.

ABOUT THE AUTHOR

Glenn Savan, the author of *White Palace,* is a graduate of the Iowa Writers' Workshop. He lives in St. Louis.